USA Today bestseller Annette Dashofy is the author of over a dozen novels including the five-time Agatha-nominated Zoe Chambers mystery series about a paramedic-turned-coroner in rural Pennsylvania. Her standalone, *Death By Equine,* won the 2021 Dr. Tony Ryan Book Award for excellence in thoroughbred racing literature. This is the third book in her Detective Honeywell mystery series set along the shores of Lake Erie. Annette and her husband live in the United States on ten acres of what was her grandfather's Pennsylvania dairy farm with one very spoiled cat.

www.annettedashofy.com

 x.com/Annette_Dashofy
facebook.com/Annette.Dashofy

Also by Annette Dashofy

Zoe Chambers Mystery Series

Circle of Influence

Lost Legacy

Bridges Burned

With a Vengeance

No Way Home

Uneasy Prey

Cry Wolf

Fair Game

Under the Radar

Til Death

Fatal Reunion

Crime in the Country

Helpless

What Comes Around

Standalone titles

Death by Equine

Detective Honeywell Mystery Series

Where the Guilty Hide

Keep Your Family Close

The Devil Comes Calling

No Stone Left Unturned

THE DEVIL COMES CALLING

A Detective Honeywell Mystery

ANNETTE DASHOFY

One More Chapter
a division of HarperCollins*Publishers*
1 London Bridge Street
London SE1 9GF
www.harpercollins.co.uk
HarperCollins*Publishers*
Macken House, 39/40 Mayor Street Upper,
Dublin 1, D01 C9W8, Ireland

This paperback edition 2025

1

First published in Great Britain in ebook format
by HarperCollins*Publishers* 2025
Copyright © Annette Dashofy 2025
Annette Dashofy asserts the moral right to be identified
as the author of this work

A catalogue record of this book is available from the British Library

ISBN: 978-0-00-871040-8

This novel is entirely a work of fiction. The names, characters and incidents portrayed in it are the work of the author's imagination. Any resemblance to actual persons, living or dead, events or localities is entirely coincidental.

Printed and bound in the UK using 100% Renewable Electricity
by CPI Group (UK) Ltd

All rights reserved. No part of this publication may be reproduced, stored in a retrieval system, or transmitted, in any form or by any means, electronic, mechanical, photocopying, recording or otherwise, without the prior permission of the publishers.

Without limiting the exclusive rights of any author, contributor or the publisher of this publication, any unauthorised use of this publication to train generative artificial intelligence (AI) technologies is expressly prohibited. HarperCollins also exercise their rights under Article 4(3) of the Digital Single Market Directive 2019/790 and expressly reserve this publication from the text and data mining exception.

Dedicated to the memory of Dawn Dowdle, who was my agent and my dear friend.

Chapter One

Matthias Honeywell couldn't remember the last time he'd been this content. Or even content in general. Stress? Anger? Frustration? Those were emotions he knew well. Mostly the only satisfaction he experienced came from being a police detective, taking bad guys off Erie's streets. Or from taking a hot woman to bed.

No, even that stirred up bad memories, which is why, until now, he'd rarely dated the same woman twice. Yet here he was on a Sunday morning, sitting opposite Emma Anderson at the island of his loft apartment's kitchen, feeling lighter and—yes, more content—than he had in a very long time.

Emma, her newly pixie-short red hair still damp from the shower, sipped her cup of coffee, an equally relaxed smile gleaming from her Caribbean blue-green eyes. "What do you have planned for today?"

"If I could talk you into sticking around, spending the day in bed sounds fantastic."

A blush crept into her cheeks. "It does. But I don't want to lose the job you helped me get, so I have to take photos of kids playing baseball."

"They're wasting your talent, you know."

"I'm the newest photographer on staff. I'm paying my dues." She set down the coffee and picked up her fork to stab the last of the cheese omelette he'd prepared for her. "We'll see what happens this week."

He tensed, trying to remember what was happening this week. Had she told him something important, which he'd forgotten? He'd been working on a homicide case for the last month, one he and his partner had cracked two days ago, so he'd been distracted.

Emma must've read the confusion in his face. "One of the other photographers is leaving for a new job."

"Right." He tried to sound like he'd known all along.

"It's okay. You've had other things on your mind lately."

Other women had given him that same line, but with ice dripping from the words. Emma, however, smiled as she gave him an out. Not only was she girl-next-door beautiful, she also sincerely did not mind him being a cop. "It's not okay. You shouldn't take a backseat to some homicidal bastard."

"You have a job to do. I'd rather you focus on it than give me your full attention and let a killer go free. Or worse yet, get killed yourself." She lowered her face, but he'd already seen the concern there. She may not mind his work, but it didn't mean she wasn't aware of the danger. Hell, she'd been in the thick of it a few times since their first encounter two months ago.

"I'm focused on you now," he said. "Tell me about the photographer who's leaving ErieLIVE."

She lifted her face. "Darcy Tomasetti. You might know her. She works the crime beat."

"Tiny little thing. Looks like she's about twelve years old?"

Emma laughed. "That's her. I think she's in her mid-twenties, but she's an amazing talent."

"So are you."

Emma eyed him flirtatiously. "Flattery will get you everywhere." She pushed her cleaned plate away. "Anyhow, no one knows who they'll pick to replace her. That's why I said we'll see what happens this week."

He transferred the plate to the sink. "If your boss is as smart as I think she is, you'll get the promotion."

"There are two others in the running, both with more seniority than me." Emma slipped off the barstool. "All the more reason why I don't want to be late to work."

Matthias came around the island to pull her into his arms. "Want me to put in another good word for you?"

"I appreciate it but no. You helped me get the job. It's all on me to keep it."

"The offer stands." He pressed a kiss to her warm lips. "See you tonight?"

"Afraid not. I'll need to edit all the baseball photos I take today. Plus, they're throwing Darcy a going-away party at the office."

He considered telling her to bring her computer back here and work from his apartment, but didn't. They'd agreed on taking things slow. It was another reason he was content with his life. A beautiful girlfriend who wasn't rushing things. A job he loved. A partner who had his back.

Life was good.

He walked Emma down the stairs to the street-level entrance. They kissed again before he held the heavy steel door for her and watched as she crossed the sidewalk and climbed into her Subaru.

He scanned his block of downtown Erie, Pennsylvania, which was quiet on a Sunday morning. A light covering of clouds appeared to be giving way to July sunshine. O'Reilly's Pub, over which he lived, was closed as were most of the other businesses along State Street except for the convenience store on the corner.

He caught Emma's wave as she pulled out. He waved back, hoping she was paying attention to traffic rather than watching him.

Back upstairs, Matthias busied himself with cleaning his kitchen after having cooked them breakfast and pondered how he'd spend his day off. Hit the gym? Take a run on the trail around the peninsula? The second option sounded better, but he'd have to head over there soon, before the summer heat turned Presque Isle State Park into a sauna.

His door buzzer interrupted his thoughts. Had Emma left something behind? No, he'd seen her grab both her purse and her camera backpack from the hooks at the top of the stairs, and couldn't see anything else lying around his wide-open living area that belonged to her. He didn't bother with the intercom, instead tromping down the steps to let her in. The words "What'd you forget?" were on his lips as he flung the door open.

The woman standing on the sidewalk was not Emma. The face, still drop-dead gorgeous after all these years, hurtled him from his cocoon of contentment into his past. It was slightly more than twenty years since Melissa Garcia had rejected his marriage proposal. He, on bended knee cradling a diamond ring that, at the tender age of twenty-two, he could not afford. She, going pale and stiff at the thought of a life with him.

Now she stood before him, the breeze tossing strands of her dark hair across her even darker eyes. Her black tank top showed every curve and not an ounce of fat. Long, tanned legs beneath very short, very tight beige shorts.

He came back to the dark eyes. "Melissa."

"Matthias."

He tried to read her expression, something he'd never been able to do. Criminals, yes. This woman? No. "What are you doing here?"

"May I come in?"

He wanted to ask, "Why the hell would you want to?" But the questions racing through his head demanded answers. He stepped back. "Sure."

Upstairs, she sashayed across the ancient hardwood floors, surveying the space. "Nice place. I'm surprised you can afford it on a cop's salary."

"The owner's a friend." His jaw clenched. Shortly after she'd turned him down, she'd accepted another marriage proposal. From a lawyer. Who could no doubt afford to buy the entire block. "He appreciates having me on the premises," Matthias added in a low growl, although he instantly wished he hadn't bothered addressing her comment. "But you didn't come all the way from Oklahoma to check out my living arrangements."

She pivoted toward him, resting her left hand—with its massive diamond-encrusted wedding band—on the back of the leather sofa where he and Emma had sat watching TV last night. "You're right. I didn't."

"Then why?"

"When was the last time you spoke to your father?"

Of all the questions she could've asked, none could have thrown him more than this one. "I don't remember." A lie.

"I gather you haven't been keeping tabs on his situation."

"Situation?" Is that what an attorney's wife called being locked up for murder?

Melissa looked away, shaking her head. "That's what I was afraid of. After what happened, you went into denial and just pretended he no longer existed."

Matthias didn't think of it as denial as much as considering his old man dead to him. "What are you getting at?"

She brought her almost black eyes back to him. "Matthias, your father was released from prison almost a month ago."

The newsroom at ErieLIVE was usually lightly staffed on Sunday evening. After hours in the sun taking photos of kids playing baseball, Emma joined almost everyone on the news outlet's staff in celebrating her coworker's departure. News manager, Laurie Kassim, had gone all out with the decorations. Helium inflated balloons floated in bunches over each chair. Streamers draped from desk lamps. Colorful confetti scattered everywhere. Trays of deli meats, cheeses, and rolls accompanied bowls of salad and boxes of pastries and cookies. One desk served as a makeshift bar with bottles of wine and soda gathered along with plastic cups. Between the confetti, the crumbs, and spilled drinks, the cleaning staff were going to demand a raise.

In the center of it all, petite Darcy Tomasetti beamed and laughed as her colleagues shared humorous stories and offered congratulatory toasts.

Emma took it all in while wading through the partygoers to fill a cup with ginger ale. She'd never handled alcohol well, and if she drank any of the wine, she feared she'd never make it home in one piece. Besides, those photos still on her camera weren't going to edit themselves.

Darcy spotted her approach and popped down from her perch on what would be her desk only until the end of the party. "Emma…" She hesitated, staring at Emma's head. "You got a new haircut. It's cute."

Emma fingered her short 'do, not wanting to explain the reason she'd had her dyed ash-blond locks chopped, leaving only her natural red as it grew back in. "Thanks."

"Cute," Darcy repeated. "I'm so glad you could make it."

"The last game was in the seventh inning when I left," Emma said, "but the score was fifteen zip and no sign of a comeback in sight."

Darcy made a pained face. "Poor kids." The smile returned. "But I'm glad you got away." She caught Emma by the elbow and guided her through the room and the reporters to a quiet corner. "I wanted to talk to you," she said in a whisper. "I know I'm not supposed to say anything yet, but I won't be here when you get the official news. You're going to be taking over my job."

Emma studied her, searching for any telltale sign of being pranked. Practical jokes were a daily occurrence around here. "You're serious?"

"Absolutely." Darcy lifted her chin, scanned the room and apparently located who she was looking for. She waved, and Emma spotted a glum-faced Preston Guilfoyle sulk their way over. Darcy reached out and slung an arm through his, drawing him closer. "Preston, isn't it true? Laurie is going to give Emma my job."

"You weren't supposed to say anything," he said.

"That's okay. She'll act surprised." Darcy looked at Emma, grinning. "Right?"

"Right." Emma wondered about Preston's downtrodden appearance. He was the reporter Darcy worked with most frequently. If what Darcy claimed was true, was Preston bummed about losing his photographer or disappointed about potentially being partnered with Emma?

Darcy seemed oblivious to his mood. She grabbed Emma's hand and practically jumped up and down. "You'll be great. Working the crime beat is so much more exciting than taking pictures of sporting events. Unless..." She scowled. "You aren't squeamish about blood, are you?"

"No," Emma replied quickly, but she let her mind go to a place she'd been avoiding. Chasing crime scenes would mean bumping into Matthias, and she had mixed feelings about that. The idea of seeing him in his element gave her a thrill. Yes, she'd seen him in action before. She could still picture him, fresh from a near-fatal car crash, his dark hair barely concealing a bandage over one of his blue eyes, as he faced down an armed killer. She'd been terrified, but nothing like that was likely to happen again. Working with him might be fun. No, she thought. Not working *with* him. Working *alongside* him.

On the other hand, they'd developed such an easy-going relationship... If he was trying to stop a killer and she, while doing her job, got in his way, would it cause a rift between them? No way did she want to sacrifice what she and Matthias had for the sake of a photograph.

Emma shook off her apprehension and brought her attention back to Darcy and Preston. "I don't understand why you're leaving. You love the excitement of the crime beat, yet you're quitting. Why?"

Preston looked even more glum. "I'm gonna get something to eat," he said and stalked away.

Darcy didn't seem to notice. "Two reasons." She held up one finger. "Passion and"—she held up a second—"money." She let go a peal of laughter. "You have to know the money sure helped the decision."

Emma recalled hearing the new job involved real estate. "You're passionate about selling houses?"

"Oh, no." Darcy waved the idea away with one hand. "Design. You know. Like on the TV shows where one half of the team is the real estate expert and the other designs the renovations." She struck a pose. "I'm the designer. It's something I've studied and played with for ages."

Matthias was right about her looking like she was twelve years old. How long could "ages" be?

"Plus, with me on the team, there won't be any need to hire a photographer once we're ready to list the houses. I'll be using both of my skillsets."

"That's fantastic."

Darcy's eyes widened. "Say, aren't you staying in a campground? Maybe we can help you find a real home."

Emma stammered. She'd come to love her little seventeen-foot camper trailer and its spot in Sara's Campground, although she realized winter would be here before she knew it, and the campground would close for the season. But purchasing a "real home" was a step she wasn't ready to take. Not when the rest of her life was so unresolved.

From across the room, Laurie called out, "Darcy! Darcy, where are you?"

She spun away from Emma and waved and shouted, "I'm over here."

"Come here," Laurie ordered with a smile on her face. "It's time to raise a toast to your future endeavors."

Darcy flounced away to join the news manager who'd climbed onto a chair. Emma moved closer. Preston, she noticed, made no move to join the circle of colleagues pressing in around the guest of honor. He remained by the food, looking dour.

"Raise your glasses, everyone," Laurie said, hoisting her own. "To Darcy. We'll miss your smiling face, your work ethic, and your stunning photographs, but we wish you well in your new career. May you make piles of money and maybe even get your own HGTV show."

The newsroom erupted in calls of "hear hear" and "cheers!" Emma joined in and sipped her ginger ale. She turned to see if Preston participated in the toast to his former photographer. Instead, he set down his glass and walked out the door.

Chapter Two

Monday morning, Matthias arrived at his desk in the Major Crimes Division of the Erie Bureau of Police more than an hour earlier than usual. The other cubicles were vacant, which suited him well. He lowered into his chair, thumbed the plastic lid from his coffee cup, and inhaled the aroma. His head throbbed with the barrage of memories from yesterday.

Melissa had only stayed long enough to answer questions. Why was she keeping tabs on his father? She wasn't, she claimed. Not really. Her husband was an attorney with connections. He tracked cases that might impact his career or his family.

Despite already having been imprisoned by the time Matthias and Melissa met, his father had made efforts to contact her, efforts she'd ignored. As a result, her husband considered him to be worthy of his attention.

Matthias then asked why she'd come all the way to Erie to tell him in person. "Because I didn't feel comfortable delivering this kind of news over the phone." Her expression softened as she added, "Your father scares me. He should scare you, too." What might have been a congenial moment ended when she added that she still had friends in Erie and was looking forward to seeing them. Her tone left little doubt that she had *not* been looking forward to seeing Matthias.

As she left, she made no suggestion about them getting together for old times' sake, having a drink and catching up, for which he was grateful.

The only good thing about her visit was something he realized once he was alone.

He had no feelings for her anymore. None. After the initial rush of bad memories, he didn't even loathe her. He'd moved on.

Not so true regarding the bombshell she'd dropped on him.

He'd spent the rest of Sunday working out his anger. He ran the entire fourteen-mile loop around Presque Isle State Park before taking a swim off Beach One. From there, he spent a couple of hours at the police station's gym, hitting the heavy bag and lifting weights. By the time he made it home, he was physically exhausted and too tired to think about his old man.

But following a fitful night of sleep, he knew he couldn't ignore the inevitable. After serving almost twenty-five years behind bars, Isaiah Honeywell, his father, was a free man once more.

The wise thing would've been to sign up for notifications about Isaiah. Instead, Matthias had chosen to push his father from his mind. To pretend he was as dead as his victim. As far as Matthias was concerned, he'd lost both his parents that night.

He almost had, until what some might say was good sense had stopped him from pulling the trigger.

Matthias scrubbed his face with both hands, struggling to wipe the memories of that night from his mind once again. After so many decades of locking his feelings away, of lying to himself, trying to believe Isaiah no longer existed, with one sentence Melissa had opened Pandora's box and released every nightmare, every boogeyman from Matthias's youth.

He brought his hands back to the keyboard and his focus to the computer monitor. He needed to catch up. No, not merely catch up. He needed to get ahead of this.

From what he could access of Isaiah's records, his old man had been a model prisoner, earning his GED and even getting a college degree in business administration. He'd participated in Bible study and was considered a leader who helped his fellow inmates find a better path.

"Bullshit," Matthias muttered. What wasn't in the reports was any mention of Isaiah's acting skills and innate ability to charm those in a position of power.

Footsteps on the stairs outside the door filtered in ahead of his partner, Detective Sergeant Cassie Malone. Lugging an oversized tote bag, she strode in through the break room. All six foot of her. She paused in the doorway between the kitchenette and the cubicles housing the Major Crimes Division. "What are you doing here so early?" she asked.

"Working," he muttered.

He caught glimpses of her moving around in the break room, pouring coffee, plating a doughnut from the box the lieutenant had left. Her white hair was even shorter than Emma's new cut and stood in stark contrast against the darkness of her skin. Part Amazon warrior queen, part mother hen, Cassie was one of—if not *the*—best detectives he'd ever worked with. She had only two flaws. She was right more often than he was. And even when she wore flats and he wore thick-soled shoes, she towered over him.

Coffee and doughnut in hand, she entered and headed for her desk in the space past his. He clicked to a different screen before she had a chance to glance at his monitor. "Digging deeper into your pet case?" she asked.

He didn't reply.

"Anything new on the Havana Carlisle murder?"

Havana's homicide was indeed Matthias's "pet case" although

having occurred in Colorado, it was nowhere near his jurisdiction. Her husband, however, was. Russ Carlisle was a smug son of a bitch and guilty of a number of crimes in Erie, from assault to drug dealing. Emma's younger sister had fallen victim to him months ago. Unfortunately, she'd been too intimidated to testify and was gone now.

Matthias knew of Carlisle's guilt, but knowing and being able to prove it were two separate issues. Havana's father owned a real estate empire and kept Russ employed and protected, despite Havana's mother's insistence that her daughter's death was not the ski accident Russ claimed.

"Did you hear me?" Cassie asked.

Matthias blinked. "Yeah, I heard. No, I haven't found anything to provide probable cause for a warrant."

Cassie huffed. "He'll slip up eventually. He's not nearly as smart as he thinks he is."

Matthias hoped Cassie was right. Until that happened, Matthias would have to satisfy himself with the memory of Emma slapping the smirk off Russ's face a few weeks back.

Cassie's ringing phone sent her retreating into her cubicle. Matthias took advantage to pull up the prison records on Isaiah again, this time focusing on the end of the report.

Early release granted, dated three and a half weeks ago.

Early release. There shouldn't have been any such thing. Not for years of brutalizing one's wife and child. Not for cold-blooded murder.

"Hey."

Cassie's voice over his shoulder made Matthias flinch and hit the key to close the window on his computer. "Christ. Stop sneaking up on me."

She looked equal parts puzzled and concerned. "I didn't sneak. I work here, remember? What's wrong with you?"

He pinched the bridge of his nose. She was right. He needed to get a grip. "Sorry."

"Don't worry about it. Come on. We have a new case." She had her handbag slung over one shoulder. "Double homicide over on Clifton Drive."

Clifton Drive was a quaint residential street with tidy homes. Close enough to the lake to crank up the real estate values, yet not so close as to make them totally unaffordable to those in the upper middle class. Most of the houses were older one-story or story-and-a-half structures. Some showed signs of remodeling over the years.

Patrol cars blocked the street leading to the address in question. Uniformed officers waved Matthias and Cassie through the barricade, and she parked in front of the house next door. Matthias sat in the passenger seat, taking in the scene. A massive dumpster took up most of the Cape Cod-style structure's front yard. A boxy tagalong trailer with ORLANDO LARSON, GENERAL CONTRACTOR emblazoned across the side filled the bulk of the rest. In the driveway, the coroner's van sat behind a white box truck with racks holding ladders on top. Whatever siding had once covered the house had been stripped, replaced by synthetic house wrap printed with the brand name Tyvek. It struck Matthias as darkly amusing that the house was covered in material made by the same company that made the protective suits worn by the crime scene techs. New windows had been installed on the first floor. Plywood filled the openings where second-floor windows and the garage doors should be.

Cassie turned off the ignition. "Maybe this isn't a double homicide after all. Maybe it's a construction accident."

"Let's find out." Matthias exited the car and started down the sidewalk. Cassie fell into step beside him.

A pair of uniformed officers, Lyle and Kollman, spotted their approach. "Honeywell." Lyle acknowledged them with a nod. "Malone."

Matthias dug his notebook from his pocket. "What've we got?"

Lyle opened his own notepad. "Electrician called it in when he showed up this morning and found them." He pointed to a young man in a T-shirt and cargo pants, sitting on the curb with his face buried in his hands. "I told him to stick around until he could give us a statement. When he tried the first time, he about barfed on my shoes." Lyle flipped a page. "Two bodies. One male, approximately fifty years old. One female, mid-twenties. Both shot execution-style."

Matthias glanced at Cassie. "So much for your construction accident theory."

"Definitely not an accident," Kollman said. "Unless two people can accidentally shoot themselves in the back of the head."

"Professional hit," Matthias said. "Do we have IDs on them?"

"Not officially. Hamilton's inside with the bodies. You can check with him."

"What about unofficially?" Cassie asked.

"The electrician over there says the man is the general contractor on this job. Guy by the name of Orlando Larson."

"What about the woman?"

"He says he doesn't recognize her."

"Anything else we should know?" Matthias asked.

Kollman hooked his thumbs in his duty belt. "We've got men canvassing the neighbors. Hopefully we'll have more for you shortly."

Matthias and Cassie thanked the officers and approached the house, ducking under the yellow police tape.

Another uniform stood guard at the open front door. Not

"open" so much as nonexistent. "They're near the back," he told them.

Inside, the house had been gutted to the studs. Interior walls were framed. Electrical work was started but consisted largely of a tangle of wires looping through the two-by-fours and dangling from the joists overhead. As the officer had stated, Erie County Coroner Felix Hamilton and a pair of his deputies were gathered at the rear of the space.

Matthias and Cassie paused to slip protective booties over their shoes, although as Matthias scanned the floor, he strongly doubted the crime scene techs would be able to discern evidence from construction debris. Sawdust coated the subflooring. Nails, screws, and scraps of wiring were scattered everywhere.

Cassie must have been thinking the same thing. "What a mess. I wonder how many people have been traipsing through here recently. They couldn't make it easy on us, could they?"

"When do they ever?"

They picked their way to the crime scene, avoiding what looked to be the most likely path the killer would've taken. Hamilton knelt next to the female victim.

"Hey, Ham," Cassie called out. "What do you have for us?"

The coroner stood, his sun-bleached blond hair askew with a bad case of bedhead. He held out a hand to one of his deputies who deposited a pair of wallets into it. In turn, he passed them to Cassie. "Male victim is Orlando Larson, which you've probably already figured out if you saw the construction trailer. Fifty-two years old. Lives down on Zuck Road. Single tap to the back of the head. No signs of a struggle."

Cassie opened the wallet as he spoke and showed the contents to Matthias. She fanned a wad of cash, and the interior slots were filled with assorted credit cards. "Doesn't look like robbery was the motive."

"What about the woman?" Matthias asked while Cassie switched wallets.

"Female victim is Darcy Tomasetti, age twenty-five," Hamilton said. "Address is an apartment on West Fifth Street downtown."

"Darcy Tomasetti?" Matthias recalled Emma mentioning the name yesterday. He leaned over to see the wallet in Cassie's hand.

"You know her?" Cassie asked.

"Yeah. You do, too. She's a photographer with ErieLIVE. Or was. We've seen her at crime scenes dozens of times."

"What do you mean, *was*?"

Matthias felt Cassie, Hamilton, and both deputies study him. "As I understand it, she quit and was taking a new job."

"Doing what?" Cassie asked.

"I don't know." Emma hadn't told him.

Lowering her voice, Cassie asked, "Would Emma know?"

"Maybe."

Hamilton interrupted their hushed discussion. "Tomasetti also exhibits a single GSW to the back of the skull."

From his tone, Matthias surmised there was more. "And?"

Hamilton pointed at the woman's body. "Her wrists are bound behind her back with a length of electrical wiring. Not a good job. If she'd had time, she would've been able to wiggle out of it."

"Any idea which of them was shot first?" Cassie asked.

The coroner shook his head. "Too early to say."

"Time of death?" Matthias asked, knowing Hamilton hated the question and would likely not be able to give an accurate answer just yet.

"Just a guess of course, but not long ago. Rigor hasn't started. Livor isn't set. The blood is only beginning to coagulate, and the bodies are still warm. Definitely not more than a few hours. I'll know more after the autopsy."

The officer at the front door leaned inside and called out, "CSU is here."

Hamilton ran a hand through his tousled mop of hair. "We're about ready to transport. Give us a few minutes and then they can have the run of the place."

"Call us when you have your preliminary report done," Cassie told him as she turned away.

"You know I will."

Matthias took another look at the littered floor. "No shell casings."

She scowled at him, surveyed the mess, and came back to him. "The crime scene guys might find them."

"Or the shooter used a revolver," he mused. "Or he policed his brass."

Matthias and Cassie backtracked the same way they'd come in. "Let's see if the neighbors have any information," she said once they'd stepped outside.

Lyle and Kollman met them halfway to the crime scene tape. "Thought you'd want to know," Lyle said. "Neighbors on both sides and across the street reported hearing what might have been gunshots about ninety minutes ago. None of them thought to call it in. Said they thought it was leftover fireworks."

Kollman gestured at the surrounding houses. "Several folks mentioned there are a couple of locals who've been doing that. Setting off firecrackers at all hours."

"Did they notice any strange vehicles parked around here?" Matthias asked.

Kollman shook his head. "With all the construction going on, this place has been Grand Central Station where traffic's concerned. Folks around here aren't happy about it."

They probably weren't happy about a killer striking in their neighborhood either.

"Uh-oh," Cassie said under her breath.

"What?" Matthias noticed she was looking toward the end of the driveway and followed her gaze. Emma stood on the opposite side of the yellow tape, camera aimed at the house. Next to her, a young man with a recorder was speaking with one of the officers. Matthias had seen the reporter before—with Darcy.

"You better go talk to her," Cassie said, keeping her voice low enough that only he could hear.

He eyed his partner. "You want me to give a statement to the press? Now?"

She gave him a look. "Don't be stupid. No, not a statement to the press. We need to let them know their colleague—former colleague—has been killed and ask if they have any idea who might've done it. I'll talk to the reporter. You talk to your cute photographer chick." Cassie's favorite nickname for Emma.

Matthias growled softly. His partner wanted him to interview his girlfriend about a homicide without giving away too much information on the case. "Fine." He hoped Emma and Darcy hadn't become too close over the last couple of months.

Emma spotted them heading her way and lowered the camera. She nudged the man with the recorder and pointed. He said something Matthias couldn't hear and must've thanked the officer he was talking to because the uniform gave a nod and walked away.

The reporter looked from Cassie to Matthias. "Detectives, Preston Guilfoyle with ErieLIVE. Can you give me a statement about what happened here?"

Cassie, all business, introduced herself and Matthias, although he was certain Guilfoyle knew who they were. He'd interviewed them numerous times at crime scenes—with Darcy at his side instead of Emma. "Mr. Guilfoyle," Cassie said. "I need to speak with you in private, if you don't mind." She gestured toward their car.

The reporter's face went still. He shot a glance at Emma, but her puzzled gaze was locked on Matthias. "I'll be right back," Guilfoyle said before trailing after Cassie.

"What's going on?" Emma asked.

Matthias looked around. Cassie had claimed the car. He needed a quiet spot where they wouldn't be interrupted and zeroed in on the dumpster. "Come with me." He took her by the elbow and guided her under the yellow tape.

There were no cops near the massive trash bin over which an enormous oak cast deep shadows. Standing behind it, they were blocked from prying eyes.

She repeated her question. "What's going on?"

He wasn't ready to tackle that one yet. "I gather you got the crime beat job. Congratulations."

"I did. Thanks." She tipped her head and fixed him with a look that let him know she wasn't backing down.

He sighed. "How much have you already learned?"

"Just what came over the police radio. Report of a double homicide at this address. The uniformed officer didn't give us anything."

He debated how to start. If he began questioning her about Darcy's new job, she'd know immediately. There was no use in trying to enter this discussion through the back door. "The victims haven't been formally identified and won't be until next of kin have been notified."

"Right." Emma dragged out the word.

"So this is off the record."

"I'm only the photographer—"

"One of the victims is Darcy Tomasetti."

Emma stiffened with an audible intake of breath. Not a gasp. More like she inhaled her words, and they stuck in her throat. She stared at him for several long moments, waiting for him to say more.

He wasn't about to tell her about the single GSW to the back of the young woman's head, nor her bound wrists. Nor was he willing to volunteer the identity of the second victim.

Her lips parted to speak, closed, opened, and closed again. She swallowed. "How? Why? What happened?" The questions poured out in disbelieving squeaks.

"I was hoping you could help me with some of that. You told me Darcy was leaving ErieLIVE for another job. Do you know what kind of job?"

Emma exhaled and looked around. "As a designer."

"What kind of designer?"

"Home interiors." Emma told him about a conversation she'd had with the victim the previous night. "Laurie Kassim joked Darcy might get a show on HGTV. You know. Flipping houses."

That explained what Darcy was doing here. Matthias glanced toward the house. "Shitty first day at the new job."

Emma's laugh was more of a choke.

"Did she tell you who she was working with?"

"No." Emma's eyes widened. "Who's the second victim?"

"I can't tell you that."

"Ongoing investigation. Next of kin notification. I get that. But—"

"Male. Early fifties. That's all I can say."

She fixed her gaze on him.

"What I *can't* say is he's the general contractor on this job."

"Orlando Larson." Not a question.

So Matthias didn't answer it.

"Got it," Emma said. "I won't say a word."

"Not even to Preston Guilfoyle."

"Not even."

Matthias managed a grin. "Good. Now, what else can you tell me that might help the investigation? Did Darcy seem concerned at all about this new job?"

"No. She was thrilled. Said it paid more money and that designing was her true passion. And she figured she could use her photography skills on the new gig, too."

"What about before? Are you aware of anyone who might've been threatening her?"

"No."

"Did she seem afraid or worried about anyone?"

Emma shook her head. "No."

"Was there anyone at ErieLIVE who disliked her? Or who she disliked?"

More head shaking. "No. No one. Besides, why would an ErieLIVE employee wait until after Darcy left if they wanted to do her harm? You'd think they'd be happy to be rid of her."

Matthias couldn't argue with her logic.

"Emma!"

The shout drew their attention. Emma walked to the corner of the dumpster and peered around it. "It's Preston." Facing Matthias, she asked, "Is there anything else you need from me?"

"Emma!" The shout was more insistent this time.

"I'm coming!" she shouted back before again looking at Matthias.

"I think we're good for now. Keep what I told you under your hat, okay?"

"Of course."

"If I have any more questions, I know how to reach you."

She blushed at his suggestive tone. "Yes, you do." With that, she slipped away and broke into a jog toward the sidewalk where her co-worker waited.

Matthias moved away from the dumpster and watched the pair have a quick conversation before Guilfoyle gestured toward the crime scene, placed a hand on his chest, and then made a looping motion with one finger. Even without hearing the exchange, Matthias could read the meaning. Guilfoyle wanted Emma to take more photos of the house while he went door to door to question the neighbors.

"Did Emma give you any information?" Cassie asked from behind him.

Matthias turned. "Yeah." He shared what he'd learned regarding Darcy's reason for being there.

"Helluva first day at the new job." Cassie surveyed the construction site.

"That's what I said."

"First and last."

"What about the reporter? Did he say anything interesting?"

"Say? No. He's a tough nut for someone so young. More interested in asking questions than answering them."

Matthias almost laughed. "Tough nut? I doubt that. Not when he's encountered a master nutcracker."

Cassie grinned. "I restrained myself."

"He didn't *say* anything interesting. I get the feeling you still got information from him, though."

"Yeah, but I'm not sure exactly what information yet."

He eyed her, waiting.

"He was trying to hide it, but I could tell he was shaken up."

"A woman he worked closely with has been murdered. I'd be more concerned if he wasn't."

"True, but my instincts tell me there's more to it than losing a colleague."

"You think they were involved?"

"Definitely. I'm just not sure that's the only thing weighing on Mr. Guilfoyle's mind right now."

"Honeywell," a voice called out. "Malone."

They looked toward the voice. Officer Kollman stood beside the same dumpster where Matthias had spoken to Emma. Another officer, who'd no doubt pulled the short straw, stood inside the dumpster with only his head and shoulders visible.

Kollman waved them toward him.

The Devil Comes Calling

"What've you got?" Matthias asked as they approached.

Kollman glanced at the dumpster diver, who replied, "A revolver. I think I found the murder weapon."

Chapter Three

After several hours at the house on Clifton Drive, Matthias and Cassie determined the shootings occurred shortly before six a.m. when the neighbors reported hearing what they thought were fireworks. The street apparently had a dearth of nosey residents. The few who admitted to seeing any unusual vehicles couldn't agree on a single make or model, let alone color. A thorough search revealed no security cameras on-site, and none of the neighbors they spoke to had anything aimed toward the construction.

The discovery of the gun—a High Standard .22 revolver with a fancy bone handgrip—answered a couple of Matthias's questions. With a revolver, there would be no brass to find at the scene. And the small caliber projectile was as likely to bounce around inside a victim's skull causing massive brain damage and becoming lodged as it was to create an exit wound like Larson's.

The crime scene techs found the bullet they presumed killed the contractor. It would be up to Hamilton to retrieve the other from Darcy. With any luck, they'd be able to match it to the gun. The lab would hopefully be able to lift fingerprints, which combined with the serial number, might lead to a quick and easy identification of the killer.

Except the crime scene techs reported the serial number had been filed off. The news brought a humorless laugh from Matthias. Homicide investigations were rarely quick and easy.

Having accomplished all they could at the scene, Matthias and Cassie returned to their car with Cassie taking the wheel. "Time to make the death notifications to the families," she said with a sour expression.

"Which one do you want to talk to first?" he asked. Breaking the news of a lost loved one was one of the shittiest parts of the job. When the victim was young with a promising life ahead of her, like Darcy Tomasetti, it was that much harder. The family would be devastated. "Larson's wife," Cassie replied. "I can well imagine how the woman's parents are going to react."

"But with a spouse, you never know."

"Exactly." Cassie started the car.

The Larson residence on Zuck Road was a modest two-story brick. Nothing pretentious. Nothing screamed *a master remodeler lives here*.

Cassie pulled into a wide driveway and parked in front of the garage door. "Let's do this."

The woman who answered the door looked to be the perfect match for the house. Medium brown hair done up in a ponytail. No makeup. An oversized T-shirt hung loose over a pair of snug capris. While she appeared plain, Matthias noted the toned arms and calves and suspected this woman could be a knockout if she wanted.

"Mrs. Orlando Larson?" Cassie asked, holding up her badge.

"Yvonne Larson," she said. "Yes?"

Cassie introduced herself and Matthias. "May we come in?"

Her icy blue eyes darted from him to Cassie. "What's this about?"

"Please." Cassie gave her a kind smile. "It would be better if we could talk inside. In private."

Yvonne crossed her arms. "Better for whom? You can say what you have to say here. I'm very busy."

Cassie shot a glance at Matthias. As usual, she wanted to remain the benevolent cop, leaving him to be the bad guy. He looked more the role, she liked to remind him. "I'm afraid there's no easy way to tell you this," he said. "Your husband's dead."

Yvonne Larson's eyes continued to shift from one of them to the other, unblinking. They settled on Matthias, and he could almost hear the mental gears grinding, processing behind those frosty irises. She stepped back, holding the door. "Come in."

She offered them seats in a living room that looked like a set from a home design magazine. Light-wood floors, light walls, and a couch with two chairs in a dark blue-green plush fabric. Yvonne took one of the chairs. Matthias and Cassie sat on the couch, half turned to face her.

"Do you know who killed him?" the widow asked.

Matthias had expected her to ask about a construction accident. The fact she jumped immediately to murder said a lot. He knew Cassie would think the same thing, but she didn't let on.

"We're still investigating," she said. "When was the last time you saw your husband?"

"Last night when he went up to bed. I stayed down here to watch TV."

"What about this morning?"

"He likes to get to his job sites early. I was still in bed." Yvonne's voice was steady, matter-of-fact. Her eyes showed no hint of tears.

"Do you know which of those job sites he was working at today?"

"No clue."

"How many jobs does he usually juggle at one time?" Matthias asked.

She looked at him and repeated, "No clue."

"You wouldn't happen to know who hired him to remodel the property on Clifton Drive, do you?" Cassie asked.

Yvonne brought her gaze back to Cassie and tipped her head.

"Let me guess," Matthias said. "No clue."

The widow heaved a sigh. "I'm sorry I'm so little help. Orlando doesn't bring his work home with him and, frankly, I don't care about his carpentry skills unless something here breaks down. Even then I practically need to make an appointment to get any work done."

Cassie's expression was fading from kind mother hen to annoyed police detective.

Matthias decided to try a slightly different angle. "Do you know any of the people your husband worked with?"

"A few."

"Do you know how he got along with them?"

"Not well."

He wasn't sure if she meant she didn't know, or he didn't get along with them. Before he could ask for clarification, she gave it to him. "Orlando isn't known for being easy to work for. He's been in this line of business a long time. He's tough. Brutally tough sometimes. His employees come and go, mostly go. He always says if they can't stand the heat—"

"They can get out of the kitchen," Cassie ended the sentence for her.

"Precisely. And most of them got out in short order."

"What about the people *he* works for?" Matthias asked. "If he was tough, but did a good job, I imagine his clients liked him better than his employees."

"You would think so, wouldn't you?" Her words carried a healthy dose of sarcasm, but she closed her eyes and sighed loudly. When she opened them again, she looked at Matthias. "My husband made a lot of enemies. The men who worked for him hated him. The people he built houses for only hired him because, yes, he's good at what he does. What he isn't good at is interacting with folks. He feels that he's right no matter what."

"Is there anyone in particular you can think of who may have made threats?" Matthias asked. "Someone who may have wanted to do him harm?"

She snorted. "Harm? Take a number. Go to his office and start questioning everyone who's worked for or with him or who has hired him. You want a suspect list? It's a long one."

Cassie thanked her for her time and expressed their condolences, although Matthias didn't see any hint of grief in the woman. Back in the car, Cassie glared at the house. "That was one cold-ass woman. If she's right, we have our work cut out for us."

"I'm keeping *her* at the top of my list for now."

"Mine, too. I sure hope the ballistics lab match the gun and hand us a nice set of fingerprints." Cassie started the car. "That may be the only way we clear this case before Christmas."

Darcy Tomasetti's parents lived on a corner lot in a two-story house that boasted a fresh coat of gray paint over what looked like cedar shingles. With the classic picket fence edging the tiny yard, the place epitomized warm and inviting. Matthias wouldn't have been surprised to smell bread baking when a woman with dark hair flecked with gray answered the door.

"May I help..." The question died on April Tomasetti's lips as she took in Matthias's and Cassie's department-issue polo shirts with the Erie Bureau of Police badge embroidered on the left chest. Her gaze slid down to the real badges clipped to their belts, the guns holstered on their hips, and came back up to their faces. "Oh, dear God," she whispered. "Has something happened to Darcy?"

"Is your husband home, Mrs. Tomasetti?" Cassie asked, her voice soft.

"Yes." Tears flooded her eyes as April braced herself with a hand on the door frame and called over her shoulder, "Steven! The police are here."

Fifteen minutes passed as Matthias watched the couple cling to each other, weeping and mumbling their disbelief. He'd seen variations of this bone-deep anguish too many times to count. The Tomasettis seemed to carry their own sorrow in addition to the grief Yvonne Larson lacked. Finally, the bereaved parents led the detectives through a screened-in porch to a surprisingly wide open floorplan. Matthias and Cassie took the offered seats on a massive sectional that backed up to a spotless kitchen with appliances similar to those in Matthias's own kitchen. The walls were covered with photographs and watercolors of Lake Erie's shores

"We're so sorry for your loss," Cassie began.

"Thank you." Steven plucked some tissues from a box on the coffee table and handed them to his wife.

Once the grieving parents had settled on one end of the sofa, Cassie began with the routine questions. They hadn't seen Darcy in a couple of weeks, which wasn't unusual. She was supposed to come for dinner next Sunday. They had, however, spoken with and texted her on a daily basis. She'd been bubbling over with excitement about this new job.

"Darcy has always been so creative." April pointed to the

framed images on the walls. "All the drawings and photographs are hers."

"She designed the remodel of this house last year." Pride resonated in Steven's grief-stricken voice.

"It's beautiful," Cassie said.

Matthias kept quiet, letting his partner take the lead, but he had to agree. Darcy had been a talented young woman.

Cassie leaned forward, resting her elbows on her knees. "I realize this is a difficult question, but can you think of anyone who might have wanted to harm your daughter?"

Both parents appeared startled by the question. "Harm Darcy?" Steven echoed. "I— We ... assumed this was a robbery ... vandals breaking into the construction site. That sort of thing. You hear of it all the time. Except Darcy and her new boss were there. Wrong place, wrong time. You know?"

Vandals didn't usually execute people they encountered with single gunshots to the back of the head.

"That may very well turn out to be the case," Cassie replied, "but we'd be shirking our duties if we didn't look into all possibilities at this stage of the investigation."

Both parents nodded.

"I see," Steven said. "No, I can't think of anyone. Darcy was always smiling. Always kind. She volunteered at the food pantry."

"And at the animal shelter," April added. "She loves animals, but I'm allergic, so she could never have pets as a kid."

Steven touched his wife's leg. "What about her cat?" He looked at Cassie and Matthias. "I hadn't thought about it before, but since she has her own place now, she adopted a cat. Someone will need to take it in."

"We can't," April said to her husband and sounded on the verge of more tears.

"I know that, but it's..."—he sighed—"one more thing."

April looked imploringly at Cassie. "Do you know of anyone who could take it? I hate to think of it being abandoned."

Cassie shifted in her seat. "My husband's a vet—"

"That's perfect! Would you mind taking the poor kitty to him until we can find it a new home?"

"He does have a young woman on staff who helps place rescue animals."

"That would be a blessing. Thank you."

Matthias interrupted in an attempt to bring the conversation back on track. "Do you know of any arguments or disagreements Darcy might've had recently?"

Steven thought about it, then shook his head. "No. I told you. Everyone loved her. She wasn't the confrontational type."

"Wait." April's eyes narrowed in a scowl. "There was that man."

"What man?" Steven asked, sounding as if this was the first he'd heard of him.

"Her boyfriend."

"Ex-boyfriend, wasn't he?"

"I'm not sure. The last time Darcy mentioned him, I got the impression they were back together."

"No, I'm sure that was over weeks ago."

Cassie shot a glance at Matthias before asking, "Do you have a name for this boyfriend?"

"Ex-boyfriend," Steven said.

"Either way. A name?"

"She works—*worked* with him," April said. "His name's Preston Guilfoyle."

Chapter Four

Emma's first day as a crime beat photographer sucked. Granted, she hadn't seen the body of her colleague, for which she was eternally grateful, but the knowledge that Darcy had been killed, murdered, on her first day of her dream job broke Emma's heart. Preston had been a bear to be around, although he apologized several times. She understood. He and Darcy had worked together a long time. First, he got stuck with Emma as a new partner. Then, he had to write a story on his previous partner's murder. Emma was having enough trouble holding it together. She couldn't imagine what was going through Preston's mind.

By quitting time, Emma had edited the pictures she'd taken of the exterior of the house on Clifton Drive, and Preston had posted them and his write-up online. The plan was for the same group who'd celebrated Darcy last night to meet at a local bar to mourn her later this evening.

First, Emma needed to unwind and was grateful her yoga instructor and friend, Kira Petersen, had a class scheduled on the beach at Presque Isle.

Kira's ever-changing hair was now pink and matched her curve-fitting unitard. She gave Emma an appraising look but didn't ask questions in front of the other students. Another thing Emma was grateful for. Kira had an uncanny ability to read people and knew when to keep quiet.

The class was a vigorous one with a series of vinyasa flows. Sun salutations with extra poses thrown in. The movements combined with finding balance and footing on the shifting sands succeeded in draining Emma of her stress.

As Kira finally brought her students down onto their beach towels and yoga mats for *savasana*—corpse pose—Emma glanced around at the others to see if they were sweating as much as she was.

They were.

Emma's gaze settled on one young woman. A relatively new member of Kira's yoga community, the woman always positioned herself at the rear of the class and would dart out as soon as it was over. Today, in the sunlight, Emma noticed something else. Bruising on her upper arms. The woman spotted Emma watching her and quickly pulled on a long-sleeved shirt before settling on her back to rest and absorb the benefits of the work. The sleeves covered the bruises on her arms, but looking closer, Emma was certain makeup concealed more bruises around one eye.

Pushing aside what she saw, she stretched out and listened to Kira's soothing voice lull her into a deep relaxation.

Fifteen minutes later, Kira brought them back with the same calm tone. Once everyone was sitting up, they said "Namaste" in unison before rising and gathering their mats. Emma glimpsed Kira striding toward the woman with the bruises. She'd noticed, too. Emma tucked her mat under her arm and joined them.

Head lowered, the woman told Kira, "I'm fine."

"I know that's what you'd like everyone to believe, but I know where you can get help."

"I don't need help."

Emma spoke up. "I've been where you are. I had a boyfriend who grabbed me hard enough to create bruises, who thought slapping me around would keep me in control—"

"You're wrong." The woman lifted her face defiantly, but the brightness of the setting sun made the purple swelling beneath one eye shine through the makeup. "I'm a klutz. I ran into a door. That's all."

"But—" Before Kira could say more, the woman wheeled and sluffed through the sand toward the parking lot.

Emma sighed. "A door with fingers. I saw her arms before she put on that shirt."

"So did I." Kira turned to her. "I've been worried about Suzanne since she started coming to the studio."

"Suzanne? I didn't even know her name."

"Suzanne Foster. Very shy. Hardly says a word."

"That much, I knew."

Kira crossed her arms. "I'm not done with her. I'm not about to let one of my students get beat up by some man."

Emma had no doubt. Kira might come across as all calmness and light, but she was a force to be reckoned with outside of the yoga class.

Which was why Emma wasn't surprised when Kira turned to her. "What about you? I saw when you got here. You look like you've been through hell." She uncrossed her arms. "Oh, God. Don't tell me you and Matthias are having issues."

"No, no. We're fine. Rough day at work." She checked her watch. "I'd tell you about it, but I'm supposed to meet some friends in about half an hour. Thanks to you and your sun salutations, I need to shower first."

Kira smiled, but Emma could tell she wasn't letting her off the hook that easily. "Okay, but call me later."

"Will do."

Emma was glad the downtown bar Laurie had selected had a parking lot behind it. While Emma had no problems parallel parking her Subaru, there weren't any available spaces on the street. She found a prime spot in the lot though, close to the rear entrance. As she climbed out of the Forester and locked it with a beep, another car rumbled in and caught her attention.

Her father had been a muscle car aficionado all his life. While Emma had never been interested in owning one, some of his appreciation had rubbed off on her. Enough that she recognized a 1969 Dodge Super Bee when she saw it. This one was a dark green rather than the more popular vivid yellow but still boasted the signature black stripe around the rear of the car along with the angry bee logo. She watched the car park across the lot from her, and Preston stepped out. Head down, he crossed toward her and the door.

"Nice wheels," she said.

He looked up and a smile briefly replaced his sullen frown. "Thanks. I inherited it from my dad."

"My father was a gearhead, too. He'd probably have traded me and my sister for a car like that."

Preston appeared on the verge of saying something but changed his mind and gestured at the door. "After you."

Emma led the way through the rear entrance, along a poorly lit, narrow hallway with public restrooms on each side, and into the heart of the dining area. A bar stretched across the wall facing the windows. She spotted the ErieLIVE gang gathered around a group of tables off to the side and started toward them. A glance behind her revealed Preston had detoured to the bar. She surmised he needed a drink before facing the others.

Laurie spotted Emma and waved her to an empty stool beside her. "Helluva way to start a new job, huh?"

The Devil Comes Calling

"Yeah," Emma said. "Poor Darcy."

"Heartbreaking." Laurie lowered her voice and leaned closer to Emma's ear. "But I meant for you. I was afraid your new position as the crime-beat photographer might pose some challenges. I never dreamed it would involve a homicide with one of our own as the victim."

"It was definitely a shock." Emma hadn't known Darcy long but had liked her. "Preston's the one who's taking it hard, though. How long were he and Darcy partnered up?"

One of the other reporters, a scarecrow-thin man with thinning red hair, shouldered in. "Partnered up? Which way? Professionally or personally?" From his slurred speech, Emma knew the amber liquid in his glass was not his first of the evening.

"Boze," Laurie said with a note of warning in her voice, "not here. Not tonight."

"Why not? Emma's teamed up with him now. She should be aware of what he's like."

While she wasn't interested in workplace gossip, this caught her attention.

One of the women, a forty-something soccer mom who wrote a regular column about parenting, joined them. "What do you mean, 'what he's like'? Preston's a professional. He and Darcy just happened to gravitate toward each other. Two consenting adults."

Boze the redhead sipped his drink. "Preston is happy to consent with any good-looking woman and doesn't take no for an answer."

Soccer mom stepped closer. "That's nonsense and you—"

Laurie put a firm hand on Boze's shoulder. "She's right. You're spewing gossip with no basis in fact. Not good for a reputable reporter at any time. Especially when we're gathered in memory of our colleague. Either tone it down or leave."

Boze glared at her, but he swayed so badly Emma thought all Laurie had to do was sneeze and he'd fall over. Hard to be intimidating when you can barely stand up. He must've come to the same realization because he lowered his face. "Fine. I'll drop it." He started to teeter away but managed to brush Emma's shoulder. "We should talk later," he whispered. "You need to know who you're working with."

She watched him circle the group, his gait unsteady, until he settled in with another pair of reporters.

"Ignore him," Laurie said. "If Preston were the womanizer Boze claims, I wouldn't have him on my staff."

Soccer Mom hiked a hip onto one of the stools. "Boze is right about one thing. Preston and Darcy were more than work partners. At least for a while."

Emma figured this was more idle gossip and innuendos and started to turn away.

"They were quite the couple for a while there. Not just a crime fighting, crime reporting team, but a pair of lovebirds as well. Preston had it especially bad."

A waitress arrived with a tray laden with drinks and deposited a beverage laced with brightly colored fruit in front of Soccer Mom before handing a glass of white wine to Laurie. To Emma, she said, "What can I get you?"

Emma thought of the drive back to Sara's Campground and her seventeen-foot Terry travel trailer and almost ordered a ginger ale. Then she thought of Matthias's apartment only a block or so away. "Can you check back after you deliver those?" She pointed at the tray.

"Sure. Back in a minute."

Emma tugged her phone from her pocket with the intention of texting Matthias only to find one from him that she'd missed.

I'm home if you want to stop by.

She smiled and texted back.

I do. See you in about an hour. Maybe less.

He replied with a smiley emoji.

"—absolutely heartbroken," Soccer Mom was saying.

"I'm sorry. I missed that. Who's heartbroken?" Emma asked, then realized why they were there. "Oh, you mean all of us about Darcy."

"That, too, but I was saying when Darcy broke things off with Preston, it really messed him up. I think he was genuinely in love with her."

Laurie shook her head. "I hate all this gossip. Preston is a good reporter. Darcy was a damned good photographer…" She shot a look at Emma. "Not that *you* aren't. You are, and I'm glad to have you on board, but we were all sorry when Darcy decided to leave. Now look what's happened. We need to focus on remembering her as our friend and coworker and leave the rumor mill out of it."

Soccer Mom sipped her fruity drink. "You're right, of course, but I have one more thing to say on the subject and then I'll shut up. Preston's had a rough go of it lately. Darcy dumping him and them still working together was hard enough. Then she tendered her resignation, basically ending any chance he had of winning her back. It's no wonder he's been a bear around the newsroom lately." She fixed her gaze on Emma. "Just tread lightly. He'll get his shit together eventually, but until then, he's likely to bite your head off over nothing."

The sound of a crash behind her spun Emma around and turned all heads toward the bar. A stool was toppled, a waitress stood over a dropped tray and shattered glasses, her hands covering her mouth, and Preston had Boze pinned to the ground.

Laurie leaped toward them. Emma followed. Laurie caught Preston's wrist as he wound up to drive a fist into Boze's face. "Stop it," she commanded in a voice that may have halted traffic on the street outside.

Preston tried to shake her off, but she held fast. His attempts grew weak until he gave up. Laurie was taking no chances and refused to release her grip. Emma stepped in and caught him under the arm. Together, the two women hoisted him to his feet.

Boze clutched his cheek and scrambled away from them, staggering to stand. "You're crazy, you bastard."

"What the hell happened?" Laurie asked Preston, who glared red-faced at Boze.

"Nothing." Preston tried again to free himself from Laurie's grasp. Emma let go of his arm, but her boss held on. "Let go."

"Not until you explain yourself."

With his free hand, he pointed at Boze. "He's drunk."

"That's no reason to beat the crap out of him."

Preston glowered at Laurie. "Isn't it?"

She must've sensed she wasn't going to get anything more from him. "You need to get out of here and cool down."

"I won't argue with that. Coming here was a mistake. This whole thing is disrespectful to Darcy's memory." He tugged against Laurie's grip. This time, she released him. He shot a look at Emma that she couldn't quite interpret. Preston turned away and started to leave, but paused and shoved a folded twenty-dollar bill at the waitress along with an apology.

Laurie shook her head and mumbled something under her breath before returning to the others, including Boze, who held a glass of ice against his cheek.

The waitress stooped to pick up the tray. When she stood, she leaned closer to Emma. "I really don't blame Preston," she said.

"You know him?" Emma asked.

"He's a regular. Always tips well." She held up the twenty. "Not this well but you know what I mean." She shook her head. "You ask me, that skinny guy had it coming."

"Why?"

A man wearing a shirt bearing the bar's logo showed up with a broom and dustpan.

The waitress clamped the tray under her arm. "Because the skinny guy accused Preston of killing his girlfriend." She shook her head. "Isn't that the stupidest thing you've ever heard?"

Emma watched her walk away and had to wonder. Was it?

Chapter Five

Matthias flinched when his intercom buzzed. He was expecting Emma, but the last time he'd assumed it was her, he'd discovered Melissa at his door. He pounded down the steps and yanked open the door.

Emma appeared startled. "If this is a bad time, I don't have to come in."

He realized he must have what Cassie called his "scary look" on his face and forced Melissa from his mind. "Sorry. It's not a bad time. I was just thinking of something unpleasant." He reached out and guided her in with a hand on her back. Not for the first time, he thought he needed to give her a key.

Upstairs, she hung her purse over one of the hooks on the brick wall and kicked off her shoes.

Matthias crossed the floor to his kitchen. "Have you eaten yet?"

"Kinda."

"What's that mean?"

"Do appetizers at the French Street Tap House count?"

He faced her, about to ask what she'd been doing there, but instead he noticed how exhausted she looked.

He was an idiot. Emma had spent her first day on her new assignment working the story about her co-worker's murder. The French Street Tap House was a known hangout for journalists, which is why he never went there. She must've been with the other employees of ErieLIVE, drinking to Darcy Tomasetti's life, taken too soon.

In her stocking feet, Emma soundlessly walked into his arms and buried her face against his neck. He enveloped her, not asking how her day had been—he knew it'd been crap. Not asking how she was holding up—clearly she wasn't. But she wasn't sobbing or shaking either. She just needed a safe place.

And he was it.

He smiled and let her cling to him for however long she needed.

An hour later, she'd devoured a plate of shrimp curry. Matthias had added a number of vegetable and seafood dishes to his repertoire of signature dishes. Emma was a pescatarian, something she always stated apologetically. Granted, Matthias preferred a rare steak to fish any day of the week, but he loved to cook for her. Those meals were a small price to pay.

With the loaded dishwasher rumbling, they moved to the sofa where she curled up against his shoulder. Life was good.

The realization immediately sent him back to yesterday morning's visitor and the news she brought.

"What's wrong?" Emma lifted her head and looked at him with concern in her almost-teal eyes. "You tensed up there for a minute."

He cupped her head with one hand, gently drawing it back against him. "It's nothing." It was far from nothing, but he wasn't yet ready to broach the subject of Isaiah Honeywell—or Melissa, for that matter—with her.

They sat in comfortable silence for several long, sweet minutes before Emma again spoke. "Have you made any progress on Darcy's murder? Anything you can tell me, that is."

"It's early in the investigation. I will say, Orlando Larson's wife is a piece of work."

"You think she's responsible?"

"I didn't say that. Do not print that in the news."

"I'm just a lowly photographer. They don't let me write copy."

"Okay, but don't repeat anything I say to Preston Guilfoyle either."

Emma lifted her head again. "I wouldn't. Let him find his own sources."

Matthias caught an odd look in her eyes. He was trying to think of a subtle way to ask about Guilfoyle but didn't need to make the effort.

"A bunch of us from ErieLIVE got together earlier this evening at the Tap House. That's why I was there."

"I figured as much."

She gazed toward the windows. From her expression, Matthias knew she was debating how much to say. "There were a lot of rumors ... gossipy stuff ... flying around."

"What kind of rumors?"

"About Darcy being romantically involved with Preston. They were partners, you know."

He did.

"And a fight broke out."

"A fight? You mean...?" He made a fist with the hand not resting on her neck.

"Yeah."

"Who?"

"Preston and another reporter. Guy goes by the name Boze."

"What happened?"

"Boze was drunk and mouthy. I know that much first-hand.

He was babbling about Preston and Darcy being involved and made it sound like Preston was a lady's man."

Matthias sensed Emma was holding back. "Did you believe this guy? Boze?"

She wrinkled her nose in thought. "He was drunk. Really drunk. I don't know how much legitimacy you can give to anyone's claims when they're in that condition. Anyhow, next thing I know, Boze is on the floor with Preston on top of him, beating the snot out of him. Laurie put a stop to it, and Preston left. A waitress who was right there when the fight started told me Boze deserved it."

"For saying Guilfoyle's a lady's man?" Hardly seemed a good reason to get into a brawl.

"That and some other stuff."

"What other stuff?"

She squirmed. "Boze was drunk."

"You already told me that."

Emma fell silent. Matthias watched her, waiting.

Finally, in an almost inaudible voice, she said, "Boze accused Preston of having something to do with Darcy's death."

Matthias pondered her words, remembering what Mrs. Tomasetti had told them. Remembering what Cassie had told him about her interview with the reporter. Matthias made a mental note to look deeper into Guilfoyle's past, both recent and more distant.

Matthias's gaze fell on the pictures hanging on the wall next to the window. There were three. One was from his first day in uniform with four of his fellow patrolmen. The second was his favorite photo of himself as a teen astride his horse back in Oklahoma. He liked to think he looked like a matinee cowboy in it, complete with hat and boots.

The third photo was the only picture he had left of his mom. Emma had taken note of it the first time she'd been here. Mom was also astride a horse—one of her championship barrel racers—in action, leaning hard into the sharp turn around a barrel. She'd brought home a trophy from that competition. One of many.

Something seemed off about that photo. He wasn't OCD by any means, but the picture was slightly—very slightly—askew.

He'd probably bumped it walking past without realizing it.

Except, his spidey senses were tingling like mad.

"Something else happened today that's bugging me," Emma said, and he reeled his thoughts back to the woman snuggled against him. "I took a yoga class with Kira over on the beach before I met the gang at the Tap House. There was a woman there. I've seen her at a couple of classes before. She's super timid. Never stays around to chat. Today, I noticed she had bruises on her arms." Emma touched her own bicep. "She had makeup on, so it was hard to tell for sure, but I'm positive she also had a black eye."

She had his full attention. "What's her name?" he asked.

She scowled, thinking. "Suzanne," she said after a few moments. "I can't remember her last name. Kira knows it. We both tried to talk to her after class, to offer help, but she claimed she'd walked into a door and that she was fine."

"Any chance that's true?"

"Not a snowball's in hell." Emma's tone left no doubt. "The bruises on her arm were shaped like fingers. Someone grabbed her. Hard." Her head dropped back against his shoulder again. "I don't suppose you know of any assault charges filed by a young woman, do you?"

"I know of lots of them, unfortunately. Some might be Suzanne's. But without a last name? I don't have a place to start."

"I figured. I'll have to ask Kira."

Emma's voice became so soft, Matthias thought she might be falling asleep. He let her. The only thing missing from his apartment to make this a perfect evening was a fireplace.

The thought rekindled his unease. Remaining still, to avoid disturbing Emma, he surveyed his living space. Everything was as it should be. Nothing moved. Nothing missing. And yet...

He hadn't survived in law enforcement for as long as he had without developing a sixth sense, and his was blaring like a claxon.

Someone had been in his apartment, touching his possessions, invading his privacy.

The next morning, Matthias fixed Emma a breakfast of scrambled eggs and hashbrowns with freshly squeezed orange juice. He loved having someone to cook for and loved watching her devour his food. After sharing a cup of coffee, he gave her a long, lingering kiss and sent her on her way. Then he grabbed his duffel bag and walked the two blocks south to the police station. He spent his usual hour in the gym, hit the showers, dressed and was at his desk early. But not early enough to arrive before Cassie.

He felt her eyes on him as he slipped into his cubicle.

"Damn," she said from her desk behind his.

He couldn't see her, yet knew the single word was directed at him. "What?"

"I knew it."

"Knew what?"

"That all you needed was a good woman in your bed to snap you out of all your anger issues."

He closed his eyes, choosing to ignore her.

Cassie rose and came around the divider to stand over him. "Your step is lighter. Your face isn't all crunched up like you want to take a bite out of anyone who crosses your path."

"Yet you have no scars matching my teeth imprints."

"That's because I'm even meaner than you are."

He snorted. "I'm not about to argue the point."

"How's Emma?"

He mulled over the question rather than snap a short, easy reply. "She told me about something that happened last night." He shared what he'd learned about the bar fight and the workplace rumors regarding Preston Guilfoyle and Darcy Tomasetti.

"Fist fight, huh?" Cassie leaned against the wall behind her. "Shows he has a temper."

His thoughts exactly. Although whoever had fired two shots into the backs of Larson's and Darcy's heads had been methodical, all business.

"I'd like to have a talk with the guy at the receiving end of that temper. What'd you say his name is?"

"All Emma said was Boze." And Matthias had been thinking the same thing. "Have you come up with the name of the owner of the house on Clifton?"

Cassie pushed away from the wall and retreated to her desk. "No, and it's beginning to annoy me. From what I've found out from Larson's subcontractors and suppliers, it was to be a standard flip. Gut remodel, modernize the design, stage, and resell, hopefully making money."

"I know what a flip is," Matthias growled.

Cassie ignored him. "If it's so standard, why hide the true ownership behind shell companies? Feels a lot like someone else we know."

He rose and circled to stand behind her, looking over her shoulder at her monitor. "Please tell me Erie Huron and Ontario Holdings is involved." They'd had no luck building a case against Russ Carlisle for any of his known misdeeds so far. Tying him and his father-in-law's conglomerate to a double homicide would make Matthias's day.

"Sorry. You know that would be too easy. From what I can tell, there's no connection between our crime scene and Carlisle."

Cassie pivoted her chair to face him. "After we talk to Boze, I think we should go have another talk with Guilfoyle. He doesn't seem like the execution-style gunman, but he's the best we have right now."

Matthias was in total agreement. Especially since Emma was now working side-by-side with this guy.

Emma arrived in the newsroom early but was still surprised by all the empty desks. Laurie's wasn't one of them. She appeared at her office door and gestured to Emma. "Can I have a minute?"

Laurie's tone was unreadable. Emma hoped this wasn't akin to being summoned to the principal's office.

Once Emma entered the small glass-walled room, Laurie took a seat at her desk. "Close the door, please."

Emma did as she was told. When she again faced her manager, Laurie had set a cardboard box on the desk. She leaned down to heft a second identical one from the floor and thumped it beside the first. "I have an assignment for you."

Emma glanced over her shoulder toward Preston's currently vacant desk.

Laurie must've read her mind. "This one's just for you. I told Preston to take some time off after what happened last night."

Emma relaxed. She wasn't in trouble with the boss, but Preston was. "What do you need me to do?"

"Don't misunderstand." Laurie gave her a kind smile. "You'll still be teamed with Preston. I told him to take a personal day. Two if he feels he needs it. Once he gets his head on straight, he'll be fine. He's a good reporter, and you'll work well together once he deals with his grief." She placed a hand on one of the boxes. "For now, I need you to go through these."

Curious, Emma stepped closer. "What's in there?"

"You're taking over Darcy's position. She was a talented photographer, but…"—Laurie sighed heavily—"God rest her soul, she was horribly disorganized." Laurie lifted the lid on the first box.

Emma peered inside to see stacks of photographs. "Are these Darcy's?"

"Yes."

"She wasn't concerned about saving trees, was she?" Emma rarely printed out her photos unless she planned to frame a few for one of the local businesses that offered them for sale. Instead, she kept them stored in the cloud. Then again, Emma lived in a seventeen-foot camper, so physical storage space was nonexistent.

Laurie chuckled. "No, she wasn't. I've also granted you access to Darcy's online storage account. I'd like you to go through her images when you have time and put them in some sort of order. If you can match these to ones already stored online, shred them. Keep anything without a jpg backup but organize them as best you can."

Emma stared into the box. There had to be hundreds, possibly thousands of prints, and that was just one of the boxes.

"There's no rush. Like I said. Whenever you have spare time. But since Preston is off today, I thought it'd be a good chance to get started." Laurie replaced the lid, lifted the box, and held it out. "Have fun."

Emma accepted the box with a weak grin. "Thanks."

Chapter Six

"According to the woman I spoke with," Cassie said from behind the wheel of the department-issued Chevy Malibu, "Guilfoyle took a personal day."

Matthias wondered how bad the bar fight had been if the guy needed to recover at home. Unless it turned out he wasn't there.

"Boze, however, is currently at the Maritime Museum working on a story about the Niagara."

"I haven't been over to see the Niagara in a while," Matthias said sardonically.

"There's no time like the present."

The museum was a four-minute drive north from the police station. The large, historical brick building that once housed an electrical power plant on the edge of Presque Isle Bay now housed exhibits of a nautical nature. Matthias and Cassie showed their badges to the man at the admissions desk, who told them they could find the reporter outside on the dock.

Most years, finding the U.S. Brig Niagara in port was a hit-or-miss proposition, but the tall ship was undergoing repairs and was currently draped in tarps. Standing on the dock, looking up at it was a red-headed man so thin he reminded Matthias of one of the brig's masts. The notebook in his hand singled him out as the person they were looking for.

"Mr. Boze?" Matthias asked as they approached.

"Just Boze," he said, turning toward them. His swollen and bruised left cheek was another giveaway that they had the right guy. He stiffened when he spotted their police attire. "What do you want?"

Matthias identified himself and Cassie. "We have a few questions for you regarding an altercation you were involved in last night."

Boze touched his cheek at the mention of the fight. "Don't tell me Preston is pressing charges for my face bruising his knuckles. I should be the one sending the cops after him."

"Do you want to press charges?" Cassie asked.

He scowled, considering it. "No. I'm sure I said some stuff I shouldn't have."

"Like what?"

Boze eyed them. "What have you heard?"

Matthias didn't answer, instead telling him, "We'd like your version of it."

Boze lowered his face. "To be perfectly honest, I'm not sure what I said. I'd had a few too many drinks. I don't remember much except that I was being an ass, and Preston took offense."

Cassie crossed her arms. "I understand you made some accusations about Preston and Darcy. Care to share what you know with us?"

"Not really."

They stared at him, waiting.

"Look. I don't like Preston. I *did* like Darcy. So, yeah, the news about her death hit me—hit *all* of us—hard. There were rumors flying around and"—he made a pained face—"in my drunken state, I probably gave them too much credence. From there, my mouth got me in trouble. My mom would tell you that happens all the time, even when I'm sober."

"Rumors," Matthias echoed. "About Preston and Darcy?"

"Yeah."

"We have a witness who says you made some accusations about him being responsible for her death."

"I'm sure I did." Boze pulled himself to his full height, which towered over Matthias and brought him eye-to-eye with Cassie. "As I told you, I was drunk. I goaded Preston because he thinks he's God's gift to the journalism world. And to women. I deserved what I got." Boze swallowed. "Darcy didn't. Beyond that, I got nothing more to say." He turned and walked away.

Once he'd disappeared through the museum's rear entrance, Cassie asked, "What do you think?"

Matthias pondered the question. "I've said some stupid shit when drunk, too. In the sober light of day?" He shrugged. "If he really believed Guilfoyle was guilty, you would think we'd be the people he'd tell."

Cassie made a face. "Doesn't mean it isn't true. Let's go see the man responsible for those bruises."

The address they had for Guilfoyle was an apartment unit outside of the downtown area. The three-story building looked like it was built in the seventies—all steel and glass—and hadn't been updated since.

Guilfoyle, wearing a Buffalo Bills T-shirt and plaid boxers, answered their knock on the second try. His eyes were mere slits and dark stubble covered his cheeks. Matthias didn't need to be a detective to know this guy had tied one on last night and was paying the price this morning.

Cassie held up her badge and introduced them. "You and I talked yesterday, remember?"

"Yeah. I remember," Guilfoyle said, sounding like he wished he didn't.

"Mind if we come in?"

He hesitated for a split second before stepping back and opening the door wide.

The apartment reeked of liquor. A nearly empty bottle of Jack Daniels sat on the kitchen counter next to an empty whiskey glass. Dirty laundry buried the sofa and recliner, leading Matthias to wonder if the place was a mess because its occupant was grieving or if he was merely a slob.

Guilfoyle excused himself to duck into one of the rooms at the rear of the apartment, allowing Matthias time to give the space a thorough inspection. Unlike the exterior, the interior had seen a renovator's hand. The kitchen was nothing fancy—builder's grade cabinets, cheap but functional appliances—but everything was in modern shades of white, gray, and black.

Guilfoyle returned wearing a flannel robe tied at the waist. "I don't know what more I can tell you beyond what I said yesterday."

Cassie folded her arms. "You failed to mention you and Darcy Tomasetti were an item."

He glanced from her to Matthias. "We weren't."

"Maybe not now, but you used to be."

"No, we didn't. We worked together. That's all."

"Do you always go on a bender when a colleague dies?" Matthias asked, picking up the bottle of Jack.

"I've never had a colleague die before, so I'll have to let you know if it happens again." Guilfoyle must've realized how he sounded. "Look. Having my partner murdered shook me up. I may not have been dating her, but I liked her well enough. It was a shock."

"But she wasn't your partner any longer," Cassie said. She plastered on her sympathetic face. "That must've hurt like hell. Having her quit and go get another job."

"Not really. It was what she wanted to do. She was excited about it. I was happy for her."

Matthias didn't buy it. "Had you ever met the man who was killed at the same time she was?"

"Orlando Larson? No. Why would I?" Guilfoyle showed no sign of changing his story.

"When was the last time you saw Darcy?"

Guilfoyle nodded at Cassie. "She asked me that yesterday. We had a going away party for Darcy on Sunday evening at the ErieLIVE office."

Matthias made a note on his pad. "You didn't run into her later?"

"Nope."

"Have you ever been to the house where she died?" Cassie asked. "Besides yesterday, I mean."

"Never."

"You weren't romantically involved with Darcy?"

"I told you. No. I never saw her outside of work."

"Don't suppose you can tell us where you were Sunday night and early Monday morning."

"As a matter of fact, I can." Guilfoyle glared at Cassie. "I met up with my cousin after the party on Sunday night. He and I went to his house and played video games. It was late, so I crashed in his spare room. I showered there in the morning and went straight to work."

"What's your cousin's name?" Matthias asked.

"Quentin Donahue," Guilfoyle said and spelled it. He volunteered the cousin's address over in Harbor Creek and looked up his phone number as well. "He'll back me up. I was nowhere near Clifton Drive."

"He's not answering," Cassie said from behind the wheel as they sat in front of Guilfoyle's apartment building.

"Of course not." This was going to be one of *those* cases. Uncooperative witnesses. Deeply buried ownership records. A crime scene so messy, discerning real evidence from construction debris was nearly impossible. He listened as Cassie left Quentin Donahue a message requesting a call back as soon as possible.

"Oh, look." Cassie flashed her phone's screen revealing her email. "We can get into Darcy's apartment now. Let's head there next." She kept scrolling and reading. "And Ham's scheduled the autopsies for ten. Perfect timing."

Matthias grunted. He hated autopsies.

"I'll take that as a yes." She started the engine.

"Do you really think Hamilton's going to tell us anything we don't already know?"

It was Cassie's turn to grunt.

Fifteen minutes later, they stood in the doorway to Darcy's downtown apartment. A uniform kept guard in the hallway. "The crime scene dudes have finished doing their thing," he said. Meaning they didn't need to put on their protective booties. "Once you guys are done, we can release the apartment to the victim's family."

Cassie thanked him, and they stepped inside. She headed for the hallway.

Matthias moved to the center of the small but open space, taking in the dozens of photos hanging on the walls. Some were duplicates of those he'd seen in Darcy's parents' home, but most were stylized versions of what could be found on ErieLIVE's website. Crime scenes but close up. A few raw emotional images of people he surmised were victims' families.

One grouping drew his attention. He moved closer. These

images were different. Smiling faces, some of whom he recognized as other ErieLIVE employees. A couple of selfies—Darcy mugging with Guilfoyle, another with Laurie.

Matthias reached up and lifted the last one off its hook.

For a moment, he flashed on the old pictures hanging in his own apartment and the feeling he'd had of someone else having been there.

"Don't suppose you've seen a cat, have you?" Cassie asked the uniform still standing at the door, her voice snapping Matthias from his reverie.

"No, ma'am."

She looked at Matthias. "You?"

He replaced the photo. "No."

"I told Darcy's parents I'd take it to my husband's veterinary clinic. There's an empty food bowl in the kitchen and a second bowl full of water. And there's a litter box back there." She aimed a thumb at the hallway off to one side. "Needs to be scooped. But I don't see the cat."

Matthias scanned the room. "Maybe the parents changed their mind and came and got it."

"Parents haven't been allowed in yet," the uniform said.

Cassie looked around. "It's probably hiding. Cats do that."

"I wouldn't know," Matthias said. "I'm a dog guy."

"You don't have a dog."

"Landlord doesn't allow pets."

Cassie heaved an exasperated sigh and crooked a finger at him. "Come check this out,"

"What'd you find? Besides a dirty litter box, that is."

Without answering, she led the way to one of three open doors —a bedroom, a bathroom, and the one she entered. An office.

It reminded him of a larger version of Emma's camper. A pair of folding tables held three monitors, a pair of keyboards, an open but dark laptop, and a computer tower. More photos hung on the walls. A large set of floor-to-ceiling shelves held several cameras, lenses, camera bags, and assorted other photo equipment.

Cassie crossed to the laptop and touched the mousepad. The screen woke up, displaying a photo of one of Presque Isle's beaches. In the center, a request for a PIN. She closed the lid. "We need to haul all of this to the station and let the tech guys go through it."

"I doubt they'll find anything useful."

She turned to him with an annoyed scowl. "I take back what I said earlier about Emma making you less grumpy. What's with you today? You don't think Ham's going to give us anything. You don't think Darcy's computers are going to give us anything…"

He wasn't about to tell her his father had been released from prison or that he had a weird feeling about someone being in his apartment. "You're right. I don't. I think both our victims were executed with single GSWs to the back of the head. I doubt there's any mysterious cause of death, and I don't think Darcy is hiding anything murder-worthy on her computers. I think we're wasting our time interviewing ex-boyfriends and her parents."

Cassie crossed her arms. "What exactly do you think we should be doing?"

"Looking into Orlando Larson. Who owes him money? Who does he owe money to? Who stands to benefit from his death? I'm thinking his widow was far from grief-stricken when we broke the news to her. And the big one. Who owns the property over on Clifton Drive? The fact you haven't been able to figure that out bugs the hell out of me."

Cassie stared at him, her lips parted. "Wow. That's the most I've heard you say at one time in … like … ever."

He gave her a dirty look. "You asked."

"I did. And I agree with you, but we can't ignore that Darcy was there."

"Wrong place, wrong time. First day on the job. I hate the phrase, but I believe Darcy Tomasetti was collateral damage."

"I do, too, but if we don't take all this"—she gestured at the room's contents—"into evidence, we'd be shirking our duties."

He surveyed the electronics filling the room. Cassie made a good point, and if he hadn't been so damned distracted and impatient, he'd have already started bagging and tagging. "You're right."

"I know I am." She grinned smugly. "So, we're admitting Darcy's computers and cameras into evidence, we're going to the morgue to oversee hers and Larson's autopsies. Then we're going to do a deep dive into Larson's life and business." She turned toward the hallway. "Did you hear that?"

"What?"

She raised a finger, listening.

He heard it. A tiny chirp of a meow.

Cassie smiled. "But first, I'm going to find the cat and we'll drop it off at Shawn's clinic."

Emma had taken up residence in one of ErieLIVE's vacant conference rooms. It was nothing fancy. A long table and some plastic folding chairs in a larger version of Laurie's office with thin half walls topped with glass. No privacy, but Emma didn't need to hide. She just needed space to spread out a few hundred of Darcy's photos.

About a half hour into her task, Laurie showed up in the open door. "Change of plans. Leave all of this. I need you on a story. There was an armed robbery at the Bay Harbor Convenience Store over on Cherry Street. Do you know it?"

"Yeah, I do."

"Good. I talked to Preston. He's feeling better and will meet you there." Laurie wheeled and hurried away.

Emma studied the photo in her hand, an image of two men on a street corner, neither of whom she knew. She flipped it over. Nothing on the back. No names. No date. No location. She tossed it on a pile of similarly unlabeled photos, shut off the lights, closed the door, and jogged to grab her camera equipment.

The police had roped off the parking lot and sidewalk around the convenience store. Looky-loos gathered outside the yellow tape, gawking at the store's entrance. Emma parked a block away and lugged her camera bag toward the crowd, digging out one of her Nikons on the way. She spotted Preston, who looked uncharacteristically rumpled, speaking with an elderly gentleman, and eased up beside them.

Preston thanked the man for his time, and Emma asked for and received permission to capture a photo of him.

"Eyewitness to the getaway," Preston said. "I got his name to go with your picture."

"Thanks." She took in the dark circles under his eyes, his mussed hair. "Are you okay?"

At first, she thought he was going to snap at her, but he drew a deep breath. "Not really, but I'm working on it."

"Good." She tipped her head toward the store. "What happened?"

He relayed what he knew. A white male in a ski mask had pulled a gun on the employees and demanded money from the cash drawer, which they had turned over without argument, and the safe, to which the two employees had no access. He'd grabbed a bunch of merchandise and got away. "The man I was talking to got a look at him, but because of the mask, he couldn't give a great description beyond what he was wearing. And his eyes. The suspect has light brown eyes." Preston gestured around. "Take some photos of the overall scene. I'm going to try to get one of the cops to give an interview."

"Got it."

He turned to leave but hesitated and faced her. "By the way, I need to apologize."

"No, you don't."

"Yes. I do. I've been a son of a bitch lately. I'm sorry you got stuck in the middle of it. Especially last night. I was drunk."

No kidding, she thought.

"I don't usually drink for that very reason. I don't handle booze well. I'm sorry, and it won't happen again. You have my word."

Before she could accept the apology, he turned and jogged away.

Emma watched him go. This was the Preston Guilfoyle she'd come to know—although not well—since starting to work at ErieLIVE. Professional. Polite.

She felt bad for ratting him out to Matthias.

A familiar-looking unmarked sedan pulled up at the end of the block. Emma knew an Erie City Police Detective's vehicle when she saw one, but neither of the two men who climbed out was Matthias. She lifted her camera and focused on the store front, snapping a few images. Then she moved behind the crowds, grabbing a shot here and there until she reached the end of the crime scene tape barricade. From that angle, she aimed her camera back toward the curiosity seekers and pressed the shutter button. A face in the crowd made her lower the Nikon and blink. She brought the viewfinder to her eye again and zoomed in as much as the lens allowed. It was Suzanne from yoga class. Suzanne with the bruises.

Emma again lowered the camera and took one step in the

direction of the young woman but froze. She didn't need a zoom lens to recognize the man who sidled up next to Suzanne and slipped an arm around her waist.

Emma's breath stopped. The man at Suzanne's side was Russ Carlisle, who'd brutalized Emma's sister as well as another woman who worked for him.

The bruises now made sense.

Emma lifted her camera, brought the viewfinder to her eye. The moment she brought Russ's face into focus, he turned his head and looked directly at her.

She snapped a photo. Then another. A smirk crossed his lips, and he tipped his head, acknowledging her with a nod.

He could be looking at someone near her in the crowd. She tried to convince herself of that. But she was well aware Russ had seen her taking his photo.

Part of her felt comforted. I have my eye on you, you son of a bitch, she thought. Part of her felt unnerved. Yes, she was watching him...

But he knew it.

And was watching her, too.

Chapter Seven

By early afternoon, the morning clouds had given way to a blue sky and brilliant sunshine. Temperatures were climbing, but the bay was less than a half a dozen blocks away, and a northern breeze kept the air comfortable. After dropping Darcy's cat off at Shawn Malone's veterinary practice, Matthias and Cassie returned to the police station. Instead of going inside, they left their car on South Park Row and walked to the morgue.

As Matthias predicted, Hamilton offered no epiphanies regarding the deaths of Darcy or Larson. The coroner had retrieved the bullet from inside Larson's skull but neither had suffered any damage other than the devastation done to the brain by a twenty-two-caliber slug.

Which reminded Matthias. They needed to check with ballistics and find out if the bullet found at the house on Clifton Drive matched the revolver found in the dumpster. If so, it was a sure bet this one would also match.

Hamilton reported finding no defensive wounds, no skin beneath Darcy's fingernails. He determined the trajectory of both

GSWs was downward and surmised both victims were on their knees when shot.

Execution style, as they'd suspected from the beginning.

Or made to look that way, Matthias thought.

With the bullet in an evidence bag tucked safely in Cassie's pocket, they walked back to the station. Instead of turning right on Peach, Cassie pointed at Perry Square Park. "Let's take the scenic route."

They crossed at the light and passed between the Civil War Soldiers and Sailors statue and the Korean War Memorial to enter the park. Folks were enjoying the sunshine, wandering the paved pathways, taking photos of the monuments, and sitting on benches. Instinctively, Matthias scanned faces and knew Cassie was doing the same. It was a cop thing. Were there signs of strain in anyone's expressions? Was anyone he'd locked up lurking about? Was anyone giving them a little too much attention? Or trying too hard to avoid eye contact?

They followed the path toward the police station and were almost on South Park Row when Matthias spotted a face that stirred a tsunami of emotions. The man appeared to be close to eighty, but Matthias knew he was ten years younger than that. With pure white hair, he was the same height as Matthias's five foot eight and every bit as muscled.

Matthias hadn't seen him in over twenty years—the last time had been in a courtroom—but even through the decades, he recognized his father.

Isaiah Honeywell sat on one of the benches and came to his feet as Matthias approached, slowing his gait with each step.

Cassie noticed and frowned at him. "What's going on?"

"Nothing," Matthias said low enough that only she could hear. "Keep going. I'll meet you inside."

"Hello, son."

The voice took Matthias back to his teens, back to the pain, physical and emotional. Back to that night.

"Son?" Cassie's voice was a mere whisper.

But Isaiah clearly heard. He held out a hand to her. "I'm Isaiah Honeywell, ma'am. This here's my boy."

Matthias reacted, stepping forward before Cassie could respond and slapped the bastard's hand away.

Cassie flinched, her shocked gaze on Matthias, but she said nothing.

Isaiah raised both hands. In surrender? Showing he was unarmed? Matthias wasn't sure. Nothing was ever cut and dried where he was concerned. "Easy, boy. I just came here to see you. To make amends."

"Amends?" Matthias stepped even closer, keeping his voice a low growl.

"Yeah. Amends. I know it's too soon to ask forgiveness. I have a long way to go to earn that."

"Like all the way to Hell."

"I've spent twenty-five years thinking about you. How I done you wrong."

Matthias glared at him, seething. He had so much he could say. So many questions he could ask. But not here in a public park with youngsters running about, within sight of his place of employment. Even if they'd been in private, there was nothing Matthias could say to make any difference.

His mother would still be dead.

"I guess you heard I got out."

"If you had … any … sense of…" Matthias stuttered. "If you had any feelings for me…"—he knew he didn't—"you would've stayed in Oklahoma."

"I needed to see you. I needed to see for myself how you're doing." Isaiah gestured at Matthias's detective's uniform—dark polo with an Erie City Bureau of Police badge embroidered on it, dark trousers with his real badge clipped to his belt—and smiled. "I should've known you'd become a cop." There was no pride in his tone.

"You've seen. Now get the hell out of Erie. Out of Pennsylvania. Out of the country would be even better."

Isaiah acted as if he hadn't heard. "Tell me about yourself, son. How are you?" He tilted his head slightly. "How is Melissa?"

Matthias realized his hands were aching from being clenched. Without breaking eye contact, he stretched his fingers.

"You're probably wondering how I know about her. I've kept tabs on you, son. More than you've kept on me, I bet. I know she left you." Isaiah tsk-tsked. "That's a shame. She's one fine-looking woman."

Matthias leaned in, his face only inches from his father's. "My life is none of your business. As far as I'm concerned, you've been dead for twenty-five years. And if I ever see you again..." He stopped before uttering the threat, although he meant it with every inch of his being. *If I ever see you again, you will be dead.* Instead, he repeated, "Get the hell out of my city."

Isaiah shrugged and stepped aside. He faced Cassie and gave her a nod. "Ma'am." Then he turned and strolled away, just another tourist taking in the sights and the sun.

A hand touched his arm. Matthias jerked away. But it was Cassie. "Easy," she said.

He realized he was trembling. In just a few minutes in his old man's presence, he'd reverted to that terrified, angry teen, seething with rage to avoid cowering in fear. He took a deep breath. Blew it out slowly. Forced every muscle in his body to relax. "Sorry," he told his partner. God, he wished she'd done as he'd asked and just kept going. He hated what she'd witnessed.

"What was that all about?" she asked. "You have a father?"

The question struck him as funny. Maybe there was hope for him after all. "You think I just hatched?"

She gave him the side-eye. "I know you had a father, smart ass. I just assumed he was dead. I know you said your mother died when you were a kid. I figured he had, too."

"It's too bad he didn't," Matthias said under his breath as he started once again toward the police station.

Cassie fell in beside him. "You still haven't said what that was all about?"

He glanced around. "Not here."

She let it drop. Or so he thought.

Once inside, they deposited the bullet at the ballistics lab. Before they started up the stairs to Major Crimes, Cassie caught him by the arm and steered him into an empty interview room.

She closed the door behind them and stood with her back against it, arms crossed. "Okay, spill."

He faced her and mirrored her crossed arms. His past, his father, the whole mess was none of her concern.

The standoff went on for what felt like minutes. Hours. Until she hiked one eyebrow. A silent, "I'm not backing down."

He knew she wouldn't. The question was how little could he get away with telling her? "My father's been in prison for the better part of the last twenty-five years."

"I gathered that much."

"He just got out."

"Tell me something I haven't already heard out in the park."

She'd already heard more than he wanted her to.

"Okay, since you aren't going to make it easy." She opened her arms wide, indicating the room they were in. "What was he in for?"

At least she hadn't insisted Matthias take a seat at the table. "Homicide."

"Whose?"

He lowered his face, not wanting his partner to see his pain.

"*Whose?*" she repeated in her annoyed cop voice.

Matthias set his jaw and met her gaze. "My mother's. I walked into their house and found the son of a bitch standing over her, holding the gun."

Cassie's lips parted. "Oh, my God. How old were you at the time?"

"Seventeen." He prayed she'd let it go at that.

But of course, she didn't. "What happened then?"

"I called the cops. They came and arrested him. I buried my mother." The truth, but not the whole truth.

He felt Cassie's eyes drilling into his brain. Instead of pressing for all the details he did not want to unearth, she asked, "Who's Melissa?"

Any other time, he'd have wanted to avoid that topic, too, but considering the alternative, this was an easy question to answer. "My ex-girlfriend. I met her shortly after I became a cop. She was from here but working in Oklahoma. I was … in love." True but hard to admit. Considering. "Within a year, she lost her job and decided to move back here. I came with her."

"I'd always wondered how an Oklahoma boy ended up in northern Pennsylvania."

He lifted one hand, palm up. "There you have it."

"What happened?"

That's where it got touchy. "I bought her a ring. Proposed. Wine. Roses. The whole enchilada. She turned me down. Said she couldn't be married to a cop. Two months later, she got engaged to a lawyer."

"Ouch."

"Yeah." He dragged the word out. "They got married and moved away. I thought about moving back to Oklahoma." Except he had nothing back there. "Decided I liked my brothers in blue here in Erie, so I stayed." He huffed, thinking he'd made the right choice, especially since Melissa and her lawyer husband had ultimately settled in his home state.

Cassie studied him, her dark eyes soft. "That explains a lot."

He wasn't sure what she meant but didn't want to keep this can of worms open any longer. "I notice you didn't tell your father about Emma."

Every muscle in Matthias's body tensed. "The less he knows about my life, the better."

Cassie acknowledged him with a nod. "Understandable. This is why you've been so jumpy the last couple of days, isn't it? You knew he'd been released."

He didn't reply but pointed at the door. "You gonna let me out now?"

"I suppose." She moved aside and opened it. As he stepped past her, she leaned closer and said, "I know there's more to this. If you ever want to talk…"

He paused in the doorway. "I won't."

Matthias shoved the encounter in the park and Cassie's interrogation to the back of his mind and focused on Orlando Larson. Cassie'd had no luck tracking down the owner of the house on Clifton, so Matthias gave it a shot. An hour later, he was even more frustrated. "Dammit."

From the cubicle behind him, Cassie's melodic voice floated out. "Told you so." She wheeled her chair into the aisle and around the partition. "Why on earth would anyone bury their ownership of a flip house so deeply?"

Matthias shook his head. "It feels like something Russ Carlisle and his father-in-law would do."

"Yes, it does, but can you find even a hint of a link to them?"

"No." Pinning a murder on Carlisle through his father-in-law's holding company would be too easy. And too gratifying.

She threw up both hands. "There you go." She reached over and thumped him on the shoulder. "But come see what I found."

He rose and followed her around the divider to her space.

"I started looking into Quentin Donahue."

"Guilfoyle's alibi? I thought we'd decided to focus on Larson."

"Well, yeah."

Her tone stirred his curiosity. "What have you got?" he asked.

She typed on her keyboard before pointing to the monitor. "Quentin Donahue isn't just Preston Guilfoyle's cousin. He's Orlando Larson's former business partner."

"What the hell?" Matthias leaned down for a better look at the screen.

"Seems Larson Building and Construction used to be Donahue and Larson Remodelers."

"When did that change?"

"According to the court records, Larson acquired a business license under the new name seven months ago."

"I wonder what happened?"

Cassie looked up at him. "I'd really like to find out."

"We need to talk to Mr. Quentin Donahue."

"Yes, we do." She picked up her phone and keyed in a number. Putting the call on speaker, she set the device on her desk.

After several rings, Matthias expected to hear a voice message pick up, so was surprised when someone answered.

"Hello?" The man on the other end sounded faintly Irish.

"Quentin Donahue?" Cassie asked.

"Who's this?"

Matthias took that as a yes.

"I'm Detective Sergeant Cassie Malone of the Erie Police. We're investigating the death of your business partner, Orlando Larson, and hoped you could answer a few questions for us."

"I don't know what I could tell you. Your information is a wee bit out of date. Larson and I parted company a while back."

She glanced at Matthias, both clearly noting that Donahue wasn't concealing the fact they were no longer partners.

"Nevertheless, we'd like to speak with you. Is there any chance we could meet? Either at your residence or here at the station?"

The line went silent for a few beats. "I suppose so. I'm remodeling a place over on Patterson Avenue." He gave them the house number. "I'll be there any time after eight a.m. tomorrow."

"We'll see you then."

Donahue ended the call before Cassie could say anything else.

She looked up at Matthias. "Looks like we're getting an early start tomorrow."

Chapter Eight

Wednesday morning, Emma had just arrived at her desk in the newsroom when Laurie barreled out of her office and looked around. "Preston," she shouted. "Emma."

Laurie and the reporter converged at Emma's desk.

"What's up, boss?" Preston asked.

Laurie produced a square of paper. "This just came over the scanner. Structural fire. Peninsula View Apartments off Raspberry Street. Sounds like a big one."

Ten minutes after receiving their assignment, they arrived at Raspberry only to find it blocked by a firetruck. Preston pulled over in a spot that may or may not have been legal. "I hope you're up to walking."

"Always." Emma climbed out and grabbed her camera gear from the back seat.

"I'm gonna try to get some interviews," he told her. "You do your thing, and I'll text you when I'm done."

She watched him jog away, then took in the scene. They were both looking for the same thing but in different ways. Preston would ask questions and get the story from residents, witnesses, and fire officials. She would tell the same story but from the visual side. First with overall views showing the structure, the flames, and the smoke. With those images secured, she switched to a longer lens and went in search of emotions. Apartment dwellers were now standing in the street, some in pajamas, some with blankets draped over their shoulders. Their faces registered shock, terror, and sorrow. Emma grabbed a few shots before letting the Nikon hang around her neck from its strap and taking out her notebook. The subjects of the photos hadn't been aware of her until she asked their names and permission to use the images. They were on a public street with no expectation of privacy—they'd lost that potentially along with the contents of their homes thanks to the blaze—but Emma still asked. It made her feel less like a vulture, preying on the most vulnerable.

It also reminded her why she'd avoided the journalism side of freelance photography for so long.

With names and permissions in hand—she would share them with Preston in case he wanted to talk with these folks—Emma moved closer to the fire apparatus and the men in bunker gear. The press badge hanging around her neck gave her access, but she did her best to stay out of their way. Instead, she used the long lens to grab images of the firefighters' faces, some showing the dirt and soot of having been up close and personal with the fire.

Her phone buzzed in her pocket with a text from Preston.

Meet me in front of the apartment. Want photos of the man in charge.

In front of the apartment covered a lot of ground. Emma made her way around the firetrucks, searching for and finally locating Preston standing with an older man wearing a white firemen's helmet.

Preston spotted her approach and waved. "Get a shot of Chief Ormand to go with my interview."

Another fireman interrupted, allowing Emma to snap a candid photo of the chief in action.

Preston thanked the chief for his time and gestured for Emma to follow him. "Did you get what we need?" he asked.

Emma hefted her Nikon. "I believe so." She pressed the review button to display the latest shot on the camera's screen and angled it so he could see it, too. Clicking through the entire morning's work, she knew Laurie would be pleased. "How about you?" Emma asked.

"Yep." He held up his phone. "The fire was mostly isolated to a second-floor apartment, although the neighboring units suffered heavy smoke and water damage."

Emma thought of the residents she'd spoken with and was glad to know they had a home to return to, although perhaps not right away.

"The unfortunate part is they found two bodies."

"Oh?" She almost made a snarky remark about burying the lede but decided against antagonizing her new partner. "Did you get the victims' names?"

"No. Neither have been identified yet." Preston took one more look at the building. "The fire's been contained, so let's get back to the office and get this story posted."

The address Donahue had given Matthias and Cassie showed none of the same obvious signs of construction as the house on Clifton. This yellow-brick ranch appeared intact with no dumpster or construction vehicles in the yard or driveway.

"Do we have the right street?" Matthias checked the time. Eight thirty.

"Right street, right house number." Cassie pulled into the driveway and parked.

"Maybe he's sending us on a wild goose chase."

"One way to find out."

They stepped out of the Malibu and approached the front door.

A sour-looking man, who appeared to be in his late sixties, answered their knock.

Cassie held up her badge and introduced them. "We're here to meet a Mr. Quentin Donahue."

The man snorted. "He's not here."

"But you know him?"

"Hell yes, I know him. He's been working on my bathroom. Been doing a damned poor job of it, let me tell you. Crappy workmanship. Cheap materials when I paid for the good stuff."

"We were told he'd be here by eight," Cassie said.

"I was told the same thing. I gave him hell on Monday. Told him to get his ass back here and fix his mess. Said he'd be here yesterday morning." The man shook his head. "Then he called around lunchtime and said something came up and he'd be here this morning." He spread his arms. "He's not. Let me tell you, this is the last straw. I'm calling the trade union and Better Business Bureau and anyone else I can think of. If I have my say, Quentin Donahue will never work on another renovation in the entire state ever again."

As Matthias and Cassie walked back to the car, the homeowner was still ranting. "I'm not sure if Donahue's ditching him or us," Matthias said.

"Both." Cassie slid behind the wheel and pulled up her notes on her phone. "If Donahue isn't at work, let's try his residence."

The address they had for Donahue's home was well east of town in a largely residential area. Cassie parked in front of a closed single-car garage.

"I hate when people make us come looking for them," Matthias grumbled as they stepped onto the concrete slab at the front door.

Cassie choked a laugh. "You, my friend, are in the wrong profession." She knocked.

When no one responded, Matthias gave it a shot, pounding loud enough to wake even the soundest sleeper.

Still no response. Cassie remained where she was and tried again. Matthias stepped off the stoop and peered through the picture window into an unoccupied living room.

"Hey!" came a nearby voice. "Hey!"

Matthias looked around and spotted the source. A scrawny elderly gentleman wearing a plaid bathrobe over what looked like pajama bottoms stood on the other side of their car.

"You the cops?" he asked, his tone eager and conspiratorial.

"Yes, sir, we are." Matthias strode toward him as he came around the front of the sedan.

"I live next door." The scrawny gent thumbed over his shoulder. "I keep an eye on things around this neighborhood and saw you over here. Nobody's home."

Cassie joined them, and Matthias introduced her.

"I'm Buddy McCall. Well, my name's George, but everyone just calls me Buddy."

"Nice to meet you, Buddy," Cassie said with her good-cop smile. "We understand Quentin Donahue lives here. Is that right?"

"Yepper." He nodded vigorously. "But he hasn't been home for a couple of days."

"When was the last time you saw him?" Matthias asked.

"Like I said. A couple of days ago."

Cassie held up her fingers, counting. "So, Monday?"

"Yepper."

Matthias bit back a smile. "How well do you know Mr. Donahue?"

"Oh. Not well. I keep to my own business, you know."

Considering how quickly Buddy had shown up, Matthias doubted it. "Do you know anything about his work?"

"He's a carpenter. Remodeling mostly. I think he's been working on a house down on Patterson Avenue."

"We checked there. He didn't show up for work the last couple of days."

"I'm not surprised." Buddy crossed his arms. "I don't like to speak ill of my neighbors, but I wouldn't want him working on my house. Not reliable, you know."

Matthias decided to take a chance. "Do you know about his previous business partner?"

"Orlando Larson? Yepper. He's the poor fellow who got shot over on Clifton." Buddy shook his head. "What a shame. But him and Quentin haven't been partners for a while. Larson figured out that Quentin liked to take shortcuts. Said it reflected badly on him. Can't say I disagree."

"How did Quentin feel about that?"

"Oh, not good. Not good at all. No sir-ree. No love lost between those two for danged sure." Buddy leaned closer, as if about to divulge a secret. "Quentin's mad as a wet hen because Larson still owes him money from their last job together. Larson told him he had to rebuild an entire kitchen because of Quentin cutting corners, so he was taking the cost of it out of his cut of the profits. Quentin didn't take kindly to that."

Buddy seemed to know a lot for someone who "kept to his own business." Matthias decided, what the hell. "Do you know Quentin's cousin, Preston Guilfoyle?"

Buddy's eyes widened in surprise. "That reporter for ErieLIVE? I read his stuff online all the time. Didn't know him and Quentin were cousins."

Matthias guessed they'd reached the end of Buddy's wealth of knowledge. He and Cassie thanked the old man for his time and watched as he tottered back to his house.

"Dammit," Matthias muttered.

"What?" Cassie asked.

"We didn't ask him if he knew where Donahue is right now."

Cassie reached for the driver's door and blew a puff of air from her lips. "Oh, he wouldn't know. He keeps to his own business."

Matthias crossed to the passenger side. "Yeppers."

Back at the station, Matthias immersed himself in social media, digging for background information on Larson and Donahue. A young woman in civilian attire and carrying a large brown envelope entered Major Crimes and strode past Matthias's desk to Cassie's.

He heard her thank the young woman, who hurried out. A few seconds later, Cassie said, "Come look at this."

Matthias rose and moved around the partition. "What?"

"It's from ballistics." She scanned the pages she'd slid from the envelope. "The bullet found at the Clifton house and the one removed during Larson's autopsy match the gun from the dumpster."

"No surprise." Matthias turned to leave.

"But this is. The lab managed to raise the weapon's serial numbers."

He came back. Minor surprise, although it shouldn't have been. Bad guys were always filing guns' serial numbers, thinking that would save their asses. What they didn't seem to realize was nine times out of ten, police labs could restore the numbers.

Cassie held up one of the pages, waving it, a triumphant smile on her face. "We have an owner along with his address. One Willis

Bryant from Mill Creek. Let's go pay him a visit." She reached for the drawer in which she stored her purse.

"First, take a look at what I've found."

She looked at him as if he couldn't possibly believe he'd come up with something more interesting than the owner of their murder weapon. But she left her purse where it was and followed him back to his desk.

Matthias slid into his chair and clicked his mouse. "Larson has an ex-wife."

"I know. Nadia. They've been divorced for over six years. She's been remarried for three. I don't see she has any motive to want him dead."

"She may not have motive, but..." Matthias clicked on one of the woman's photos, an image of her and Larson, arms around each other, smiling broadly.

"Look at the date." Cassie pointed. "That's from ten years ago."

"Yet she reposted it less than a week ago." Matthias clicked to the next picture, another of the couple during happier times. "This is another one from her memories, reposted on Sunday." He continued to scroll through her recent posts, all pictures with her ex-husband, all smiling.

Cassie fell silent, watching. Frowning.

"Everything she posts is a memory from her marriage to Orlando Larson. Not to mention the fact she kept his last name when she remarried."

"Are there any pictures of the new husband?"

"If there are, they're from further back than I've been able to find."

Cassie bent down, bracing one hand on his desk, taking the mouse from him with the other. She continued what he'd begun, scrolling back into Nadia Larson's history. There were some modern photos without her ex, but most of those were posted by others tagging her. Cassie finally gave up and straightened. She pulled her notebook from her pocket and thumbed through its pages. "Her current husband is a guy named David Pankowski. Have you found anything on him?"

"I've tried. He doesn't have a social media presence."

"Smart man."

"But it doesn't help us."

Cassie replaced her notebook. "Definitely makes you wonder though. Does he know his current wife still has such fond memories of her ex?"

Matthias was thinking of yet another suspect and a new motive. "And if he does, how does he feel about it?"

"Exactly." Cassie met Matthias's gaze. "I can't imagine he'd be too happy."

Chapter Nine

Willis Bryant lived in a boxy two-story house with green aluminum siding that begged for a power washer. Wooden steps to the front porch gave Matthias pause. He put one foot on the bottom step and tested its weight-bearing capabilities. The rasping sound of cracking timber confirmed his trepidation. "Is there a back door?"

Cassie walked to the corner and looked alongside the house. "Probably, but there's also a chain link fence, a gate, and a Beware of Dog sign."

"Hey," a man coming down the sidewalk called to them. "Hey. What do you want?"

"We're looking for Willis Bryant," Matthias replied.

The man thumped himself on the sternum. "That's me. Who are you?"

They held up their badges, and Matthias made the introductions. "Mind if we talk?"

Bryant folded his arms over his ample girth. "I guess that's what we're doing now."

"How about we go inside?" Cassie brushed her fingers over her forehead. "It's hot out."

"Whatever you want to talk about, do it here. Unless you have a warrant, I'm not inviting you into my house."

Matthias noticed Bryant didn't invite them to sit on his porch either but considering his size and the condition of the steps, Matthias suspected the man hadn't used it in years. "Fine. We understand you own a High Standard .22 double nine revolver."

Bryant's mouth pressed into a thin inverted U. "You understand wrong. I don't have any guns like that."

"Really?" Cassie feigned puzzlement. "Because we show a High Standard .22 bearing a serial number that's registered to a Willis Bryant at this address." She tipped her head toward the house.

His chin jutted. "Where'd you get that information?"

"From our ballistics lab," Matthias said. "The gun in question was used in a double homicide earlier this week."

"Someone," Cassie continued, "tried to file off the serial number, but that doesn't really work."

"I don't suppose that 'someone' was you, was it?" Matthias asked.

"No," Bryant sputtered, the color draining from his face. "Double homicide? Oh, hell no." He wiped a hand across his mouth and shot a glance around.

Checking to see if his neighbors were watching, Matthias thought.

"Okay, yes, I did own that gun, but I don't anymore."

"You're still the owner on record."

"I swear to God. I sold it to a pawn shop."

"How long ago?"

"A month. No, five weeks. I loved that gun and the fancy bone handgrip. Reminded me of the cowboy shows my pop and I used to watch when I was a kid. But I was late with my car payment, so I sold it."

"Which pawn shop?"

"Cash and Dash. Out toward Avonia."

Matthias looked at his partner. They knew the place. And not in a good way.

"Do you have a receipt for the sale?" Cassie asked.

If possible, Bryant paled even more. "No."

"Any documentation that you sold the weapon?"

"No." His voice was steadily rising in pitch. "Hey, look. I'm not responsible for someone else using that gun. I haven't had it in my possession for weeks now."

"Legally, it's still in your name."

"I swear to God, I sold it. You go to that pawn shop and talk to Big Dan. He'll tell you."

"Big Dan," Matthias echoed under his breath. "Ambrose Daniels."

"I don't know his real name. Just Big Dan. That's who I dealt with."

Ambrose "Big Dan" Daniels owned Cash and Dash. Matthias, Cassie, and three-quarters of law enforcement in northwestern Pennsylvania and northeastern Ohio regions knew him. Half of those had arrested him at one time or another.

Emma had edited her photos from the apartment fire and submitted six to Laurie. "Excellent work," she'd proclaimed.

With that done, Emma returned to the boxes of Darcy's photos. While her colleague had a fantastic eye for color, light, and composition, she was horrible at organization. After an hour of sorting, an eye strain headache simmered, and Emma wished for a bottle of eye drops. Instead, she left the photos on the table and crossed to Laurie's office.

Emma leaned into the open doorway and rapped lightly on the frame.

Laurie looked up. "What do you need?"

"I've been working on Darcy's photos, and my eyes are ready to fall out of my skull," Emma said with a grin. "I was thinking I'd take a walk to the coffee shop. I'll take my camera in case I see any newsworthy images along the way."

"No problem. You are allowed to take a coffee break."

"Can I bring you anything?"

"That would be great. How about a large white chocolate mocha."

Emma's favorite. "A woman after my own heart. Back in a bit."

Emma slung her purse over one shoulder, draped her camera strap around her neck, and headed for the elevator.

On the ground floor, she stepped through the glass doors onto the Eighth Street sidewalk and lifted her face to the sky. It was a glorious day for a walk. The mid-summer heat was tempered by a stiff breeze. One of the downsides of having a full-time job was no longer having the freedom to bike the peninsula loop at will. She definitely would've been out there today. On the other hand, she did not miss living off her savings. Now that she wasn't afraid of being found by her stalker, she'd moved her cash from its hiding spot inside her camper to a bank account.

The memory of that murderous ex-boyfriend gave her a chill. She shook it off and started strolling down the street.

Benny Bean's coffee shop was only a block south on the corner of Ninth and State Streets. She turned left and strolled along Eighth to the intersection with State.

As she waited for the light, she contemplated heading north and taking a longer hike to the police station. And Matthias. She hadn't seen him for a couple of days, settling for a pair of texts and a quick phone call. He was busy with Darcy's homicide. She was busy with Darcy's photos.

The crosswalk light indicated it was safe to cross Eighth, and she chose to keep to her original plan, ambling south toward the coffee shop.

Halfway to the next block she came to a full stop at the entrance to a private parking lot. The skin on the back of her neck prickled. She spun to look in the direction she'd just come, expecting to see … who? No one was there. No one in the lot either. Scanning across the street, she noticed two white-haired men standing in front of the old Warner Theater engaged in conversation, paying no attention to her.

She exhaled. That fleeting moment spent thinking about her stalker must've rekindled her paranoia.

Emma kept walking but stayed more alert to her surroundings and the other pedestrians. A woman in a business suit stepped out of a lawyer's office and bustled past her, going in the opposite direction. An elderly couple approached from the south but stepped into a convenience store between Emma and the coffee shop.

She froze again, the feeling of being watched even stronger now. Not Clay, of that she was sure, but she'd learned during those terrible months not to disregard her intuition. She studied each person she saw. Young and old. Male and female.

None of them were paying any attention to her, all busy with their own lives.

Across the street, the two older men were still there, laughing about something. Not her.

The sense of eyes on her remained. But whose?

Her breath caught in her throat. Russ Carlisle had seen her watching him yesterday. Knew she'd taken his photo. Had his new girlfriend told him about the questions Emma had been asking?

She again searched the crowds, looking specifically for one man.

And not finding him.

Convinced she was working herself into a PTSD-driven panic attack, Emma focused on her breathing, as Kira had taught her to do. Inhale slowly, consciously. Exhale even slower. The tension drained away, allowing Emma to look down State Street and see shoppers rather than monsters lurking behind utility poles and garbage cans. The thought of Kira gave Emma an idea. She needed to find Russ's girlfriend and warn her. Emma had failed at saving two other women from the brute. This time, she wouldn't let him get away with the abuse.

That evening, Matthias stood in the middle of his loft, his phone to his ear, listening to Emma telling him about her day.

"I know I'm just overly anxious," she said after sharing her sense of being watched, "but I really wish you could arrest Russ Carlisle."

Matthias wished the same thing. "I'm working on it." He wanted to tell her not to worry. That Carlisle wouldn't be stalking her. But he wasn't so sure. She'd slapped him in the middle of his own restaurant in front of his employees and guests after all. Now, Emma believed he'd seen her taking his photograph. Matthias wasn't at all certain of Carlisle's limits. He *was* certain Carlisle had killed his own wife even though there was no evidence, no witnesses. The man was smart. Too smart.

"I know you are. Anyway, I made it to the coffee shop and back to work in one piece, so it's all good."

Not all, Matthias thought. "Why don't you come over here? For supper."

"I already ate."

He lowered his voice. "For dessert then."

From the sultry note in her laugh, he knew she understood his interpretation of dessert. "I wish I could, but I brought home a box of Darcy's photographs to sort. I can't believe how many images she printed out. Not to mention, once I get through these, I have all her digital files to organize."

"Are you sorry I helped you get this job?"

"Not at all."

"If you can't come over tonight, how about we plan on going out after work tomorrow?"

"I'd like that."

"Good. Text me when you're done for the day."

"Will do."

He opened his mouth, three words trying to form in his throat, but sticking there. "Have a good night. Bye."

"You, too."

He ended the call and contemplated what she'd told him about feeling she was being watched. He couldn't very well tell her she was being ridiculous when he felt much the same way. Not that he was being watched, but that someone had been in his apartment.

He set the phone on his kitchen island and began to stalk around his loft. He didn't keep a lot of possessions out on display. Two guitars he rarely played anymore hung on a wall. A couple of small, framed photos of Cassie's Army Sergeant daughter and eight-year-old granddaughter—gifts from his partner—sat on an oak table along with a lamp. Bookshelves held a variety of legal and police procedural tomes plus his favorite classic novels and a few mysteries. Craig Johnson's latest Longmire perched bookmarked next to Matthias's reading chair. The trio of old photos hung on the wall.

At those, he paused. They were perfectly level as always. Everything was exactly as he always kept it. Why the hell did he think his home had been breached?

Paranoia? Emma had given that name to her anxiety. But Matthias was a cop. *Can you call it paranoia when they really are out to get you?*

He let out a growling exhale and made a decision. He strode into his bedroom, ripped open the closet door, and yanked out the fingerprinting case he kept there.

Why did he keep his own private fingerprinting kit? Paranoia? No. To keep the paranoia at bay.

He lugged the case back out to the open living area, set it on one of his barstools, and popped it open. For the next hour, he went over every inch of his place more thoroughly than the city's forensics team, dusting and lifting prints. He labeled the print cards with the location of every lift before tucking them back into the case. By the time he finished, he'd created a mess of black fingerprint powder. His cleaning lady was due tomorrow and would have a stroke when she saw this. He'd double her pay for the week. It would be worth the extra expense if running these prints eased his mind. Either they'd all match his, Emma's, and the cleaning lady's, in which case, yes, he was paranoid. Or he'd find one that belonged to someone else. Someone who should not have been in here.

Chapter Ten

The next morning, Emma arrived at Kira's yoga studio with coffee and a box of pastries. Kira unlocked the front door before Emma had a chance to juggle their breakfast and knock.

"Come in, come in." Kira stepped aside, allowing Emma to enter. After locking the door, Kira took the two coffees and led the way through the studio to a small office in the rear. "Have a seat."

"I'm glad you could meet me before work." Emma broke off a piece of cheese Danish and popped it in her mouth.

"Hey, you offered to bring breakfast. I'm always available when food's part of the deal." Kira spread a paper napkin on her desk and picked out a blueberry muffin from the box. "What did you want to talk about?"

Emma had spent all last evening and most of the morning trying to decide how best to broach the subject without sounding like she was seeing monsters in every shadow. But this was Kira. She knew all about Emma's monsters. "I have a feeling I'm being watched."

Kira lowered the muffin. "Oh? Who?"

"I'm not sure. It's probably just my imagination—"

"No. Don't say that." She tapped her breastbone. "We need to listen when our heart is talking to us."

"I am, but the thing is, I didn't see anyone. It was just a feeling."

"Okay. Who do you *feel* is watching you?"

Emma wasn't ready to divulge her suspicion yet. "Remember that woman in class on Monday? The one with the bruises?"

Kira's expression darkened. "You mean Suzanne Foster. Sure, I remember her. I haven't seen her since then."

"Well, I have." Emma told her about spotting her the next day with Russ Carlisle.

Kira inhaled sharply. "Not *that* Russ Carlisle?"

"God, I hope there isn't more than one. But now we know who gave her the bruises."

Kira swore. "Next time I see her in class, I'm taking her aside and giving her a piece of my mind. She needs to get away from that man."

"That's the problem. I don't want to wait."

Kira's expression shifted from angry to puzzled before her eyes widened in realization. "You think Carlisle is the one following you."

"I took a picture of the two of them on the street. I'm pretty sure he saw me."

"You're right. We can't wait. Do you have a plan?"

"Only that I want to talk to Suzanne. Tell her what I know about this guy. What he's done to other women."

Kira nodded slowly. She picked up the muffin and nibbled on it, thinking. "Here's what we're gonna do," she said after swallowing. "I'll call her. Right now. If he answers, I'll tell him I'm Suzanne's yoga teacher and I need to talk to her about a change in scheduling."

Emma liked it. "Good. He might actually let you talk to her then. But what if he listens in?"

The Devil Comes Calling

Kira ran a finger over her lips. "I'll tell her I'm offering her a free private class and have an opening this morning. Try to get her to come here as soon as possible. What do you think?"

Emma nodded at the phone on Kira's desk. "Do it."

Kira deposited the half-eaten muffin on the napkin, brushed crumbs from her hands, and opened a folder, which she thumbed through. "Found it." She picked up the phone and keyed in a number.

Emma waited, holding her breath. She wanted to—no, *needed* to—save this young woman from the fate that had befallen her sister.

Kira made a face. "Hi, Suzanne, this is Kira Peterson from Namaste Erie Yoga. You've won a free private session with me, and I wanted to set up a time that's good for you. Call me back as soon as you get this." She set down the phone and scowled. "I don't like it. I don't like it at all." She looked at the student registration form in her hand. "I have her address here. I'm going to her apartment. If Carlisle answers the door, I'll claim I'm there to talk about the yoga class. If she's alone, I'll sit her down and tell her who and what her boyfriend really is."

"I'll come with you."

Kira shook her head. "Bad idea. What if he's there?"

"If he's there, you're walking into a lion's den alone." Emma shook her head. "It's too dangerous." She needed to save Suzanne but not at the risk of Kira's life.

"I'm not going to put myself in harm's way. If he's there, I'll use the free yoga class ruse and get her to come to my studio. I've got this." Kira gave Emma's arm a playful jab. "Don't worry about me. I'm tougher than I look."

Emma laughed in spite of her concern. "You're right about that."

"Of course, I'm right." Kira grinned. "I'm always right."

"Let me know as soon as you finish talking to her."

"Deal. Now eat up. We both have places to go and people to see."

Matthias walked to work with the box of fingerprint cards tucked under his arm. He made his way through the cavernous underground garage and into the station, keeping his head down, slightly embarrassed by what he was doing. He imagined the conversation.

Hey, Honeywell, what've you got there?
Oh, fingerprints from my apartment.
Did someone break in?
No. I'm just imagining someone's been in my place.
Paranoid much?

He ducked into the lab and set the box on the front counter.

Lab Tech Todd Jackman looked up. "Hey, Honeywell. What've you got there?"

He fought the urge to roll his eyes. "I need a favor."

Jackman strode to the counter and placed his hands on either side of the box. "What can I do for you?"

"I need you to run these prints. Some of them are going to be mine. Some of them will match Emma Anderson." They had hers in the system from a few months back when her camper had been broken into and trashed. She'd been printed to eliminate hers from the investigation. "And some will match my cleaning lady."

"Okay." Jackman eyed him. "What case is this for?"

"That's where the favor comes in. It's not for an official investigation." He paused. "Yet."

Jackman held his gaze, one eyebrow raised.

How could Matthias explain this without sounding like he'd taken a dive into the shallow end of the pool? Headfirst. "I suspect someone's been in my apartment. Before you ask, no, the door wasn't forced."

The lab tech continued to look at him. Just about the time Matthias expected him to push the box away, he drew it toward him. "Okay. But you owe me a beer."

Matthias exhaled. "You got it, man. Call me the minute you find anything."

"Yeah, yeah."

Leaving the lab behind, he climbed the stairs to Major Crimes and found Cassie waiting for him with her purse slung over her shoulder. "About time you got here."

He checked his watch. "I'm not late."

"We have a busy day ahead." She grabbed him by the shoulders and turned him to face the door. "I want to see what Orlando Larson's ex has to say."

The woman who answered the door was so pale and her eyes so red Matthias was certain she must be ill. Her dark brown hair needed to be washed. Her black oversized T-shirt and jeans were rumpled as if she'd slept in them.

For a week.

Cassie introduced them and asked if the sickly woman was Nadia Larson.

"I am." She swiped a strand of hair away from her face. "Please, come in."

Matthias followed Cassie across the threshold into a narrow entryway and came face to face with a large, framed photo of Nadia and Orlando. The Nadia in the professional portrait was younger, blonde, and smiling. He caught Cassie studying it, too.

They followed the ex-Mrs. Larson into a sitting room filled with dainty antique chairs upholstered with floral fabric. Matthias hoped Nadia didn't offer one of those to him, fearing he'd end up on the floor. She might've had the same thought because she gestured toward a sturdier sofa covered in the same fabric.

Seated, he took in the room. More photos hung from the walls and filled the end tables. Every one of them was of Nadia and her ex, smiling radiantly.

She sat on one of the delicate antiques, withdrew a tissue from her pocket and wiped her nose. Matthias realized she wasn't ill. She was in mourning.

"I hope you don't mind if we ask you a few questions," Cassie began.

"Not at all. I expected to hear from you—the police, I mean—sooner. Orlando was killed days ago."

"I gather you and your ex-husband were still close." Cassie emphasized the "ex" part of her statement.

Nadia reached over and picked up a five-by-seven from the stand next to her flimsy chair and looked at it. "Not as close as I'd like. Not anymore."

"I'm sorry, but I have to ask," Cassie said. "You're remarried. What does your current husband think of all"—she waved a hand at the photograph-covered walls—"this?"

"We're separated. Have been for over a month. I plan to file for divorce as soon as I can get myself together."

Matthias caught the glance Cassie shot his way and the silent comment, *Jeez, I can't imagine why*.

He decided to jump in with the questions. "When was the last time you saw Orlando?"

Nadia pressed the five-by-seven to her chest. "We had coffee two weeks ago."

"Was that common? You two meeting for coffee?"

"Common? I suppose so. We'd either have coffee or lunch once every week or two, depending on his work schedule."

Matthias wondered what the current Mrs. Larson thought of

these "dates". Or if she knew about them. "What did you talk about?"

"Oh, you know. The usual."

What the hell was usual about having coffee and lunch dates with your ex? "Be more specific."

"His work. My job. The house." She pointed upward. "I'm having some plumbing issues in the upstairs bathroom. He was going to talk to one of his guys about giving me a hand."

"You say he talked about his work. Did he happen to mention any problems there? Any disgruntled employees?"

Her forehead furrowed in thought. "Not that he told me."

Cassie, who'd been jotting notes, leaned forward. "Would you happen to know who owns the property on Clifton Drive? The one he was working on?"

"I have no idea. When we talked about his job, it was little stuff. Funny anecdotes, you know? Like the nest of squirrels they found in the chimney. That sort of thing."

Cassie scratched her chin with her pen. "Nothing about his employees? Subcontractors?" She waited a beat and added, "Business partners?"

Nadia continued to scowl and think. "He may have mentioned one of his subs having a birthday."

Matthias seriously doubted a birthday would help their investigation.

She brought her hand lightly to her mouth and fingered her upper lip. "The last few times I saw him, he seemed happier than he'd been in a while."

"He'd been unhappy?" Cassie asked.

"Not necessarily *unhappy*." Nadia made air quotes. "Concerned might be a better word. He had some big bills he owed money on. I mean, he never wanted to worry me about such things. Even when we were still married, he'd make light of financial issues, but I could tell he was troubled. Then, all of a sudden, he was happy. He told me this house was going to get him out of the red and provide a nice bit of cash on the side."

"This house?" Matthias asked. "You mean the one on Clifton?"

"I assume. As far as I know, it was the only one he'd been working on."

"Did he mention having a buyer for it?" Cassie asked.

Nadia's frown lines deepened again. "No. I don't think so." She shook her head. "I honestly don't know. As I said, he didn't like to worry me where money was concerned."

Matthias looked at Cassie, wondering if she'd found any red flags while digging through Larson's records. But she didn't meet his gaze, instead focusing on the ex-wife. "Thank you," Cassie said. "You've been very helpful."

She had?

"If you remember any specifics he may have mentioned, please give me a call." Cassie stood and held a business card out to her. "Something you don't think of as important might help us catch his killer."

Nadia rose and accepted the card, her eyes brimming. "I will. Thank you so much. I truly don't know how I'm going to go on without him."

Matthias stood as well, still puzzled by the photo gallery of this woman and her ex.

"I do have one more question," Cassie said, sounding apologetic. She pointed at one picture in particular, showing Orlando and Nadia wrapped in each other's arms, on a beach—possibly at Presque Isle—at sunset, appearing head-over-heels in love. "You two look so happy. You still saw each other regularly. If you don't mind me asking, why did you ever get divorced in the first place?"

Nadia's expression turned dark, brooding. "Because of a filthy slut who seduced him away from me."

Matthias again looked at his partner, gauging her reaction.

The Devil Comes Calling

Cassie appeared sympathetic. "I'm so sorry. Who is she?"

Nadia averted her gaze. "I shouldn't say."

"That's incredibly noble of you. If someone made a move on my husband, I'd splash her name and face on every billboard in town."

Nadia's face came up, tears streaming down her pale cheeks. She nodded in agreement. "You're right. There's no reason in the world I should protect her name. It's Yvonne. His current wife." She spit out the words.

Now Cassie looked at Matthias, a glimmer of triumph in her eyes.

"And," Nadia continued, "as if that wasn't bad enough, the bitch has been sleeping with someone else."

"Who?" Cassie asked.

"I don't know." Nadia must've caught the skepticism in Cassie's expression. "Honestly. I don't know. If I did, I would tell you."

"Then how do you know Yvonne's having an affair?" Matthias asked.

"Orlando told me."

Matthias resisted an urge to glance at his partner. "Was he upset about it?"

"Not at all. I believe the idea of getting free from her was another reason he was happier lately."

They thanked her once more for her time, and she showed them out with a promise to call if she thought of anything else. At the car, Matthias gazed back at the house. "We sure got handed a shitload of motive in there."

Cassie rested an arm on the driver's doorframe. "Money owed. Big haul coming in."

"Jealousy," he added.

"Nadia? If she's to be believed, Orlando was about to come into a nice chunk of change and leave Yvonne."

"No, not Nadia. Not unless she's a much better actress than I think she is. Besides, if she was going to go *Fatal Attraction* on anyone, it would be the wife."

"Agreed." Cassie slid behind the wheel.

Matthias climbed into the passenger seat and pulled up his phone's browser. "On the other hand, what about Nadia's current, soon-to-be-ex-husband? If she had all those pictures displayed while he was still in the house, he'd have good reason to snap."

Cassie's mouth slanted in thought. "Another person to question." She started the car. "But first, let's go see a pawnbroker about a gun."

Matthias raised a finger. "Hang on a minute."

"What?"

He enlarged the screen and read. "David Pankowski, Nadia's husband, is employed as a groundskeeper at Waldameer. Why don't we stop there on our way?"

Cassie gave him a snide grin. "Too bad Emma's at work. We'd be so close to her camp."

Matthias ignored her. He pulled up the water park's website and tapped on the phone number. "Let's see if Pankowski's on duty."

Chapter Eleven

David Pankowski was indeed working at Waldameer, and the woman Matthias spoke with said she'd have him meet them outside the admissions gate.

Cassie drove through the busy lot with her window down and her badge in her hand, flashing it at parking attendants who tried to redirect them. She pulled into a no-parking zone and shut off the engine. They stepped out of the car, passed under the welcome sign, and stopped before reaching the booths selling admission tickets.

From inside, the sounds of carnival-like music and the joyful screams of park guests mingled with the mechanical rumblings and whooshing of roller coasters and other nausea-inducing rides. There used to be a time when Matthias loved this place, but that was more than a decade ago.

"Shawn and I are supposed to bring Alyssa here at the end of the month," Cassie said. "Don't suppose you and Emma would want to come along and take her on the rides."

He huffed. "Not on your life."

Cassie lifted her chin, looking toward the sidewalk leading deeper into the park. "I bet that's him."

A dark-haired man with a deep tan and wearing a Waldameer Park uniform strode their way, a scowl on his face. Matthias stepped toward him. "David Pankowski?"

"That's me." He looked from Matthias to Cassie after they'd introduced themselves. "Excuse me for asking, but what do a couple of police detectives want with me?"

"We're investigating the death of Orlando Larson," Matthias said.

Pankowski reacted as if a foul aroma had settled around them. "Good riddance," he said. "Other than that, I have nothing else to tell you."

"You're married to his ex-wife, right?" Cassie asked, feigning a puzzled expression as she scanned her notes.

"Not for much longer."

Cassie continued to maintain the clueless façade. "What can you tell us about her relationship with Mr. Larson?"

Matthias caught his lip between his teeth to keep from grinning. His partner was anything but clueless.

Pankowski, however, was buying the act. He studied her as if she'd grown a second head. "You surely don't suspect she had anything to do with Larson's death. The woman was obsessed with him. She'd have slain a dragon for him. She would *not* have killed him."

Cassie made a note. "I hope you don't mind my asking, but if she was so devoted to him, why on earth did you marry her?"

He ran a hand through his hair and looked around at the crowds, then gestured for them to follow him toward a cluster of well-manicured trees. Matthias wasn't sure if it was the shade that drew Pankowski or the semi-privacy.

"When I met her, she was lost. Lonely. I didn't realize it at the time—although I should've—but I was her rebound romance. She was devastated when Orlando left her for Yvonne. She was needy, and I was foolish enough to think that I could pick up the pieces of her broken heart." His voice turned melodic, as if singing the lyrics of a country song. "I proposed a few months later, and she said yes." He huffed. "The first red flag should've been when she refused to take my last name. Granted Pankowski might be harder to spell, but it's a good solid name. Nadia preferred to keep Larson. The name, I mean. Although later I realized she preferred the man as well."

"When was that?" Matthias asked, keeping his tone sympathetic.

Pankowski shifted his gaze, thinking. "I had a feeling something was off about a year ago."

Cassie dropped the clueless act. "I assume she didn't have his photos all over the house back then."

He looked at her, surprised. "You've been to the house."

"We spoke with her earlier."

"I see."

Matthias wasn't sure he did but wanted to keep him talking. "What made you suspect she was spending time with her ex?"

Pankowski squirmed. "I didn't know she was back to seeing Orlando, but she started... Well, let's just say she started withholding marital favors."

"Ouch," Cassie said.

"Yeah. Anyhow, I hired a P.I. He reported that she and Orlando were meeting for coffee, lunch, dinner. He didn't catch them sleeping together, but I wouldn't be surprised if they were. I started snooping through her social media and found she was posting old photos of the two of them."

Cassie was back to acting oblivious. "Oh, dear. What'd you do?"

"I confronted her." Pankowski's jaw grew tense.

"What happened?" Matthias asked.

"She came right out and told me she was still in love with him."

"What'd you do?"

"I asked her to go to marriage counseling with me. She refused. I tried going to therapy sessions alone for a while, but when she started breaking out the old photos, I threw in the towel. Packed my stuff and moved out." His voice and expression were bitter.

Matthias shook his head. "Man, that sucks. Must've really pissed you off."

Red-faced, Pankowski looked at him. "It did. That bitch."

"I can understand you being angry at your wife," Cassie said, laying on the empathy.

"I am. I'm mad at her, but I'm furious with Larson. That no-good bastard could've put an end to it. *Should* have put an end to it. Stayed with his own wife." Pankowski turned to Matthias, fists clenched and trembling. "But you know what? I swear to God, he was encouraging her to leave me."

"Why do you say that?" Matthias asked.

"That's just the way he was. He wanted it all. Wife. Mistress. Hell, I heard he was planning to pitch his business to a television producer." Pankowski spat into the grass at their feet.

Matthias caught Cassie's eye. She nodded. "We appreciate your time," he said.

Pankowski swiped his mouth with the back of his hand. "Sure. Hey, if you catch whoever popped Larson, do me a favor."

"What's that?"

"Shake his hand for me."

As Cassie made the right out of Waldameer's parking lot,

The Devil Comes Calling

Matthias called Detective Brad Frazier back at Major Crimes and asked for a background check on David Pankowski.

"On it," Frazier said. "Let me get back to you in a few minutes."

By the time they arrived at the pawn shop, he'd returned the call.

"Well?" Cassie asked as Matthias hung up and tucked the phone back in his pocket but held on to his notebook.

"We aren't the first cops Mr. Pankowski has encountered. He served five years for armed robbery and has been up on charges of both aggravated and simple assault. He pled out to both of those and received community service."

Cassie parked the car, cut the engine, and stared out the front window. "I'm not surprised. The man was seething. I could see him losing his shit and beating the hell out of Larson."

"Or Nadia. Agreed. Except Larson's murder was cold. Execution-style. Not a jealous rage."

She looked at him askance. "Unless Pankowski hired someone to do the job for him."

"I was thinking the same thing. He hired a P.I. Maybe he prefers to get the job done without getting his hands dirty."

"Except real dirt." She smirked. "Groundskeeper. Dirt. Get it?"

Matthias groaned. "I got it." He stepped out of the car before Cassie continued her comedy routine.

Cash and Dash and the store's owner, Ambrose Daniels, had been on the Erie Police Department's radar for as long as Matthias could remember. Even when he was new to the department, Big Dan would be the first stop in a burglary investigation. Back then, he should've carried the moniker Skinny Dan, but he'd grown into his chosen nickname, at least in girth. Height-wise, even Matthias towered over him.

Which was why Big Dan mostly stayed seated on a high stool

behind the display counter and had his employees do the footwork around the store.

"Detectives Honeywell and Malone," he called out jovially as they came through the door.

Matthias aimed a thumb at Cassie. "Detective *Sergeant* Malone these days."

"My apologies. Congratulations on the promotion."

She grunted at him. "Don't blow smoke up my skirt, Danny boy."

A nickname everyone knew Big Dan hated. "What can I do for you today?" he asked, his tone decidedly less jovial.

"You sold a gun. A High Standard .22 revolver with a bone grip." Matthias made a show of checking his notes, as if the make, model, and now serial number weren't permanently etched in his memory.

"Sorry, detectives. Excuse me. Detective sergeant and detective. I don't know anything about a .22 revolver."

Cassie looked at Matthias. "Have you noticed how nobody knows anything about anything where this case is concerned?"

"I have. Especially this particular gun." Matthias leaned an elbow on the glass counter and narrowed his eyes at the pawnbroker. "At least at first. But we do eventually get the truth. For instance, a man by the name of Willis Bryant sold this gun to you. Funny thing is, the serial numbers were filed off."

Big Dan's eye twitched, a nervous tick he'd had since the first time Matthias had met him.

"Even funnier, the gun's registration was never transferred out of his name."

"Then you can't prove I ever had possession of it."

Matthias pointed at the security camera above them and looked at Cassie. "How long do you think it would take to get a warrant for that footage?"

She acted thoughtful. "Considering Bryant is willing to swear that he sold it here, I can probably have a warrant in under a half hour." She pulled out her phone. "You wanna keep Danny boy company while I swear out the affidavit?"

"No problem."

"I mean, you don't look scary or anything." Cassie eyed Matthias but her caustic tone was all for Big Dan's benefit. "Especially with your badge hanging out. I doubt you'd run off more than five or six paying customers."

"Maybe closer to ten or twelve. It's almost lunchtime. Pinning down a judge might take a little longer. But I'll wait. I bet we spot evidence of at least a couple illegal transactions on that footage. It'll be worth killing some time here." Matthias turned to give Big Dan his best rattlesnake smile, knowing Cassie was matching it. All three of them knew the warrant wasn't happening.

However, Big Dan was sweating just thinking about it.

"Look." Matthias turned serious. "We're not here to bust you."

"This time," Cassie added quickly.

"*This time*," he echoed with more emphasis, "we just want to know who you sold the gun to."

"What's so special about this piece anyway?" Big Dan's voice had risen an octave.

Matthias shrugged nonchalantly. "Not much. Other than it was used in two homicides earlier this week."

The pawnbroker's eyes bugged. "No shit?" He braced his hands on the counter as he slid down from the stool. "I'll be right back with my sales records."

Matthias watched the not-so-big man scurry into the back room.

"Should I go cover the rear entrance?" Cassie asked.

"Might not be a bad idea, but I doubt it's necessary." He extended both arms in a grand gesture, indicating the store and its merchandise. "This is his entire world. It's all he's been known for as long as I've been in Erie. Unless he's done more than buy and sell a firearm without registering it, I can't see him running out."

She eyed a taxidermized ferret or weasel or some other such vermin perched on a shelf next to the counter. "Yeah. Who would want to give all this up?"

Big Dan shuffled back through the door, carrying a plastic storage bin. He hefted it onto the counter, climbed onto his stool, and popped the lid. "I remember the piece. Nothing especially valuable about it, but it had that nice bone handgrip. I hadn't had something like that in the shop for ages." He riffled through pages of sales receipts, occasionally licking his thumb and withdrawing a sheet of paper to scrutinize the writing. Then he'd shake his head and return the page to its spot. After the fourth try, he perked up. "Ah. Here we are." He smoothed the page and placed it in front of Matthias.

Cassie leaned in to read alongside him. "Zane Norris." She held her phone above the receipt to scan it.

"Yeah." Big Dan tapped the paper with one finger. "I remember him now. Young guy with white spiky hair and weird eyes."

"Weird how?" Matthias asked.

"Like they had no color at all."

"Albino?" Cassie asked.

"No, not like that. His hair was bleached. I know because he had dark roots. It's just his eyes were a super light blue. Or maybe gray." Big Dan shook his head. "Weird-looking."

Matthias again pointed at the security cameras, but before he could ask, the pawnbroker flashed a palm at him.

"Not without that warrant we were talking about. Besides, you got his name and address. You two are detectives. Look him up in your database."

"Is there anything else you can tell us about this guy?"

"You're lucky I can tell you that much. I remember the gun

because it was unusual. Not valuable, but unusual. I remember the buyer because he looked weird. He paid cash, so you're really lucky I got as much on him as I do."

"Fair enough." Matthias aimed a finger at him. "I expect a phone call if this Zane Norris comes back in."

"Sure, sure." The pawnbroker fluttered a hand at them.

Cassie held up her phone. "If this address turns out to be a vacant lot, we will be back with that warrant."

"Hey, it ain't my fault if he gave me false information."

"No," Cassie said, "but it's your fault not getting the gun registered when you bought it and not running a background check when you sold it."

Big Dan folded his arms over his belly and gave them a scowl that looked more like a pout. "You promised you weren't gonna bust me on that if I gave you what I had on this dude."

Matthias followed Cassie to the door. "Yes," he said, "but only if the information pans out."

Back in the car, Matthias listened as Cassie called Frazier and put him on speaker. "Are you near a computer?"

"What do you need?"

"Run a background on one Zane Norris." She read the address. "At least that's the address we were given."

"Hang on a minute." The rapid-fire click of keystrokes filtered through the phone's speaker. "Got it. That is the address on record for Zane Norris. He served five years for aggravated assault." After a pause, Frazier added, "Looks like he was released two months ago."

"Do me a favor and get in touch with his parole officer. Find out if he's aware Mr. Norris purchased a High Standard .22 revolver from Cash and Dash."

"A .22 revolver? You mean like the one we have in evidence on the Larson/Tomasetti case?"

"Not like. That gun."

Frazier whistled. "On it."

Cassie ended the call and turned to Matthias. "Let's go see if Zane Norris is home."

The address was in a rundown part of town. The house was a boxy, shingled two-story structure with a distinct lean. If anything, it looked even worse than Willis Bryant's place.

Matthias studied the building. "If Norris is our shooter, he should've been hiring Larson to fix his house rather than blowing him away."

Cassie didn't reply but stepped out of the car.

At least someone had nailed replacement boards on the front porch steps. A screen door allowed a view inside. Matthias knocked and stepped out of the way. Norris might not have the murder weapon in his possession any longer, but that wasn't to say he didn't own another firearm. Catching a shotgun blast through a door wasn't on Matthias's agenda for the day.

Heavy footsteps from inside approached and a man with a wrestler's physique, wearing a Gannon University T-shirt and a pair of baggy knee-length shorts, appeared inside the door. With a shock of bright orange hair sticking out at odd angles and narrow slits for eyes, he looked like he'd been rousted from bed.

He slammed through the screen door, looked at Matthias, then Cassie, then back to Matthias. "What the hell do you want? I was asleep."

Cassie held up her badge. "Detective Sergeant Malone." She thumbed at Matthias. "Detective Honeywell. Erie City Bureau of Police."

Instantly wide awake, the man stiffened. "Whatever you're here for, I didn't do it."

Matthias exchanged an amused glance with his partner. If they weren't on such serious business, he could have fun yanking this guy's chain. Instead, he said, "We're trying to locate Zane Norris. We were told he lives here."

The man visibly relaxed. "Yeah, well, join the club."

"He doesn't live here?" Cassie asked.

"Oh, he lives here all right. At least I think he does."

"And you are?"

He grew cautious. "Why do you want to know?"

Cassie gave him her best motherly smile. "Because I told you who we are. It's only good manners for you to do the same."

His eyes shifted between them. "You can call me Red. Everyone does."

"Okay, Red. Is Zane here?"

He planted his hands on his hips, flexed his muscles like some bodybuilder, and gave her a smirk. "No."

Cassie turned to Matthias, silently turning this discussion over to him.

He broadened his stance and crossed his arms. If Red wanted to play the intimidation card, Matthias knew the muscles knotting his own forearms made promises his Mixed Martial Arts background and Krav Maga training could keep.

The posture worked. Red eyed him, his gaze sliding down to those forearms before coming back up to the look Cassie always said scared people. "All right. Zane lives here, but he's not here now."

Matthias didn't budge. "When was the last time you saw him?"

"I dunno." Red stuffed his hands in his shorts' pockets. "We both live here, but we don't hang together, you know?"

Matthias's phone vibrated in his pocket. He ignored it.

Red heaved a sigh. "Lemme think. He was here Sunday morning. Wait. Monday. No, Tuesday. When I got up on Tuesday, he was packing a bag. Said he was taking off for a few days. Said he'd come into some money and was gonna have a good time." He snorted. "Right. Rat bastard came into money and is out spending it on God knows what. But I can tell you what he ain't spending it on. His rent, that's what. He still owes me the two hundred bucks I loaned him for last month."

"See," Matthias said. "Was that so hard?"

"Just, when you find him, tell him to pay me what he owes."

"One more thing."

"What?"

Matthias held out a palm. "Let me see some ID."

Red stepped back and collided with the screen door. "Why?"

"I doubt your legal name is Red. I want to know who I'm dealing with."

On their way back to the station, Matthias checked his phone and found a message from Todd Jackman.

Got a hit.

Matthias's pulse quickened. He texted back that he would be there in fifteen minutes.

At the station, Cassie headed for the stairs, but Matthias stopped at the bottom. "You go on. I'll be there in a couple minutes."

She eyed him. "Why?"

"I need to check on something." He aimed a thumb over his shoulder in a non-definite direction.

"*Something*, huh?"

He fixed her with the scary look, knowing it never worked on her.

"Fine. Just don't come back with that expensive crap coffee you like to waste your money on."

"Okay, *Mom*." He watched her ascend the stairs before reversing directions and heading to the lab.

The Devil Comes Calling

Jackman looked up from his computer when Matthias strode in. His expression grew wary at the sight of the detective.

Matthias feared his paranoia was about to be proven legit. "You said you had something for me."

Jackman stood. "I do. But I'm not sure what to make of it."

Matthias had a feeling he knew exactly what Jackman had found and what to make of it. He held out a hand. "Let me see."

Jackman picked up a sheet of paper from his desk and set it on the counter in front of Matthias.

He didn't have a long list to go through. Most of the prints were his own. A number belonged to Emma. A few to the woman who cleaned his loft once a week. She'd worked as a custodian at a couple of area schools and had been printed as part of a background check. There was a set listed as unknown. Those, he suspected, belonged to Melissa, left during her brief visit Sunday morning.

It was the remaining name identified on the list that tensed every muscle in his body despite it being no real surprise.

Isaiah Honeywell.

Jackman was still watching him when he lifted his gaze from the page. "Thanks," Matthias said and started to turn away.

"Wait. You can't just say thanks and leave it at that." Jackman pointed at the report. "Not when that name's on the list."

"What name?" Matthias hoped the tech would take the hint.

"Your father's name."

Dammit. If Jackman knew who Isaiah was, it meant he'd done some digging and no doubt also knew where he'd been for the last few decades.

And why.

"Hey, I understand you not wanting to talk about it. From what popped up in the database, I wouldn't either. Sounds like your father was a real—"

"Drop it, Jackman. All I wanted was the prints run. You did that. I'm grateful."

"As a favor." Jackman emphasized the last word.

"Fine. I owe you a whole dinner instead of just a beer."

"Damn straight. Prime rib at that." Jackman glanced around, apparently to make sure they were still alone, placed his palms on the counter, and leaned closer. "I'm not trying to extort you … well, except for dinner … but if he's gained access to your apartment without you knowing, you need to be careful. If it's true what he was convicted of—"

"It's true. Don't worry about me. That's why I wanted this. Forewarned is forearmed, right?"

"Right." Jackson sounded doubtful.

Matthias started to turn away but paused and came back. "If I'm shelling out for prime rib, I need one more favor."

Jackson stuffed his hands into his pants pockets. "What?"

"Keep this between us."

The tech held his gaze. "Deal. Unless Isaiah Honeywell becomes a danger to the citizens of this city. That includes you. Then all bets are off, and you can forget about the prime rib."

Chapter Twelve

Emma arrived at O'Reilly's Pub well before the time she and Matthias had agreed upon. Kira had called earlier in the day, sounding strange, but refused to talk over the phone. They'd agreed to meet here ahead of Emma and Matthias's date.

Siobahn O'Reilly, the owner's daughter and primary waitress at the establishment, greeted Emma with a smile.

"I'd be guessing you're the second person in Matthias's reservation for two. Am I right?"

"Yes, you are." Emma knew Matthias was a regular here since he lived upstairs and was flattered that the owner now recognized her as well.

Siobahn led Emma to a table for two in a quiet corner near the rear of the dining room and deposited a pair of menus on the table. "I'll be back in a jiffy with your water."

Emma took a seat and inhaled the mouthwatering scents of roasting meats and herbs. She didn't eat chicken or beef, but still enjoyed the aromas. As she gazed out across the quaint, dimly lit room, she observed only a few empty tables remained open. Most of the others were occupied by couples and downtown employees stopping for a bite before heading home after work. She recognized a few other regulars, but most of the patrons were strangers to her. She'd only lived in Erie since February, and most of that time had been spent lying low to avoid her stalker ex-boyfriend, so she didn't know a lot of people here.

Kira appeared in the doorway, hard to miss in her trademark unitard and gauzy, flowing tunic. She scanned the room. Emma waved to catch her attention. Kira waved back and glided over to Emma's corner.

Emma rose and accepted Kira's hug. "I promise I won't interrupt your dinner with our favorite hot cop."

Emma cringed. Kira had dated Matthias briefly but had strongly encouraged Emma's relationship with him. She knew the Kira-Matthias fling was over, but couldn't help but feel that Kira, with her skin-tight outfits hugging those curves, was a darned hard act to follow.

She must've read Emma's mind. "Don't tell me you're still worried about me and your man. I told you, that's been over for ages. Besides, all he ever talked about was you. Kind of puts a damper on the romance."

Heat seared Emma's cheeks. "I'm not worried, but look at you. How could any heterosexual man resist?"

Kira dismissed her with the flutter of a hand and slid into an empty chair. "I'm glad you agreed to meet me."

"Did you talk to Suzanne?"

"No." Kira's face held no sign of her usual lighthearted, easy-going attitude.

"Oh, God. You ran into Russ."

"No. There wasn't anyone there."

Emma waited, knowing something bad was coming.

"When I went to the address I had for her, I couldn't get in. There'd been a fire."

The Devil Comes Calling

Emma's breath settled to her feet. "Don't tell me. Peninsula View Apartments off Raspberry Street."

"How'd you know?" Kira rolled her eyes before Emma could reply. "You work for ErieLIVE."

"I was at the scene after it happened."

Siobahn arrived with Emma's water. She turned to Kira. "Are you going to be joining them? Can I bring you something to drink?"

"No to both. Thanks."

"Let me know if you change your mind." Siobahn hurried away.

Emma took a long drink, wishing she had something stronger in the glass.

Kira rested her elbows on the table, leaning forward. "I heard there were two fatalities in that building," she whispered. "Do you know who—"

"The names haven't been released yet."

"You don't suppose…"

"I sure hope not."

Kira slumped back in the chair. "It can't be, can it? Suzanne, I mean."

Emma didn't reply. Of course, it could be, she thought, but she refused to voice the possibility.

They sat in silence, the clink of glasses and the soft rumble of conversation fading into the background of Emma's consciousness.

Kira broke the stillness. "I'm sure it's not her. I mean, how many people live in that building? At least half of them had to move out due to smoke and water damage, according to what I was able to learn. Suzanne's probably one of those."

Emma nodded. "I'm sure you're right." Another thought struck her. "She's probably staying at Russ's place."

Kira groaned. "I guess that's better than the alternative." She shook her head. "I wish Matthias could put him in jail."

"Put who in jail?"

Emma looked up to find her dinner date standing over them.

"Speak of the sexy devil himself." Kira rose from her seat, making even the simple movement appear provocative. "Detective Honeywell, how are you tonight?"

Emma noticed how he battled to keep his focus on Kira's eyes. But failed.

And Kira wondered why Emma couldn't let go of that minute bit of envy.

He recovered quickly and repeated, "Put who in jail?"

"Russ Carlisle," Kira replied.

"Oh." Matthias said flatly, clearly in agreement. He looked at Emma.

"I don't suppose you're working on the case of the two bodies found in the Peninsula View Apartments?" Emma asked, hopeful he could provide answers.

"No. Brad Frazier and Vince Roth are assigned to it."

"Do you know the victims' IDs?"

"What's this about?"

Emma shot a glance at Kira before replying, "Remember I told you about the woman with bruises?"

"Yeah."

Emma told him about seeing her outside the robbery at the Bay Harbor Convenience Store on Tuesday. "She was with Russ."

His jaw clenched. "Didn't you say her name was Suzanne?"

"Suzanne Foster," Kira said. "Timid little thing. Just the type a control fiend like Carlisle loves to seduce."

Emma didn't say anything but thought Carlisle didn't need his women to be timid. Her younger sister had never been timid.

She'd been wounded. And he'd made those wounds deeper.

"What do she and Carlisle have to do with the apartment fire?" Matthias asked.

Kira told him about the conversation she and Emma had earlier about wanting to hold an intervention for Suzanne.

He narrowed his eyes at Emma. A cautionary glare. She knew he didn't want her anywhere near Carlisle.

Kira either. He gave her the same dark look. "You two need to stay out of it."

"No, wait," Kira said and continued her story, telling him about Suzanne not answering her phone, concluding with Kira's visit to her home address. "We're afraid she might be one of the victims."

Matthias shook his head. "More than half of the tenants had to relocate because of the fire." He pulled out his notebook and pen. "What was Suzanne's unit number?"

"Three sixteen." Kira stood and watched over his shoulder as he wrote it down.

"I'll talk to Frazier tomorrow morning."

"And another thing," Emma said. "We thought she may be staying with Russ."

Matthias gave her the look again. "Please tell me you two aren't planning to go there."

Kira grinned sheepishly. "I was thinking about it. Like I said, I'd claim to be there on yoga business."

"And how would you explain having *his* address?"

"I haven't thought that far ahead yet."

"Don't." His tone left no room for debate. "Either of you. I'll have a talk with him. I've been looking for an excuse to put some pressure on him."

"Just don't punch him," Emma said. She'd seen him come close.

"I won't." Matthias's scowl morphed into a wicked grin. "That's *your* department."

Emma lowered her face. She could still feel the sting in her hand from when she'd slapped that smug-faced bastard. Given half a chance, she'd do it again.

Kira brushed a strand of pink hair from her face. "Okay, then, that's settled. You'll let us know about Suzanne's apartment tomorrow, right?"

"Yes, ma'am."

"Then I'm going," Kira said, "so you two can get on with your date." She blew a kiss in Emma's direction and gave Matthias a teasing nudge with her elbow before sashaying away.

Matthias claimed the chair Emma had saved for him. "Let's make a pact," he said.

"What kind of pact?"

"No more talk of Carlisle tonight."

"Deal." Nothing killed a romantic mood like the thought of that man.

Siobahn appeared within seconds with a second glass of water. "I'll give you a few minutes."

Matthias reached toward her. "Not necessary. We know what we want."

Emma gave him a look. *We do?*

His mouth twitched into a grin. "I'll have the Irish Chicken."

Siobahn held her pen poised over the order pad.

"Emma will have the fish and chips."

He *did* know.

"Any appetizers?" Siobahn asked.

Matthias handed her the menus. "Provolone sticks with marinara. And two beers."

"I'll get this in." The waitress hurried away without having written a thing.

He braced his forearms on the table. "I either order the Irish Chicken or the house macaroni and cheese with pulled chicken.

The Devil Comes Calling

And you"—he winked—"have ordered fish and chips every time I've brought you here."

Emma snorted a laugh. "See, you should've kept that to yourself and let me go on believing you're a mind reader."

He smiled and reached over, placing a strong hand over hers.

Then his eyes shifted. The smile faded. Although he never tightened his fingers on her hand, she felt his grip turn to stone. She watched as his eyes lifted and his expression turned menacing.

"Well, hello, son."

Emma whipped around to see the man behind the voice. Son? Surely, this was merely a term any older man might use when addressing someone much younger. But one look told her otherwise. While decades older than Matthias, the resemblance was unmistakable. Broad shouldered, built like a bulldog, same blue eyes.

No. Not the same. While Matthias's eyes radiated all of his emotions from kind to playful to furious, this man's eyes were veiled. Secretive despite his smile.

He extended a hand to her. "Hello, young lady. I'm Isaiah Honeywell. Matthias's dad."

Before she had a chance to reach for the offered hand, Matthias reacted, coming to his feet and stepping toward the older man. "Get the hell out of here," he growled so low no one beyond the three of them could hear.

The senior Honeywell raised both arms, palms at shoulder height, and aimed at Matthias. The universal gesture for *I mean no harm*. "Easy, boy. I just saw you two sitting here and wanted to meet your girl, seeing as you never mentioned her to me."

Emma's mind raced. Matthias had never mentioned his father to her either. She knew his mom was dead and had assumed his dad was, too. Yet, here he stood, and Matthias, while looking more menacing than she'd ever seen him, wasn't exactly surprised by his father's appearance.

Isaiah brought his attention back to her, ignoring his son. "You sure are a pretty thing." His Oklahoma drawl was more pronounced than Matthias's. "I didn't catch your name."

"Emma—"

"Don't talk to him," Matthias snapped, his eyes still on the older man.

She swallowed, aware of surrounding conversations falling quiet and patrons' attention turning their way.

Isaiah, however, seemed oblivious, watching her with a charming smile.

Or it would've been, were it not for the coldness of his eyes.

He reached over and clamped a hand on Matthias's shoulder. "People tell me that me and my boy here look a lot alike. What do you think?" Without giving her a chance to answer, he added, "I can tell you this for certain. Matthias and I are exactly alike."

With a move so fast, she wasn't sure she'd seen it, Matthias whipped his arm around, snatching his father's hand from his shoulder and locking it behind the older man's back. Isaiah didn't yelp but his smile jerked into a sneering grimace.

Holding him there, Matthias met Emma's gaze for the first time since Isaiah's appearance. "Excuse me just a minute. I have to take out the trash."

Chapter Thirteen

Matthias kept his father's arm in a shoulder lock as he marched him to O'Reilly's front door.

"Enough already, boy," Isaiah said through a tight jaw. "You don't have to throw me out on the street. I can leave on my own."

Matthias caught a glimpse of shock on Siobahn's face as she scurried away from the bar, and felt a rush of embarrassment. He released his grip with a shove.

Isaiah staggered but righted himself and cradled his arm against him. "Damn. You darn near dislocated my shoulder. Guess I forgot about your inability to control your temper."

Matthias caught the innuendo but wasn't going to mention the one time Isaiah had benefited from Matthias's ability to restrain himself. "In that regard, maybe I *am* a little like you."

That brought a smile. "The apple don't fall far from the tree, you know." He patted his chest.

Becoming more aware of drawing the full attention of those seated nearby, Matthias gripped the same shoulder he'd held in a lock and propelled Isaiah outside. Thankfully, the sidewalk was deserted. He fixed his father with a hard glare. "I don't know what kind of bullshit you're trying to pull, but it stops here. I know you've been in my apartment. I have your fingerprints."

Isaiah didn't even blink.

"I could arrest you for breaking and entering right now—"

"Didn't break anything." Isaiah extended a hand, indicating the door to Matthias's loft. "Anyone can see. The lock wasn't jimmied or forced."

Matthias wondered if his father had learned lock picking while incarcerated. "Unlawful entry then. The point is, you just got released from prison. The fingerprints I collected will send you back."

The corner of Isaiah's mouth twitched. Matthias had struck a nerve.

"Unless you leave town. I never want to see your face again."

Isaiah's gaze grew menacing, a look Matthias had seen too many times as a kid. "I leave town when I want to leave town." The hatred transitioned into a sneer. "And you're not gonna do anything about it. You know why?"

Matthias didn't answer.

Isaiah's tone turned mocking. "Because you're in love with that little gal in there. It would be a crying shame if something tragic were to happen to her."

Matthias battled his rage. "If you touch—"

Isaiah flashed a palm in Matthias's face. "I would never harm a woman you loved, son. I'm just sayin'. It *would* be a shame."

Before Matthias could react, Isaiah stepped back, turned, and sauntered away without glancing back.

Matthias realized his hands, arms, and entire upper body were clenched, ready to pummel the life out of the man he'd called father. He inhaled. Exhaled. Consciously released the tension.

I would never harm a woman you loved, son.

He already had. It's why he'd been convicted of murder.

Once his breath became more regular, Matthias walked stiffly back into O'Reilly's, half expecting Emma to have escaped through the rear entrance. Instead, she sat in the same spot, her hands folded around one of the two mugs of beer that had appeared in his absence. God, he did not want to explain his father to her. To anyone. But especially to her.

He slid back into his chair. "I'm sorry about all that."

"Are you okay?" Her voice sounded strained.

He tried to smile. "Define 'okay.'"

She didn't return the smile but studied him as if trying to read the past written on his face. Whatever she interpreted would be wrong.

He was going to have to do this. Explain what happened all those years ago. He opened his mouth.

Siobahn saved him by arriving with the provolone sticks. She placed them and two small plates on the table. "Can I get you anything else right now?" Her words were directed at Matthias and carried a bigger question than the simple offer to bring another beer.

"We're good. Thanks." He was anything but good and feared the same was true of Emma.

Once Siobahn left, Emma reached over, resting a hand on his arm, her touch feather soft. "It's okay. You don't have to tell me anything," she said, her voice as soft as her touch. "I just want to be sure you're all right."

He stared at the plate of breaded cheese and marinara. "I'm not." He lifted his gaze to meet hers and gave her a smile. A real one this time. "But I will be."

Emma turned down Matthias's invitation to spend the night—much as she'd have liked to—and drove home to the Campground and her seventeen-foot camper. The campground's sister business,

Sara's Restaurant, was crowded and alive with oldies rock music that matched its red, white, and chrome diner décor. Emma kept to the slow speed limit through the campgrounds, waving to some of the residents she'd become friendly with, and made the right turn up the hill to her lot. The site above hers remained vacant although she'd heard rumors of someone moving in within the next week or so. To her relief, the next neighbor uphill, boorish Mick Harper, hadn't been at his camp for several days and still wasn't.

She parked and climbed out into the sultry evening air. At least the breeze kept the mosquitos at bay. She thumbed through her keys as she stepped onto the covered wooden deck, but instead of inserting the key into the door's lock, she slumped into one of the molded plastic chairs, exhaled, and buried her face in her hands.

The mental image of Isaiah Honeywell's deceptive eyes chased the image of Matthias's barely restrained rage through her head. She'd wanted to ask Matthias a million questions when he'd returned from escorting his father from O'Reilly's, but she'd sensed talking about it was the last thing he wanted to do, so she'd honored that. She remembered how he'd looked when she'd declined his invitation to go upstairs to his place. He probably thought the incident with his father was the reason.

It was.

Only not in the way he believed.

At first, she thought Isaiah looked familiar because of his resemblance to his son. As the evening went on, as she sat across from Matthias for dinner and studied his scarred but handsome face, she realized, no. There were some familial similarities...

But she had seen Isaiah before. Recently. If only she could remember *where*.

An idea struck her. She leaped to her feet and wheeled, catching her toe on the chair leg, sending it toppling with a sharp plastic-on-wood thunk. Fumbling, she managed to stuff the key into the lock and yank the door open. Inside, she pulled it shut and flipped the deadbolt.

The stagnant, humid air in the camper nearly choked her. She clicked the switch on the air conditioner, and it whirred to life. In such a small space, the unit would have it comfortable in a matter of minutes.

Emma had brought one of Darcy's boxes of photos home with her and stored it under the kitchen table that doubled as her workspace, holding two laptops and monitors. She moved the computers to one of the bench seats and slid the monitors as far to one side as she could without tipping them off the table. Then she dragged out the box, slammed it on the table, and removed the lid. After turning on the overhead light, she started through stacks of prints she'd already sorted.

Fifteen minutes later, she found what she was looking for.

Like the majority of Darcy's photos, these three had no label, no hint as to their context. Emma held the first one up to the light for a closer look.

All three had been taken with a long lens, capturing unobtrusive candid images of two men on a downtown Erie sidewalk. At work, Emma had bundled these and several other photos obviously taken at the same shoot. The background was too blurred for her to recognize the street. Matthias might. If she showed them to him.

She had to show them to him. One of the two men in the three photos was Isaiah. The other had his back to the camera.

Matthias would want details. Even if he identified where the pictures had been taken, he'd want to know when. Emma had no idea. Not from the unmarked prints. Which meant she would spend tomorrow at ErieLIVE, going through Darcy's digital files. If Emma located the digital images from which these photos had been printed, she would be able to access the metadata, including the day and time the images were captured as well as the GPS coordinates.

She dropped onto the bench not holding her laptops and studied the images. In the first of the sequential captures, Isaiah's intense expression strongly suggested he and the other man were having a heated discussion. In the second, his mouth was open in what looked like a snarl.

In the third, he turned his head slightly and appeared to be looking straight into the camera's lens with an expression that chilled Emma to the bone.

Even more chilling, she realized another reason Isaiah looked familiar to her. He was one of the two older men she'd seen talking in front of the theater yesterday when she went for coffee.

Russ Carlisle wasn't watching her. Matthias's father was.

Matthias paced his apartment, trying and failing to tamp down his anger. He'd spent his entire adult life acting as if his father was dead. If he'd learned Isaiah had died in prison, he wouldn't have mourned his loss. Not for a single minute. Some humans were beyond redemption. Isaiah Honeywell was one of them.

Despite Matthias denying his father's existence all this time, Isaiah was here. He'd first claimed he wanted to make amends. Matthias hadn't bought it. Then the old man had managed to gain access to this very apartment, Matthias's sanctuary. His escape from the brutal world he worked in.

And now, Isaiah knew about Emma.

Matthias's gut told him Isaiah already knew about her, though. Tonight, he'd made contact. Had used the same charm that had won over so many others. Matthias didn't think Emma bought it. She had experience with a charming, abusive man. They hadn't discussed Isaiah over dinner. Matthias knew she was dying to ask, but she'd kept her questions to herself. How the hell had he lucked out to find a woman like her?

He would eventually have to come clean and tell her about the night he'd come within a hair of committing murder. But not right now. Right now, he needed to sleep. He laughed out loud at the thought. Sleep was not happening.

The clock read nine-thirty. He considered going to the station. Take out his frustrations and aggressions on the heavy bag. Possibly work on the Larson case.

He stopped pacing as a better idea struck him. Russ Carlisle. Emma and Kira were digging into Carlisle's involvement with a woman who bore bruises. Bruises Carlisle surely inflicted.

Matthias checked his service weapon, grabbed a light jacket from the bedroom, and pounded down the stairs.

He didn't need the jacket, especially after the brisk hike to South Park Row to retrieve his Jeep.

The last time he'd been on Sixteenth Street, he'd caught a bullet. He'd also caught a killer. Tonight, as he pulled into the lot facing The Blue Pike Restaurant, he was about to face another, except gathering evidence on this one had proved challenging.

He stepped out of his vehicle and slipped into the jacket, although the muggy night air made it completely unnecessary. Still, he didn't want to walk into the restaurant with his weapon in full view.

Nothing had changed inside The Blue Pike since his last visit. If it weren't for the manager, he would gladly frequent the place. Brick walls, exposed ductwork, and the overall industrial tone appealed to him. It should. His apartment looked much the same.

Unlike his first time here, he stopped at the PLEASE WAIT TO BE SEATED sign. The hostess who approached him at the podium wasn't the same young woman who'd once promised him and Emma free meals for life.

"Do you have a reservation?"

"I'm not here to eat. I need to speak with your manager."

"Mr. Carlisle?"

Matthias gave her a tight smile. "Yes."

"I'm sorry. He's not here this evening."

"Can you tell me when he'll be in?"

The young woman appeared on the verge of tears. "I wish I knew. We haven't seen him since Saturday. He never told anyone he was taking time off. He just hasn't shown up."

"Is that common for him?"

"No." From the note of hysteria in her voice, Matthias wondered if she was another of Carlisle's conquests. "Ordinarily, I'd be thrilled for the peace and quiet of him being gone, but he left without completing the employee schedule for the week. I've been losing my mind trying to make sure the shifts are all covered."

Matthias ran his fingers across his upper lip to conceal a smile. No, this young hostess wasn't frantic with concern for Carlisle's wellbeing. Rather she was pissed about the added work he'd dumped on her. Regaining his cop face, he asked, "Do you know a young woman by the name of Suzanne Foster?"

She huffed. "That would be Russ's current lady friend. I suppose she's missing too."

"Not that I know of," he lied. Sort of.

"Then you might want to ask her. They're probably together. In Fiji."

Matthias slid a business card from his pocket and set it on the podium in front of the waitress. "Do me a favor. If either of them shows up, give me a call."

"Me? Or do you want me to have Mr. Carlisle call you?"

"*You* call me. I suspect Carlisle would toss my number in the trash."

She grinned. "Ah. Gotcha. Will do."

He thanked her and stepped back out into the muggy night air.

Russ Carlisle was missing. Since Saturday. Except...

Matthias climbed into his Jeep before pulling up Emma's number. Her voice sounded odd when she answered. His first thought was that Isaiah had followed her to the campground and was standing next to her. "Are you okay?"

"Yeah."

He almost asked if his father was there, but imagined how that would sound if he wasn't. "You sure?"

"I'm positive."

He detected no sign of distress or deception.

"What do you need?" she asked.

"When did you see Russ Carlisle at the convenience store robbery?"

"He wasn't the one doing the robbing. He and Suzanne were on the sidewalk, watching."

"I know that. But when was it?"

"It was Tuesday."

The same day Isaiah had shown up in Perry Square Park. "You're sure it was him?"

Her annoyed sigh breathed into his ear.

"Never mind. Stupid question."

"It was him," she answered anyway. He thanked her and was about to hang up when she said, "Hey."

"Yeah?"

She didn't answer right away, and he wondered if the call had dropped. When she did speak, her voice was soft, strained. "Is it okay if I stop by the station tomorrow? I have something I need to show you."

"Do you want me to come by your place now?"

"No." Her tone turned flirtatious. "I need to get my sleep."

"I didn't mean..." He'd never spent the night in her crammed camper. He'd seen her so-called bed, which was more of a futon, with a lumpy not-even-full-size mattress. Snuggling close was one thing. Not being able to stretch out was another.

"I know you didn't. But I need to go to the office and dig up some more information first. I'll see you tomorrow."

More information? On what? But he sensed she didn't want to divulge anything tonight. "Text me when you get there. I'll come down and escort you inside."

"Okay. Goodnight."

Those three little words stuck in his throat again. "Goodnight."

Chapter Fourteen

Once again, Emma was at her computer in the ErieLIVE office ahead of anyone else. While she had no desire to be the early bird on a regular basis, she preferred solitude for this kind of research.

She hoped finding the digital files of the three images would be easy. Of course, it was not. With the three photographs spread on the desk beside her keyboard, she moused back through time scanning the images Darcy had shot in recent weeks.

Emma liked to take four times more photos than she needed just to get one sellable picture. If that was true, Darcy took ten times that amount.

After what felt like hours, Emma found what she was looking for—the digital files matching the prints. She clicked through them, then reversed, stopping on one image. On the computer screen, Isaiah's face loomed larger than on paper. In spite of the obvious distance between photographer and subject, he appeared to look straight into the lens. And he did not appear happy.

Emma swallowed hard and clicked the arrow to advance to the

next picture. He no longer eyed the camera but was conversing with the other man, still looking miffed.

Along with the three photos matching the prints, Emma found another six images taken at the same time, but those images didn't show Isaiah's face. Nor did they give a good angle on the other man. The metadata revealed the pictures were taken one week ago. Last Friday. The location was identified as State Street, just south of Eleventh.

Less than three blocks from where she'd seen him outside the theater.

She made a note, copied all nine photos onto a USB drive, and logged out of the system.

Rather than move her car and risk losing her parking space, she decided to walk, keeping vigilant in case Isaiah was lurking in the area. By eight a.m. she'd reached South Park Row and texted Matthias, telling him where she was. He responded within seconds.

Be right down.

She clamped the manilla envelope holding the photos and flash drive under her arm and gazed north, beyond Perry Square Park toward the lake. The morning air was every bit as humid as it had been yesterday, but the billowing gray clouds rolling down from Canada promised the relief the weathermen were forecasting.

She turned her back on the park and surveyed the brick, concrete, and glass structure housing the municipal offices and police station. She'd never been inside it before and was eager to see where Matthias worked, but also felt a little intimidated.

Not even two minutes passed before he appeared at the corner of the building and strode toward her.

"Hi," he said.

"Hi."

The Devil Comes Calling

He pointed at the envelope. "Is that what you want to show me?"

"Yeah." Suddenly, she didn't want to go inside. This was Matthias's dad, not a criminal. "Last night, when your father showed up at O'Reilly's, I had a feeling I'd seen him before."

Matthias's expression darkened.

"At first I thought it was because he looks a little like an older version of you." Emma waited for a reaction or a reply, but none came. "Then I remembered where I'd seen him. I told you about being assigned to go through Darcy's photos." She held out the envelope. "He's in several of them." When Matthias stared at the envelope without reaching for it, she added, "I thought you should see them."

After several long moments, he gave one quick nod of agreement. But instead of taking the envelope from her, he tipped his head toward the station. "Come on. Let's go inside."

Emma fell into step beside him as he led the way down the sidewalk to the West Seventh Street side of the building and down a ramp into an underground garage. She concealed her curiosity as best she could, keeping her head down, but sneaking furtive glances at the police cruisers. Without a word, he led her up several flights of poorly lit concrete stairs. At the top, he held a heavy fire door for her.

"Welcome to Major Crimes."

She flashed him an uneasy smile. Was he taking her to an interrogation room?

Instead, he escorted her into a small kitchenette complete with a coffee urn and an open box of doughnuts. She continued to follow him into a room with a row of three-sided office cubicles along a windowed wall.

Matthias grabbed an empty chair from one of the vacant cubbies and parked it at one of the desks. "Have a seat."

A familiar face—Detective Sergeant Cassie Malone—appeared from the next cubicle. "Hi, Emma. What brings you here?"

"I do," Matthias answered before Emma had the chance. He slid past her and took a seat at the desk. "Let's see what you have."

She turned the envelope over to him. "For some reason, Darcy liked to print a lot of her photos. The ones with your father are in there along with a USB drive containing more images taken at the same time."

Cassie rose and joined them. "Pictures of your father?" she said to Matthias.

He grunted as he dumped the contents on the desk and picked up the prints.

Emma watched his face, but it might as well have been carved from stone.

"Do you know when these were taken?" he asked.

"According to the metadata, last Friday on State Street between Eleventh and Twelfth."

Cassie leaned over his shoulder as he thumbed through the images. He settled on the photo in which Isaiah appeared to look directly into the lens with an expression that still gave Emma chills. It reminded her of the look Matthias had given her when she'd first spotted him in the cemetery, only ten times scarier.

He handed the image to Cassie and looked at Emma. "Are there any that show the guy he's talking to?"

"No. His back's to the camera in all of them." Emma pointed at the USB drive. "There're a few more pictures on that but still not even a profile view of the second man."

Matthias picked it up and inserted it into his computer. When it loaded, he clicked to open the folder Emma had copied. He and Cassie stared at the monitor. He zoomed in, which only pixelated the image.

"Emma's right. I can't make him out," Cassie said. "He's wearing a ball cap, so I can't even tell his hair color."

Matthias studied the images as if willing the man to turn around.

"Do you have an idea of who he might be?" Emma asked.

"No." He clicked back to the image of Isaiah staring into the lens. Matthias turned to her. "I need you to do me a favor."

"Anything."

Cassie snorted.

"Stop," he growled at his partner before coming back to Emma. "We have Darcy's photographic equipment here in evidence. Can you take a look at it? Let us know if there's anything there that shouldn't be." He held her gaze. "Or anything that's *not* there that *should* be."

Emma glanced at Cassie hoping to get a clue as to what he was thinking, but her face remained as still as his. "Sure, but I don't know how much help I can be. We don't keep track of each other's camera equipment."

"I realize that, but you might see something we've missed."

"I'll do my best."

Matthias and Cassie escorted Emma to an interrogation room.

"We'll be right back," Cassie said. She and Matthias closed the door and left Emma alone.

She paced the floor, taking in the table, the chairs, the dreary and faded paint on the walls, grateful she wasn't claustrophobic and that she wasn't here for the room's usual purpose.

After what felt like ages, the door opened and Matthias and Cassie entered, each carrying a large cardboard box, which they placed on the table.

Matthias removed the lid of the first box. He lifted the camera bodies and lenses out and arranged them in front of Emma. He did the same with the second box. When the boxes were empty, he faced her. "What do you think?"

She stepped closer and exhaled. Darcy had been passionate about her profession. Passionate about only using the best equipment. She and Emma shared a love of Nikon. Darcy's Nikon bodies were newer than Emma's. Emma remembered joking with her, telling her not to turn her back and not to come looking for her if one of them went missing. It was all in jest. Except now, it wasn't.

"There's a Z8 body missing."

"A what?" Cassie asked.

"A Nikon Z8 camera body. It was her newest and her favorite. Two weeks ago, she was showing it off to me, which is how I know about it. The darn thing retails for close to four grand."

"Four thousand dollars?" Cassie blew a low whistle. "My phone takes nice enough photos for me, thank you very much."

"Is it possible she left it at the newsroom?" Matthias asked.

Emma shook her head. "ErieLIVE has cameras for us to use if we want, but they're mostly old junkers. Like me, Darcy always used her own. She was fastidious about keeping her stuff separate from theirs."

"Is there anywhere else she might have left it?"

Emma thought. "I assume this is from her apartment."

"Yeah."

"You searched her car?"

"We did."

"I'm not sure what her new job entailed, but she might've had it with her. I can't imagine where else it would be."

Matthias turned to his partner, and they once more exchanged a silent conversation.

"Do you think the person who killed her took the camera?" Emma asked. "I mean, yes, it's an expensive piece of equipment, but hardly worth killing two people over."

Cassie huffed. "You'd be surprised."

Matthias waved a hand over the table. "Do you notice anything else missing?"

Emma exhaled and took another long look, mentally inventorying what she'd seen Darcy use. The long lenses, like the one used to photograph those two men at a distance, were all there. "No," she said, then stopped. "Wait. I don't see her wide-angle lens. She rarely used it for ErieLIVE work." Emma met Matthias's eyes. "But it would be perfect for photographing the inside of a house."

"What are you thinking?" Cassie asked after Matthias returned from walking Emma back to her car.

He dropped into his chair, jiggled his computer mouse and watched his father's image fill the monitor. "I'm thinking I'd like to know who Isaiah was meeting and why."

Cassie picked up one of the prints and studied it. "You know how I always tell you that you have a look that scares people?"

"Yeah?"

"You got nothing on your father." She turned the image toward him.

The photo she referred to was the one in which Isaiah appeared to look directly into the camera lens.

Directly at the photographer.

Cassie positioned herself to face Matthias. "Your father was angry about something. Was he upset at the man he was with?" She left the rest of the question hanging.

Or was he outraged at being photographed?

She didn't say it out loud. Didn't need to. He knew where she was headed and said it for her. "We may be looking at this case all wrong."

"We've been *assuming*—" Cassie shook her head. "I hate that word—Orlando Larson was the intended target and Darcy Tomasetti merely picked the wrong day to start a new job."

Matthias stared into the soulless eyes of Isaiah Honeywell glaring at the photographer through her lens. "Darcy could've been the real target, and Larson just got in the way."

"There's something else," Cassie said.

Matthias knew what she was thinking. "Darcy's missing camera."

"Right. Maybe the killer took it—"

"Not because it was worth four grand," Matthias said, "but because they wanted what may or may not have been on the memory card." Like the image he was looking at right now. Another thought struck him. He swore and bolted from his seat.

"What is it?" Cassie called after him.

He pounded down the stairs, and through the hallways, shouldering uniformed officers out of his way.

Matthias burst out of the station into a downpour. Ignoring the soaking rain, he strode across South Park Row to Perry Square and stalked the paved paths through the park, searching the few faces of people braving the weather.

His father was not one of them. Why had he thought he'd find Isaiah here?

The answer was simple. He sensed his old man was following him, spying on him. He'd run into him in the park before. If Isaiah truly was lurking, watching Matthias, this would be the best place to do it.

If Isaiah *had* been here, he would've seen Emma. He'd have seen Matthias walk her out of the station, press a gentle kiss to her lips. He'd have seen Emma walk away while Matthias went back inside.

He'd have followed her.

Matthias's first instinct was to jump in his Jeep and drive to

ErieLIVE's offices. That's where she was headed. He unlocked his vehicle and climbed behind the wheel, out of the rain.

His phone buzzed with a text. It was from Cassie.

Where the hell did you go?

He stared at the words. Felt his breath and heart rate slowing.

Back in a minute.

Instead of returning the phone to his pocket, he pulled up Emma's number and pressed the call button.

She answered immediately. "What's up?"

Thank God. There was no stress radiating from her voice. "Where are you?"

"At work. I'm going through more of Darcy's photos."

"Find anything else?"

"Not yet. I'll let you know if I do."

"Good." His mind returned to Isaiah and imagined him sitting outside ErieLIVE, watching Emma's car, waiting for her. "I need you to do something for me."

"Do you have more evidence for me to look at?"

He could hear the smile in her voice. "This is serious."

"Okay. What do you need?"

It was a good question. What exactly did he want her to do? Stay safe? Too generic. Don't leave the building? Impossible. She had a job to do. A job that required her to follow the news. Move into his apartment and lock herself in?

Isaiah had already proved he could access the loft, come and go as he pleased.

Matthias needed to make some calls and get his locks changed. Install a security system.

"Matthias? You there?"

"I'm here. Sorry."

"What did you need from me?"

He squeezed the bridge of his nose. "Keep your eyes open for my father. If you see him, go the other way. Call me immediately. No matter what, do *not* go anywhere with him."

The silence on the line screamed at him. After several painfully long moments, she responded, "Okay."

"I mean it."

"I know you do. I wish you'd tell me why."

"You don't want to know."

Another long silence. Then she said, "I'll be careful."

"Thanks. I'll talk to you later." He ended the call, pocketed his phone, and gazed through the rain-streaked windshield at the mostly deserted park.

Where the hell was Isaiah? And how the hell could he find out?

Chapter Fifteen

Emma sat at her desk, staring at the image on the computer monitor. What was the deal with Matthias and his father? Clearly, he didn't want to talk about it, and at this early stage of their relationship, she didn't feel she was in a position to press. If he wanted her to know, he'd tell her.

But he was worried about her. Worried about his father doing something to her.

Why on earth would Isaiah Honeywell want to do anything *to her*?

She looked around at the reporters in the room, on their phones or tapping away on their keyboards. Preston was at his desk, engaged in what appeared to be an intense phone call.

The only person not occupied with their work was the red-headed scarecrow, Boze.

She stood and was halfway across the room on her way to his desk when she stopped and reconsidered. Boze would have easy access to all the news outlets' archives. He could easily look up Isaiah Honeywell and any stories he was mentioned in. But what if there was something big? Boze would jump on it, turn it into an online news blast. Matthias would be furious.

Even the simple act of delving into Isaiah's past was an invasion of Matthias's privacy. She couldn't do that to him.

"Emma!"

She turned toward the source of the shout and spotted Preston jogging toward her. "What is it?"

He stopped in front of her and waved his notebook. "I just spoke to the fire marshal. They've ID'd one of the victims from the structural fire we covered on Wednesday."

Emma swore under her breath. She'd meant to ask Matthias if he'd spoken with Detective Frazier and had forgotten with all the drama surrounding the photos. She'd also forgotten to tell Matthias about seeing his father on the street the other day. That part could wait. "And?" she asked Preston.

"The woman's name was…"—he looked at his notes—"Suzanne Foster."

Emma swore out loud this time.

"You know her?" Preston asked.

"She took yoga classes with me."

He lowered his head. "I'm sorry."

"What about the other victim? The man."

"No ID on him yet. They were both badly burned. The only reason they were able to determine the woman's identity this soon is because the fire originated in her apartment."

"Did she have a roommate?"

"I wondered the same thing. You know, maybe she lived there with a guy but apparently not." Preston eyed her. "Did she have a boyfriend that you know of?"

Emma's mind raced. "I don't know," she lied. "Maybe."

"What does that mean?"

Russ Carlisle could be the second victim. Was Emma a horrible person for hoping that was the case? If she gave his name to

Preston, he'd run with it. Emma wasn't a reporter, but this story had just become personal. She wanted to be the one to find out if her biggest nemesis was truly out of her life.

"Emma?"

She blinked and looked at Preston. "I'll ask around and let you know."

He gave her a good-humored side-eye. "You trying to steal my job?"

Emma forced a laugh. "I don't want your job. I don't want to waste your time, either. I'll see what I can find out and then the story's all yours."

"What was that all about?" Cassie demanded when Matthias returned to his desk after stopping at his locker to change into a dry shirt and towel dry his hair.

How could he explain without sounding like he'd lost hold of his senses?

His partner stood over him, arms crossed. "You think your father is wasting his time sitting in the park, waiting for you?"

Matthias tensed. "How— How did you..." he stuttered.

"I'm a damned good detective, remember? I connected the dots." She pointed at the computer screen, which showed the image of Isaiah glaring into the camera lens. "If looks could kill, the person behind the camera would be dead. Oh, wait. She is. We've already found him waiting for you in the park once. Maybe he claimed one of the benches as his own."

"The park isn't the only place he's been."

Cassie raised one arched brow. "Oh?"

Matthias exhaled and, keeping his voice low, told her about the fingerprints in his apartment and about Isaiah's appearance in O'Reilly's.

Midway through his tale, Cassie wheeled the empty chair Emma had vacated back to Matthias's cubicle and slumped into it. When he finished, Cassie asked, "How much does Emma know?"

He shook his head. "Nothing."

"Oh, come on. This is a woman who's been stalked by a maniac. I imagine she can spot one a mile away."

Cassie had a point.

"I told her to call me if she sees him," Matthias said. "And to stay the hell away from him."

"Good." Cassie stood and rolled the chair back to its assigned desk. "Do you have any idea where he's staying?"

"None."

"We need to figure that out."

"We don't have enough for a warrant."

Cassie nodded in agreement. "Let's put out an ATL bulletin."

Attempt to locate. Matthias had to admit it was a good option. "As long as it's clear we only want an address or a make, model, and plate number of whatever vehicle he's driving. Do not detain. Contact one of us." He waggled his finger back and forth between them.

"Agreed. Once we get that much, we'll set up surveillance." Cassie's gaze returned to the photo. "I'd also like to know who the other guy is."

Matthias faced his computer and clicked through the rest of the images on the flash drive. "His back's to the camera in all of them." He stopped on one, magnified it, and tapped the screen. "He's almost in profile here. Almost, but not quite."

"I know. It's too bad. I have a feeling the real key here is him more than your father."

"Do you know something I don't?"

She grinned. "I know lots of stuff you don't. Comes with age."

"I mean—" He was going to say "about this case" but knew she was yanking his chain.

"Isaiah Honeywell hasn't been out of prison long, so he can't have been in Erie all that long either. Why was Darcy Tomasetti taking his picture? Or was she trying to get a shot of the other guy?"

"She was in a lousy position if she was trying to get a photo of the other guy."

"Maybe she was like us—hoping he'd turn around." Cassie reflected for several moments before giving one determined nod. "I want to talk to Darcy's parents again."

Not what Matthias expected. "Why?"

"It's been four days since they lost their daughter. The initial shock has worn off. I'd like to know if they've thought of anything new now that we think Darcy may be the center of the investigation."

April Tomasetti led them into the house Darcy had designed, for the second time that week. She'd looked devastated the first time. Today, she seemed several inches shorter, as if the heavy hand of grief was slowly smashing her into the ground.

Matthias surveyed the room. Black ribbons hung over most of the photos on display. Heavy draperies that had been open during their first visit were now closed, blocking out the gray light of the rainy day.

"Is your husband home?" Cassie asked.

Pressing a tissue to her nose, April mumbled something and left them alone. Her voice reached them as she called out, "Steven. The police are here."

A minute passed before both of Darcy's parents joined them. "Have you found our daughter's murderer?" the father asked, his voice equal parts eager and anxiety-filled.

"Not yet," Cassie said. "We're chasing down some leads and hoped you might answer a few questions."

"Anything to help." Steven guided his wife to the same sofa on which they'd sat on Monday. It struck Matthias how utterly lost April looked, as if she couldn't find her way around, even in her own home.

Cassie flipped open her notebook. "First let me ask if either of you have thought of anything new since we last spoke?"

"Nothing beyond trying to figure out how to live without our little girl," April said.

Matthias slid his phone from his pocket, pulled up the photos, and handed the device to April. "Do you recognize either of the men in this picture?"

April studied the images as Steven put on his glasses. They each went through the photos before exchanging frustrated looks. "No," April said. "Then again, it's hard to tell when one fellow has his back to the camera." She lifted her gaze to Matthias and Cassie. "Did our Darcy take these?"

"We believe so, yes." Cassie leaned forward, perching on the edge of her chair. "Did she seem nervous or upset in recent weeks?"

Steven shook his head.

"Did she mention being afraid of anyone?"

The father again shook his head.

"Yes." April's reply was sharp.

He looked at his wife. "What? Who?"

She lifted her chin defiantly. "I told you before. That man she was dating."

Cassie flipped back through her notebook.

"Preston Guilfoyle?" Matthias asked.

"Yes," April said. "Him. I told you last time." She looked from Matthias to Cassie. "Have you questioned him?"

"We have," Matthias said. "He claims to have an alibi for the time of the homicide."

"Oh." April leaned against her husband, who appeared pensive.

Cassie looked at Matthias, a gleam in her dark eyes.

He knew exactly what she was thinking.

It was an alibi they had yet been able to substantiate.

Steven returned Matthias's phone. "I truly wish we could be more help."

Matthias thought of another question they hadn't asked. "Did Darcy happen to leave any of her camera equipment here? Specifically a Nikon Z8?"

The couple looked at each other, frowning in thought. "No," April said. "I think she may have left a couple of older cameras here when she moved out. They're up in the attic if you want to see them."

"That won't be necessary," Cassie said and started to rise.

April stopped her with an outstretched hand. "How's Darcy's cat? I know you said your husband's a vet—"

"She's fine. My husband's taking good care of her until he can find her a new home."

A sad smile crossed April's face. "That's good. Thank him for me."

Back in the car, Matthias tried Quentin Donahue's phone only to listen to his voice message for the umpteenth time.

Matthias ended the call without speaking after the beep. "I get the feeling he doesn't want to talk to us."

"Ya think?" Cassie backed out of the driveway. "Let's track him down anyway."

Their next stop was the yellow brick ranch Donahue was

supposedly remodeling. The homeowner visibly seethed as he told them he still hadn't seen or heard from the contractor. Next, they drove west to Donahue's home residence only to get no answer at the door. Buddy McCall, the next-door neighbor, waved at them as he pruned a shrub in front of his house.

"Mr. McCall," Matthias shouted, then raised a hand when the man struggled to his feet. "Don't get up."

"Too late." Buddy chuckled, dusting off his knees. He shot an upward glance. "Just trying to get some work done between rainstorms."

"I won't keep you." Matthias strode toward him. "Don't suppose you've seen your neighbor since we last spoke."

"No, sir-ree, I have not. I would've called you if I had."

Matthias thanked him and let him get back to his gardening. Cassie waited by their car, her arms crossed. "Now what?" she asked.

"Let's go talk to Preston Guilfoyle again."

Cassie slid behind the wheel. "I would give you grief for disliking this guy simply because he works with Emma, but I have to admit, with his missing alibi who also happens to be his cousin—"

"Who also happens to be Larson's ex-partner."

"Right. And Guilfoyle's denial of being involved with Darcy while her parents insist he was." Cassie shook her head. "Something's off with him."

"You forgot to add he happens to work with Emma."

Cassie glanced at him and snorted. "And then there's that."

Matthias and Cassie made it as far as the receptionist's desk at ErieLIVE before being stopped by a stern-looking woman with short hair and large glasses.

The Devil Comes Calling

"How may I help you, detectives?" The woman, whose name tag read LeeAnn, jutted her jaw as if daring them to punch her.

Matthias forced a smile. "We need to speak with Preston Guilfoyle."

"I can't let you back there." LeeAnn reflected his not-quite-sincere smile back at him. "Unless you have a warrant."

"Seriously?" Cassie feigned frustration. "We're not here to arrest him. We just need to talk to him. Besides"—she elbowed Matthias—"this one's good friends with Emma Anderson. She'll vouch for us."

Considering the look the receptionist gave Matthias, she believed Emma should have better taste.

He wasn't sure he disagreed.

"I'll call and have Mr. Guilfoyle come out here to meet you." LeeAnn picked up a phone and punched an extension. "Mr. Guilfoyle, there are a couple of police detectives here to see you." After a pause, during which Matthias pictured Guilfoyle climbing down a fire escape, the receptionist said, "I will tell them." She replaced the phone in its cradle. "He'll be down shortly."

As the minutes ticked by, Matthias's vision of Guilfoyle on the fire escape felt more realistic. He was about to pull out his cell and call Emma when Preston stepped out of the elevator and strode their way.

He directed them to a small office just off the lobby. The news outlet's version of an interrogation room, Matthias mused. None of them moved toward either the desk or the chairs.

"We wanted to ask you a few more questions about your relationship with Darcy Tomasetti," Cassie said.

"I told you before. We were co-workers. Nothing more."

"Are you sure about that?"

"Very." Guilfoyle looked at Matthias and back at Cassie. "What's this about?"

"We're just having a hard time believing you." She placed her hands on her hips. "Darcy's parents are quite certain you and she were seeing each other."

"We weren't."

"Not even in the past?" Cassie asked. "I can see why, under the circumstances, you wouldn't want to admit to being involved with her now. Maybe you'd been seeing each other, maybe secretly, but one of you broke it off a while back."

"I don't know why her parents believe we were 'involved,' as you say, but we weren't. Ever."

Matthias studied him, thinking he was a good liar. Damned good. But not good enough. Matthias wasn't buying it and doubted Cassie was either.

Guilfoyle snapped his fingers. "I bet I know what was going on. Darcy said her folks were always pressuring her to settle down, find a nice guy, get married, have kids. The whole nine yards, you know? I bet she told them we were seeing each other just to get them off her back."

Cassie made a show of considering his theory. "You might be right. That makes sense."

Guilfoyle flashed a relieved smile.

"Except we've spoken with them. If she lied about being involved with you to please them, it doesn't appear to have worked."

The smile vanished.

"Besides, we're having a problem with something else. You told us you were with your cousin, Quentin Donahue, Sunday night through Monday morning."

"That's right. I stayed at his house after a party and came to work straight from there. Didn't you check with him?"

"We've tried," Matthias said. "He was supposed to meet us at one of his job sites but didn't show. He's not answering his phone, and he's not been home for days."

The puzzled look on Guilfoyle's face was the first genuine

expression Matthias had seen from the reporter. "That can't be right." Guilfoyle pulled out his phone, keyed up a number, and waited.

And waited.

"Hey, Quent, it's Preston. Where the hell are you, pal? Give me a call as soon as you get this." He pocketed the phone. "That's really weird. He always answers his phone for me."

"Just not for the police," Matthias added.

"I didn't mean that." Guilfoyle squirmed. "I don't know what you want me to say. Darcy and I never dated. We weren't involved outside of work. As soon as Quentin returns my call, I'll have him get in touch with you."

"You do that." Cassie pocketed her pen and notebook. "We'll be in touch."

Matthias concealed a smile. The way his partner said it, it sounded very much like a threat.

Because it was.

"Are we done here?" Preston asked.

"Not yet." Matthias pulled out his phone and pulled up the photos of Isaiah and the unidentified man. "Who are these guys and why was Darcy photographing them?"

Guilfoyle maintained a passive face as he accepted the phone and looked at the images, but his Adam's apple rode the wave of a big swallow. "Darcy took these?"

"She did."

Shaking his head, he returned the phone to Matthias. "I can't help you there either."

"You're a reporter. Darcy was the photographer you worked with." Matthias held his phone in front of Guilfoyle. "You must've been working on a story about these men. Or at least one of them."

"No. I swear. Yes, Darcy took photos of the scenes I wrote about, but she also took photos for other reporters and random pictures for her files. Some she'd sell to stock-photo distributors. Some she kept for her own portfolio. Those must've been for one of those. I'm sorry I can't be of more help."

"What other reporters?" Matthias asked.

"Any of them. All of them. It's not like being married."

Matthias thanked him for his time.

"*Now* are you done with me?" the reporter asked.

"For now," Matthias replied, dropping his voice to its deepest growl and watching as Guilfoyle hurried from the room and back the way he'd come.

Chapter Sixteen

Matthias faced his partner. "I noticed you didn't mention April Tomasetti's accusation about Darcy being scared of him."

"I'm saving that tidbit for a future conversation. Besides, I'm curious about the father's reaction to the mother's statement. I'd like to talk to him alone." Cassie reached for the handbag she'd placed on one of the chairs. "You ready?"

"Not yet." He needed to find out who Darcy was working with when she took those photos.

"You want a few minutes with Emma."

"Yeah, but not for the reason you think." He tapped a text into his phone, asking Emma to come down to the lobby if she wasn't busy.

She responded within seconds.

On my way.

He looked up to find Cassie scrutinizing him. "What?" he asked.

"If you ask Emma for information to help with a case, she's going to expect the same in return for a story."

"I thought you were happy she and I are dating."

"I am. She's good for you. But conflict of interest where our jobs are concerned is tricky. I don't want to see it ruin things for the two of you."

"I'm not asking her to divulge a confidential source."

"Okay." Cassie's tone was dubious.

He spotted Emma exit the elevator and caught her eye, waving. She veered in their direction.

"What's going on?" Emma asked, her gaze darting from Matthias to Cassie. "Why are you questioning Preston again?"

Cassie shot him a look that clearly said, *I told you so.*

"It's an ongoing investigation. You know I can't talk to you about it."

Emma scowled at him. "I'm not asking for a statement for the press. I'm asking because I work with this guy."

"I know. That's—"

"If this is still because of what I told you about the bar fight, Boze was drunk when he said what he did. Preston's been nothing but professional and civilized and … and…"—she stammered—"and gentlemanly since we've been partnered up. I can't believe he would harm anyone."

Matthias took a step toward her, holding up both hands in surrender. "Just because someone you work with is professional with you doesn't mean he's not capable of taking a life."

Emma inhaled sharply.

He needed to regain control over the conversation. "None of this is what I asked you to come down here for. I'm trying to find out why Darcy took those photos of my father. I asked Guilfoyle if he was there. If he was working on a story about either of the men in the photo. He said no."

"Oh." Emma calmed down, apparently assuming that was the sole reason they'd spoken to the reporter.

"He also said Darcy sometimes worked with other reporters."

"That's true."

"Do you think you could ask around?"

She thought about it and nodded. "Sure."

"Thanks. Let me know what you find out."

"Wait," she said. "There were two things I forgot to ask you about earlier. Well, one thing I wanted to ask and another I meant to tell you."

"What's that?"

"Did you talk to that other detective about the victims from the fire?"

Dammit. He'd forgotten. "I will as soon as—"

She shook her head. "No. I mean, I found out they released the name of the woman. It *was* Suzanne."

Russ Carlisle's girlfriend.

"As far as I know, they haven't identified the man yet, so if the detective on the case happens to—"

"I'll check and let you know." Matthias could read Emma's face. She wanted the second victim to be Carlisle. He did, too. "What was the other question?"

She blinked. "That *was* the question. What I forgot to tell you was..." She caught her lip between her teeth for a moment. "Remember when I told you I had a feeling I was being watched?"

"By Carlisle."

"Right. Well, it wasn't." Emma glanced at Cassie and came back to Matthias. "That photo isn't the only place I remembered seeing your father before. He was across the street from me the other day, talking to another older man in front of the Warner Theater. Neither of them was looking my way, so I didn't give it another thought at the time."

Matthias inhaled slowly. Isaiah *was* following Emma. Had been for days. Last night at O'Reilly's he'd acted like he'd never seen her before. Yet another lie. "If you see him again—"

"I know. Avoid him and call you."

Despite Cassie's presence and the clear view from the receptionist's desk, Matthias pulled Emma to him and held her to his chest. "That's right," he whispered. "Stay as far away from him as you can."

Emma watched Matthias and Cassie leave through ErieLIVE's glass doors. Her head was swimming. He'd wanted her to believe that photo of his father was the only reason they were questioning Preston. She wasn't buying it. If Matthias wouldn't tell her, she'd get answers from Preston himself.

She took the elevator up to the newsroom, thinking about Matthias's reaction to her seeing Isaiah on the street. What was it about his father that freaked him out so badly? The temptation to use her news sources created an itch. Heck, even a Google search might provide some insight. But she wasn't ready to scratch that itch just yet. Matthias would tell her when he was ready.

The other issue swirling through her head was the fire. She needed to know if Russ was dead … for the sake of her younger sister as well as her own peace of mind.

First things first. The elevator doors swished open. She stepped out and looked around. Preston was nowhere to be seen.

Laurie stood in the doorway to her office and scowled at her. "Are you all right?"

She wasn't sure. "Where's Preston?"

"He left. Came back from meeting with someone downstairs, said he had to take care of some personal business, and took off."

He must've used the back stairs. Emma hadn't seen him come

through the lobby. She stared at his empty desk. So much for asking him why Matthias and Cassie had questioned him.

"Emma?"

She flinched and met Laurie's troubled gaze.

"Are you sure you're all right?"

"Yeah." Emma remembered Matthias's request. If anyone knew what assignment Darcy'd been working on, it would be their boss. "Are you busy? Can I talk to you for a minute?"

Laurie tipped her head toward her office. "Come on in."

Emma detoured to her desk and grabbed one of the photos of Isaiah before joining her manager.

"What can I do for you?" Laurie gestured to one of the chairs.

Emma didn't sit. She held out the picture. "This is one of Darcy's images that you asked me to organize."

Laurie accepted the photo.

"Do you know what story she was working on when she took it?"

Laurie studied the print. "I have no idea. There had to be other images captured at the same shoot. Where are they?"

"On her computer."

"Let's have a look."

Emma followed Laurie to the desk Darcy used to occupy. Without a word, Emma slid into the chair, woke up the computer, and pulled up the photo files from that day. Then she stood and let Laurie take her place. Emma watched as her manager clicked through the photos including those taken before and after the pictures of Isaiah. Laurie reached the end and reversed through the same images, settling on the one with Isaiah glaring into the lens. She shivered. "I don't know who that man is, but he looks none-too-pleased to be having his picture taken."

"Do you remember what story she was working on?" Emma repeated.

"No." Laurie snatched a notepaper from a stack on the desk.

She squinted at the metadata and jotted down the date. "Let me check my records. I'll be right back."

While Emma waited, she scanned the rest of the room.

"Got it." Laurie's voice behind Emma startled her.

"That was fast."

"I'm afraid I don't have much. At the time Darcy was taking those photos, she was working with Boze. It wasn't a story I assigned. All I have in my records is that Boze was looking into something on spec. As far as I know, the piece never panned out."

"Thanks. I'll check with him."

"What's this all about?"

"I'm not sure yet. I'll let you know if it turns into anything."

Laurie eyed her. "You do that."

Emma snatched the print and crossed to Boze's desk.

He lifted his head at her approach. "What's up?"

"A couple of things." She debated which subject to broach first and held out the photo. "Laurie says you and Darcy were working together the day she took this."

He pulled a pair of reading glasses from his shirt pocket, stuck them on his nose, and took the print from her. "Yeah. I remember. I wanted to do a story on the misappropriation of funds meant to subsidize public transit for Erie residents with lower incomes. I hoped to uncover a big conspiracy."

Emma remembered hearing about the case.

"But my source was a no-show. Darcy shot a bunch of photos of the area. Random pictures in case I needed them." Boze returned the photo to Emma. "Seems the guy with the sticky fingers had a guilty conscience and turned himself in. No big exclusive scoop for me after all."

She held the photo toward him. "So, you weren't trying to get anything on these two men?"

"Nope. Why? Who are they?"

Emma lowered the picture. "Probably no one."

"Hey, if you've got a lead on a story, let me know."

"If it turns out to be anything interesting, I will."

Boze removed his glasses. "You said you had a couple of things on your mind. What else?"

She paused.

Boze smirked. "Let me guess. You wanna ask me about the fight between me and Preston."

From the way he spoke the name, Emma knew he had nothing good to say. "You were both drunk. *You* especially."

"That's true. I don't do a good job of controlling my tongue when I've had too much alcohol."

Emma waited, knowing there was more.

"I shouldn't have said what I did, but I meant every word of it."

She gawked at him. "You believe Preston killed Darcy?"

Boze flushed a bright crimson. "I didn't know you heard that."

"The waitress told me that's why Preston had you pinned on the floor."

The red-headed reporter scanned the newsroom. "I can't talk to you about this here. You want to know about your new partner, meet me for a drink after work."

"A drink after work is what got you into trouble the last time."

"True. Just don't bring Preston and we'll be fine."

She considered the request. "Where?"

"Your choice."

An idea whispered in the back of her brain. There was one place that could allow her to get answers to two questions at the same time.

Matthias stared at the images from Darcy's camera on his computer screen. His eyes and his mind bounced from his notations about the Tomasetti murder to those damned pictures. None of it made sense.

Who was the man in the photo with his father? Why didn't Isaiah want to be photographed with him? Or photographed at all? Was his reason strong enough to lead to murder? Why kill Darcy and Orlando Larson?

No. Why *execute* them? This hadn't been a crime of passion. The victims hadn't been beaten, hadn't fought back.

A long-ago memory flashed across Matthias's mind. His mother. His father. Her death hadn't truly been a crime of passion either. It had been a crime of unbridled rage.

Unlike the current homicide. A single gunshot wound to the back of the head wasn't Isaiah's style.

Except Matthias didn't truly know his father anymore. Those decades in prison would've altered him. Helped him learn new skills. Matthias already believed the old man had learned to pick a lock—namely Matthias's.

Could being a hitman for hire be another new skill?

Matthias clicked on the x in the corner of the screen, closing out the photo file. If only he could blot Isaiah from his mind and his life as easily.

Time to change focus and take a closer look at Preston Guilfoyle. Matthias dived into the reporter's social media presence and quickly learned there was damned little of a personal nature. There were links to news stories he'd written, but nothing showing him with Darcy or any other woman. Or man for that matter.

On to Darcy Tomasetti.

Her social media offered only slightly more, but nothing about Preston. Was it possible he was telling the truth?

Detective Brad Frazier breezed into Major Crimes clutching a USB drive. Before he could speak, Matthias stopped him with a raised hand. "You're working on that apartment fire, right? The one with two victims?"

Frazier scowled. "The Peninsula View Apartments? Yeah."

"Do you have a name on the male victim yet?"

"No. Hamilton's office is having trouble confirming the ID. He's supposed to call me as soon as they know for sure."

"Did you know the Foster woman was dating Russ Carlisle?"

Frazier blanched. "*The* Russ Carlisle?"

Matthias didn't bother answering.

"No, I didn't know. I guess it would be too much to hope…" Frazier let what Matthias knew was their mutual wish that Carlisle no longer walked the earth go unspoken.

"Let me know when you find out."

"Will do."

Matthias started to turn his focus back to his computer, but Frazier waved the USB drive in front of him.

"You need to see this," Frazier said.

"What is it?"

"I may have gotten a break on the Larson-Tomasetti murders."

Chapter Seventeen

The rain had ended as Emma sat in her car looking across the street at the front of The Blue Pike. She'd only been here once before and not to dine. She rubbed the palm of her hand, which still stung at the memory of slapping Russ Carlisle's smug face.

As she studied the restaurant's exterior, other memories washed over her, nearly drowning her. Memories of her younger sister, who'd worked here. Who'd been seduced by Russ.

Emma would never find peace for the life his actions had taken. But she vowed to find justice, if not for her family, at least for Suzanne Foster.

Unless justice had already been dealt by a higher power, in which case the second body in the apartment house fire was his.

Her phone rang, interrupting her thoughts. Kira's name lit the screen. Emma had texted her earlier, asking her to give her a call when she was free.

"What's up?" Kira asked, sounding perky.

Emma exhaled, searching for the right words.

"What's wrong?" Kira no longer sounded perky.

"It's Suzanne. She died in that fire."

"Oh, God. Oh, no." After a few moments, Kira asked, "What about the other body?"

"No word yet on his ID."

Kira didn't have to say she shared Emma's hope that Russ had perished alongside his latest victim. Emma knew.

"You'll call me when you learn anything?" Kira asked.

"You know I will," Emma said. "And I'm sorry."

"So am I."

The call ended. Emma pocketed the phone and steeled herself for what came next.

She stepped out of the Subaru, crossed the street, and pressed through the doors. Two young women stood at the hostess's podium. One looked up as Emma approached.

"Do you have a reservation?"

"No—"

"Then I'm sorry. We're booked solid."

Emma glanced toward the dining room. Only half of the tables were occupied, but she wasn't going to argue the point. She took a longer look at the bar. Boze wasn't there yet. Good. "I'm not here to eat," she told the hostesses. "I need to see Russ Carlisle."

The second woman at the podium made a grumbling noise in the back of her throat.

"Mr. Carlisle isn't in," the first one said. "May I take a message?"

"When do you expect him?"

The two women exchanged a look. "I'm not at liberty to divulge his schedule."

"He's the manager. How can he do business if you won't give out the times he's available?"

"If you have business with him, you can leave your name and contact info, and I'll see he gets it."

Emma sighed. "Can you tell me when he was last here?"

The Devil Comes Calling

The second woman reached an arm across in front of the first one as if blocking her and said, "Why do you ask?"

Because I hope he's dead and want to know if he might be didn't seem like a proper response. "I just want to know if you've seen him since Tuesday."

The second woman faced the other. "I'll take care of this. You seat Mr. and Mrs. Roth."

Emma realized an elderly couple had entered and were waiting behind her.

The hostess scooped up two menus and smiled at the Roths. "Please follow me."

When they were alone, the second hostess motioned for Emma to step to one side with her. "What's going on? There was a cop in here last night asking about Russ. Now you."

"Detective Matthias Honeywell?" Emma asked, surprised.

The woman pulled a business card from her pocket and looked at it. "Yes. Do you know him?"

"I do. We're friends."

"Are you a cop, too?"

"No." Emma hesitated. "I'm with ErieLIVE."

"Really?" the woman flashed a smile that quickly faded. "Please don't quote me on anything. I need this job."

"I understand. This is just background for a story. Totally off the record."

The hostess blew out a relieved breath. "In that case, Russ hasn't been in since Saturday, which is what I told the detective."

"Did he say he was going out of town?"

"No. Not a word. He simply never showed up for work."

"Is that odd or does he disappear on a regular basis?"

"It's very odd. As much as I—" She clamped her mouth shut, then said, "Off the record, right?"

"Absolutely."

"Good. As much as I despise the man, he never misses a day without letting everyone know ahead of time."

"Have you tried calling him?"

She choked a laugh. "Only about twenty times. The calls go to voicemail. Like he's turned his phone off. It occurred to me that he might be on some tropical island with his girlfriend. I told the detective that, too."

"Girlfriend? You mean Suzanne Foster?"

"That's her. Poor thing."

Emma almost blurted out that Suzanne was dead but decided to keep the news to herself. "Okay. Thanks for your time."

A voice behind her said, "Emma, am I late?"

She wheeled to find Boze. "Not at all. In fact, you're early."

The hostess grabbed a pair of menus. "Mr. Bozwell, it's good to see you again. Your table's ready."

Mr. Bozwell? "You made reservations?" Emma asked.

"This is one of my favorite restaurants. When you suggested meeting here for drinks, I figured we might as well have dinner, too."

Emma's shoulders tensed. Dinner at The Blue Pike felt too much like a date, and she didn't want Boze getting ideas. "I'm not hungry."

"Well, I'm starved." He turned to the hostess and swept an arm toward the dining room. "After you."

The hostess took a step, then paused at Emma's side and asked softly, "Do you want me to call you when Russ shows up?"

"No, thank you. I'm sure Detective Honeywell will keep me in the loop." Emma gave her a weak smile.

Once they were seated, had been informed of the daily specials, and left alone again, Boze picked up one of the leather folios containing the menu and held it out to Emma.

"I told you. I'm not hungry." Even if she was, she didn't think she could bring herself to eat anything that put money in Russ's pocket. Except it was beginning to look like he really was the second victim. She should celebrate.

Boze shook the menu. "Oh, come on. At least have an appetizer. I'm buying."

She took the folio. "I can pay for my own food." But she set it down in front of her without looking at it and folded her hands on top. "Tell me about Preston and Darcy."

"After dinner."

Emma fixed him with a determined glare. "Now."

A young man wearing all black arrived at their table. "Good evening. My name is Justin, and I'll be your server tonight. What can I get you to drink?"

"I'll have bourbon. Neat. And the lady will have…"—he paused, studying her as if reading her mind—"a Mai Tai."

Her patience wearing thin, she narrowed her eyes at the waiter. "The lady will have a glass of water."

"I told you I'm buying," Boze said, a note of protest in his voice.

She held the waiter's gaze. "I'm driving. Unless you want to be responsible for me getting into an accident, you'll bring me water."

Justin flushed. "Water it is." He looked apologetically at Boze. "And a bourbon, neat. I'll be right back with your drinks."

Boze pouted. "You're no fun."

"I'm not here for fun. This is not a date, and I'm not hungry. Deal with it."

He huffed. "Fine."

"Now, Darcy and Preston."

Boze leaned back in his chair and crossed his arms. "They were quite the item at one time. They tried to keep their relationship a secret, but no one was fooled."

"Is there a company policy against coworkers dating?"

"No." He came forward again grinning at her. "Is that what

you're worried about? You won't lose your job for having dinner with me."

She ignored the innuendo in his tone. "Then why the secrecy? Why didn't they want anyone to know?"

"Her parents."

"What about them?"

"They never liked him."

Emma closed her eyes. At this rate, she wasn't going to get any real answers until the waiter was serving dessert. She glared at Boze. "Why didn't they like him?"

"I don't know. You'll have to ask them."

She was starting to get a headache. "Why did you say he killed her?"

Boze raised both hands. "I never claimed that."

"Why did he slug you the night of Darcy's wake?"

"Because he's got a temper. He doesn't like to hear the truth."

"Which is?"

Justin returned and set Emma's water in front of her before placing Boze's bourbon on the table. "Are you ready to order?"

Before she could say anything, Boze replied, "Yes, we are. I'll have the New York Strip Steak and my lady friend will have the Duck Breast." He grinned suggestively at her. "It's amazing. You'll love it."

"I'm a pescatarian," she said.

"What's that?" Boze asked.

Justin squirmed. "We have a wonderful Chilean Sea Bass with jumbo lump crab and grilled asparagus."

She picked up the menu and opened it long enough to take note of the prices before handing it to the waiter. "No, thank you. Just the water is fine."

He accepted both menus and strode away.

"You're hurting my feelings," Boze said.

Emma wasn't about to point out yet again that this wasn't a

date, nor was she hungry. Especially for sea bass that cost at least as much as two-weeks-worth of groceries. "Are you going to tell me about Preston and Darcy, or am I wasting my time here?"

Boze sighed. "Fine. I truly don't know why her parents don't like him, but she broke up with him a while back."

Emma studied him and had an epiphany. "You dated her."

He didn't reply. From his expression, he didn't need to.

"You were in love with her."

He sighed. "I thought we were in love with each other. Then Preston decided he wanted her back, and she went." Boze muttered something under his breath.

Emma thought it was *bitch* but didn't ask him to repeat it. "That must've hurt."

He lowered his eyes. "She got what was coming to her though, didn't she." Not a question. "She got that new job and put in her notice at ErieLIVE. Her leaving ripped Preston apart. He wasn't going to have her at his side all day, every day, anymore. Knowing her, she probably had plans to seduce her new boss. Sleep her way to the top."

Emma studied him, aghast. His tone was bitter, petty.

Jealous.

Boze met her gaze. "Your turn."

"Excuse me?"

"Why were you asking questions about Russ Carlisle? And what's going on with you and Detective Honeywell?"

Boze's tone and expression raised a whole fleet of red flags. Anything she said was going to be instant fodder for a potential news story. She took a long sip—her first—of the water, set the glass back down, and stood. "Enjoy your meal."

He gave her a predatory smile. "I will. See you at work."

Emma turned and strode away from the table. As she pushed through the restaurant's doors, questions circled within her mind. One settled to the forefront.

How could Boze afford this place on a reporter's salary?

Matthias pointed at the flash drive in Frazier's hand. "What've you got?"

"Security footage."

Cassie came to her feet as Frazier passed her cubicle to take a seat in his own. Matthias and Cassie gathered behind him.

"I canvassed all the neighbors along Clifton for the third time," Frazier said. "No one had a camera aimed in the right direction." He inserted the USB into the computer and pulled up a view of the house in which Darcy Tomasetti and Orlando Larson had died. "However, this guy lives right across the street"—Frazier pointed at the video on his monitor—"and wasn't home the first two times I knocked. He was shocked to learn about the murders. Said he was on an Alaskan cruise. Anyway, he was happy to hand over this footage from Monday morning, once he learned what happened."

The image was better quality than most, although distorted by the wide-angle view. Along with the front porch of the house across from the crime scene, it also picked up the street. On fast-forward, occasional cars sped across the screen.

"Have you looked at it already?" Matthias asked.

"Yeah. On the homeowner's tablet." Frazier tipped his head at the monitor. "Just watch what I found."

Matthias watched a car zip into the frame and stop.

Frazier hit pause. "Check it out." He rewound, and the car reversed out of view. Then he clicked play.

Matthias and Cassie leaned in and watched an older model sports car roll up to the end of the driveway. It sat there for a minute before the passenger door opened and a woman stepped out. She leaned down, saying something to the driver before pivoting and flouncing toward the crime-scene house. The sports car drove away.

And the footage stopped.

Matthias pointed at the screen. "Where's the rest of it?"

Frazier looked at him, wide-eyed, his mistake visible in his flushed cheeks. "That's all I got. I figured it showed this car, so that's all…" His voice trailed off.

"That's all you got," Cassie echoed. "How do we know he didn't circle back? Go inside? *That* is the evidence we need."

Frazier lowered his face. "You're right. I got ahead of myself. I'll go back and get the rest."

"Everything up until the first responders arrive," Matthias said.

Cassie turned to him. "In the meantime, did you catch who was driving?"

"No," Matthias replied. "But I can tell who the woman is."

"So can I."

In unison, they said, "Darcy Tomasetti."

Cassie pointed at Frazier's computer. "Play it again."

Matthias focused on the driver's window during the second viewing, but the distorted camera lens combined with the distance made it impossible to make out even a silhouette behind the glass.

As the car drove out of the range of view, Cassie said, "There's no angle showing the plate number."

Frazier rewound the footage. "At least the car is unique."

"True." Cassie scowled. "I'm not a car person. What kind is it? Looks like something from the early seventies."

Frazier froze the video and zoomed in on the car.

"Hard to tell." Matthias squinted. "It's definitely Mopar."

She swiveled to look at him. "Who?"

"Not who. What. Mopar refers to Dodge, Plymouth, and Chrysler vehicles. I'd have to say it's one of the first two. Late sixties or early seventies."

"At least I was close on the model year. Shouldn't be too hard to track down the owner. There can't be a lot of those in the area." She patted Frazier on the shoulder. "Go collect the rest of the footage and see if you spot anything else. Then try to clear up the image of the car and driver." She shifted to Matthias. "You know more about cars than I do. Find out who in Erie owns a sixty-year-old Mopar." Her voice softened as she added, "I want to know who drove Darcy Tomasetti to her death."

Matthias did, too, and on a Friday night in Erie, he had a pretty good idea of where to start looking.

Chapter Eighteen

Emma gazed across Lake Erie toward Canada, which was well beyond the horizon. Sunset was still an hour or so away, but the day's clouds giving way to clearing skies promised it would be a spectacular one. She took it as a sign she was becoming a local, taking Presque Isle's setting sun for granted, that she didn't have her camera draped over her neck. She had her phone tucked in the side pocket of her yoga pants should a breathtaking image present itself, but she wasn't here to take pictures. She was here to let the cool waves lap over her feet and clear her mind as she tried to make sense of the day.

Preston and Darcy really had been seeing each other romantically. Emma realized she'd known it all along. His off-kilter reaction to Darcy leaving her job at ErieLIVE. His stunned reaction to learning of her death. His drunken despair the evening of her wake. It all made sense.

Except for his denial of the relationship.

Then there was Boze. What the heck was going on with him? More importantly, did she truly want to know? Not really. If she never had to spend another minute alone with him, she'd be happy. The way he'd insisted she have dinner with him when she'd told him she wasn't interested. The presumptuous way he'd ordered for her.

Matthias had done the same thing at O'Reilly's, except he'd gotten it right. And she'd agreed to dinner with him.

Boze had been in love with Darcy. That tidbit combined with his obvious bitterness nagged at Emma.

She took one step deeper into the water and closed her eyes, listening to the soft rush of the waves rolling in, the hissing splash as they broke, spraying her rolled-up pant legs.

Her mind drifted to her other reason for visiting The Blue Pike. Even though she hadn't encountered Russ, her presence there stirred up a tsunami of emotions. Nightmarish memories of what had happened to Nell thanks to that bastard. Memories of a loss that proved to be a mistake followed by one that was all too real. If it wasn't for Russ Carlisle, Emma might have her sister here at her side. Or they might be back home, a hundred and fifty miles to the south, rebuilding their family farm.

Which brought more nightmarish memories to the surface.

Emma opened her eyes to focus on the horizon. *Breathe. Pay attention to the sensation of the waves kissing your ankles and calves*, she told herself. She tried to focus her attention on the way the sand beneath her feet washed away with each retreating wave, letting her sink deeper into the earth. Inhaling with each incoming wave, which brought the sand back and deposited on top of her feet. Exhaling with each outgoing wave, letting those nightmares wash away into the lake.

Her phone vibrated against her thigh. She considered ignoring it, but even though she knew the call wasn't from Nell, she still had to check.

Matthias's name and number flashed on her caller ID.

She swiped the green icon. "Hi."

"Hey." He sounded genuinely happy to hear her voice. "Where are you?"

"Standing on the beach."

"Which one?"

The beaches within Presque Isle State Park were numbered, but she wasn't in the park. "The one right across from Sara's." This was a stretch she considered hers, nestled between the posted private beach reserved for the lakeside condo residents to her left and the Presque Isle beaches to her right. It was a short stroll from her campsite.

"Want some company?"

"Sure."

"See you in a few."

The call ended. She slipped the phone back into her pocket and again closed her eyes, this time concentrating on the warm sunshine on her face.

A full minute couldn't have passed before she sensed more than heard someone approaching. She half-turned to see Matthias, still wearing his official polo shirt and tactical pants, closing the distance between them.

"When you said 'in a few', you really meant it," she said. "Where were you?"

He stopped just short of the waterline and gazed out at the lake as she had done. "Over at Sara's."

She freed her buried feet and moved to his side. "My campsite?"

"No. The restaurant. There's a classic car show going on."

During the summer, local car owners frequently flocked to Sara's or to other parking lots around Erie, showing off their beloved coupés and sedans, polished to a high sheen. "I'm glad you're here. There's something I want to talk to you about."

His gaze shifted from the lake to her. "Oh?"

"I heard you were at The Blue Pike yesterday looking for Russ."

His expression darkened. "Yeah."

She waited for him to elaborate. He didn't. "I drove over there a little while ago."

"And?"

"He wasn't there. Hasn't been there for almost a week. The hostess told me you'd been asking about him, too, so you already know that much."

He studied her with that old intensity that still unnerved her. "Why were you looking for him?"

"Because of Suzanne Foster and the fire."

"You're thinking he's the other victim."

"Have you heard anything from the coroner yet?" Emma asked.

"No. I guess we'll find out soon enough."

"You didn't say why you went looking for him."

The corner of his eye twitched. "I've never stopped looking for him. We didn't know his girlfriend was dead at that point. You'd told me about the woman with him being bruised. I wanted to have another talk with him."

"You expected him to admit to beating her up?"

"No."

Emma grinned. "You know what they say about repeating the same actions and expecting a different outcome."

"Einstein's definition of insanity. I know. I've been called worse than insane."

She laughed. Thoughts of Boze and Darcy sobered her.

"What's wrong?"

She debated how much to tell him and decided she needed more time to sort it out before sharing with a cop. "Nothing's wrong. I just have some stuff on my mind."

He raised an eyebrow at her.

"I'll tell you later, once I make sense of it."

He didn't press. Instead, he slipped an arm around her waist. "Let's go walk around the car show."

She leaned against him as they made their way across the sand with uneven strides, the ground beneath their feet shifting with each step. When they reached the edge of Peninsula Drive, Emma dropped her canvas boat shoes onto the ground in front of her. She held on to Matthias's arm and balanced on one foot, brushing the caked sand from the other before slipping into a shoe and repeating the process on the second side. Grit clung to her soles, and it felt like the shoes were lined with sandpaper. Such was life at the beach.

Once they spotted a break in the slow-moving traffic entering and exiting the park, they jogged across the road to the parking lot of Sara's Restaurant.

The rows of classic and antique cars took Emma back to her teen years when her dad would drag her, Nell, and their mother to these rallies. He would linger at certain vehicles, engaged in deep conversation with owners. Emma had vague memories of her dad's pink DeSoto, a much loved and cherished boat of a car he'd owned when she was small. Then one day it was gone. Dad would occasionally gripe about having to trade the DeSoto for a college fund after Nell came along, but he said it with a sly wink. Thinking back, Emma believed he mourned the loss of his beloved old car more than he ever let on.

After the sale of the pink monstrosity, his next passion was the muscle cars of the 1960s. As a teen, Emma found those much more appealing than the boxy DeSoto. She began to tag along with her father when he'd stop to admire a Ford T-bird or a vintage Corvette while Nell and their mother would wander off to find shade and something to eat.

Matthias stopped at an aqua Chevy.

"That's a '55," Emma said.

He looked at her in surprise. "You know old cars?"

"Some." She shrugged. "My dad took us to car shows when I was a kid."

He appeared impressed, but he turned from the '55 Chevy Bel Air and scanned the various cars.

"Are you looking for something in particular?"

"Yeah, and I'm not seeing one."

"One what?"

"I'm not exactly sure. Late sixties, early seventies Mopar. I'm thinking either a Plymouth Road Runner or a Dodge Super Bee."

"Cool cars. My dad loved those, too. Heck, he loved all old cars. Are you planning to trade in your Jeep for a muscle car?"

He chuckled. "No way."

She searched the parking lot for one of the cars Matthias mentioned. "I saw Preston's '69 Super Bee earlier this week. Sweet car."

Matthias grabbed Emma by the arm. Too hard if her grimace was any indication. He jerked his hand away. "Guilfoyle has a Super Bee?"

Emma's almost-teal eyes grew wide and anxious. Obviously, she knew she'd said more than she should have. She swallowed. "He inherited it from his father." She turned back toward the '55 Chevy.

Matthias wasn't about to back down. "Where did you see it?"

"The night we had the wake for Darcy? Preston and I pulled into the parking lot at the same time, and I admired his wheels."

Matthias yanked his phone from his pocket and scrolled to find the still from the security footage. He aimed the screen at her. "This car?"

Emma studied the image. "Maybe. I can't tell for sure." She looked from the phone to him. "Where is this?"

He considered not telling her. Would she run to Preston and tell him what she'd learned? Or would she finally realize why Matthias had been warning her to be careful around this guy? He gambled on the latter. "Outside the house where Darcy and Larson were executed."

She took a sharp inhale of breath and studied the phone more intensely. He let her take the device from his hand and watched as she scrutinized the image.

"Well?" he asked.

"Honestly, I can't be positive." Her shoulders sagged under the weight of realization. "But the color looks right."

"What color is Guilfoyle's car?"

"I don't know what it's called, but it's a dark, mossy green."

Good enough for him. He reclaimed his phone. "I shouldn't have to tell you, but don't say anything to Guilfoyle about this."

"I won't."

"And for crying out loud, don't let yourself be alone with him."

"Are you going to arrest him?"

Matthias stuffed his phone back in his pocket. "Not yet." No judge would sign off on an arrest warrant on the basis of a car that may or may not belong to Guilfoyle. "Not yet," Matthias repeated.

But he definitely planned to have another talk with the reporter.

Chapter Nineteen

Saturday was not a day off for detectives working an active investigation. Matthias arrived at his desk early. Cassie wandered in fifteen minutes later, in time to find him watching the footage of what he now knew was a Super Bee over and over.

"What's with the text you sent me?" she asked and then quoted, "'Break in the Tomasetti case. Come in early.' What break?"

"I know who's driving the car that dropped Darcy off at the construction site."

"Who?"

"Preston Guilfoyle." He told her about the car show and Emma divulging what kind of car the reporter owned. "I've pulled up the '69 Super Bee online and compared it to that." He pointed at the paused image on his monitor. "It's the same car."

Cassie fell silent, pensive. "How many of those are registered in the area?"

"Exactly three. One belongs to a sixty-nine-year-old gentleman near the New York border. His, a yellow one, is locked in a storage unit and hasn't been on the road in ten years. The second belongs to a seventy-year-old woman from all the way down in Albion. Hers happens to be green, but her grandson wrecked it six months ago and she hasn't gotten it repaired yet. Says the entire driver's side is smashed."

Cassie pointed at the car in the video. "Driver's side looks fine to me."

"Which brings me to Super Bee number three, registered to one Preston Samuel Guilfoyle."

"Bingo." She looked at Matthias with a grin. "What do you say we go have a chat with our favorite reporter?"

There was no telltale Super Bee parked outside Guilfoyle's apartment building. The reporter answered the door wearing khaki cargo shorts and what appeared to be the same Buffalo Bills T-shirt he'd worn last time they'd come to call. Unlike last time, he was clean-shaven and exhibited no signs of being hung over.

He also exhibited no sign of being thrilled to see them. "Now what?" he demanded.

"May we come in?" Cassie asked.

Guilfoyle shot quick glances up and down the hallway, checking for nosey neighbors, Matthias guessed. With a huff, Guilfoyle stepped back and let them enter. The place had been tidied up. No piles of dirty clothes—or clean—were evident in the living room. Once more, Matthias was aware of what appeared to be a recent remodel. Darcy's doing perhaps?

Guilfoyle didn't invite them to sit and stood with his arms across his chest. "I haven't heard from my cousin, if that's what you're here about."

Matthias fingered the phone in his pocket, eager to show the video from the crime scene.

But not yet.

The Devil Comes Calling

Cassie took the lead, slipping her notepad and pen from her purse. "We're still trying to get our timeline straight and hoped you could help us out. Tell us your whereabouts from Sunday night following the going-away party for Darcy through Monday morning."

"I already told you."

"I know." She gave a dramatic sigh and rolled her eyes. "This is how we spend our days. Listening to people tell the same story over and over. If you think you have it bad having to repeat yourself, imagine being on the receiving end."

Guilfoyle eyed her, clearly trying to decide if she was bullshitting him.

She was, Matthias thought, and she was enjoying every minute of it.

"Like I told you, after the party, I met up with Quentin. We went back to his place and played video games."

Cassie held her pen over her notebook. "How long did you play those video games?" she asked, as if it was an important detail.

"Um." Guilfoyle scowled, his eyes shifting. "Until we fell asleep. I slept on his sofa—"

"What time did you fall asleep?"

"I don't know exactly. One a.m. maybe?"

Cassie wrote it down. "Okay. Keep going."

"The next morning, I got up and showered at his place and went to work."

"What time did you get up?"

Guilfoyle's annoyance was showing. "I guess around seven."

"Then you showered."

He glared at her. "Do you need to know what time I stepped into and out of the shower?"

She jiggled her pen. "No. I'm good. Then what?"

"I drove to work."

Matthias interrupted. "What kind of car do you drive?"

Guilfoyle's expression turned from annoyed to uneasy. "A silver Hyundai Elantra."

Matthias grunted and motioned for Cassie to write it down.

She did. "What time did you arrive at work?"

"A little before eight?"

"You don't know?"

"Yeah, I do. I was at my desk by eight."

"Did you stop anywhere between your cousin's house and work?"

"No."

"You didn't pick up any coffee?"

"No." Guilfoyle sounded less and less certain.

"You didn't have breakfast?"

"Oh. Yeah. I ate at my cousin's before I left."

"Ah. There." Cassie acted—over acted—pleased. "See. That's the kind of variation that's throwing me off."

Guilfoyle visibly relaxed.

"You said you drive a Hyundai." Matthias calmly brought his phone out and cradled it in his hands. "That's funny. I had you pegged as a Mopar guy."

The color drained from Guilfoyle's face. Gotcha, Matthias thought. The reporter kept his gaze on Cassie as if hoping for another question he could handle, unlike Matthias's comment.

But Matthias was only getting started. "You're the owner on record of a dark green 1969 Dodge Super Bee, are you not?" He recited the plate number from memory.

Guilfoyle's reply was barely audible. "Yes."

Matthias pulled up the security cam footage on his phone, starting with the still image of the car in front of the Clifton Drive address. He aimed the screen at Guilfoyle. "This car." He didn't pose it as a question. Let Guilfoyle think they'd positively identified it.

Unless he chose to deny it.

He glanced at the photo and looked away, saying nothing.

"That is your car, isn't it?" Cassie asked.

He still didn't reply.

Matthias clicked to the next file on his phone, queuing up the portion of the video showing Darcy stepping out of the Super Bee. He turned the screen toward the reporter, who kept his eyes lowered.

"Look at it," Matthias ordered in his lowest growl.

Guilfoyle flinched and obeyed. Matthias tapped the play button and watched Guilfoyle's expression dissolve from uneasy to guilty to distraught. His chin quivered, and when the video ended, tears were gleaming on his lashes. He took two staggering steps to his kitchen table and sank into one of the chairs.

"That is you, right?" Matthias asked, daring Guilfoyle to deny it.

Cassie moved to take a seat across from him. Her voice was less accusatory than Matthias's. Good cop to his bad cop. "Mr. Guilfoyle, we've caught you in a lie. You need to come clean right now while we can still help you out."

No, they couldn't, but Guilfoyle didn't need to know that.

He swiped a hand across his eyes, drying the tears, and sat a little taller. "Okay. Yes. I lied about dropping Darcy off. She asked me for a ride." He locked eyes with Matthias, who remained standing. "Only because we were friends. Nothing more. I swear, we were never romantically involved."

Most people would've bought it. The whole business about looking a person straight in the eyes meant they were telling the truth. But Matthias had been lied to too many times. Guilfoyle could swear on his mother's grave and Matthias would still know he was lying his ass off.

"Then why not just tell us?" Cassie asked.

Guilfoyle sighed dramatically. "Because of her parents. They hate me. No, we weren't dating, but that didn't stop them from despising me. If I'd admitted to dropping her off at her new job the morning of the day she ended up dead, they'd be screaming at the tops of their lungs that I did it."

Which they were doing anyway.

Cassie raised a finger. "I have one question about that."

More than one, Matthias thought, but they needed to start somewhere.

"Why do they hate you? If you're only colleagues, as you claim, why would they care?"

Guilfoyle opened his mouth, then closed it, obviously contemplating his answer before simply saying, "You'll have to ask them."

"Darcy's mother told us something else." Cassie leaned forward, her gaze intensifying. "According to her, Darcy was scared of you."

Guilfoyle inhaled sharply.

"What did you do to scare your co-worker?"

"Nothing. She wasn't." He stuttered. "I didn't. Honestly." He looked back and forth between Cassie and Matthias before settling on the phone in Matthias's hand. "Look, you watched that video. I dropped her off and drove away. I never came back."

Thanks to Frazier's shortsightedness, they hadn't watched the rest of the video, but Matthias wasn't going to admit it. "Unless you spotted the security camera and drove around the block," he said. "You could easily have parked out of sight and walked in from the blind side of the house."

"Except I didn't. Go ahead and scan every home security camera you can find. I dropped Darcy off and left."

"Where'd you go?" Cassie asked.

"Back here. I don't drive the Super Bee to work because I don't trust those idiots I work with. I've seen how they park. So, I put it back in the garage and took my Hyundai to work."

Cassie's phone rang. She glimpsed at the screen before giving Matthias a go-ahead nod to continue the interview while she took the call.

Once she'd moved out of hearing range, he claimed her chair and asked, "What garage?" He hadn't noticed one.

Guilfoyle aimed a thumb at the rear of the apartment. "There's a garage on the adjoining property out back. My landlord owns it, too, and has assigned each tenant one bay. I keep my Super Bee in there and park my Hyundai out front."

"Why not drive Darcy to work in the Hyundai? Why break out the cool car?"

Guilfoyle's expression shifted, and Matthias knew he had him.

"A Super Bee," Matthias said, "is the kind of car you drive to impress a woman." He shrugged. "Or a man. You've already said you don't trust the people at ErieLIVE to not damage it in the parking lot. Why pull it out of the garage to pick up a woman you claim is nothing more than a co-worker?"

Guilfoyle lowered his face, and for several long moments, Matthias thought he wasn't going to respond. When he did, his voice was strained. "Because Darcy loved that car."

Matthias became aware of Cassie's return, but she stayed at the edge of the room, not interrupting.

Meaning Matthias had to drop the hard-ass bad cop routine if he wanted to keep Guilfoyle talking. "And you loved Darcy."

Guilfoyle's face was shielded from view, but Matthias noticed his shoulders jerk and realized he was sobbing. "Yes," he said, his voice little more than a squeak.

Cassie moved to Matthias's side while Guilfoyle wept. Matthias looked up at her, silently asking about the phone call. Her expression suggested that she knew something he did not.

Guilfoyle managed to collect himself. He pulled the neck of his shirt up to dry his face and sat taller looking very much like a man facing a firing squad.

"How long were you and Darcy seeing each other?" Cassie asked, her tone soft.

"About six months the first time. Her parents pressured her to stop going out with me. After a while, she caved and told me it was over."

"That must've pissed you off," Matthias said.

Guilfoyle shot him a look that held more pain than anger. "I didn't exactly celebrate. But I respected her decision." He lowered his head, hiding his expression for a second. "About five or six weeks later, she told me she'd made a mistake. Despite her parents' objections, she wanted us to get back together."

"How long ago was that?" Cassie asked.

"A month or so."

"At what point did she decide to change careers?"

"It was something she'd been talking about all along, but I thought it was just a dream. Then she came to me a couple weeks ago and told me she had an opportunity to make that dream come true." He looked at Matthias. "And before you ask, no, I wasn't happy about it. I liked— loved working with her." He shrugged. "But I loved seeing her so excited even more."

Matthias wasn't so sure but nodded. "Okay. Let's get back to the morning of the murder."

Guilfoyle winced at the word.

"Where did you pick Darcy up?"

"I didn't. She'd spent the night here. With me."

Cassie leaned down, bracing one hand on the table. "Mr. Guilfoyle, now that you admit you were at the crime scene—"

"I didn't kill her," he said.

She lifted her other hand. "That's not what I was going to ask. Did you see anyone else around the house when you dropped Darcy off?"

The question brought a puzzled frown. He thought about it. "No one out of the ordinary. A neighbor was walking his dog."

"What about other cars on the street?"

He thought some more. "It was early. No, I didn't notice anyone." He scowled at Cassie. "Why?"

She straightened, jotted a note, and shook her head. "Like I said. I'm trying to fill in a few blanks in our timeline."

Now that Matthias believed the words coming out of Guilfoyle's mouth, he had another big question. "What about your cousin?"

Guilfoyle's eye shifted. "What do you mean?"

So much for believing him. "You know exactly what I mean," Matthias said. "You claimed you were with him Sunday night. Now you're saying you were with Darcy."

"I was. With Darcy, I mean."

"Is that why Quentin Donahue is dodging us? Because he didn't want to cover for you?"

"No. He promised to tell you I was at his place all night. I don't know why he's been avoiding you."

"Have you heard from him lately?"

"No. I told you that."

Cassie gave Guilfoyle a look. "You've told us a lot of things that weren't true."

He nodded. "I know. I'm sorry. But Darcy's parents really do hate me. And I'm not lying about Quentin. He's never called me back after I left that message."

Matthias looked at Cassie, who met his gaze and blinked a nod. He knew she was thinking the same thing he was. "Why," Matthias asked Guilfoyle, "was your cousin willing to lie to the police to provide you with an alibi in your girlfriend's murder?"

The reporter reacted to the question by squirming and looking away.

"Preston..." Cassie dragged the name out using the same tone as Matthias's mother used to use on him when he was being evasive.

Guilfoyle leaned forward, resting his elbows on the table, studying his interlaced fingers as if they were fascinating. "It was his idea."

"Why?" Cassie again dragged the word out, letting Guilfoyle know she wasn't backing down.

He blew out a breath. "It wasn't the first time." He must've realized how that sounded because he sat bolt upright. "Not that he covered for me because of a murder."

"Glad to hear it," Matthias said. "What exactly do you mean, 'it wasn't the first time'?"

"We covered for each other … because we were both involved with women … and needed to keep it quiet."

"Keep what quiet?"

"The relationships."

"Why?" Cassie asked once more.

"I told you. Because Darcy's parents didn't want her seeing me."

Cassie's patience was quickly thinning, a fact that was evident with one glance at her face. "Your cousin, Preston. Why did your cousin need to keep his relationship quiet?"

Matthias had a feeling Guilfoyle also recognized that Cassie was growing irritated by his clueless act. "Because—" He stuttered. "Because he was seeing a married woman."

"Who?"

He shifted in the chair. "I shouldn't say."

Cassie may have claimed Matthias had a look that struck fear into even the most hardened criminals, but what she'd never admit was that she had an expression that worked equally well. She now directed the full impact of that look at Guilfoyle.

He caved. "Her name's Yvonne."

Yvonne? Not a common name but one they had recently encountered.

"Yvonne Larson?" Cassie asked.

Guilfoyle nodded.

"Orlando Larson's wife?" Cassie's voice rose in pitch.

He nodded again. "You can see why Quentin wanted to keep it a secret. Please don't let him know I'm the one who ratted him out."

Cassie turned to Matthias and rolled her eyes.

"We'll do our best," Matthias told the reporter.

Cassie composed herself and returned her attention to Guilfoyle. "You have our cards, right?"

"Yeah, I do."

"Good. I'd appreciate a call when you hear from your cousin."

"Sure."

Matthias rose. He'd bet a month's salary that phone call would never happen.

They thanked Guilfoyle for his time. Cassie promised—threatened—to be in touch, and they left the reporter in his apartment.

Back in the Malibu, Cassie stared at the apartment building with narrowed eyes. "You know what I'm thinking?"

"Yeah."

"Quentin Donahue was providing an alibi for Preston Guilfoyle. Which also means Guilfoyle was providing an alibi for Donahue."

"And Donahue was not only Orlando Larson's disgruntled ex-business partner—"

Cassie filled in the rest. "He was screwing his ex-partner's wife."

"We need to talk to Yvonne Larson again." Matthias remembered something else. "What was that phone call about?"

"An interesting development." She met his gaze with a cryptic grin. "We were right to make Frazier go back for the rest of that security footage. He got it and found something else."

"Oh?"

"A few minutes after the Super Bee pulled away from dropping off Darcy, another car pulled up and parked out front. Someone, presumably a male, got out and went inside. Seven minutes later, the same person returned to the car, got in, and drove away. No other vehicles stopped at the address until the electrician arrived. Not long after that, the first police units pulled in."

"That's why you asked Guilfoyle if he'd seen anyone else in the area."

"Yep."

Matthias pondered the news. "This guy in the car that shows up after Guilfoyle left is our killer."

"Yep."

"Could Frazier give us an ID?"

"Nope."

Matthias looked at his untalkative partner. "I think I want to take a look at that footage before we go visit Yvonne Larson."

Cassie met his gaze with a grin. "Yep."

Chapter Twenty

The ErieLIVE newsroom was lightly staffed and quiet on a weekend, which suited Emma just fine. Laurie wasn't there. Preston wasn't there. Even better, Boze wasn't there.

Emma still didn't know what to make of what Matthias had told her last night. A Super Bee had been at the crime scene. Considering what Boze had told her, it had to be Preston.

But Preston had nothing to do with what Emma was up to. She took a seat at her desk and booted up her computer. Usually, she only used it to edit photos. Today, she logged into the news outlet's list of contacts and found the coroner's office phone number.

A secretary answered the phone.

"I'm Emma Anderson with ErieLIVE. Do you have an ID on the second victim from Wednesday's apartment fire?" She read the address.

"Emma Anderson?" The secretary sounded skeptical. "I don't believe I've spoken to you before."

Because you haven't, Emma thought. "I'm assisting Preston Guilfoyle. It's Saturday, so he's taking the weekend off and left me to follow up on a list of stories we're working on." A small percentage was true. It was Saturday. Preston was taking the weekend off. Emma sort of assisted him.

The secretary breathed a sigh over the phone. "Girlfriend, I feel your pain. Hang on while I check."

Emma breathed her own sigh of relief.

"Okay, here we go. The female victim was Suzanne Foster, who resided at the apartment where the fire was determined to have started."

Emma knew about Suzanne. "Yes, we have the information on Ms. Foster. What about the male?"

"We do have an ID on him, but I'm afraid I can't release it to the press until the next of kin has been notified. Sorry."

Emma chewed her lip, contemplating what kind of lie might entice the secretary to bend the rules. She settled on thanking the woman for her time and promised to call back later.

"I'm sure you'll receive the information from Mr. Hamilton directly."

"Thank you." Emma ended the call and stared at her phone. Next of kin. Did Russ Carlisle have parents? Siblings? Or was he truly the devil's spawn?

In that case, notifying his family could prove troublesome.

He had a wife who'd predeceased him.

At his hand, most likely.

His late wife did have family. Family for whom Russ worked. Elias Nelson owned a major real estate holding company with properties all over northwestern Pennsylvania, as well as Ohio and New York. The Blue Pike was one such property. Russ served as manager for it as well as several others to the best of Emma's knowledge.

If anyone would be notified of Russ's death, it would be Elias Nelson.

The Devil Comes Calling

Matthias wished like hell the neighbor across the street from the Clifton Drive crime scene had placed his camera at a better angle. He studied the footage for the fourth time, hoping to catch a glimpse of the second car's plate or the driver's face and knowing he wouldn't.

Cassie and Matthias flanked Frazier's chair, leaning closer to the computer screen as the video played. A small white sedan, make and model as yet undetermined, pulled over at the edge of the driveway, giving them only a distorted view of the passenger side. A male wearing a ball cap and a windbreaker jacket exited the car, strode away from the camera, and entered the house. There was no audio, so they could only guess as to shots being fired.

Frazier sped through the next seven minutes, slowing the playback to reveal the same person leaving the house, head down. As they watched, he veered to one side of the driveway, pulled something from the windbreaker's pocket, and flung it into the dumpster. The gun.

As the killer tossed his weapon, he lifted his face for a split second, giving them a partial view of his profile.

A distorted partial view. Not enough to positively identify the man, but from his height and athletic build, Matthias at least ruled out Isaiah.

Frazier paused the replay once the small car had driven out of the frame. "I'm afraid that's all there is."

Cassie patted his shoulder. "It's more than we had before. Good job."

Matthias continued to eye the frozen image on the screen. "Something's not right."

Cassie turned to him. "You're thinking the same thing I am."

Frazier's gaze shifted between them. "What'd I miss?"

"Darcy and Larson were shot execution style," Matthias said. "But this dude disposes of the gun in plain sight in a dumpster right outside the house. Not the move of a seasoned professional."

"Unless he's intentionally trying to send us down the wrong path," Frazier offered.

"Or he's just not the brightest bulb in the box." Cassie patted Frazier's shoulder. "Get this down to the IT department and see if they can enhance it."

"I have my doubts."

"So do I. Do it anyway." She turned to Matthias. "Okay, now let's go talk to the bereaved widow."

A half-hour later, they stood at the front door of Yvonne Larson's home. The first time they'd seen her, she'd looked impassive. When she responded to their knock today, she appeared on the verge of a meltdown.

"Mrs. Larson, are you all right?" Cassie asked.

Her hand trembled as she swept a strand of brown hair from her face, tucking it behind one ear. "No, I'm not all right. My husband is dead."

Matthias thought back to Monday when they'd delivered the news. She hadn't displayed any of the signs of shock or grief they usually encountered. Now? She didn't look like a mourning widow so much as a woman battling a panic attack. Still, everyone handled the loss of a loved one differently.

Unless the man Yvonne loved was responsible for the death of her husband and she was terrified of his imminent arrest.

"May we come in?" Cassie asked.

"Why? Do you have news about the person who killed my husband?"

"It's still an ongoing investigation."

"I take that as a no."

Matthias thought he noted a hint of relief in her pale eyes. "We need to ask you a few more questions," he said.

"I don't know what more I could tell you." She huffed and stepped back. "But come in. You're letting all the cool air out."

Matthias and Cassie took the same seats on the dark blue-green plush sofa as the last time. Yvonne, however, remained on her feet, pacing, her arms wrapped around herself. She seemed so jittery that Matthias wondered if she was on something.

"Mrs. Larson," Cassie began, "when we were here last time, you said your husband had made a lot of enemies in his line of work."

"It's true."

"You also said you know a few of the people he worked with."

"Very few."

With pen poised over her notebook, Cassie asked, "Give me their names."

Yvonne froze in place. "What?"

"You know only a few of his colleagues. It shouldn't be too hard to name them."

She ran a tongue over her lips. "I'm not good at remembering names. I remember faces."

"Fair enough." Matthias pulled out his phone. "I'm the same way. I'll recognize a face and can't come up with the person's name to save my life." It was a lie. He rarely forgot a face or a name, but Yvonne relaxed. He brought up a photo of Quentin Donahue and held the phone out to the widow. "How about this guy?"

Yvonne's eyes widened at the sight of the man. She staggered back a step as if shoved. Her attempt to recover and appear nonchalant failed on a grand scale. "Yes, he used to be my husband's business partner. They had a falling out as I recall. I think his name is Donahue." She tugged at the collar of her T-shirt with a shaky hand.

"That's right." Matthias lowered the phone. "Quentin Donahue. Tell us about him."

She dropped her chin and walked away a few steps, pivoted, and paced back. "I don't really know him. Orlando mentioned him from time to time is all."

"Are you sure about that?" Cassie asked.

Yvonne looked at her, unblinking. A deer in headlights, Matthias thought. A tractor-trailer was barreling her way and she wasn't sure which way to jump.

"Of course, I'm sure." Her voice wavered.

"I'm only asking," Cassie said, "because we were talking to Quentin's cousin. A young man by the name of Preston Guilfoyle. Have you heard of him?"

Yvonne shook her head. "No."

"Huh. That's interesting. Because Guilfoyle's heard of you."

Matthias faced his partner. "Not *that* interesting. Guilfoyle only knows who she is because his cousin bragged about his sexual conquests. It's not so likely Donahue would brag on his cousin"—Matthias fixed his gaze on Yvonne—"to his lover."

Her sharp intake of breath sounded ragged.

"Remember Donahue now?" Cassie asked.

The widow looked around as if searching for an escape. Finding none, she sank into one of the plush chairs and buried her face in her hands.

They gave her time to get a grip. Matthias was about to say something to shake her out of her stupor, but she lifted her head before he had the chance.

"All right. Yes. Quent and I have been seeing each other for quite a while now."

Cassie glared at her. "Your husband found out."

"It wasn't the only reason he ended the partnership, but it didn't help."

"What were some of the other reasons?"

She opened her mouth but closed it again. "I don't know."

Matthias didn't buy it. "I guess we'll have to ask Donahue."

Yvonne shot a glance at him, then lowered her face again.

"Where is he?" Matthias asked. When she didn't move, he asked again more forcefully. "Donahue. Where is he?"

Keeping her head down, she said, "I don't know," in a quivering voice.

This time, Matthias believed her.

Cassie leaned forward. "When was the last time you saw him?"

"Sunday night. We had dinner together."

Matthias and Cassie exchanged a look. He knew she was thinking the same thing he was. "Before your husband's murder," he said.

Yvonne nodded without looking up.

"Did Donahue say anything to lead you to believe he planned to kill your husband?"

This brought her bolt upright. She stared at Matthias, her lips parted. "Quent didn't kill Orlando."

"What time did he leave you on Sunday night?"

She scowled in thought. "We had dinner at one of the restaurants by the mall. Then we went to his place and…"—a hint of a smile crossed her face—"you know."

"You had sex," Cassie said.

The smile faded as she shot a dark look at Cassie. "We made love."

"Tomatoes, tomahtoes," Cassie said with a smirk.

"What time did you leave?" Matthias asked.

"I guess it was around midnight."

"Was your husband here when you got home?"

Yvonne gave a disgusted huff. "He was already in bed. Asleep."

"He didn't wonder where you'd been all evening?" Cassie asked.

"I told him I was getting together with some girlfriends."

Cassie raised an eyebrow. "He believed you?"

Yvonne shrugged. "Don't know. Don't care." Her gaze shifted from Cassie to Matthias and back. "You have to understand. Orlando wasn't an easy man to live with. Or work with. I was in love with him when I married him, but he destroyed that love within a year. I was miserable. Until Quent came along. He's attentive. Strong, but kind." Her voice cracked. "I'm in love with him, and I'm sick with worry. It's not like him to not answer my calls or texts. Something's wrong. I know it."

Matthias and Cassie again exchanged looks. Something was wrong, all right, Matthias thought. Quentin Donahue had killed his lover's husband and was on the run.

Cassie flipped back through her notebook. "Can you tell me anything about David Pankowski?"

Matthias had already determined that Yvonne was a terrible liar, so he bought the blank look on her face. "Who?" she asked. "Is he one of Orlando's employees?"

Cassie kept her pen poised. "Actually, he works maintenance at Waldameer."

"You might know his wife," Matthias said. "Nadia Larson." He expected Yvonne to spit and fire off some expletives as Nadia had about her.

But all she said was, "Oh. Her."

They waited for more, but Yvonne made no move to volunteer her feelings for the woman.

"You do know Nadia Larson, don't you?" Cassie finally asked.

"Orlando's ex."

"Are you aware she'd been seeing your husband?" Cassie tapped her chin with her pen. "Before he was killed, obviously."

Yvonne had recovered from her concern about Donahue's absence. "Am I aware? No. Do I care? Also, no. She would have been welcome to him as far as I'm concerned."

Matthias brought the subject back to their maintenance man. "David Pankowski."

Yvonne brought her cold focus back to Matthias. "You said he's Nadia's husband." Her eyes shifted, and Matthias watched the puzzle pieces floating inside her mind settle into place. "You also said Nadia was seeing Orlando. Did this Pankowski guy know his wife was cheating on him?"

Matthias didn't reply. He didn't need to.

"He did." A slow smile spread across Yvonne's face. "That means I may have him to thank for getting rid of my husband for me." She didn't add that he also provided the police with another viable suspect besides her beloved Quentin Donahue.

"If you hear from your boyfriend," Cassie said, coming to her feet, "we'd appreciate it if you'd have him contact us. We need to clear him before the two of you can run off to Vegas and live happily ever after."

Yvonne stood, still smiling. "*When* I hear from him," she corrected. "I will make sure he gets in touch."

Chapter Twenty-One

Emma cruised along Niagara Point Drive and expected to be pulled over by the police at any moment. Her older model Subaru didn't fit in with the Mercedes and Porsches. The residents in these multimillion-dollar homes would surely see her and place a call to the Erie PD. Or, more likely, their own private security firm.

She stopped across from a massive stucco mansion and checked the address she'd written down. Yep. This was it. The Nelson residence, home to Russ Carlisle's in-laws. She debated whether to park here on the street or pull into the wide circular drive. Street parking didn't appear to be a "thing" in this neighborhood, so she eased into the driveway only far enough to get her car off the road.

She shut off the engine and sat motionless. What the heck was she doing? The body in the morgue had been identified. The information would be made public soon enough. If she had any sense, she'd wait and find out with everyone else. Except where Russ was concerned, her good sense evaporated into mist. She needed to know. She owed it to Nell. She owed it to herself. If

Russ was truly dead, she could once again breathe without worrying what he might do next.

Bracing against whatever would happen in the next few minutes, Emma stepped out of her car and approached a pair of pillars topped with angry lion statues. She reconsidered her decision to park so far away. Images from an old television show her mom had loved leapt to mind. Images of a handsome, mustached private investigator on a Hawaiian estate, being besieged by a pair of barking Dobermans. Did the Nelsons have Dobermans? Rottweilers? Pitbulls?

Alert for barking, she continued between the pillars, through a beautifully maintained garden complete with benches for enjoying the shade of several exotic trees, to a pair of massive doors with leaded glass in the top halves. She reached toward the doorbell, the type with a built-in camera, but one of the doors swung open before her fingers could touch it.

A woman, who Emma judged to be her age or perhaps a little younger, stood there wearing black slacks and a white button-down blouse. A name badge labeled her as Juliette. "May I help you?"

"I'm here to see Mr. Nelson."

"Is he expecting you?"

"No."

"Then I'm sorry. You'll need to call his office during business hours and make an appointment." Juliette started to close the door.

"Wait." Emma reached out placing a palm on the leaded glass.

From Juliette's expression, Emma surmised the woman had just polished that window to a high sheen and didn't appreciate the handprint. "I'm sorry." Emma snatched her hand back. "But could you please ask Mr. Nelson if he'd give me just a couple minutes of his time? It's about his son-in-law. Russ Carlisle."

Russ's name did nothing to brighten Juliette's face. "Who may I say is calling?"

"Emma Anderson." She searched for some reasonable excuse why Elias Nelson should care. Nothing she could think of would make him want to let her in. More than likely, he'd go out and buy a pair of Dobermans to attack her right here by his front entrance. Instead, she blurted the same excuse she'd been using all week. "I'm with ErieLIVE."

Juliette made an annoyed face. "Wait here." She closed the door with a heavy thump.

Emma stood stock still, listening for barking dogs. Minutes ticked by, and she grew more convinced that Juliette wasn't coming back in the hope that Emma would grow weary and leave. The longer she waited, the more alternate plans she devised. Plan B involved traipsing around the huge grounds in search of a back entrance or an open window.

The door swung open again. Juliette tipped her head. "Follow me, please."

Emma stepped into a grand foyer and felt her mouth drop open. A dark wood spiral staircase with a swirling black iron railing swept upward to a second-floor balcony. She followed Juliette across a marble floor, through a formal living room, into a less formal but equally large and ostentatious seating area, to a pair of glass sliding doors. Without looking to make sure Emma was still behind her, Juliette stepped outside onto a multi-tiered patio. Emma hesitated on the threshold, gawking at the stunning view of Lake Erie.

"Mr. and Mrs. Nelson will give you five minutes," Juliette told her and indicated a U-shaped outdoor seating arrangement that could easily hold two dozen guests with room to spare.

At the moment, only a middle-aged couple sat there, as far apart as two people could get and still be on the same piece of humongous furniture. Juliette disappeared back inside and closed the sliders behind her. Emma approached the open end of the U-shaped couch. Mrs. Nelson eyed her with a look of disdain.

Elias's expression was more amused and assessing, making Emma feel like a rabbit being studied by a hawk. "Juliette tells us you're with ErieLIVE," he said.

"I am." She reached out a hand. "Emma Anderson."

He remained still except for his narrowing eyes. "I know every reporter on staff at ErieLIVE. You are not one of them."

She lowered her hand. "I'm not a reporter. I'm a staff photographer."

His smile was more of a sneer. "Yet here you are without a camera."

"I didn't come to take photos. I wanted to ask about your son-in-law."

"Russ. Yes. Juliette mentioned that, too."

Mrs. Nelson blew out an annoyed breath and stood, tossing her book onto the seat she'd vacated. Without a word, she stormed from the seating area, and Emma watched her retreat inside.

Once the sliding door closed, Elias clucked. "My wife is not as fond of Russ as I am." He gestured to the seat across from him. "Please. What would you like to know?"

Emma lowered onto the outdoor sofa, but balanced on the edge, sensing she wasn't going to be here long enough to get comfortable. "When was the last time you saw Russ?" If he'd been notified of Russ's death in the fire, she expected now was when he'd say so.

"Saw?" He looked into the distance as he traced his upper lip with one finger. "Not recently. Last month, I believe. Yes. We had dinner together."

"So, you haven't heard from him in several weeks?"

His gaze came back to her, amused once more. "Now that isn't what you asked. You asked when I last saw him. I speak to him several times a week." Elias Nelson showed no indication of having learned of Russ's demise.

"You're right. My mistake," she said. "When was the last time you were in touch with him?"

"Why do you want to know?"

Emma debated her response. She sensed this man had a stronger than normal bullshit meter. But she didn't want to mention her hatred of Russ Carlisle or his connection to what had happened to her sister. She doubted Russ had told Elias of his sins. "There was a fire downtown on Wednesday."

"An apartment building. Yes. I read about it in the news."

"There were two fatalities as a result. One, a young woman by the name of Suzanne Foster, had been romantically linked with Russ. The second was an as-yet-unidentified man."

Elias leaned his head back. "Ah. You think Russ might be the second victim."

Emma didn't feel a need to answer.

Elias brought his hawk-like gaze back to her and came forward, resting his elbows on his knees. "I can assure you, Ms. Anderson, Russ Carlisle is alive and well. I spoke with him two days ago, on Thursday. Believe me, he wasn't calling from the great beyond."

"You're sure it was Russ?"

Elias broke into a guffaw that blossomed into a rollicking belly laugh. As the mirth died away, he stood. "I do know the voice of my son-in-law when I hear it. Yes, I'm sure. Russ is very much alive."

Emma studied the millionaire. Most men didn't reach his level of business acumen by being honest. Was he telling her the truth and Russ was alive? Or was he lying, and if so, why?

He obviously knew what she was thinking and aimed a palm at her. "Before you ask anything else, I must end our conversation now." He glanced toward the house and bellowed, "*Juliette*."

Either the house had paper-thin walls or Juliette had been poised inside the sliding doors. They opened immediately, and she stepped through them.

"Show Ms. Anderson out." To Emma, he tipped his head. "Good day."

Feeling fortunate that she hadn't been devoured by the hawk, Emma did her best to not sulk her way to the open door. Juliette stood aside, allowing her to enter.

To Emma's surprise, Mrs. Nelson sat in the more informal of the two living rooms, fingering a pendant hanging around her neck. "Juliette," the woman said, "I'll take it from here. You're excused."

Juliette appeared uneasy at the idea of ignoring her master's orders.

"You're excused," Mrs. Nelson repeated, sharper this time. The young woman lowered her chin and hurried into another room. Mrs. Nelson came to her feet with the grace of a ballerina. Or a leopard. "Walk with me."

Emma fell into a slow step beside her, moving toward the front of the huge house in no hurry.

"Why are you here asking about Russ? And before you answer, rest assured I heard everything you and my husband discussed."

Had she been eavesdropping? Then Emma caught a glimpse of a security camera mounted in the corner of the room. There was probably a similar set-up outside, complete with audio. Elias's bellowing for Juliette was all for show.

Mrs. Nelson chuckled. "Don't worry. I've muted the sound. My husband won't be privy to our conversation." She stopped and faced Emma, waiting for an answer to her question.

An answer Emma hesitated to give.

"Let me help you out." Mrs. Nelson folded her arms. "Like you, I am no fan of the man my daughter married."

Emma gasped, startled that her feelings were so evident.

In response, Mrs. Nelson gave her a kind smile. "You're Nell Anderson's sister."

Now Emma was really startled. "I can't believe Russ would've mentioned her."

"He didn't." Mrs. Nelson continued toward the front door. "Come with me."

Emma followed. Mrs. Nelson led her through the front door, into the garden Emma had admired on her way in, but instead of continuing out through the pillars, Mrs. Nelson guided her along a flagstone path to a shaded and private spot with two wrought iron benches.

"Have a seat." She circled a hand over her head. "This is the one spot on our estate with no cameras, no microphones. We can speak freely."

They sat facing each other, Emma uncertain and anxious, Mrs. Nelson stroking the gold pendant hanging from her neck. No cameras, no security against Mrs. Nelson being as predatory as her husband.

"As I said, Russ never told me about your sister. However, I do frequent The Blue Pike. One of my charity groups lunches there. I insist Russ not be around during those meetings. A few of the staff have…"—Mrs. Nelson paused, considering her words—"confided their grievances to me."

"Nell?"

"No. I never spoke to her, but I did hear from others what happened. I'm so sorry."

Tears warmed Emma's eyes, and she blinked them away. "Thank you."

"Therefore, I know why you loathe my son-in-law as much as I do. What I don't know is why you're here asking about him."

Did Mrs. Nelson truly loathe Russ? Emma knew Matthias had

been trying to uncover what part, if any, Russ had had in this woman's daughter's death, his efforts coming up dry. "You said you overheard me talking to your husband."

Without breaking eye contact, Mrs. Nelson gave a nod.

"I saw Russ on the street Tuesday morning. He was with Suzanne Foster. Suzanne attends the same yoga classes as I do. I'd seen her the day before. She was badly bruised."

"You think Russ caused the bruises."

"I do."

Mrs. Nelson shook her head in disgust. "I'm sure he did."

"When I learned Suzanne had died when her apartment burned, I—" Emma licked her lips. "I hoped he'd died in the fire, too."

Mrs. Nelson didn't react in shock or revulsion. Instead, she sighed. "I wish he had. But if Elias says they spoke this week, I'm afraid Russ is alive. Elias wouldn't lie about that."

From her intonation, Emma filled in the blank. *He would lie about other things, though.*

Mrs. Nelson lifted the gold necklace away from her chest, allowing Emma to see it wasn't merely a pendant but a locket. The older woman thumbed it open and stared at whatever was inside, a wistful look on her face. Then she removed the chain from her neck and held the piece of jewelry out to Emma.

She hesitantly took it and looked at a small portrait of a beautiful young woman with haunted eyes. "Your daughter."

"Havana."

"She was lovely."

"Yes. She was. And she was brilliant, at least where finances were concerned. She would've been a much smarter business entrepreneur than her husband."

Emma noted Mrs. Nelson left off *had she lived*.

Instead, she added, "If my husband … and hers … weren't so misogynistic."

The Devil Comes Calling

Emma met the older woman's eyes.

"Both of them believe a woman's place is in the bedroom or the kitchen. Anywhere but in the board room." Mrs. Nelson held out a hand.

Emma deposited the locket and chain into Mrs. Nelson's open palm.

"I should've stood up for her." The woman stared at the image. "I should have backed my brilliant, beautiful daughter. I should have supported her instead of sitting back like the weak fool that I am."

"I'm sorry."

"As am I. Although, I believe if I had stood up to them, I would be dead as well." Mrs. Nelson slipped the chain around her neck, came forward on the bench, and leaned toward Emma. "You seem like a nice young woman, so I'm going to give you a word of advice and pray you heed it."

Emma braced.

"Let this go."

"This?"

Mrs. Nelson fluttered a hand. "This search for information about Russ. This ... vendetta, if that's what it is. We share a loss because of him. I want my revenge, too, but I've learned to wait it out. Do you believe in karma?"

Not a question she'd expected from this millionaire's wife. And not one Emma truly had an answer for. Kira was a strong believer in it. Nell as well.

"Never mind." Mrs. Nelson shook her head. "What you do or don't believe isn't important here. What is"—she reached over and tapped Emma's knee—"is staying safe. That means staying away from Russ Carlisle. Far away. Do you understand?"

Emma nodded.

"Good." Mrs. Nelson rose again with that lithe grace of a dancer. "Then I don't expect we'll see each other again." She tipped her head and gave Emma a sly wink. "Unless it's to dance on Russ's grave." She pivoted and strode away, calling back over her shoulder. "You know your way out."

Chapter Twenty-Two

"Could be Yvonne Larson really does know where Donahue is," Cassie said on their way back to the station, "and now that she believes we have a better suspect, she can tell him to come out of hiding."

"I don't know about that."

She shot a look at Matthias. "Why?"

"You saw her when we first got there. She was on the verge of a meltdown."

"Because she thought we were there to put her boyfriend under arrest."

Matthias had considered the option. "I don't think so."

"What *do* you think?" Cassie asked.

"That Donahue had a lot of reasons for wanting Larson dead." Matthias started counting on his fingers. "Larson dumped Donahue as a business partner, still owed Donahue money, and was married to the woman Donahue loved. Then Donahue provided an alibi to his cousin for the time of the murder, which conveniently gave himself an alibi as well."

Cassie sighed. "Until Guilfoyle caved and admitted it was a lie."

"You ask me, Donahue's on the run, laying low from the cops and from his girlfriend. I don't think she has the faintest idea where he is."

"You might be right." Cassie drummed on the steering wheel. "Go ahead and do it."

Matthias didn't have to guess what she meant. He picked up his phone and put out a BOLO on Donahue, letting all area law enforcement officers know to be on the lookout for the man now listed as a person of interest in the Larson-Tomasetti homicides.

Once he ended the call, he shifted in the seat to look at his partner. "Speaking of Larson and Donahue, I remember Nadia mentioned Larson was concerned about owing a lot of money. Did she mean what he owed Donahue or was he in debt to others as well?"

Cassie's jaw tensed. "I don't know. I started digging into his finances but got sidetracked. You can be damned sure that's the first thing I'm going to check when we get back."

"While you're at it, Nadia mentioned Larson was expecting a windfall."

"From flipping the Clifton house?" Cassie mused. "Or some other source?"

"Follow the money."

"Always." She continued her drum solo on the steering wheel. "As if these aren't all good questions that need to be answered, there's that video. We can't tell for sure who the man arriving at the Clifton house was, but we can tell who he wasn't. I've not met Donahue, but from his description, he's too heavy. The man we believe to be the gunman was thinner, more athletically built."

The single gunshot wounds to the back of the victims' heads nagged at Matthias as well. "Hit man," he said under his breath.

"Yeah. Which makes me think about Pankowski, Nadia's jilted

husband. He admitted to hiring a P.I. Maybe investigators aren't the only help he likes to hire. It would accomplish his mission without him getting his hands dirty."

They arrived back at the station twenty minutes later. "Divide and conquer," Cassie told Matthias. She would take a deeper dive into Larson's financials. Matthias accepted responsibility for digging into Donahue's and Pankowski's recent posts on social media.

He started with Pankowski and came up blank. The groundskeeper apparently was not interested in putting his life out there in front of the public. He had no accounts on any of the social platforms Matthias accessed. Smart man, he thought.

He switched to Donahue. At first, all Matthias could find was business stuff. Photos of remodels Donahue had done, five-star reviews and high praise from satisfied customers, before and after shots of smaller jobs like replaced windows and doors. Matthias scrolled back and found similar images but including Orlando Larson, prior to their split. The latest of those posts revealed forced smiles. Earlier ones showed the two men, arms slung over each other's shoulders, laughing. Matthias wondered at what point Donahue had started bedding Larson's wife.

And at what point Larson had found out.

Matthias's cell vibrated. The screen identified the caller as Cash and Dash. His pulse quickened. "Detective Honeywell."

"Detective, this here's Big Dan. You asked me to let you know if I saw the guy who bought that bone-handled High Standard .22 revolver. You know. Zane Norris."

Matthias reached around the wall behind him that separated his space from Cassie's and snapped his fingers twice. She appeared at his side, scowling. "Yes." Matthias scribbled BIG DAN on a slip of paper and held it up for his partner. "And have you?" He hit the speaker button and set the phone on his desk.

"He was just in here. Had some snazzy camera he wanted to sell."

Matthias met Cassie's eyes. "What kind of camera?"

Cassie's phone buzzed.

"A Nikon Z8," Big Dan said as Cassie muttered an oath and ducked back into her cubby.

"Is he still there?" Matthias asked.

"No. I tried to chat him up to get him to stick around, but he wasn't having any of it. Asked if I wanted the camera or not. I did. We agreed on a price. Man, I got a steal on it. I'm gonna make a tidy profit, I'm telling you. Anyway, I paid him, and he took off."

"I hate to tell you this, Dan, but that camera is not only stolen, it's evidence in our homicide case."

There was a pause before Big Dan swore. "You're kidding me, right?"

Matthias pinched the bridge of his nose. "Sorry. I need you to hang on to the Nikon until we can get there."

Big Dan's groan filtered through the phone. "Fine. That'll teach me to cooperate with the law." The line went dead.

Matthias rose and circled to Cassie's desk where she was still on the phone. "Yes, Red," she said, "I know where it is."

Red? Matthias searched his memory to figure out who the hell Red was.

As he'd done, she put the call on speaker, scribbled a note, and held it up.

Norris's roommate.

"Zane was headed there. He's sweet on one of the girls tending bar and said he wanted to see her." Red huffed. "If he still has any of that dough he came into, he'll probably give what's left to her instead of helping me with the rent."

"Got it," Cassie told him. "I appreciate you getting back to me."

"Hey, man, is there any kind of reward for me turning him in?"

"I'm afraid not."

"Aw, shit. Is there any way you can make sure I get some of the cash he's got on him? Just for the rent, I mean."

"We'll see what we can do."

Which Matthias knew was absolutely nothing.

"Thanks, detective."

Cassie ended the call and looked at Matthias, her dark eyes gleaming.

"Well?" he asked.

"According to Red, Zane Norris came back to their apartment about an hour ago. He's not there now, but went over to Beach Bums, that biker bar on West Twenty-Ninth."

Matthias knew of it. Knew better than to step foot inside it without backup. "Why don't we let the uniforms bring him in while you and I go collect Darcy's camera from Big Dan."

Cassie grinned. "Sounds good to me. Hot damn. We might finally have a break in this case."

They made the trip out to Cash and Dash, collected the Nikon Z8 and its wide-angle lens—but no memory card—and returned to the station, where they learned the uniforms who were assigned to pick up Zane Norris at Beach Bums did indeed have to call for backup. What started as simply bringing a person of interest in for questioning quickly escalated to an arrest for assaulting an officer when Norris threw a punch that broke a nose. From what Matthias was told, three other bar patrons were hauled in for doing their best to assist Norris.

"Seriously," Cassie grumbled as they waited for their

suspected gunman to be brought to the interview room. "What did they expect to happen?"

"Norris and his friends or the uniforms?" Matthias asked.

She thought a moment before shrugging. "All of the above. We should've sent SWAT."

He knew she was only half joking. "Looks like you were right."

"Of course. I'm always right." Cassie cocked an eyebrow. "About what?"

"The shooter not being the brightest bulb in the box."

"Criminals fall into one of two categories. Brilliant or stupid." She snickered. "Thankfully, Norris lands solidly in the second category."

From the observation room, they watched two uniforms, one of them wearing a bandage across his nose and looking pissed off, escort Zane Norris into the room and seat him at the table. He held up his handcuffed wrists. They ignored him and walked out.

"Let's give him a few minutes to think about the direction his life has taken," Cassie said.

Matthias leaned closer to the monitor, squinting at the image. The man in the frame was tall and rangy with light spiked hair. He was too far away from the camera to tell, but Matthias was sure he had the "weird" eyes Big Dan had described.

Almost a half hour later, they joined Norris. Cassie carried a bottle of water and held it out to him. He told her where she could stuff it.

Matthias tamped down an urge to do some stuffing of his own and placed the folder containing Norris's arrest history on the table. He let Cassie choose the chair directly across from their suspect. Matthias moved his chair closer to the table's corner before lowering himself into it. He clicked the remote to start the audio and visual recording. Cassie listed the day, time, and each of their names for the record, then read Norris his Miranda Rights.

The Devil Comes Calling

When she asked if he understood them, he turned and spat on the floor. He licked his lips. "I ain't stupid. I understand just fine." He did not jump on the get-me-a-lawyer bandwagon—yet—and they hoped to keep it that way.

"Where've you been?" Cassie asked with the inflection of an old friend curious about what this guy had been up to lately.

"Outta town."

"Where?"

"None of your business."

She shrugged. "Okay. You're right about that. How about this past Monday morning?"

"That ain't none of your business either."

She made a pained face. "I'm afraid it is. And I'm afraid I need you to tell me where you were." She held up both hands. "In your own words."

He glared at her with almost colorless eyes. The pawnbroker had been right about that. "I got up around seven. Took a piss." He smirked at Cassie, clearly expecting her to react. She didn't so he continued. "Had some bacon and eggs for breakfast."

"Then what?" Cassie asked.

He again displayed his cuffed wrists. "How about you take these off, and I'll tell you anything you want to know."

"Sorry. Can't do that."

"Then I can't talk."

Matthias forced his voice to be calm. "You're cuffed, not gagged."

"And we saw what you did to that officer." Cassie touched her nose with an exaggerated wince. "See, my husband likes my looks just the way they are, so I'm taking no chances."

Norris looked at Matthias. "You her husband?"

He snorted. "Hell no."

That brought a grin and a chuckle from Norris. "Okay. I'll tell *you.*" He looked straight at Matthias. "I spent the entire time on the couch watching Netflix."

"Was anyone there who can confirm that?"

"Nope. I had the place all to myself. Don't even have a dog."

"Okay," Matthias said, pretending to buy it. "What kind of car do you have?"

Norris appeared disoriented by the change in subject, which was exactly what Matthias intended. "Car?" Norris frowned. "A white Kia Forte. Why?"

Matthias glanced at his partner who gave him a faint nod. He picked up his phone and thumbed to the video from the security camera, already paused at the image he'd prepared. "This car?" He turned the screen toward Norris.

The light-eyed, spike-haired man's lips pressed into a thin, quivering line at the sight of the car he'd just described parked in front of the house on Clifton.

Matthias angled his phone so both he and Norris could see it and tapped play, pausing it a moment later when the driver stepped out. "That looks a lot like you, Zane."

Norris caught his lower lip between his teeth. Matthias expected him to scream for a lawyer, but he said nothing.

Matthias set his phone back on the table, screen down. Time to change topics again. "Your roommate told us you came into a bunch of money recently. What'd you do? Win the lottery?"

Cassie elbowed him. "That would be pretty easy to check, don't you think?"

"Yeah," Matthias said. "It would." He fixed his gaze on Norris and waited.

But Norris was studying his own hands with an intensity that rivaled an air traffic controller on Thanksgiving weekend.

Cassie shifted to face Matthias instead of their suspect. "You know what I think?"

He played along. "No. What?"

"I think his windfall came from doing a job."

"You think?" Matthias looked at Norris. "Is that true?"

The suspect brightened as if he'd been offered a life saver. "Yeah. I got a job."

"Doing what?" Matthias asked.

Norris sputtered, still too rattled to come up with a quick lie.

"Jobs require tools," Cassie said to Matthias. "You know where's a good place to get specialty tools when you're low on funds?"

Matthias made an exaggerated show of snapping his fingers. "I hear Cash and Dash has quite the inventory."

"And good prices," Cassie added.

At the mention of the pawn shop, Norris stopped fidgeting, his colorless eyes wide.

Both Cassie and Matthias turned to him. Norris's gaze darted back and forth between them.

"We have the bone-handled High Standard .22 that was used to shoot Orlando Larson and Darcy Tomasetti. As of an hour ago, we also have Ms. Tomasetti's Nikon Z8 that was taken from her when she was killed." Matthias lowered his voice to a growl. "The owner of Cash and Dash described the guy who bought the gun and sold the camera. Same guy. Funny thing. You match his description to a T."

Cassie shifted back to her mother-hen act, leaning forward and resting her forearms on the table. "Look, Zane, we understand. We really do. A guy like you, low on funds, can't even pay the rent. You get desperate."

Norris nodded.

"Someone waves a nice chunk of change in front of you. What's a guy supposed to do? You don't want to find yourself out on the street."

He continued nodding.

"The people you're paid to get rid of aren't nice people to begin with. No one liked Larson. And Darcy Tomasetti—"

"She was a mistake," Norris blurted.

Matthias resisted the urge to smile triumphantly.

Norris leaned toward Cassie. "I didn't know there was gonna be a girl there. I was told Larson would be alone. I was only paid to do him, but the girl saw me. I had no choice. I had to take her out, too. And that camera? It only made sense to take it with me. I knew it would bring in some big bucks."

Cassie leaned back and draped one arm over the back of the chair. "You had no choice."

"None. You understand, don't you? You're right. I was broke. My idiot roommate was threatening to kick me out."

They had his confession. They only needed one more bit of information. "We understand," Matthias said. "We'll do what we can to get you a lighter sentence." A lie. Only the DA had that kind of power. "What we need from you is a name. Who paid you?"

Norris sat back as if the table had become electrified. "I can't tell you that."

Matthias looked at Cassie, who sighed dramatically. "That's a shame," she said. "Looks like you'll be taking the full brunt of the prosecution. Death penalty for sure."

"Or worse," Matthias said. "Life without the option of parole. Probably served in solitary." He looked at Cassie. "Is the rat problem still as bad in the state penitentiaries as it used to be?"

"I heard it's gotten progressively worse. I heard about an inmate who got his pinky toe chewed off—"

"Wait," Norris said, his voice as high-pitched as a little girl's. "If I talk, you can keep me out of a place like that?"

"We'll do what we can," Cassie said.

A very pale Norris nodded. "Fine. I'd never met him before, but the guy who hired me was a dude named Donahue. Quentin Donahue."

Chapter Twenty-Three

After leaving the Nelsons' home, Emma headed to Sara's Campground, but continued past the entrance and into Presque Isle State Park. She had no destination in mind but pulled into one of the bayside parking lots, locked her car, and strolled along the paved trail. A few minutes later she reached the Feather —part art installation and part observation deck—overlooking the wetlands and beyond to the bay. She and Nell loved it here. During long-ago family vacation trips, they'd come here with their yoga mats to practice as the sun rose.

Today, Emma meandered up the wooden walkway alone, reading the words of a Native American Seneca verse etched into the decking. *The feather unto the Heavens I will soar with the water at my feet to humbly flow with the balance of nature as my guide.*

At the railing, she rested her forearms on a horizontal brace and gazed out at the gray sky reflected in the lagoon. The calls of waterfowl filled the air around her.

Despite the peace and serenity of this spot, Emma's mind continued to swirl.

She thought about the haunted eyes of Havana Nelson Carlisle in that photo and about all she already knew about the woman. Matthias had shared mere tidbits of what his investigation had uncovered, but it was enough. Emma recalled the grieving mother's warnings to stay away from Russ. To wait for karma to settle their debts. Lives lost, if not directly by his hand, then indirectly, the result of falling dominos. One tipped over resulting in miles of toppled victims.

"Stay away," Mrs. Nelson had said. Far away.

A very large part of Emma continued to hope Russ was the body from the fire. But Elias had been convincing. How many other women would become his victims, their lives lost, literally or figuratively, if Russ remained unrestrained? If he was still alive, Emma needed to find him. And see him locked up.

Mrs. Nelson, however, had made Emma aware of one thing. Going it alone was a bad idea.

Her thoughts drifted to ErieLIVE and its resources. Maybe she could involve Preston in her quest, but it was another man who made his way into her consciousness.

What the hell was it with Boze? Twenty-four hours after last night's encounter with the reporter, she was still uneasy. Not only had he been putting the moves on her even after she'd repeatedly told him she wasn't interested, but he'd asked her about Russ with that hungry newshound gleam in his eyes. And he'd asked about Matthias. How had Boze found out about their relationship? She'd kept her personal life a secret from her coworkers.

Added to his inherent intrusiveness, he apparently had an income source above and beyond his work at ErieLIVE. She couldn't afford the kind of meals they served at The Blue Pike. She doubted even Laurie could. How did Boze manage to live so large on a reporter's salary?

Behind Emma, heavy pounding footsteps, the kind that can only be made by a herd of elephants or small children, interrupted her thoughts. The delighted squeals confirmed she was not being joined by a troop of pachyderms. As the youngsters galloped to the raised platform on the observation deck, Emma nodded a greeting to the trailing parents and retreated down the walkway to the paved trail. She dug her phone from her pocket once she returned to her car and called Matthias. She knew he couldn't help her find Russ. She had nothing new in the way of information, and he'd already tapped out his resources on the investigation. Still, despite Mrs. Nelson's admonishment to stay away, she couldn't.

"What's up?" he asked instead of a simple hello.

"You sound busy," she said, already regretting bothering him.

"Little bit." The line became muffled for a moment. When it cleared, the background noise was slightly different.

"What's going on?" she asked.

His voice was hushed as he replied, "We have a suspect in custody for Darcy's homicide."

"Oh? Who?"

"You know I can't tell you."

She sighed. "Would you be able to tell me if it was Russ Carlisle?" Another name came to mind. "Or Preston?"

"No." A soft chuckle filtered through the phone. "But it's not."

"Understood. Thanks."

"What do you need?"

She hesitated, considering her answer. "Nothing that can't wait. You go do what you have to do."

"I'll talk to you later."

"Okay. Bye." She ended the call.

Russ wasn't in jail, and he was probably still alive. An arrest had been made in Darcy's murder, and it wasn't Preston.

Emma keyed in another number. She hadn't wanted to involve him in her unofficial investigation, but she needed help. When he answered the phone, she said, "Preston, it's Emma. I may have a story for you."

"Where the hell is Quentin Donahue hiding?" Cassie asked in a huff once they returned to their desks. "I can't believe we haven't gotten a hit from the BOLO yet."

Her words floated into Matthias's consciousness without completely registering. "Huh?"

She appeared next to his desk. "I said, where the hell is Donahue hiding out?"

"I wish I knew."

Cassie gave him the same kind of look he remembered getting from his mom when he would skip out after supper to ride his horse instead of doing homework. "We've broken this case wide open," Cassie said, "and you're over here lost in thought. About who? Emma?"

"No." He'd much rather have been thinking about her. "About Norris."

"Oh. Well, that's different." Cassie crossed her arms. "What about Norris."

"He looks familiar."

"He should. He matches the description Big Dan gave us. His build matches the video from the house across Clifton Drive of the crime scene."

"That's not what I mean. It started bothering me when I played the video of him getting out of the car." Matthias rubbed his upper lip. "I could swear I've seen him before."

Cassie's phone rang and she stepped to her desk to answer. "Hey, Ham," Matthias heard her say. "Yeah, that's right." A long pause followed. Then he heard Cassie's chair squeak as she sat down hard. "You've got to be shitting me."

Matthias rose and moved to her side. She looked equal parts exasperated and defeated.

"When was that?" She waited, listening. "Well, that's just

great." From her tone, it was *not* great. "Okay. Thanks for letting me know." She ended the call. To Matthias, she said, "We can cancel the BOLO on Quentin Donahue."

She'd been talking to the coroner, so it was an easy assumption. "He's dead?"

"Yep. Has been since Wednesday. He died in that Peninsula View Apartments fire."

Matthias stiffened. "He was in Suzanne Foster's apartment?"

"I don't remember the other victim, but yeah, there was a woman whose identity was released a couple days ago."

"Suzanne Foster," he repeated. "She was Russ Carlisle's current battered girlfriend."

Cassie's dark eyes widened. "You're kidding."

He shook his head. "Emma knew her from yoga class and was on the scene taking photos during the fire. She's been—" He almost said *hoping*. "She's been wondering if the second body might have been Carlisle's since he's been MIA since Tuesday."

"No such luck," Cassie said. "The coroner's office hasn't publicly released Donahue's name as the second victim because they were having trouble reaching his next of kin. Apparently, they didn't know about his cousin. His parents are dead, and he has no siblings. Ham found out about the BOLO." She tapped her phone. "That's why he called me."

"What the hell was Quentin Donahue doing in Carlisle's girlfriend's apartment?"

"Good question." Cassie faced her computer and started pounding the keys. She pulled up, scanned, and dismissed several databases and shook her head after the fourth one. "There's no obvious connection between Donahue and Foster."

"What about between Donahue and Carlisle?"

Cassie kept searching and shook her head. "Nothing. I've already determined there's no record of Donahue working for Carlisle or Erie Huron and Ontario Holdings. God knows I've been trying to link them all week with no luck. Granted, I'm only doing a quick search here, but at first glance I don't see any evidence of the Foster woman working for Donahue either. I'll keep digging."

Matthias wiped a hand over his face. "We have the man who pulled the trigger and killed Larson and Tomasetti. We know from him that Larson was indeed the intended target. We know Donahue paid for the hit."

"Now we can't question him about the case." Cassie swiveled to face Matthias. "I think it's awfully damned convenient."

"So do I." Matthias arched his back sending a series of rapid-fire pops down his spine. "Did we ever find out how the fire started?"

She riffled through her notes. "No, but that's a very interesting question." She picked up her phone.

While Cassie tracked down the fire investigator, Matthias turned to his computer for another look into Larson's mysterious employer on the Clifton Drive house. An image of Zane Norris kept swimming into Matthias's mental field of vision distracting him from his search. Norris was under arrest. They had the murder weapon downstairs in the evidence room. They had a witness to his purchase of the gun at the pawn shop. Hell, they had his confession. Norris would do considerable time.

Matthias heard Cassie end her call and wheeled his chair into the aisle to face her. "Norris was the gunman. Donahue paid him, but I'll bet a month's salary Donahue was just a middleman."

She didn't look up from the note she was scribbling. "No bet."

"I'll bet another month's salary that whoever paid Donahue is responsible for the fire."

"Again, no bet." She set down her pen and lifted her gaze to his. "You'll never guess what the fire investigator told me," she said, her tone dripping sarcasm.

"The fire that killed Quentin Donahue and Suzanne Foster was arson."

"Yep. He told me they detected substantial amounts of accelerant—he used the word 'overkill'—within Suzanne's unit at the point of origin." Cassie's eyes narrowed in thought. "Ham mentioned only Donahue showed evidence of soot in his airway, meaning he died of smoke inhalation. Suzanne's cause of death is undetermined pending toxicology findings. According to Ham, neither victim showed any signs of a struggle."

Matthias leaned back and traced the stubble on his upper lip. The more they learned, the less they knew, he thought.

Cassie pushed the notepad away. "Anyhow, since Darcy Tomasetti was only collateral damage at the Clifton house homicide, I guess Preston Guilfoyle is off the hook."

Matthias huffed a laugh. "Seriously? His cousin paid for the hit. Maybe his girlfriend wasn't the target, but with that familial connection, I'm not ready to take him off the suspect list."

"Somehow, I knew you'd say that." Cassie gave him a borderline evil grin. "I forgot to tell you earlier, when I informed Ham that Donahue has a cousin in town, I told him we'd make the notification."

Matthias usually tried to avoid telling family members that a loved one had died. This time, he didn't mind. He wanted to observe the reporter's reaction to the news.

The ErieLIVE offices were nearly vacant when Emma arrived. Laurie's office was dark, the door closed. Most of the lights in the newsroom were off. The windows faced west, but clouds blocked the setting sun. The only pool of illumination came from Preston's desk, where he sat, staring intently at his computer. She crossed the room toward him, her sneakers making no sound on the industrial carpeting.

Preston looked up. "Good. You're here."

"Find anything yet?" She dragged an empty chair to sit next to him.

"I only arrived a few minutes ago. I've pulled up Carlisle's bio, and I know about the death of one of his restaurant employees last month. But I need to hear more of this story you're talking about."

Emma had only given Preston the bare bones over the phone—the part about Russ possibly being the second victim in the apartment fire and about his history of abuse. No specifics. No names. "He was married to Havana Nelson—"

Preston stopped her with a raised hand. "I already know that. I told you I read his bio."

"Did you read the part about her death?"

"Skiing accident. Yeah."

"Did you know she wasn't a skilled skier? That Russ insisted they make a run on an advanced slope? That there was no one else around to corroborate his version of the accident?" Emma could tell this was all news to him. "That Havana's mother is staunchly convinced it was no accident? He killed her." Emma left Matthias's failed investigation out of it.

"None of that means anything," Preston said, but his curiosity was clearly piqued.

"No, which is why he's still walking free. He's guilty of a lot of crimes, none of which he's paid for."

"You said that on the phone. I need more."

There was no way to avoid sharing her personal story. Not if she wanted Preston to help take Russ down. Even if it meant she had to slice open her chest and hand over her still beating heart to a news reporter. She sighed and launched into the story of her younger sister and what Russ had done to her. The tiny lost life Russ had helped create and had taken away.

She told him about Suzanne and her bruises. About seeing her with Carlisle at the convenience store robbery.

"And now she's dead," Preston said.

"Maybe Russ is, too."

Preston looked at his phone. "I might be able to get someone at the coroner's office to confirm his identity if I promise to hold the story until after they release the information to the public."

From behind her, a voice boomed, "Make what information public?"

Emma wheeled to find Boze striding toward them, and from the look of his eyes, he'd already spent time at a bar.

"What are you doing here?" Emma asked.

"I work here." Boze took one off-balance sidestep, confirming Emma's assessment, before continuing toward them. "Now answer *my* question."

Preston's face could've been carved in stone. "I don't think I will."

Boze pulled up in front of him, too close, but Preston didn't move other than folding his arms across his chest. "You hogging a good story for yourself?" Boze asked, slurring his words.

Preston managed a tight smile. "It's what we do, right?"

Boze spun to face Emma and his alcohol-laden breath made her blink. "And you. You're falling for his good-guy act, yet you won't so much as let me buy you dinner."

Emma spotted the puzzled look creasing Preston's forehead but kept her focus on Boze. "We're working," she said.

Boze sneered. "Sure you are. All cozy and alone." He looked at Preston. "You planning on taking her on one of the desks?"

Preston struck out as quick as a snake. Emma gasped at the thud of bone against flesh followed by the crash of metal, plastic, and wood when Boze stumbled backward into another desk, toppling a chair, and sending a computer keyboard smashing to the floor. He landed on his back, moaning and cussing and clutching his face. "You son of a bitch, Guilfoyle. I'm calling the cops. Kassim talked me into dropping it last time, but I'm pressing charges for assault."

Preston's phone rang, stopping him from responding. He picked it up, turned, and walked away.

Emma stood, paralyzed, wondering what on earth had just happened. Boze was drunk and bleeding on the floor for the second time in a week, both thanks to Preston's fists.

And Boze's inability to keep his mouth shut.

He thrashed unsteadily, reminding her of a turtle on its back. "Help me up, bitch."

The paralysis released its grip. Emma planted her hands on her hips and glared down at him. "Way to make friends and influence people, Boze."

Preston returned, pocketing his cell.

"I'll see you arrested," Boze continued to rant. "Gimme my phone. I'm calling the cops."

"You don't need to bother," Preston told him. "They're already on their way."

Chapter Twenty-Four

"I should be home with my husband and granddaughter," Cassie muttered as she parked in front of the ErieLIVE offices.

"I can handle talking to Guilfoyle on my own." Matthias knew she wouldn't let that happen. She might miss something.

"No way."

He smiled to himself. "To be honest, when I called him, I expected he'd put me off until tomorrow. Or longer."

Cassie turned off the engine. "Wonder why he's so eager to meet with us this evening."

"Let's find out."

Guilfoyle was waiting for them inside the glass doors, which he unlocked and held open. "Thanks for agreeing to meet me here."

Matthias surveyed the empty reception area while Guilfoyle locked up behind them. Minimal lighting. No one at the desk. The meeting room where they'd talked to him before was dark.

Guilfoyle started toward the elevator. "Come with me."

"Your receptionist isn't here to guard the gates to the freedom of the press," Cassie said.

Guilfoyle pressed the up button and gave them a tired smirk. "I won't tell her if you don't."

When the elevator doors opened on the second floor, they stepped into a large open space filled with desks and dividers. A few long folding tables were set up here and there holding boxes and files. It reminded Matthias of some areas in the police station. What grabbed his attention, though, was a pair of desks. The first was lit by a lamp. The one next to it was a mess with papers scattered on the floor along with a keyboard that had seen better days. Next to it, Emma stood cross-armed over a seated man, who was holding something to his face.

He looked up when they arrived, and Matthias recognized him as Boze, the man they'd met at the Maritime Museum. Boze lowered his hand clutching what Matthias now saw was an ice pack and revealed a bloody nose. "Arrest him," Boze said, pointing at Guilfoyle.

Emma met Matthias's gaze and rolled her eyes.

"Maybe later," he said.

He and Cassie put their heads together briefly. A few minutes later, she took Emma and Boze to the far side of the room to handle his complaint. Whatever it was.

Matthias claimed the chair Boze had vacated. Guilfoyle sat at the desk. Matthias hiked a thumb toward the others. "Wanna tell me what that's all about?"

"Boze is an ass. I punched him. He deserved it."

"Still, if he wants to press charges…"

"Let him. Frankly, I don't give a flying f—" He cut himself off. "Sorry. Rough week."

Matthias considered switching to the subject he'd come to talk about, but he gazed across the room. Emma, Cassie, and Boze were seated. Emma was speaking softly to Cassie. Boze clearly didn't like what she was saying. Matthias came back to Guilfoyle. "Why'd you hit him?"

"Does it matter?"

When Matthias's girlfriend was involved, it sure as hell did. "Maybe. Maybe not. Try me."

Guilfoyle sighed. "It's not the first time, okay? Boze gets drunk and says stupid stuff. He makes unfounded accusations."

"For instance?"

"He suggested there was something going on between me and Emma Anderson." Guilfoyle tipped his head in that direction. "He made an inappropriate comment about the two of us in front of her. Like I said, it's been a long week, and I've had about all I can take. So, yeah. I punched him. I know you're going to say it shows I have anger issues. I guess I do, where drunken assholes are concerned."

Matthias studied Guilfoyle. He looked exhausted. Beaten. Matthias was only going to make his day worse, but Guilfoyle claimed he was defending Emma's honor. "What were you and Ms. Anderson doing here after hours?"

"She called me. Said she had a story idea and wanted me to dig into some guy. Russ Carlisle." Guilfoyle's mouth slanted. "Know him?"

"Yeah, I know him." Matthias wasn't about to delve into that conversation right now. He cleared his throat. "The reason I wanted to talk to you tonight... I'm sorry to have to tell you that ... Quentin Donahue's dead."

The color drained from Guilfoyle's face. "Dead?"

"Yeah."

His eyes shifted. His jaw slackened. In a barely audible whisper, he swore. Then he brought his gaze back to Matthias. "How? When? What happened?"

He told Guilfoyle about the apartment fire.

"I know about that fire. I've been working the story. They hadn't released the second victim's name."

Matthias nodded. "Pending notification of next of kin." He raised a hand. "Here I am."

"I was just about to call the coroner's office when Boze showed up." Guilfoyle swallowed hard. "I was there, watching it burn, and my cousin was inside." He choked, bent over, braced his elbows on his thighs, and buried his face in his hands.

Matthias gave Guilfoyle time to compose himself, listening to bits of the conversation from across the newsroom, most of it too distant to make out. Except when Boze spoke. His words were loud, angry, and aimed at Guilfoyle and Emma. Matthias considered punching him in the nose as well.

Guilfoyle sat up with a ragged exhalation. "The woman who died in the fire, Suzanne Foster? Emma said she was involved with Russ Carlisle."

Matthias could tell Guilfoyle was processing the information and waited for the reporter to continue.

When he did, his voice was thinking-out-loud soft. "Why was Quentin at Carlisle's girlfriend's apartment? How did they know each other?"

Matthias had another question to add. "Did your cousin have any dealings with Carlisle?"

Guilfoyle reacted as if he'd forgotten Matthias was listening. "I don't know." From his tone, he wanted to find out.

"He never mentioned Carlisle to you?"

"No." Guilfoyle shook his head slowly, back and forth, like a pendulum.

"How about Suzanne Foster?"

"No. Never."

Matthias studied him. "How about a man by the name Zane Norris?"

Guilfoyle's brow furrowed in thought. "I don't think so."

"Spiked hair." Matthias gestured to his own not-spiked head. "Eyes so light they look clear."

"No. I'd remember someone like that. Who is he?"

"He's the man we have in custody for shooting Orlando Larson and—"

"Darcy." Guilfoyle's voice came out in a breathless huff, as if he'd been slugged in the gut.

"Yes."

"Do you believe he did it?"

"He confessed."

Guilfoyle blew out a breath. "Good." His face stilled. "Any chance he also killed my cousin?"

"We're looking into it, but I doubt it."

"Why? If he's already killed once, it would make sense he could kill again."

The reporter wasn't wrong. Matthias had to admit that much. "Norris claims your cousin paid him to commit the murders."

Guilfoyle stared at Matthias, aghast. "No way," he said once he found his voice. "Quentin wouldn't be involved in something like that. He wouldn't ... arrange to have Darcy..."—his voice cracked—"killed."

"I don't believe he expected Darcy to be there. According to Norris, Larson was supposed to be in the house alone."

"I don't believe it. Quentin isn't— *wasn't* like that."

No one ever wanted to believe a loved one, be it a child or, in this case, a cousin, was capable of brutality. Matthias shot a look across the room at Cassie, glad she was otherwise occupied. She'd give him hell if she knew he was volunteering information. "I have a feeling the buck didn't stop with Donahue."

"What do you mean?"

"I suspect Donahue was a middleman."

Guilfoyle's face turned to granite. "It's that woman, isn't it?"

"What woman?"

"Quentin's girlfriend. Yvonne." Guilfoyle ran a hand through his hair. "Yvonne Larson had them both killed. She gave Quentin the money to hire a hit man to take out her husband." His eyes shifted. "Then she arranged to have Quentin killed, too. Maybe she used the same guy. Norris, you said?" Guilfoyle was clearly piecing his suspicions together on the fly. "She probably inherits a pile of money from her husband and now she doesn't have to split it with my cousin. Plus, with him dead, there's no one to rat on her."

"Do you have any evidence to back up your theory?"

Guilfoyle locked his gaze on Matthias. "Evidence is your job, but I'm a darned good reporter. I probably have more contacts than you guys do. I'll dig up every bit of dirt that exists on her."

A crash from the other side of the room interrupted the discussion. Boze was standing, the chair on which he'd been sitting tipped over on the floor. Emma and Cassie scrambled to their feet.

Boze, fists raised and clenched, took one unstable but threatening step toward Cassie. "You bitches all stick together."

Matthias charged toward them, but before he got there, Cassie caught one of Boze's wrists and cranked, spinning him around, eliciting a drunken howl.

"Who you calling a bitch, bitch?" she hissed.

All the fight, verbal and physical, drained from him, leaving him whimpering. "You're breaking my arm."

"Not yet, but I might," Cassie said.

Matthias gave her a grin. "Looks like you have this under control."

"But he hit me," Boze said.

"We'll deal with that," Cassie said, "but for now, I'm focusing on you threatening an officer of the law."

"Don't forget drunk and disorderly," Matthias added.

"Oh, I'm not forgetting anything." She leaned closer to Boze's ear. "Are you going to behave yourself, or do I have to put cuffs on you?"

"I'm sorry. I'm done. Just let me go."

She gave him a shove away from her. He staggered but managed to stay upright. Rubbing his shoulder, he glared at Cassie, then Matthias, and settled on Emma. He looked like he wanted to call them all a few more names but thought better of it.

Emma bent down, picked up the ice pack Boze had dropped on the floor, and held it out to him. He knocked it away.

"Hey," Matthias growled.

"I have your statement, Mr. Bozwell," Cassie said. "I suggest you go home—"

"Take a cab," Matthias added.

"Yes, by all means. Take a cab home. Tomorrow, after you've slept it off, if you still want to file charges, come to the station. I'll have your statement typed up, ready for you to sign. But if you decide you should let it go—"

"And join AA," Matthias again interjected.

"And join AA," Cassie said, "we'll pretend this never happened." She looked across the room. "Unless Mr. Guilfoyle wants to file his own charges."

Guilfoyle gave a dismissive wave.

Cassie turned to Emma. "How about you?"

She glared at Boze. "I won't pretend none of this happened, but I'll let it go as long as it doesn't happen again."

Matthias wondered what exactly had happened. From Emma's expression, he sensed it was more than the scuffle between Boze and Guilfoyle combined with some name calling.

Slumping, Boze continued to hug his shoulder. He eyed Cassie. "I'll see you tomorrow." He shuffled away from them, toward the elevator.

"I guess I'm done here," Cassie said. She looked at Matthias. "You?"

"Yeah. I've notified next of kin and gotten all the information from him that I could for now."

Emma reached out to him, her fingers lightly brushing his arm. "Next of kin? Preston?"

Matthias shot a look at the reporter, who'd sunk into his chair and was again covering his face with his hands. "Turns out the second body from the apartment fire wasn't Carlisle. It was Guilfoyle's cousin, Quentin Donahue."

Her face paled. "Oh," she said in a whisper.

Matthias couldn't tell if she was upset that her colleague had lost a family member or was disappointed Russ Carlisle was still alive. A little of both, he suspected.

Cassie gathered her phone and notebook. "I'm going to make sure that idiot doesn't try to drive home on his own," she said, giving Matthias a knowing look. "You take your time wrapping things up here." She started toward the elevators and called over her shoulder. "Just don't take *too* much time. I'm tired and want to get home to my family."

Once the elevator doors closed with Cassie inside, Matthias glanced at Guilfoyle before settling his attention on Emma. "What was all that about?"

"All what?"

"What you're pretending didn't happen."

"Oh," she said again. "Boze has been acting"—she wrinkled her nose"—weird."

"Define weird."

Keeping her voice low, she told him about wanting to meet Boze for drinks to discuss Preston and Darcy, but how he'd tried to turn the evening into a date. "I forgot to tell you. According to Boze, Preston and Darcy really did have a relationship outside of work."

"I know. He already confessed it to us."

Emma appeared surprised. "Oh. Okay. Well, I also found out

Boze dated Darcy after she and Preston split up. Then Preston came back into the picture, and she dumped Boze."

"Explains the bitterness."

Emma caught her lower lip between her teeth.

"What is it?" Matthias asked.

"Apparently, Boze is a regular at The Blue Pike. The dinners he tried to order for both of us cost a lot."

"I've seen their menu."

"He kept insisting he was picking up the check. Where's he getting that kind of money?"

It was a good question. Matthias studied Guilfoyle, still slouched over his desk, head in hands. He may have been the aggressor in both encounters with Boze, but Matthias sympathized. Guilfoyle's reaction to the news of Donahue's death felt genuine. Matthias wasn't removing him from the suspect list just yet but wondered if his own concern for Emma's safety was misplaced.

Perhaps Boze was the one he needed to worry about.

"Let me see what I can find out," Matthias told her. He tipped his head lower. "How about you come over to my place after you're done here."

Her smile was damned sexy. "I want to make sure Preston's okay. And we were working on a story. Raincheck? Tomorrow maybe?"

He shot one more look at Guilfoyle to make sure he wasn't watching, then pressed a quick kiss to Emma's lips. "Deal. Oh, and do me a favor?"

"Sure."

"Tell Guilfoyle I plan to talk to Larson's widow tomorrow. If I learn anything, I'll let him know… And he should do the same for me."

Chapter Twenty-Five

Sunday morning, Matthias found Cassie waiting for him at Major Crimes, a large cup of coffee from Matthias's favorite café in hand. Her eyes were bloodshot, and her forehead was etched with deeper than usual creases. "Are you okay?" He pointed at the coffee. "You usually give me hell for paying for that stuff."

"I got an hour of sleep last night. At most. I needed a couple extra shots of espresso."

"Why no sleep?"

She sighed. "Alissa was up all night with some stomach bug."

Alissa was Cassie's granddaughter, who lived with her and her husband while their daughter was deployed overseas. "You should be home with her," Matthias said. "I can handle Yvonne Larson on my own."

"You'll do no such thing."

"I can roust Frazier from bed and take him with me."

"It's fine. Alissa finally managed to keep down some tea and toast at about three a.m. She was sound asleep when I left. Shawn's off today. He'll let me know if she relapses."

Matthias was fighting a losing battle, but once they reached the garage and their vehicle, Cassie tossed him the keys. "You drive. I'm not missing this interview, but I do know my limitations."

The sun shone down on them promising a gorgeous summer day as he drove south on State Street. Cassie shifted in the passenger seat to look at him. "Have you talked to Emma since last night?"

"If you're asking whether she spent the night with me, none of your business."

"I'm not, and you know it. Don't mess with me. I'm sleep deprived and cranky."

He chuckled. "No, I haven't spoken to her. We texted earlier, but nothing I'm going to share with you."

In his peripheral vision, he saw Cassie nod and face front. "That Bozwell dude is seriously messed up."

They hadn't had a chance to discuss their separate interviews at ErieLIVE. "Emma told me he had a thing for Darcy," Matthias said. "And Emma mentioned he wanted to buy her an extravagant dinner at The Blue Pike. She's curious about where he gets his money."

Cassie grunted. "Huh. So am I."

"What was your impression of him?"

"He's one of those guys who blames everyone else for his problems. Last night was all Guilfoyle's and Emma's fault." She shook her head. "He's unhinged. At least when he's drunk. While I was sitting up with my sick baby girl last night, I read some of his stuff on the ErieLIVE website. He's good. Probably good enough to write for a larger news outlet than where he is."

"Could be he's only unhinged when he's under the influence."

"Could be his alcohol problem might explain why he hasn't gotten a better job." Cassie turned to look out of her window. "His pricey spending habits are interesting."

Matthias braked for a red light on Twenty-Sixth Street. "Emma said he's a regular at The Blue Pike."

"I wonder if he knows Russ Carlisle."

Exactly what Matthias was wondering.

"I noticed you were willing to leave Emma alone with Guilfoyle at ErieLIVE last night," Cassie said. "Has your opinion of him changed?"

The light turned green, and Matthias made the right turn, heading west. "He seemed genuinely upset when I told him about Donahue."

"Or he's acting that way."

"I don't believe he's that good of an actor."

She shot a look at him. "You're risking your girlfriend's safety on that assumption, you know."

He thought about it. On one hand, Cassie was right. On the other... "Emma trusts him. I think she's had enough experience with madmen to know when she's dealing with one."

"Yet, she still hangs out with you," Cassie said with a snicker.

He gave her a dirty look. "Drink your coffee."

Matthias grew serious again. "Guilfoyle had an interesting theory."

"About what?"

"Yvonne Larson." He told Cassie what Guilfoyle had speculated regarding the widow's role in the deaths.

"Interesting," Cassie agreed. "I can't wait to hear what she has to say and assess her acting skills."

It took another five minutes to reach the brick house on Zuck. The front door swung open before they had a chance to knock. Yvonne wore a shapeless gray shirt that matched the circles under her eyes.

"If you're looking for Quent, he's not here." Her voice was higher pitched than Matthias remembered. "I still haven't heard from him."

"Do you mind if we come in?" Cassie asked.

Yvonne studied her for a moment before pushing open the screen door and stepping back. Once they were inside, she asked, "What's this about?"

"I'm afraid there's no easy way to tell you this—"

Cassie didn't have a chance to finish the sentence. Yvonne's eyes rolled back, and her knees buckled. Matthias dove and managed to catch her before she hit the floor.

"I don't need an ambulance." Yvonne pushed away the damp washcloth Cassie had placed on her forehead.

Matthias had carried her to the blue-green plush sofa while Cassie placed a call to emergency medical services.

"I'm sure you don't," Cassie said softly, "but let's allow the professionals to make the final decision."

Yvonne pushed up to sit. She held out a palm into which Cassie deposited the washcloth. "What happened? How did he…?" She choked a sob.

"His body was discovered inside an apartment that had burned."

Yvonne paled. "What? That can't be right. You've got the wrong person."

"I'm afraid we don't," Matthias said. "The coroner positively identified Quentin Donahue as the second victim."

She turned to him, her mouth agape. He tensed, expecting her to pass out again.

Yvonne might've felt on the verge as well. She held the washcloth in her hands and buried her face in it. "You must be wrong." Her words were muffled. "Quent can't be…"

Matthias watched her weep and thought about how unemotional she'd been when they'd told her of her husband's death. He could buy that she may have asked her lover—or even paid him—to dispose of Orlando Larson, but this raw emotion was too genuine for her to have been involved in Donahue's murder.

"Are you up to answering some questions?" Cassie asked.

Yvonne didn't reply for a few long seconds, then scrubbed her face with the washcloth and lifted her gaze to Cassie. "I guess so."

"Do you have any idea who might've wanted him dead?"

"Who wanted him—?" Yvonne hiccupped. "You make it sound like he was murdered. I thought you said he died in a fire?"

"It was arson," Cassie said. "Did you hear about the fire on the news? The apartment building over on Raspberry?"

Yvonne appeared dazed. "Yeah. I mean, I think so. But that can't be right. Quent had no reason to be there."

"Did he ever mention a woman by the name Suzanne Foster?"

"No. Why?"

"She was the other victim. Quentin was found deceased in her apartment."

"That can't be right," Yvonne said for the third and most forceful time.

Cassie again asked, "Do you know of anyone who might've wanted him dead?"

Yvonne studied the washcloth cradled in her hands. "Only one person that I know of. Orlando."

Matthias folded his arms. "I think we can cross him off the list." From the corner of his eye, he spotted flashing emergency lights outside.

Cassie saw them, too. "There's the ambulance. I'll let the paramedics in."

Once Cassie headed for the door, Matthias took a seat next to Yvonne. "Besides your husband, who else might've disliked Quentin enough to want him dead?"

"I have no idea. Orlando was a bastard. Hard to work with.

Impossible to live with. Quent was just the opposite. Attentive. Protective. Good to his employees."

Which was exactly the opposite of the picture others had painted of the man, but before Matthias could ask his next question, Cassie returned with two women, a blonde and a brunette, in gray EmergyCare uniforms. He rose and stepped away, letting the medics examine Yvonne.

"She's painting Donahue as a saint," Matthias told Cassie sotto voce.

"You know what they say. Love is blind." Cassie shook her head. "I'm not buying her as his killer."

"Tears can be faked. But that fainting spell was the real thing."

The paramedic's examination turned into a verbal battle as Yvonne insisted that she was fine. She'd received shocking news, she told them. They cajoled her into at least letting them take her vitals. After determining her pulse, blood pressure, and blood oxygenation were well within normal ranges, they had her sign a release and packed their gear. Cassie showed them out.

Matthias reclaimed his seat beside Yvonne. "You mentioned Quentin was protective."

"He was. Unlike Orlando who never gave a shit about how I felt, Quent would stand up and defend me to his death." She froze, realizing what she'd said, and covered her face. "Oh, God. He's gone. He's really gone."

Matthias looked at his partner who stood in the doorway between the living room and foyer, apparently content to let him conduct the interview.

The muffled sobs receded, and Yvonne lowered her hands, still clutching the washcloth. "I'm afraid I'm not much help. I don't know who would want Quent dead."

Matthias dug his phone from his pocket and scrolled to find Zane Norris's mugshot. "Have you ever seen this guy before?"

Yvonne dropped the washcloth onto the coffee table, took the device, and enlarged the image. "No. Never." She looked at Matthias. "Is this the man you believe killed Quent?"

"No." Matthias looked at Cassie who scowled at him. A warning to not reveal too much. He brought his focus back to Yvonne. "This is the man who allegedly killed your husband." He held back the part about being hired by her boyfriend.

"Oh," she said, her voice flat. Before he could retrieve the device from her hands, she thumbed to the next image. Darcy's shot of Isaiah on the street with the unidentified man. Her reaction was faint and fast. A twitch of one eye. A slant of her lips. Then her expression reset to neutral.

Except Matthias recognized the façade. A mask of disinterest. The raw grief had been real. The lack of caring about her late husband's killer was real. The fleeting response to Isaiah's image was real. A slip-up on her part.

She shoved the phone back at Matthias without meeting his gaze.

He woke up the device, brought the picture back up, and turned the screen toward her. "Do you know this man?"

She didn't look at it. "Never saw him before."

If he hadn't witnessed her responses when being truthful, he might not have caught the lie.

Yvonne Larson knew—and might very well be acquainted with—Isaiah Honeywell.

The line at Benny Bean's front counter was longer than Emma had anticipated for a late Sunday morning. She took her place at the end and searched the occupied tables. Preston hadn't arrived yet. She still had two people in front of her when he shuffled through the door wearing a ball cap and sunglasses. He spotted her and approached.

"Get me a large black house blend," he said, shoving a twenty into her hand. "I'm buying. I'll get us a table."

She stared at the cash, mildly amused that men kept trying to pay for her food. In this case, she didn't mind. One cup of coffee was reasonable. She could return the favor, and they'd be even. A fifty-dollar dinner? Not so much.

A few minutes later, Emma joined Preston and deposited his beverage and change onto the table he'd claimed in the back corner of the coffee shop. He thanked her and removed his glasses to reveal haggard eyes.

"You've had a rough week," she commented, sipping her white chocolate mocha.

"You could say that." He took a long drink, making Emma wonder how he wasn't scalding his throat on the steaming brew. "I'm sorry about last night at the office."

"It wasn't your fault. Boze is an ass."

"Mostly only when he's drunk." Preston huffed. "Which seems to be most of the time lately. Some of the gang have started calling him Booze instead of Boze."

"Not to his face, I gather."

"No. Definitely not to his face. But I need to learn to ignore him or control my temper when he's around. That's what I'm sorry about. I shouldn't have slugged him."

"How about we forget it happened and move on?"

Preston nodded. "Thanks." He eyed her over his cup. "Have you heard anything from your boyfriend cop about Yvonne Larson yet?"

She choked. "Who said he was my boyfriend?"

Preston tipped his head. "Get real. I saw the way he looked at you. The way you looked at him. That kiss before he left. You both suck at hiding it."

Emma lowered her face. "Oh."

"Hey, if you don't want anyone to know, I'm cool." He stared wistfully into his coffee. "Been there, done that."

Emma lifted her gaze. "Darcy."

"I guess there's no sense in denying it anymore."

"Why deny it in the first place?"

"Her folks. They had high expectations for their daughter, and I wasn't part of the equation. At first, we were above board with them, but they made life miserable. For her and for me. Darcy and I started having arguments, mostly about them. We split up for a while."

"That's when Boze started dating her."

Preston huffed a sad laugh. "They disliked him even more than they disliked me. Darcy finally told me she realized she didn't care what her parents thought. She wanted to be with me. Keeping the whole thing hush hush was just easier for everyone." His voice caught, and he covered his eyes with a trembling hand. In a ragged whisper, he said, "I'm sorry."

"Don't be." Emma looked around at the others in the café, letting him battle his way back to composure.

Minutes passed before he lifted his face and sniffed. She handed him a paper napkin, which he accepted and pressed to his nose. "I want to catch whoever did this to her." He gestured to her phone on the table next to her coffee. "You never said. Have you heard anything from your cop about Yvonne Larson?"

"Not yet."

Preston nodded, took a deep breath, and blew it out. "Okay, then. Let's get to work on locating Russ Carlisle. I know tracking him down, finding something on him, is personal for you. It's personal for me now, too. I want to know how he's connected to my cousin and what Quentin was doing in Carlisle's girlfriend's apartment."

"The number of possibilities is mind-blowing." Emma didn't like any of them.

"What do we know?" Preston pulled a notebook from his pocket. "When was the last time anyone saw him?"

"Tuesday at that convenience store robbery. But I went to his in-law's house and Elias Nelson claims he spoke with him by phone on Thursday."

Preston set down his pen and picked up his cup. "Three days ago. You mentioned going to The Blue Pike to look for him."

Emma winced at the memory of Boze and the dinner he'd tried to buy her. "That was Friday. The hostess hadn't seen him since the previous Saturday."

Sipping his coffee, Preston thumbed back a page. "I have an address for him. Bay Front Place. Did you try him there?"

"No. The last thing I wanted to do was put myself in the position to be alone with him."

"Smart. What do you say we start there?"

"It's as good a place as any." Emma rested an elbow on the table and her chin in her palm. "I hate to keep bringing up Boze, but I have to ask. Where does all his money come from? Does he have a wealthy family?"

The question appeared to surprise Preston. "Not that I'm aware of. What makes you think he has money?"

She told him about the dinner date that wasn't, skirting over the part about Boze pressuring her to let him buy. "Apparently, he's a regular there. I can't afford to be a regular at Taco Bell."

Preston traded his coffee for his pen. "Interesting." He scribbled a note. "I have no idea where his money comes from, but I plan to find out."

Emma's phone buzzed. Only a number lit the screen, no name. She swiped the green button.

"Hello, Emma." The male voice coming through the speaker was low, suave, and vaguely familiar.

"Who is this?"

"You don't know? I hear you've been looking for me."

The Devil Comes Calling

She fought to keep from gagging. "Russ."

Preston's head snapped up from his notes.

"That's right. I'm flattered you've been trying to track me down. How about we get together?"

Emma met Preston's gaze. "Where and when?"

"How about right now at my restaurant?"

"I'm on my way."

"See you soon." The line went dead.

"Well?" Preston asked.

"He's waiting for us at The Blue Pike." Not entirely true. She hadn't mentioned she was bringing Preston.

The reporter drained what was left of his coffee. "Let's go."

Chapter Twenty-Six

Back at the station, Matthias stared at the image of his father staring back at the camera lens. Yvonne Larson had a decent poker face, but Matthias knew in his gut, she'd recognized Isaiah in this photo.

From the cubicle behind him, Matthias could hear Cassie grumbling to herself as she again struggled to connect the financial dots.

Matthias picked up his phone and punched in the number he had for Guilfoyle. When the reporter answered, Matthias identified himself. "I told you I'd call after we'd spoken with Yvonne Larson."

From the background noise, Guilfoyle sounded like he was in his car on speaker. "Let me guess. She denied everything."

"Pretty much."

"You believe her?"

Matthias measured his words. "Some of what she said rang true."

"Some? But not all."

"No. Not all. Sorry I can't be more specific."

"I understand. As long as you aren't dropping her as a suspect."

"No one's getting dropped."

Guilfoyle chuckled softly. "Not even me. I get it. Thanks for keeping me in the loop, detective."

"I'd appreciate it if you did the same."

"A deal's a deal."

Matthias ended the call and contemplated those last words. Some deal. Neither of them would or could give the other the full story. That was the dance law enforcement did with journalists.

Which now included Emma.

"How do you want to play this?" Preston asked as he pulled into the almost-full parking lot across from The Blue Pike.

Emma looked at him. "You're asking me? You're the reporter. I'm just the lowly photographer."

He huffed. "Let's not even pretend either of us is here for a story. This is personal. I want to know Carlisle's connection to my cousin, which, honestly, I don't know if there is one. You, on the other hand, have lost a great deal more to this guy than I have."

Emma pictured her sister curled up in a hospital bed. She closed her eyes, forcing the image away. When she opened them again, she looked at Preston. "More to the point, he called me. He asked me to come meet him. He has no idea about you."

Preston eased into a parking space. "If you're suggesting you go in there alone—"

"I'm not. Like I said, the last thing I want is to get caught alone with him." She surveyed the cars in the lot. Sunday's brunch crowd was booming, but she had a feeling Russ wouldn't want to address her in front of his guests. He wouldn't risk having a restaurant full of witnesses to another slap. "But I don't know that he'll talk to me if I have a reporter at my side."

Preston turned off the ignition. "Do you have a voice recorder app on your phone?"

Emma pulled her cell from her pocket. "I don't think so."

He sighed in exasperation. "How on earth do you ever expect to do investigative journalism if you don't have a recorder." He held out his hand.

She placed her phone in his open palm. "I'm not an investigative journalist. I'm a photographer."

"Well, guess what. Today, you're going undercover. As yourself."

She watched as he pulled up her Google Play store, located the app he wanted, and downloaded it.

He returned the phone to her. "It's simple. Click record before you go inside."

"Where will you be? I mean, this is a recorder, but you won't be able to listen in."

Preston unclicked his seatbelt. "I'm going in first. I'll say I'm waiting for someone, so I won't be pinned down to a table until I see where you and Carlisle end up."

"You don't have a reservation, so they probably won't seat you."

"You worry about you. This isn't my first covert operation. Just know I won't be far away."

Emma hoped so. She also wished she was working with Matthias instead of Preston. She trusted Matthias to keep her safe. He'd proven himself more than once. "Okay."

"Give me two minutes, then come on in." Preston opened his door and stepped out.

Emma waited, as told, for the longest two minutes she could remember. For a hundred and twenty seconds, her imagination took her on a wild ride of being kidnapped and brutalized by

Russ Carlisle. Grateful when the time was finally up, she climbed out and crossed the street, pausing to turn on the recorder before tucking the phone in her pocket and entering the restaurant.

Preston stood off to one side, looking at his own phone. He met her eyes for a split second before lowering his gaze. She saw no hint of recognition in that furtive glance. Damn, he was good.

The hostess was the same young woman Emma had spoken to on Friday. Her eyes were wide with worry as she came from behind the podium. "Ms. Anderson. Mr. Carlisle is expecting you. Follow me, please."

She noted the woman did not snatch up a menu to carry with her like she had the last time. Resisting the urge to look at Preston, Emma followed the hostess through the dining room, past the bar, and down a hallway. By the time they reached a door marked Private, Emma's heart was thudding against her breastbone. This was a bad idea. A very bad idea.

Cassie appeared next to Matthias and slammed a handful of printouts on his desk.

"What's this?" he asked.

"The widow Larson's financials. What I could find of them, at least. Guilfoyle suggested she's the one footing the bill for our hitman, but if that's true, I can't see where the money came from. We already know Orlando was hurting for cash, and his bank records confirm he was scraping the bottom of his savings account to get the house on Clifton finished."

"Guilfoyle mentioned Yvonne might've killed him for his money."

"Doubtful. She'd have paid more to the hitter than she'd have made back."

"Don't suppose Larson had a big life insurance policy."

"He did, as a matter of fact. Not huge. But get this. He changed the beneficiary to his ex-wife about six months ago."

"Nadia?"

"That's the one."

Matthias rubbed his jaw. "Huh."

Before he had a chance to give this tidbit full consideration, Brad Frazier burst through the door. "Good morning, you two."

Frazier was too damned chipper for being at work on a Sunday.

"What brings you in?" Cassie asked.

"My Dodge Ram," Frazier said and snickered at his joke.

Matthias closed his eyes. Frazier had no sense of humor even when he tried.

When no one joined in his laughter, he glared at them. "I'm on vacation beginning tomorrow and need to finish up a few reports."

"Ah." Cassie stepped back against the wall, allowing him to pass.

No sooner had Frazier done so than he pivoted back to them. "Since my apartment fire case has merged with your homicide case, you might be interested in what I dug up on Suzanne Foster."

"Did you find anything useful?" Cassie asked.

He held up one finger and ducked into his cubby, coming back with a folder, which he opened and thumbed through. "Suzanne Rebecca Foster, age twenty-seven, grew up in Lancaster, Pennsylvania. She attended college at Ohio State in Columbus. Her grades were unremarkable, but she managed to earn a degree in education. After graduation, she moved to California." Frazier looked up. "The state, not the town in Washington County."

"Got it," Matthias said.

"While there, she bumped around as a substitute teacher at several different school districts. She moved back here last August and took another substitute teaching job at Iroquois Junior-Senior High. At the same time, she also worked at a Mexican restaurant down by Splash Lagoon. Her checking account never had more than a couple hundred dollars until two months ago, when suddenly she began depositing a thousand bucks here and a thousand bucks there."

"Russ Carlisle," Matthias grumbled. "He likes to take care of his women until he has no further use for them."

"That would be my guess, too," Cassie said.

Frazier looked from her to Matthias. "Do we have a BOLO out on him?"

"Not yet, we don't," she said, reaching for her phone. "But I think it's time we track Carlisle down and have a serious talk."

Matthias's cell buzzed. He didn't recognize the number. "Detective Honeywell."

"This is Amber," a whispered voice said. "From The Blue Pike?"

He snapped his fingers at Cassie before signaling her to wait. "Yes, Amber. What can I do for you?"

"You wanted to know when Mr. Carlisle returned? I just came in to work, and he's here."

"I'll be there as soon as I can." He thanked her and ended the call. Looking at his partner, he said, "Never mind the BOLO. Russ Carlisle's at his restaurant."

Russ sat behind a mammoth black desk with a surface so tidy and organized Emma had to wonder if he did any real business at it. Once the hostess retreated and closed the door behind her, leaving Emma to face the beast alone, he stood. He looked the same as the last time she'd seen him. Expensive suit, neatly trimmed beard, dark hair in the latest style, slicked back on top.

"Ms. Anderson, Emma, I understand you've been looking for me."

Had the hostess ratted her out? Quickly she decided, no, not the hostess. Elias Nelson. "I have," she said.

He smiled the smug smile she remembered. "I'm flattered. Please, sit down." He reached a hand toward one of the two chairs across from him.

She debated, not wanting to agree to anything he asked, but remembered her phone and the voice recorder. Better to be closer, as long as she had the desk between them.

Except once she sat and placed her phone in her lap, screen down, he came around from behind the behemoth to perch one hip on the desk's corner.

"Can I get you anything?" he asked, his voice as smooth as his red silk tie. "Coffee? Water? Something stronger perhaps?"

"No." She refused to fake civility she didn't feel by adding a thank you.

"All right then." He crossed his arms. "What can I do for you?"

"We have a mutual acquaintance."

He gave her a smile that turned her stomach. "I believe we have a number of mutual acquaintances."

"I'm speaking of Suzanne Foster. She and I take yoga classes together." Emma waited for him to react to her use of the present tense.

He didn't. In fact, he brought a finger to his lips and made a show of thinking. "The name doesn't sound familiar."

"You dated her. I saw the two of you on the street at that convenience store robbery last week."

"Oh. Her." He waved a dismissive hand. "We only went out a time or two. I broke it off, probably later that same day."

Emma's anger began to rise. "She died the next day."

"Really?" His surprise was an obvious act. "I didn't know. I've been out of town on vacation. That's why Suzy and I broke up. She got upset because I didn't invite her along."

Emma could believe that part of it. "You never were very good at monogamy."

"Why should I be? I'm not married."

"Anymore."

"It's not my fault that my dear wife passed away."

Emma almost blurted that his mother-in-law didn't believe he held no blame in his late wife's death. Nor did Matthias. But Emma was treading a fine line already.

Russ smiled again. "I know what you're thinking."

She hoped not.

"It's unfortunate that several women I've been involved with have met with untimely deaths."

"Unfortunate?" she echoed, immediately annoyed with how chirpy her voice sounded.

"Yes." The smile faded into an equally disingenuous look of sadness. "Merely unfortunate coincidences. Speaking of, I wanted to tell you how sorry I am for what happened to Nell."

At least he remembered Emma's sister's name. "*You* happened to Nell. You knew she was a recovering addict, yet you plied her with drugs and alcohol."

He held up both hands. "Whoa. I did no such thing. I tried to give your sister a better life. She fell back into bad habits all on her own."

Emma came to her feet. "You beat her."

"I would never—"

"Just like you beat Suzanne. I saw her bruises."

Russ's expression was no longer hidden behind a façade. Fury glimmered in his dark, soulless eyes. He stood slowly, intentionally, and loomed over Emma, fists clenched. "You saw nothing."

Where the hell was Preston?

Russ inhaled and managed to regain his poise. He closed the distance between them, a smirk on his lips. She instinctively took a step back only to encounter the chair she'd vacated. He bent closer to her face. "Anything you *think* I might have done, I did not." The smirk blossomed into a venomous smile. "Even if I did, neither you nor the police can do a thing about it. There is no evidence. No proof. I defy you to find even a scrap."

Emma became aware of shouts and thuds coming from the other side of the door. Russ must've heard them, too. He lifted his gaze just as the door slammed open.

She spun in time to see Matthias storm through, Cassie on his heels, closely followed by Preston. The hostess, her face blanched white, remained in the hallway.

Chapter Twenty-Seven

Cassie's fingers tightened on Matthias's arm, stopping him from doing what he wanted, which was to pummel Carlisle.

Perhaps sensing Matthias's inclination, Carlisle backed away from Emma and opened his arms wide. "Well, well, well. Detective Honeywell. Detective Malone. What brings you here?"

Emma scrambled around the chair, putting more distance between her and the smug son of a bitch.

"We've been trying to track you down," Cassie said, stepping in front of Matthias. "And it's Detective *Sergeant* Malone."

Carlisle pressed a hand to his chest and bowed his head. "My mistake. I apologize."

Matthias snorted.

"You've succeeded in tracking me down. To what do I owe the pleasure?"

Cassie faced Emma. "If you'll excuse us." She turned to Preston. "You, too. We'll give a statement to the press at a later time."

Matthias met Emma's eyes, and he spotted a blend of relief

and terror. She lowered her face and headed for the door. He reached out as she passed. "Are you okay?" he asked softly enough that only she could hear.

She looked at him, gave a quick nod that he didn't believe, and continued out of the office.

Cassie followed her to the door, which she closed and returned to Matthias's side.

"Please, have a seat," Carlisle said, gesturing to the chairs as if he was merely a congenial host.

Matthias didn't budge. Neither did his partner.

"Where've you been?" Cassie asked. "We've been trying to track you down for the better part of a week."

Carlisle prowled around his desk and lowered into his expensive-looking leather chair. "I've been away on vacation."

"Where?" Matthias asked.

"I don't believe you need to know that."

Cassie planted her hands on her hips. "We do if you want us to confirm your alibi."

"Alibi for what? I haven't done anything."

Matthias resisted the urge to slug Carlisle's smug face. The man had that effect on him. "When was the last time you saw Suzanne Foster?"

"Ah." He wheeled his chair back from his desk and crossed an ankle over a knee. "Sweet Emma asked me the same thing. I saw Suzy on Tuesday, which is when I broke up with her. Poor thing was devastated."

"So you left for your vacation after that," Cassie said. "Thursday, maybe?"

Carlisle smirked. "Nice try, detective. Excuse me. Detective *sergeant*. No, actually. I left later that day."

"Tuesday?" Matthias asked.

"That's right."

"Is there anyone who can confirm that?"

"This," Cassie said, "is where you tell us where you went on your supposed vacation."

"Along with what airline you flew and who went with you," Matthias added.

The smirk faded to a glare. "I was at a private home owned by a lovely lady who happens to be married. I promised to be discreet. And I didn't fly. I drove." He uncrossed his legs and came forward, placing both palms on the desk. "I know why you're asking. Emma told me about the fire. I swear, that was the first I'd heard of it. I'm so sorry to hear about Suzy, but I had nothing to do with her death."

"What about Quentin Donahue?" Matthias asked.

"Who?" Carlisle's tone was a little too innocent.

Matthias and Cassie waited for the quiet to get to him.

But unlike most criminals, Carlisle showed no signs of discomfort with the game of "who breaks first." After a very long minute, he shrugged. "I'm sorry, I really have no idea who you're talking about."

"Quentin Donahue," Cassie said, "died in the same fire as Suzanne Foster."

"Ah." Carlisle slapped the desk. "There you have it. He and Suzy must've been seeing each other. This Donahue character was probably jealous, so to get his revenge, he torched her apartment and ended up dying in the effort. It's tragic, don't you think?"

Matthias gave Carlisle a smirk of his own. "We never said Donahue and Suzanne were in the same apartment."

He didn't blink. "I made an assumption. My bad."

"We didn't mention the place was torched either."

Carlisle shrugged. "Sweet Emma told me." He looked at his oversized gold wristwatch. "I'm sorry, but I'm afraid I have a meeting I must attend." He lifted his gaze to Matthias. "If either of you have anything else you want to ask me, my attorney's name is Farrell Owen. You can speak with him, although I doubt that will be necessary. I've done nothing wrong, and you have no evidence to the contrary. Now, please." He extended an arm to the door. "Show yourselves out."

As they stepped onto the sidewalk in front of The Blue Pike, Cassie exhaled a loud breath. "I hate to say it, but he's right about one thing. We have no evidence."

"Again," Matthias growled.

"If we press about his alleged vacation, he's just going to call his lawyer."

"Do you believe he didn't know who Donahue was?"

"Not even slightly."

Matthias spotted Emma leaning against the grill of a small SUV in the parking lot. Guilfoyle stood by the driver's door. "I want to talk to her," Matthias said.

Cassie snickered. "I just bet you do."

He crossed the lightly traveled street with Cassie right behind and strode toward the SUV. As he drew close enough to read expressions and body language, he got a strong sense that Emma was pissed off at Guilfoyle. And Guilfoyle was doleful.

"What were you thinking?" Matthias asked as he approached. "Letting yourself be alone with that man?"

The look she shot at Guilfoyle spoke volumes. "It wasn't supposed to happen that way."

If Guilfoyle's head hung any lower, his chin would touch his chest. "I tried to follow," he said, "but the damned bartender wouldn't let me back there."

Emma came back to Matthias. "Not that I'm complaining, but what are you doing here? I thought at first Preston had called you, but he says he didn't."

"The hostess did."

Emma nodded. "Did you get anything from Russ? Because I sure didn't." She held up her phone.

"He threatened to lawyer up." Matthias scowled at her cell. "You took pictures of him?"

"No. I recorded our conversation, if you could call it that."

Matthias held out his hand. She woke up the device, punched in her code to unlock it, and handed it to him.

Cassie moved closer as he tapped the arrow.

Emma was right. While infuriating, Carlisle didn't give up anything.

Until he did.

When the recording picked up Matthias and Cassie busting in, he stopped the playback and looked at his partner. "Did you catch that?"

"What?"

"He told us he knew the fire was arson because Emma told him."

"No, I didn't," she protested.

Matthias held up the phone. "No, you didn't."

Cassie huffed. "You're right," she told Matthias. To Emma, she said, "But he didn't know you were recording him, so this isn't admissible in court. We can't use it to prove he lied."

Emma looked on the verge of tears. "Which means Russ is right, too. We don't have a thing on him."

She didn't say the rest of what she was thinking, but Matthias knew.

Russ Carlisle was going to get off scot-free yet again.

It had been one miserably long, frustrating day. Emma returned to the campground without having accomplished a thing. Russ was still free to roam the earth, seducing and abusing women.

Women like Emma's sister.

The only thought keeping Emma afloat was her impending date with Matthias. Before parting company back at The Blue Pike, he'd asked if they were still on for this evening. Her cheeks had warmed, knowing that Preston and Cassie were watching as she confirmed their plans. They warmed again now as she unlocked her camper while thinking of spending the night in Matthias's arms.

Inside, she checked the clock above the table. She had plenty of time to grab a shower.

Emma ducked into her tiny bathroom, set her phone on the edge of the sink, and shut the door. She popped open her closet and inspected her wardrobe before selecting a pair of black jeans and a slinky turquoise off-the-shoulder blouse. As she reached into the shower to turn on the water, someone pounded on her door so hard, the entire camper quivered. "Just a minute," she shouted and turned the water back off. Who would be paying her an unexpected visit? Matthias? She hoped, but they'd agreed he was cooking them dinner at his place, and she'd meet him there.

Emma stepped out of the tiny room and leaned to look through the large window over her dining table. A man stood on her deck, his back to her. Not Matthias, but older with a similar build.

Isaiah Honeywell.

She whispered a curse, wishing she hadn't called out and could pretend no one was home. Taking a deep breath, she unlocked the door and pushed it open while keeping the flimsy screen door latched. "Mr. Honeywell. What brings you here?"

He gave her a smile she didn't trust. "Let's not be so formal. Call me Isaiah."

"Isaiah," she said and then repeated, "What brings you here?"

"I need to talk with you." He stepped back and indicated her deck. "Please."

It was better than being stuck inside with him. "Okay." She

pushed through the screen door, closed it behind her, and moved toward the pair of lawn chairs.

"No." He wrapped strong fingers around her upper arm. "Not here."

She froze, staring at the hand gripping her. She lifted her eyes to meet his, which were nearly the same shade of blue as Matthias's. The smile was gone, his expression dark and dangerous. She'd seen that same darkness in Matthias but knew it was only a small part of who he was. In Isaiah's case, she sensed the darkness reached all the way to his bones.

Matthias's warning echoed through her memories. *If you see him, go the other way. Call me immediately. No matter what, do not go anywhere with him.*

Keeping her voice steady, she said, "No one will interrupt you here. You're safe." As was she.

The smile returned and reminded Emma of a wolf baring its teeth. "There's nowhere I'm safe. Definitely not here. I can see you're scared of me. Bright girl. But you have my word, I have no intention of harming you."

Said every serial killer from the start of time, she thought.

"You will come with me. It's for your own good." He pulled her arm.

She planted her feet. In a tug of war, she didn't stand a chance with this man. But the battle would draw the attention of her campground neighbors.

"You're a feisty one, aren't you?" Isaiah stopped applying force but didn't release her. He leaned closer. As she shrunk back, he whispered into her ear, "If you refuse to go, fine. Just don't be surprised when that son of mine turns up dead in the next day or so."

Emma couldn't breathe. Was he serious? He would kill his own son if she didn't cooperate? Or was he conning her, playing on what he perceived was her weak spot? Studying him, she saw no hint of a bluff. Yes, she believed Isaiah was serious in his threat. Deadly serious.

Matthias had saved her life on more than one occasion. She needed to call him. Warn him. But somehow, she suspected Isaiah would get to him, forewarned or not. With her free hand, she touched her hip pocket. No phone. She hadn't thought to grab it from the sink when the knock came at her door. She needed an excuse to slip inside. "I need to lock up my camper."

He reached over, grabbed the door, and slammed it shut. "You live in a safe neighborhood. No need to lock it. Now come on."

Isaiah was right about one thing. Her neighborhood was safe. It was the outsiders who caused trouble.

He gripped her arm even harder. "Let's go."

She allowed herself to be led to the black Camry parked next to her Subaru, and as he held the passenger door for her and "helped" her in, she wondered if this was the last car ride she'd ever take.

Emma sat quietly in the passenger seat of Isaiah's Camry, watching the outskirts of Erie pass her window. He drove along West Lake Road, past businesses and residences. She gave serious thought to leaping out at one of the stop lights.

Then she pictured Matthias, dead, a gunshot wound to his skull. Isaiah long gone. She remained in the car. In her peripheral vision, she noticed Isaiah glance her way. Somehow, he knew what she was thinking. She was sure of it. Matthias could read her mind. So could his father.

He made a right turn onto a road Emma had never been on before. A stray house or two gave way to an expanse of trees and thick underbrush. She felt like they were driving through a forested tunnel and knew they were heading toward the lake.

Less than a half mile later, the trees opened to a mowed parklike field. Isaiah veered left at a Y in the road. There were a couple of houses on a sharp bend, then another expanse of grass edged by more trees. She found herself thinking this would make a nice horse pasture. That thought morphed into the realization she may never ride or even see a horse again. She turned toward Isaiah. "I understand you had horses when you lived in Oklahoma."

He huffed but otherwise didn't reply.

So much for drawing her captor into conversation.

He made a sharp right into a long driveway at the end of which a post had been planted into the ground. Two eyebolts indicated a sign had once hung from a crossbeam. They continued for a minute or so until a house came into view. Beyond it, the lake.

Isaiah braked, shifted out of gear, and shut off the engine, pocketing the keys. "Get out."

Emma released her seat belt, stepped reluctantly from the car, and surveyed her surroundings. The house looked deserted. No curtains in the windows. No other vehicle in the driveway.

He rounded the car to her side and took her arm. "Come with me."

Every fiber of her being screamed *run*! But to where? She knew she couldn't overpower Isaiah. He had the car keys. If she broke free and ran as fast as she could back down the driveway, he would have time to get in the car and catch her before she made it to the next residence.

The hand on her arm tightened, forcing her to walk with him toward the house. No way was she going inside. She'd been trapped in a house with a madman back in May. If she was going to draw a proverbial line in the sand, it would be at the threshold.

Except Isaiah continued past the sidewalk and alongside the structure. Emma spotted a real estate sign lying against the foundation. She'd be willing to bet it had hung on the post at the end of the driveway until Isaiah had decided to take up residence.

His grip remained firm as he guided her beyond the house, toward the lake's edge and two Adirondack-style chairs and a fire pit. He stopped to give her a gentle shove toward one of the chairs. "Have a seat."

She rubbed her released arm, thinking of Suzanne Foster's bruises.

Thinking of other bruises Emma had received, courtesy of another man.

Isaiah claimed the second chair. He looked up at her, waiting.

Now would be the opportune chance to bolt. She could be halfway back to the house before he lumbered out of the low Adirondack. With that kind of head start, she stood a chance of beating him to the nearest neighbor.

"Oh, for Christ's sake. Sit down. I only brought you out here so we could talk uninterrupted. Once we're done, I'll drive you back to your camper. You have my word."

Which meant nothing.

"I bet my boy hasn't told you much about his past. About his mama and me."

Isaiah would've won that bet, but she said nothing.

He chuckled. "I reckoned as much. Sit the hell down. I'll tell you everything you want to know."

"If Matthias wants me to know, he'll tell me." But she lowered into the chair.

"Trust me. What I'm gonna tell you, he *never* will." Isaiah looked out at the lake, his expression contemplative. "What exactly *has* he told you about me?"

"Nothing." She glared at the side of his face lit by the golden light of the sun setting over the lake. What she and other photographers called sweet light—the time just before sunset and just after sunrise. Only she didn't have her camera or her phone,

The Devil Comes Calling

and the last person she wanted to make portraits of was this man. Swallowing, she said, "Up until Thursday evening at O'Reilly's, I assumed you were dead."

He turned to her, his expression unreadable. "I'm not dead."

"I gathered that much."

"I've been in prison."

Emma fought to maintain her own unreadable façade. Inside, her mind raced, remembering Matthias's reaction that night at the bar. His uneasiness when he'd returned to the table. She'd known he felt he should tell her. She also sensed he didn't want to, so she hadn't pressed. Right now, she wished like hell she had.

"For murder." Isaiah's tone sounded a lot like that low, gravelly growl Emma had heard from Matthias. "I was in prison for nearly twenty-five years for murdering my wife. Matthias's mama."

Emma pictured the woman in the photo. The woman mounted on the barrel horse, frozen for all eternity in the middle of that winning run.

"But you see," Isaiah went on, "I was framed. I didn't kill my wife." He shifted, leaning on the wide armrest closest to her, and sneered. "Matthias did."

Chapter Twenty-Eight

Emma's throat closed. She'd seen the anger Matthias carried inside him. But murder? His mother? "That's a lie."

Isaiah sat back, lifting his face to the sky, and laughed a deep belly laugh. After a minute, he looked at her again. "Is it? Has Matthias told you about his old girlfriend? Melissa?"

Emma couldn't breathe, couldn't even squeak out "no."

She didn't need to. "Clearly, he hasn't," Isaiah said. "Melissa Bowers. It was Garcia back then. She's a real beauty." He eyed Emma. "Same as you. He wanted to marry her, but she was too smart to marry a man who beat her senseless over and over again. So, she left him." Isaiah shifted toward Emma and lowered his voice even more. "You'd be wise to do the same."

Emma avoided Isaiah's eyes, her mind spiraling. He was lying. He had to be. Yet she remembered being the victim of another man's charm followed by his brutality. It wasn't so distant in the past that she couldn't still see the fury in her ex's dark eyes, couldn't still feel the searing pain of his blows. Isaiah was playing on those memories. Had to be. Matthias was no abuser. No murderer.

Was he?

Angry tears burned her eyes. Isaiah was lying, but he'd succeeded in planting seeds of doubt. Seeds of distrust in the man she loved. She hated that she was allowing Isaiah to get inside her head and do that.

He settled back into his chair, gazing out at the setting sun. "Tell me about your job," he said. "You're a photojournalist, right?"

The change in subject jarred her from the mental nightmare. "Huh? What?"

"You're a photojournalist," Isaiah repeated. "Isn't that right?"

"Yes."

"Good." He pushed forward to perch on the edge of the seat. "Because I have a scoop that's going to launch your career into the stratosphere."

For a dreadful moment, she feared he meant the story he'd just told her about Matthias.

Instead, he said, "I know who killed Orlando Larson and that young woman. What was her name? Oh, yeah. Darcy. Darcy Tomasetti."

Emma's breath caught in her throat. Darcy. That photo. "You? You killed them. Because Darcy caught you on camera."

Isaiah threw his head back and laughed a raucous, sidesplitting laugh that subsided into quieter snickering. He met her gaze and wiped a tear from his eyes. "Me? Hell, no. I'm no killer. But I can tell you who is."

"Well, I'll be damned," Cassie said from her cubicle.

Matthias stared at Darcy's photo of his old man glaring at the camera. "What?" he asked.

"Come have a look at this and tell me I'm not seeing things out of sheer exhaustion."

Groaning, he rose and stepped around the partition. "What've you got?"

"I've been following the money."

"Donahue's?"

"No. Not directly anyway." Cassie rolled her chair to the side, allowing Matthias a view of her computer monitor, which was a jumble of spreadsheets.

"What am I looking at?"

"Bank records for one Humphrey Bozwell."

The name meant nothing for a second. "Boze?"

"Yeah. No wonder he goes by a nickname. You mentioned Emma's been wondering where he gets all his money."

Matthias nodded and leaned closer, squinting at the numbers before again asking, "What am I looking at?"

Cassie huffed and pointed. "This is what grabbed my attention. His credit card records."

Matthias scanned the transactions. Lots of online purchases including a big screen TV with extra speakers, a gaming system, and subscriptions to several streaming services. "He likes his home entertainment."

"He does, but three things about his purchases interest me."

Matthias looked at her. "It's getting late. I have dinner to fix for my girl. Can you just tell me instead of playing games?"

"Spoil sport," Cassie grumbled. She clicked through a few pages. "First, these high-ticket items show up in Boze's two most recent statements. Prior to that, his charges were what you would normally expect from someone scraping by. Fast food, groceries, beer, that sort of thing. Second, he generally only paid the minimum or slightly over, but here—" She pointed at his June statement. "—he pays off this credit card and all his others."

"Boze came into some cash." Matthias traced the stubble on his upper lip, which he'd need to shave before dinner. "Did he win the lottery?"

"Not of any legal kind." Cassie tapped the screen with one finger. "Can you figure out number three?"

He scanned the purchases, annoyed that she'd found something he couldn't.

"I'll give you a clue. It's not something he charged. It's something he didn't."

Matthias looked at her. "There are no charges from The Blue Pike."

"Ding, ding, ding. Give the man a prize." She clicked through more of the pages. "I dug through every charge card, every bank account. All those expensive meals he claimed to eat at The Blue Pike? No record."

"Maybe he has another account we don't know about?"

"Not very likely. Unless he's got a card in someone else's name. Except why not charge some of these big electronic purchases on it?"

There was another possibility. "Or management at The Blue Pike is comping Boze's dinners."

"Now you're catching on. *But wait. There's more,*" she said, mimicking the generic male voice used on every stupid buy-this-product commercial on every cable television channel. "You know I've been pulling my hair out trying to uncover who the hell owns the property on Clifton."

"Boze?"

She grinned without taking her eyes from the computer. "There are a half dozen shell companies in the loop." She clicked to another screen. "Then this caught my attention."

Matthias read the report. "EHB Holdings?"

"It's the name that shows up most prevalently when I ran title searches on the Clifton house, but it's just a name with a post office box."

From her tone, Matthias could tell it was much more than that.

"EHB," Cassie said. "B is for Bozwell. H is for Humphrey."

"What's the E stand for?"

"Eleanor Bozwell. Boze's mother." Cassie smiled. "You'll never guess who she is."

Matthias glared at her.

"Okay, fine. Eleanor Bozwell's maiden name was Nelson. She and Elias are twins."

The puzzle pieces clicked into place. "You've got to be kidding me."

"Nope."

"Elias set up a real estate holding company for his sister," Matthias said, his mind racing ahead. "And his nephew. Boze is Elias's nephew."

"I still have more digging to do on the family connections, but considering how Boze lived up until recently, I'm guessing they weren't close."

"Until Elias needed him." Another thought slammed Matthias. "No. Not Elias."

Cassie flashed a smile at him. "Now we're thinking the same thing."

"Russ Carlisle?" Emma said, stunned at the name Isaiah had dropped on her. "No, that can't be. The police have the man who shot them in custody."

"That's right. They do. A young punk by the name of Zane Norris. Stupid kid doesn't have the IQ of a green tomato."

She eyed Isaiah.

He gave her that predatory smile again. "You're wondering how I know."

She swallowed but didn't say anything.

"I know because I'm the one with the connections. I'm the one who made all the arrangements."

Emma stared at him, stunned.

"After twenty-five years in a state prison, a man picks up skills he lacked when he first went in. For me, I learned to network. To make friends. Useful friends." He leaned toward her. "And to solve problems. I think of myself as a professional problem solver. I use bits and pieces I overhear to my advantage and to the advantage of others. I came here to make amends with my boy. In the meantime, I made some new acquaintances—friends of friends—who introduced me around."

Friends of friends, she thought, meaning friends of his fellow inmates. She remained still, her mind spinning, but she forced it to settle. To pay attention.

"Russ Carlisle had a problem by the name of Orlando Larson. Russ was Orlando's silent partner in a number of properties. Orlando did the work, got the credit for the remodels. Russ funded the projects and collected a hefty percentage of the profits. It was all well and good until Russ tried to withdraw money from an escrow account and learned it had already been paid out." Isaiah chuckled. "Orlando transferred the funds to his construction company's account. Claimed he needed to raise his remodel budget. Russ didn't take the news too well, as you can imagine."

She could but didn't say so.

"Russ decided he couldn't trust Orlando anymore and wanted him gone, but he was under the scrutiny of some Erie detective." Isaiah cast a grin in Emma's direction. "Don't suppose you know who that might be."

She fought the urge to give him the reaction he wanted.

"Besides, Russ didn't want to get his hands dirty. At that point, a mutual acquaintance introduced us. Russ was a man with a problem." Isaiah touched his sternum. "As I said, I know how to solve problems. I learned that Orlando had made a number of enemies in his past, including a former business partner he'd screwed over. Man by the name of Quentin Donahue."

Emma sensed Isaiah was again waiting for a reaction. She refused to give it.

"Quentin claimed Orlando owed him money. Whether that was true or not made no difference. Russ had set a healthy budget to solve his problem. I introduced the two and a deal was struck."

Emma wanted to interrupt, to point out that Zane Norris was the gunman, but remained silent.

Isaiah smiled. "I can hear you thinking. That stupid kid pulled the trigger, right?"

She didn't reply.

"Yes, he did." Isaiah gazed toward the lake. "Russ paid Donahue. The deal was half up front. The rest after the deed was done. But now Donahue was the one with the problem. He knew the cops would like him for the murder. He and Orlando had a past, so I did what I'm good at. I found him someone to be the gunman. Zane's an idiot. A broke idiot. He gladly accepted part of Donahue's downpayment as payment in full. I coached the kid on how to do it. Single tap in the back of the head." Isaiah mimed the act on himself, pressing a finger into his skull.

Emma's brain spiraled out of control. "That photo Darcy took," she said, "Zane Norris is the man you were talking to."

Isaiah looked at her. "That's right."

"That's why you had him kill Darcy, too."

"Oh, no." He shook his head. "The Tomasetti girl wasn't supposed to be there. Orlando was always the first one on the job in the morning and was always alone. Zane freaked out a little. He made her kneel like I'd told him to do with Orlando and had him tie her wrists. While he was focusing on that, Zane popped him. Then the girl. Not a bad job of improvising. Except he got greedy and decided to take her camera. Even worse, he sold it to the same damned pawn shop where he'd bought that damned fancy gun."

Emma wasn't convinced. Her memory of Isaiah's expression in that photo haunted her. But she wasn't about to call him on it. Not here. Not now.

"When Quentin Donahue found out about Zane offing the girl, he had a conniption. Seems his cousin was sweet on her. Russ was worried Quentin might do something stupid, like go to the cops as penance for his part in the girl's death. He made arrangements to meet Quentin at an apartment, supposedly to pay him the rest of the money. Offered him something to drink to calm his nerves." Isaiah chuffed. "The stuff he put in the drink calmed him all the way to unconscious. Then he doused the apartment with gasoline and…" Isaiah mimed striking a match.

"And Suzanne?"

"She was already dead. Same cocktail. Same results."

"Why are you telling me this?"

"Like I said. You're a journalist. I like you despite your poor taste in men. I know you want Russ Carlisle out of your life for what he did to your sister." Isaiah braced both elbows on his knees. "I'm giving you what you need to put him away for life." With a smile, he added, "I'm solving your problem. Now that you know the truth about my son, if you want me to solve that problem for you, too, I'd be more than happy to oblige."

Chapter Twenty-Nine

Emma hadn't showed up at Matthias's apartment as planned. She wasn't answering her phone, wasn't replying to Matthias's texts. It wasn't like her. The only time she'd been unreachable in the past had been when she was in trouble. He struggled to keep his concern at bay by focusing on the meal he was preparing. And on his case.

He and Cassie had put together the pieces in a way that made sense. Russ Carlisle owned the Clifton property, was Larson's secret partner in the flip, and for whatever reason, had decided to end the partnership. Permanently. To keep his hands clean, he'd hired Donahue as a middleman. Donahue, in turn, had hired Zane Norris.

Sometimes the simplest answer was the right one. Sometimes it was not. Proving any of it would be tricky with Donahue dead. Convenient for Carlisle. Too damned convenient. Matthias wanted nothing so much as to snap the cuffs on the smug bastard.

Until then, Carlisle was out there somewhere.

And Emma was incommunicado.

The dinner Matthias had prepared was congealing into an

unappetizing glob. He looked at the clock on the wall of his loft. It was already eight-thirty. Where the hell was Emma?

Matthias checked to make sure the oven and stove were off. He retrieved his sidearm from the safe in the bedroom, grabbed his jacket, and pounded down the stairs and out of his apartment. The air was cooler than it had been all day, but still dripped with humidity. He jogged the two blocks to where he'd parked his Jeep. By the time he reached it, he'd broken a sweat. If he hadn't been in a hurry, he'd have removed the ragtop roof. But he was, and he didn't.

The traffic between downtown and Peninsula Drive was light. He rolled into Sara's Campground shortly before nine. Shades of orange and pink painted the sky to the west, fading to deeper hues of blue and purple sweeping overhead.

Emma's Subaru sat in its usual spot in front of her camper. Matthias expected to see her sitting on her deck. She wasn't. Maybe she was on the beach like she had been last night. Or out riding her bike. Probably not. It was too late for that. Besides, they had a date.

He climbed out of the Jeep and looked around. Music from a live band at Sara's Restaurant drifted up the slope and competed with the uphill neighbor's radio. Matthias ignored the music and stepped onto Emma's deck. One glimpse of her Trek bicycle propped against the far railing confirmed she wasn't out on the trail.

He pounded on the door. No answer. No sound from inside. The lights were out. Force of habit from his old patrol officer days had him test the doorknob to make sure it was locked.

It turned and clicked open.

What had been a mild case of uneasiness exploded into anxiety, putting him on high alert. He stepped inside and looked around. No sign of Emma. Her keys hung where they always did,

The Devil Comes Calling

just inside the door. The window shades above the kitchen table holding her computers were wide open.

Emma would not leave her camper unlocked and unattended with all her computer gear in full view.

He pulled out his phone and called her again.

The rock and roll tune she used as her ringtone filled the small space. He followed the sound into the bathroom and located her phone on the edge of the sink, the screen lit with his name and face. Unease and anxiety settled into a lead block of dread pressing on his heart. He silenced the ringtones by stabbing the red button on his cell. "Where are you?" he asked out loud.

He debated what to do. He had no legal grounds to file a missing person's report just yet. He considered taking Emma's phone but resisted. If he had the device in his pocket, and she returned with a perfectly reasonable excuse for going MIA, she wouldn't be able to call him.

A loud guitar riff filtered through the camper's walls and sparked an idea. As much as Matthias hated dealing with Emma's radio-playing neighbor, Mick Harper might have information on her whereabouts.

Matthias left her phone on the sink and strode outside, around the front of the camper and across the vacant lot between the two sites.

Harper spotted his approach, snatched his radio from his porch railing, and headed into his massive rig.

"Harper!" Matthias bellowed at his retreating back.

The screen door slammed behind the man as the radio fell silent.

Matthias stopped at the bottom step to Harper's deck and called his name again.

This time, he appeared at the door, glaring at Matthias through the screen. "I wasn't playing my music too loud. If you think I was, you're too damned sensitive."

Harper was right about that. Compared to the volume he'd cranked the radio to back in May—when Matthias had forcibly removed and pitched its batteries—the music had been almost soothing. "I'm not interested in your radio," Matthias said. He aimed a thumb over his shoulder toward Emma's camper. "Have you seen her this evening?"

Harper cautiously stepped outside and scratched the stubble on his jaw. "A while ago. Yeah."

"Do you know where she went?"

"I don't keep tabs on her. Some old fellow came and picked her up. I figured it was her father paying her a visit."

Considering Emma's father had died several years ago, that was highly unlikely. "What did he look like?"

"I dunno. Old." Harper eyed Matthias. "Come to think of it, he kinda looked like an older version of you."

Matthias swore under his breath. Isaiah. "How long ago was this?"

Harper scratched his jaw again. "Maybe an hour ago? Maybe more, maybe less. Ain't my job to keep tabs on my neighbors."

Matthias hesitated before asking the next question. "Did she appear to go with him of her own volition?"

Harper snorted. "He didn't have her slung over his shoulder like a sack of potatoes, if that's what you mean."

Of course, he wouldn't. Isaiah would never be that blatantly abusive. Not where someone else might see him. "What kind of car was it?"

"Small. Black. Foreign."

"Can you be more specific?"

"All them little cars look alike."

"I don't suppose you caught a plate number."

Harper snorted again.

Matthias took that as a no. He slid a business card from his pocket and held it out to Harper. "Do me a favor. Keep an eye on her place and call me"—he almost said *if*—"when she comes back. Better yet, have her call me."

"What's in it for me?"

Matthias battled to control his temper and his words. "I'll make it worth your while." Even if it meant draining his budget for paying informants for the next six months.

"Cool." Harper took the card. "Anything else I can do for you?" His voice dripped with sarcasm.

Matthias thought of the unlocked door and the computer equipment in plain view of anyone who stepped onto Emma's deck. Alerting Harper to the situation didn't feel like a good choice. "Yeah. If you see anyone else around her place, call me asap."

Harper raised his hand as if to salute Matthias. Instead, he flipped him off before turning and going back inside.

Matthias returned to his Jeep, debating his next move. Lock Emma's trailer? No. Her keys were still inside along with her phone. He could only hope Harper would be the nosey neighbor he'd proved to be in the past.

Where had Isaiah taken her? And who might know? Melissa had been aware of his release from prison. Would she have more information on him? Matthias exhaled an exasperated breath. Even if she did, he didn't have a phone number for her.

All he had was Harper's description of a small, black foreign car.

Matthias stormed onto the deck and into the camper to make one more quick check for a note or clue about where Emma had gone. Finding nothing, he closed the blinds to conceal the computers from outsiders, pulled the door shut behind him, and headed for his Jeep. He would drive around Erie all night and all the next day if that's what it took to find that car, his father, and Emma.

It was dark by the time Isaiah returned Emma to her camper as promised. She sat motionless in his passenger seat, afraid to reach for the door handle.

He rumbled a laugh. "You really thought I was gonna hurt you, didn't you?"

She didn't answer.

"I explained everything to you. I'm not the dangerous one. My son is. I just wanted to let you know who you're sleeping with."

Emma didn't believe him. Didn't *want* to believe him. Hated that even a part of her had doubts. The part that had once been in love with a man who'd turned violent. And deadly. A niggling voice in the back of her consciousness kept whispering, was she repeating old patterns? "I can go?" she asked, her voice a squeak.

"Absolutely. It's been nice getting to know you."

She wasn't a good enough liar to return the sentiment. Instead, she pushed open the door and climbed out.

"The offer to solve your problems stands," he called after her.

She shivered at the insinuation and moved to the front of her Subaru as Isaiah reversed out of the parking spot and rolled down the hill, away from her.

"Hey, Emily," came a gruff shout.

Only one person called her that. Her pain-in-the-ass neighbor, Mick Harper. She'd given up correcting him ages ago. She waved at him and moved toward her deck.

"Emily," he called again. "Wait! I got a message for you."

She reversed course and stepped clear of her trailer. He sat on his own deck, dimly lit by an ancient set of twinkle lights hanging from the rafters and the glow of a citronella candle. "What message?"

"That cop boyfriend of yours was looking for you. Said either you or me need to call him when you got back from your date with that older guy."

Date? She waved again. "Thanks. I'll call him."

He waved back. "Remind him that he promised to pay me."

She exhaled and returned to her trailer, realizing the only music filling the night air came from Sara's, not from Mick's radio. Had Matthias hurled it into the woods like he had with those batteries the last time?

She stepped into her camper and flipped on the lights. Her computers were still there. Nothing was missing, but the blinds above her table were drawn.

Matthias had been here. He'd been inside. He knew she'd left without locking up. Without her phone.

According to Mick, on a date, but if he'd described the man she was with, Matthias would've known.

She closed and locked the door. Her phone was right where she'd left it in the bathroom. A quick check showed a half dozen missed texts and voice messages, all from Matthias.

Call me.
Where are you?
Urgent.

Were these from before he found out his father had taken her?

She collected her phone and flopped onto the futon. As much as she wanted to hear his voice, it was Isaiah's that filled her head.

No. Matthias was no killer. He'd saved her life. He'd sat by her side in the hospital with Nell. He'd been shot and added to his scar count thanks to her.

Matthias was a hero in her mind.

Except she'd thought the same about someone else not all that long ago and been proven wrong.

She shut her eyes, and Isaiah's face floated into the darkness behind her closed lids. The sneer. The loathing. The deceit. All the traits she'd finally come to see in her ex. Her past experience had left her alert to spotting evil. It had also left her with a distinct lack of trust. In men. And in her own judgment. For now, she needed to cling to her absolute conviction that Isaiah fit into the evil category and would deal with her trust issues later.

She inhaled, exhaled, and pulled up Matthia's number and pressed Call.

Chapter Thirty

Matthias was on his second pass through Presque Isle. The park's gates closed at sunset, but he'd made it in before the rangers locked up. The peninsula was close to the campground and, at this hour, deserted. Lots of places for Isaiah to take Emma.

And do what? Matthias forced his emotions aside and focused on what he could see in his headlights. The people had cleared out, but the wildlife roamed freely. So far, he'd had to stop for a deer and for a turkey to cross in front of him. Even a normally skittish coyote that had become acclimated to having humans nearby watched him pass from the edge of the road.

On the passenger seat, his phone rang. When he looked over and saw Emma's face on the screen, he braked to a stop and scooped it up. "Emma?"

"Yeah."

Her voice was tight, but he closed his eyes in relief at simply hearing it. Opening them again, he asked, "Where are you?"

"I'm home."

"Alone?"

"Yeah. Mick said you stopped by."

"I did." He had too many questions to ask over the phone. Besides, he needed to see her and make sure that son of a bitch hadn't done anything to her. "Stay where you are," Matthias ordered. "I'll be there in five minutes." He ended the call before she could protest.

With no one in the park—save for the park rangers who thankfully weren't around—he ignored the twenty-five mile-per-hour speed limit. At the gate, he broke all the rules and veered onto the grass and the bike trail to get around it.

Emma sat on the deck when he pulled in next to the Subaru. Harper, he could see, was on his own deck. Matthias stepped out and called to her, "I'll be right there," before striding across the empty site. He pulled out his wallet and thumbed out fifty bucks. Way more than he usually paid an informant, but it was money well spent.

Harper met him at his steps, hand out. "I wondered if you'd keep your word."

Matthias slapped the money into his palm. "Thank you." He wheeled around and headed back toward Emma's camper. From behind him, Harper called out, "Pleasure doing business with you."

She hadn't moved, sitting stiffly, hands folded around her phone in her lap.

He moved her second chair to face her and sat. "Where did my father take you?"

She kept her eyes lowered. "Some vacant house on the lake west of here."

Matthias felt sick. "He took you to a vacant house?"

Her face lifted, her gaze meeting his. "Not inside the house. There were chairs at the lake's edge. We sat there and talked."

"About what?"

She shifted in her seat. "Russ. He's behind Darcy's and Larson's murder."

"I know."

"You know?"

"Cassie finally linked Carlisle as Larson's silent partner." Matthias didn't mention Boze's connection.

"Oh."

"How did my father know about it?"

"He introduced Russ to Donahue and Donahue to the gunman." Emma again dropped her gaze to her lap. "He claims he's a professional problem solver."

Her obvious anxiety made Matthias wary. Looking around he whispered, "Is he still here?"

"No." She shook her head. "He dropped me off and left."

Matthias scooted his chair closer and reached for her hands.

She pulled them away before he could touch her. "Emma? What's wrong? What did Isaiah say to you?"

She continued to avoid his eyes. She opened her mouth then closed it, pressing her lips into a tight scowling line. Silence hung between them, broken only by the driving drum beat and whining guitars of the band down at Sara's. If Emma was waiting for him to give up and go away without an answer, she had a long wait ahead of her. Outlasting a reluctant suspect was one of his strong suits. Emma was no suspect but his drive to keep her safe was stronger than any desire he'd ever had to wheedle a confession from a bad guy.

She must've finally realized his tenacity. "He told me he's been in jail."

Matthias remained quiet.

Her gaze lifted to his. "For murdering your mother."

A lump formed in Matthias's throat. He should've been the one to tell her. He knew that. But he hated going back to that black day in his life.

"He says he was framed."

Matthias blinked. "He *what*?"

Emma remained almost motionless. Almost. Except he caught the slight stiffening of her posture. The miniscule lean away from him. Most revealing though was the flash of apprehension in her eyes.

She didn't need to tell him what Isaiah had claimed. He knew from her reaction. Isaiah had told her Matthias had killed his mother.

And nothing he said right now would put her at ease. "The house he took you to. Where is it?"

The shift in subject drained some of the tension from her shoulders and face. "I don't know the address or the exact name of the road we were on. It was off West Lake Road, past the Walnut Creek Access Area. He made a right on Lakeland Drive, but after that I lost track of the turns. The house had a post at the end of the driveway. You know, the kind real estate companies hang their signs on. The sign wasn't there, but I spotted it leaning against the foundation. The house sat down a long driveway with a lot of trees edging it."

Matthias tried to picture the area. Emma's description was a good one even without an exact street name.

"I'm sorry I'm not more help."

He wanted to take her in his arms but knew better. "Don't apologize. I'll find it." He thought but didn't add, *I'll find him.* "What kind of car was he driving?"

"A black Camry. I don't know the year."

"That's okay."

She appeared on the verge of saying more, so he waited. After a few false starts, she said, "You had a girlfriend. Melissa."

"Yes."

Emma's voice became so soft and strained, he almost couldn't hear her next question. "Did you beat her?"

The Devil Comes Calling

Bile rose into his throat. "Beat—?" He sucked in a breath of night air. "No. Never. What the hell did he tell you?"

She recoiled, and he realized his hatred of his father saturated his words.

He took a deep inhalation, a slow exhalation to calm his mind. When he spoke, he made sure his tone didn't convince her that his father was right. "I never laid a hand on Melissa. Or my mother. I can only imagine what Isaiah said to you. He's a killer and a master liar. His biggest talent in life is figuring out a person's weakness. Their greatest fear. And playing on it."

She stared down at her hands, but he could tell she was thinking. She heard what he was saying and was weighing his words.

Matthias could hope for nothing more right now. He stood. She remained seated. He wished like hell that he'd told her how he felt, said those three terrifying little words, last week, last weekend, last month, because this sure wasn't the time. After Isaiah had played his mind games on Emma, Matthias wasn't sure it would ever be the time again. "I'm going to find him. You lock yourself inside. If he comes back—" He almost said "call me." "If he comes back, call 911."

She nodded without looking up.

He remained rooted to the deck. Finally, he placed his hand on her shoulder. A light touch. She didn't flinch, so he pressed his luck, bent down, and kissed the top of her head. Then he strode away, off the deck, and climbed into his Jeep. He had only one thought on his mind as he drove away. Find Isaiah Honeywell and make sure he never spent another day as a free man.

Even in the dark, Matthias was able to find the house Emma had described. Except she said the post at the end of the driveway had no sign attached. This one did. A placard with an unfamiliar logo.

He turned into the lane and followed it through the trees she'd mentioned. The house at the end was dark. A waning moon did little to light the landscape as Matthias stepped out, flashlight in hand. He swept the beam, searching for some sign of Isaiah's presence and found none.

Matthias approached the porch. The front door held one of those lock boxes real estate agents use to gain access for house tours. As he had with Emma's camper, he tried the knob. This one didn't click open. The jamb appeared unmarred. He stalked to the large picture window. His flashlight revealed a few sheet-covered furnishings. He moved around the side of the house and pieced the day's events together. Isaiah had taken down the sign out front and moved in hours or days ago. How had he gained entrance? Did he have the code for the lock box? After he'd brought Emma here—and released her—he knew Matthias would come looking for him, so he left, rehanging the sign on his way out.

Yet Matthias's spidey sense sizzled beneath his skin. He swung the flashlight's beam around, searching the side of the house, the driveway behind him, the trees in full foliage and the shadows of the underbrush. He aimed it toward the lake, spotting the murky shapes of the chairs Emma had mentioned. Drawn to them, he prowled in their direction, expecting ... what? Isaiah to be seated in one, waiting for him? As he grew closer, he saw that wasn't the case. No surprise. Both chairs were vacant. Still, he continued, shining the light out toward the lake, listening to the soft *whoosh* of the low waves washing in. No one strolled along the water's edge. No one, nothing, moved.

Matthias let out a breath, rested a hand on the back of one of the Adirondack chairs, and lowered the flashlight to his side. The beam passed over a small lump on the chair's seat. He brought the light to bear on the object. A rock the size of his fist. Beneath it, something white. He bent and scooped up the rock and the piece of folded paper. Pinning the flashlight's barrel against his side, he unfolded the note and read the words scrawled across its surface.

> *You took everything away from me. Now I've taken the one thing that matters most to you. She'll never completely trust you again.*

The note wasn't signed. Didn't need to be.

Matthias resisted the urge to crumple the paper. Instead, he refolded it and slid it into his hip pocket, his fingers trembling with rage. The rage that no one could stir in him the way his father could. He looked out toward the water, steadying his breath. Emma said the lake calmed her. He tried to draw the same tranquility from it as she did.

He wondered if she'd ever allow him to stand next to her on the beach again.

Matthias stepped back with his right foot, cranked that arm around and over, and with a roar that rose from the soles of his feet, he pitched the rock into the blackness of the night.

Matthias dragged into Major Crimes the next morning, clenching a cup of coffee from the shop down the block, and found Cassie on her phone.

"Yes, I understand," she said. "I appreciate your willingness to talk to me." After hanging up, she took a long appraising look at Matthias. "You look horrible."

He grunted and dropped into his chair with a thud.

She rose from her seat and moved to stand over him. "You don't look like you slept a wink."

He hadn't but didn't feel up to discussing why. "How's Alissa?"

"Back to her old self, as if nothing had happened. Thanks for asking but stop changing the subject. What's wrong?"

Matthias logged into his computer, ignoring Cassie's question.

"Oh my God. Did something happen with Emma?"

"Emma's safe." He tossed his phone onto his desk.

Cassie cocked her head. "Then something *did* happen. What?"

So much for not discussing last night. "My father showed up at her trailer and took her for a little ride."

Cassie's intake of breath was audible. "Is she okay?"

Matthias gave her the short version, telling her about the house on the lake, Isaiah returning Emma unharmed but shaken. He told her about going there and finding Isaiah gone.

He left out the part about the note.

"Why," Cassie asked, "did he take her there?"

"I'll ask him when I find him."

"But you saw Emma afterwards. What did she say?"

Matthias pictured her face, her eyes. The uncertainty and doubt he'd seen there. "Not a lot."

Cassie leaned a shoulder against the cubby's partition wall. "She must've said something."

"Isaiah filled her head with lies."

"About?"

Matthias swallowed. "Me."

"What on earth did your father say to her?"

"I don't know all he told her. She isn't talking."

Cassie looked at him, waiting.

"She asked me if I'd been abusive to my ex-girlfriend."

Cassie snorted. "You? Abusive to a woman? Emma has to know you better than that."

He looked up at her, raising an eyebrow.

After a moment, Cassie sobered. "I get it. Emma trusted that monster she was dating before she moved here."

"The one she came here to hide from."

"So, she's questioning her judgement."

"Yeah."

Cassie swore. "Your old man's a piece of shit, you know that."

It was Matthias's turn to snort. "Cassie, I've known that since I was eight years old."

She pushed off the partition. "Give her some time. She'll come around."

He sure as hell hoped so.

"In the meantime, we have bad guys to put in jail. We have an arrest warrant for Russ Carlisle, if we can find him. He's not at his apartment, not at his in-laws, not at the restaurant, but it's only a matter of time. We also have a warrant for Mr. Humphrey Bozwell, AKA Boze. I have a good idea where to find *him*. I say we start there."

Which meant going to ErieLIVE. Which meant facing Emma.

Cassie must've read his mind. "While we're doing that, I can have a little chat with your cute photographer chick and clear things up."

"Don't."

It was her turn to hike an eyebrow. "Whatever you say."

He pinched the bridge of his nose, recognizing her tone. "Cassie," he growled, knowing she was going to butt in, no matter what he wanted.

Her phone rang, interrupting his protest. She darted from his cubby to hers to answer, leaving him to eavesdrop on her side of the conversation.

"Yes, Ham." After an extended silence, she said, "Interesting… Yes, absolutely. Thanks so much for getting this to me." She ended the call but stayed at her desk.

Matthias wheeled his chair into the aisle. "What's going on?"

She looked up from the note she was scribbling. "The labs on Donahue and Foster came in. Both had alcohol and barbiturates in their systems."

"They were drugged."

"Yep. In addition, Suzanne Foster's cause of death was the combination of drugs and alcohol, which is no surprise since Ham already said there was no evidence of soot in her lungs or trachea. Smoke inhalation was definitely COD for Donahue though."

"He was knocked out first."

"Yep. Killer probably offered him a doctored drink."

"Killer," Matthias echoed. "You mean Russ Carlisle."

"That would be my guess." Cassie set down her pen. "There's something else you should know. That phone call I was on when you came in? I was talking to Steven Tomasetti."

"Darcy's father?"

"Yeah. The last time we talked to him and April, she claimed Darcy had been scared of Guilfoyle."

"I remember."

"Something about the look on Steven's face nagged at me."

Matthias remembered that look, too.

"I called him this morning and guess what. He told me April had Darcy's boyfriends mixed up. She wasn't afraid of Guilfoyle—"

"She was afraid of Boze."

Cassie gave Matthias a wicked grin. "Yep. Let's go have a chat with Humphrey Bozwell."

Chapter Thirty-One

Emma had lain awake most of the night, staring at the ceiling above her futon, imagining Matthias as a killer. An abuser. No different than Clay had been.

Somewhere around two, she finally gave up, pulled a light fleece over the T-shirt and pajama bottoms she'd worn to bed, and made a pot of coffee. Cup in hand, she moved outside to sit on her deck. She even considered taking a walk to the Feather, but good sense prevailed.

About four a.m., her caffeinated mind cleared. The picture Isaiah had created of his son was painted in hues of deception. While he'd attempted to plant seeds of doubt in her fertile mind, one thing she had no doubt of was Isaiah. He was evil. Deceptive. Manipulative. Those were traits she was all too familiar with. His eyes might be the same color as his son's, but he'd looked at her like prey.

Something Matthias had never done.

As the sun began to brighten the eastern sky, she realized she hadn't told him all of Isaiah's revelations. She would need to call Matthias with what she'd learned.

By nine o'clock, Emma sat at her desk, battling a killer headache and trying to focus on the last of Darcy's photos yet to be sorted. Trying, but failing. She kept replaying last evening at the lake. Isaiah telling her about being a problem solver, solving all of Russ's problems. At least Matthias had reached the same conclusion about Russ's involvement in the murders.

The elevator doors at the far end of the newsroom pinged and slid open. Matthias, Cassie, and LeeAnn, ErieLIVE's bespectacled receptionist, stepped out. LeeAnn was clutching a paper and protesting loudly. "You can't just barge in here."

Matthias tapped the paper in her hands. "That says we can."

"You need to go back to your desk," Cassie added and veered toward Boze's. Matthias looked Emma's way, meeting and holding her gaze for a long second, before trailing after his partner.

LeeAnn stood, rooted in place and sputtering. When Laurie appeared in her doorway, the receptionist tottered her way. "Ms. Kassim, I tried to stop them, but they—"

Laurie raised a hand. "It's okay. Go back to your desk."

Once LeeAnn had sulked to the elevator, Laurie shot a glance at Emma and headed toward the detectives and Boze.

Emma flinched as a hand touched her shoulder. She looked up at Preston, whose gaze was locked on the police activity. "Grab your camera," he whispered.

"Seriously?"

"Yes, seriously. We have a news story breaking right under our noses. It wouldn't look good if we got scooped."

From a newsperson's perspective, he had a point. But Emma wasn't so sure Laurie would agree.

"Come on," Preston said quietly but insistently before striding toward Boze's desk.

Emma snatched her camera from the backpack at her feet, checked the settings, and followed.

"That's bullshit," Boze was saying. "I had nothing to do with a murder, especially Darcy's." He hiccupped. "I loved her."

At Emma's side, Preston emitted a sound from his throat, half gasp, half choke. She noticed he held his phone aimed at their colleague and realized he was using the same recording app as the one he'd loaded onto her cell.

"We need you to come to the station with us and answer some questions," Cassie said, her voice almost too soft for Emma to hear.

"You're a photographer," Preston hissed. "Take some damned pictures."

She lifted her Nikon and zoomed in on Boze's face. He looked shattered, terrified, trapped. Despite her dislike for the man, she wanted to look away from his pain, not capture it for the reading public. She shot a glance at Laurie, hoping her manager would signal for her to put the camera away, but Laurie was closer to the action and was glaring at Boze.

Not at the detectives. At Boze.

With a resigned sigh, Emma pressed the shutter, watched Boze's shoulders sag, captured the light glisten off a tear. At least Matthias and Cassie didn't place him in handcuffs. It would've made a great photo, but not one Emma wanted her name attached to.

Cassie took one arm, Matthias the other and guided a compliant Boze toward the elevator.

Emma remembered what she'd neglected to tell Matthias. Gripping the Nikon, she jogged after them and caught them while they waited for the elevator doors to open. "Detective Honeywell, can I have a moment?"

Cassie shot her a sympathetic look, and Emma wondered if he'd told her what'd happened.

"Sure." To Cassie he said, "I'll catch up to you."

She gave him the same sympathetic look and added a nod. The doors pinged open, and she escorted Boze inside.

Emma glanced around to make sure no one was listening. At least half of the newsroom's staff were watching her, but none were close by. Moving nearer to Matthias and keeping her voice soft, she said, "Your father told me something else last night."

Matthias visibly tensed.

"Russ also killed Quentin Donahue and Suzanne."

Before she could elaborate, he nodded. "We already suspected as much. Toxicology came back earlier. Suzanne died from a combination of drugs and alcohol before the fire. Donahue was drugged, probably unconscious, but died of smoke inhalation."

Exactly as Isaiah had said.

Footsteps drew her attention, and Preston appeared at her side. He held his phone toward Matthias. "Can you give us a statement, Detective Honeywell?"

Matthias kept his gaze on Emma. "Not right now. The investigation's ongoing. The department will make a public statement soon."

She understood. What he'd shared with her wasn't to be repeated. She gave him a nod, and he turned away to punch the down button.

As soon as the doors closed behind Matthias, Preston nudged her. "Grab what you need. We're going to the police station to follow this story."

Emma watched him jog back to his desk and realized two things.

Preston believed Boze had an active part in Darcy's death and would chase this story all the way to Boze's future prison cell.

And Isaiah's knowledge of Donahue's and Suzanne's deaths was awfully detailed—and obviously accurate. Russ wouldn't have shared those details with someone else. How did Isaiah know?

The Devil Comes Calling

Unless he'd been there.

Matthias should've felt relieved. Emma was still speaking to him, except the only reason was to share more of her encounter with Isaiah. That fact left him feeling no relief at all.

Bozwell babbled denials and nonsense the entire way to the station until, in the garage, he must've been struck with a moment of prudence. He shut up, looked around, announced he wanted an attorney, and then shut up again.

After letting him use the phone, Cassie and Matthias deposited him in an interview room and left him to ponder his poor judgment while they put together a plan. They made a list of what they knew and what they needed to know.

On the first list, they had the money trail. In theory, Boze's cash flowed from one of Elias Nelson's companies. On the second list, they needed to confirm the cash passed through Carlisle's hands. On the first list, they knew Boze was Elias's nephew. On the second, they needed to know where the hell Carlisle was hiding. On the first, they had Steven Tomasetti's accusation that his daughter had been afraid of Boze. On the second, did she have a good reason to be afraid?

Over the course of the next hour, the attorney Boze had called refused to take his case. Shortly afterward, another stepped in. Matthias learned from one of the officers standing guard that the first lawyer was on retainer to Uncle Elias, who refused to let his attorney represent his nephew. Potential conflict of interest. The second lawyer was secured by Elias's wife, a tidbit Matthias found interesting.

Finally, the call came through. Boze and his attorney were ready to talk.

Matthias followed Cassie into the room. Boze slumped in his

chair, his elbows braced on the table possibly the only thing keeping him from face planting. The attorney, a stern-looking brunette with bright red lipstick, sat at his side, spine ramrod straight. She introduced herself as Ms. Ruffino. Cassie started the recording and stated the details for the record. She opened with the softball questions. Where he lived. Where he worked and for how long.

Then she said, "Tell us about your relationship with Elias Nelson."

Boze's eyes grew wary, and he looked at his attorney.

She arched one eyebrow at him.

"He's my uncle. My mother is his sister."

"Yes. But tell us about *your* relationship," Cassie repeated, speaking slower. "How do you get along? Did you spend time with the Nelsons when you were a kid? That sort of thing."

"Oh. Yeah, when I was younger, we used to visit them quite a bit. Havana and I were close."

"Their daughter, Havana?"

"Yeah. We played together."

Matthias made a note.

"After I graduated high school, I rarely spent any time with them. They sent Havana off to Brown University." His mouth slanted into a peeved scowl. "I went to Slippery Rock."

One of the priciest universities for Elias's daughter. One of the least expensive for the nephew.

"When was the last time you saw your uncle?"

Boze shot another look at his attorney, but she was doodling on a legal pad. "I don't know. A month ago?"

Cassie and Matthias remained silent, staring at him.

As expected, he squirmed and caved. "We met for coffee."

Matthias jumped in. "When was the last time you saw Havana?"

The question seemed to startle Boze. "She's dead."

"We know that," Matthias said and repeated the question.

Boze's forehead creased in thought. "I don't know. A couple of months before she died, I guess."

"How was she?"

He ruminated for a few more moments. "She was ... sad."

"Did she tell you why?"

Boze licked his lips. "She didn't come right out and say."

"Oh, come on." Matthias deepened his voice. "You're an investigative journalist. She was your cousin. You were close as kids. She was unhappy, and you didn't even ask?"

Boze turned to his attorney, his gaze pleading with her to intervene. She didn't. He came back to Matthias and blew out a breath. "Okay, yes. I asked. She said her marriage wasn't what she'd thought it would be."

From under the table, Cassie kicked Matthias's leg. He looked at her. She tapped her notepad, and he read the message she'd scrawled to him.

Save it for later.

He understood. She wanted to ask about Russ, but not regarding Havana. Not yet. Matthias nodded to his partner and sat back, taking notes as she drew more out of Boze. During the aforementioned coffee meeting, he and his uncle had discussed a business proposition. Elias wanted to invest in a home remodeling business but wanted to keep his name and companies' names off the record. "They offered to pay me quite well if they could funnel money through another company that would be owned by me. On paper at least."

Matthias caught Cassie's eye. She picked up on Boze's slip as well and nodded to Matthias. "They," he said. "Who else?"

Boze's eyes widened. "No one."

"You said, '*They* offered.'" Matthias came forward to lean an elbow on the table. "Who was there besides your uncle?"

"Do I have to answer that?" Boze asked Ms. Ruffino.

She leaned over and whispered something in his ear. He whispered something back. She returned to her perfect posture and said, "Go ahead."

Boze looked from Cassie to Matthias and back. "I swore I wouldn't tell. He'll kill me if he finds out I did." He turned again to his attorney. "I won't do it."

Ms. Ruffino heaved an exasperated sigh. She interlaced her fingers on the table and addressed Cassie. "My client is genuinely concerned for his safety. Why don't we put our cards on the table? You tell me what you think you have on Mr. Bozwell, and perhaps I can find a way to make all of us happy."

Cassie looked at Matthias ceding their interrogation to him.

"All right," he said. "We're already aware Mr. Bozwell financed Orlando Larson's remodel of a house on Clifton. We know that money originated from Elias Nelson. So far, your client hasn't given us anything we don't already have a record of. We suspect there is another party or parties involved." Matthias paused, holding the attorney's attention.

She raised one hand, signaling for him to continue.

"Orlando Larson and Darcy Tomasetti were gunned down on the construction site, as I'm sure you're aware."

"I'm also aware you have the killer in custody."

"We have the man who pulled the trigger. We're looking for the man who paid for the hit."

"Quentin Donahue." The attorney sounded bored. "Deceased."

"Murdered," Matthias corrected. "By the same person who arranged to have Mr. Larson and Ms. Tomasetti killed. We've determined the motive to be money." Matthias turned his gaze on Boze. "And the money, as we've stated, came from Mr. Bozwell."

"No," Boze squeaked. "I didn't have anything to do with

anyone's murder. I swear. My God, I loved Darcy. I got her that job with Larson. I would never have done that if I'd known what he had planned."

"We have it on good authority that Darcy was scared of you."

No longer bored, the attorney placed a hand on the table in front of Boze. "Enough. Don't say another word." She shifted her gaze to Matthias and Cassie. "Let me speak with my client. In the meantime, I suggest you have a chat with the DA and come up with a deal."

Within a half hour, Matthias and Cassie reconvened with Boze and his stoic attorney. The DA had signed off on a deal that would keep Boze out of jail provided he gave them what they wanted.

What Matthias wanted was Russ Carlisle.

Pale and drained, Boze closed his eyes and nodded. "Yes. Uncle Elias was the source of the money, but Russ managed the whole deal. He made sure I had access to the funds needed and oversaw everything. He called himself the silent partner and made it clear if there were any issues, I was the one who would take the blame." Tears glistening, Boze locked gazes with Matthias. "I meant what I said. If he finds out I gave him up, he'll kill me. That bastard is crazy. He has no soul."

Boze reluctantly admitted that Darcy may have been frightened of how he acted when he was drinking, but insisted he'd never hurt her. He continued to deny having any personal knowledge of the plan to kill Larson or Donahue. Matthias believed him. Carlisle had used Boze the same as he used everyone else.

Matthias needed two more bits of information before they wrapped this up. "Where is Carlisle right now?"

Boze shifted uneasily.

"Look, you claim he'll kill you for ratting him out. The only way we can protect you is to put him behind bars. I can't do that unless I know where to find him."

Boze's sigh reminded Matthias of a man who'd exhausted all appeals, being walked to the electric chair. "Uncle Elias keeps a yacht at the marina. Russ has been staying on it. I can get you the slip number, but he might've taken it out."

Cassie gave Matthias a victorious smile.

But he wasn't done yet. "Tell me about your cousin, Havana," Matthias said. "You mentioned her marriage wasn't what she had expected."

Boze closed his eyes for a moment before reopening them and looking at Matthias. "The last time I talked to her, she told me if she turned up dead, Russ would've been the one to kill her."

Chapter Thirty-Two

Emma sat on the curb in front of the Erie Police Department, watching Preston pace the sidewalk, his phone pressed to his ear. His expression looked borderline homicidal. She couldn't blame him. While she didn't think he believed Boze had anything directly to do with Darcy's murder, there was a lot of bad blood between the two reporters. Preston wanted the responsible party locked up. If Boze was in an adjoining cell, Preston would count it as a double win.

Emma's phone vibrated with a text message from Matthias.

Not for public knowledge yet. Boze gave up Russ. Arrest is imminent.

She noticed Preston watching her, so she held her best poker face and texted back.

Thanks.

The prospect of Russ finally paying for his crimes, even if only part of them, should've made her happy. Except an arrest wasn't a conviction. She suspected that would be more challenging.

When Preston pocketed his phone and took a seat next to her, she studied his determined profile. "Do you mind telling me why we're here?" she asked.

He looked at her as if she'd grown a second head. "You're serious?"

She met his glower with one of her own. "Yes, I'm serious. We don't normally camp out in front of the police station when a suspect is being questioned."

"The person being questioned isn't usually one of our own."

"That's not why we're here and you know it."

"It would look pretty lame if another news outlet scooped us on a story about one of our reporters, don't you think?"

She made a show of looking around. "I don't see any of the competition lurking in the bushes. The police will let us know when they're ready to give a statement. Our air-conditioned offices are less than two blocks away. We could sit on our phones there and still beat any other reporters here once an announcement is made."

"We could, but I don't want to miss a minute of this."

She looked up at the cloudless sky. The shade was quickly receding, offering little relief from the July mid-day heat. Soon, she'd either be in full sun or she'd have to find a new perch.

More than an hour later, with Preston still insisting they keep their vigil, Emma managed to convince him to relocate across the street to the park. They claimed a bench under a tree where they had a clear view of the police department.

Emma knew the police would bring Russ in through the underground parking lot at the rear entrance where Matthias had taken her last week. She longed to text him and ask what was going on, but Preston sat beside her. If Matthias slipped her off-the-record reports, it would be impossible to hide.

Preston's phone rang. He jumped to his feet and walked away to answer.

Emma checked her own phone. Nothing new from Matthias. A few minutes later, Preston returned wearing a tight smile. "My informant says an arrest has been made. Russ Carlisle."

Preston had an informant inside the department. How had she not realized that?

He fixed her with a hard stare. "But you already knew, didn't you." Not a question.

So, she didn't answer. Preston had his confidential informant. She had hers, although it didn't require a degree in rocket science to figure out his identity.

"Carlisle was out on a yacht owned by his father-in-law," Preston said. He held up his phone. "As I understand it, they sent out the Coast Guard. They have him and are bringing him in."

A yacht. Emma was tempted to ask if Russ had been alone, but didn't think she wanted to know.

Another half hour passed before a white Mercedes backed into a spot along South Park Row. Emma lifted her camera and snapped the shutter as Elias Nelson climbed from behind the wheel. His wife stepped out from the other side. Emma lowered the Nikon and watched as he stormed toward the station, a man on a mission. Mrs. Nelson appeared more resigned. She draped a designer handbag over her shoulder and took a look around, her gaze settling on Emma. A smug smile crossed her lips, and she tipped her head in acknowledgment. Then she mouthed a word Emma was too far away to hear, but even without lip-reading skills, could understand.

Karma.

It was midafternoon by the time Matthias and Cassie entered the interrogation room to face Carlisle and his high-powered attorney, who'd arrived well ahead of the suspect. Farrell Owen, Esquire, wore a charcoal gray suit worth more than Matthias's entire wardrobe. He had little doubt this was the same attorney who'd declined to represent Boze. Elias was holding him in reserve for his favored relative. The man who'd likely killed Elias's daughter.

"Mr. Carlisle," Cassie began.

"Detective Sergeant Malone," he replied, his gaze shifting to Matthias. "Detective Honeywell. How's your father?"

Cassie reached out to lightly brush Matthias's arm. A silent warning he didn't need.

Once seated, Cassie again stated the details of the date, time, and who was in the room for the record.

Matthias was content to let her take the lead while he sat back and glared at Carlisle, using the look Cassie claimed scared people. If Carlisle was scared, he showed no sign.

"Tell us about Humphrey Bozwell," Cassie said.

"He's my cousin by marriage."

"When was the last time the two of you spoke?"

"I don't remember."

"Was it a week ago? A month ago? Last year?"

"I don't remember."

"Do the two of you have any business dealings?"

"No."

Matthias noticed Cassie's fingers tightening on her pen. The questioning went on with similar non-responses. Carlisle claimed he didn't know Orlando Larson, nor did he have any knowledge about the house on Clifton beyond what he'd heard on the news.

Cassie flipped to a different page in her notebook. "All right then, tell us about Suzanne Foster."

Carlisle made a point of examining his manicure. "As I've told you before, we dated a few times. I broke up with her almost a week ago." He lowered his hand to look at Cassie, feigning sadness. "And as you know, she died in a fire the next day. How tragic."

Matthias leaned forward on the table. "Tell us what you know about that fire."

"Nothing really."

"When we spoke at your restaurant yesterday, you suggested that Suzanne and Quentin Donahue may have been romantically involved, and that he may have torched her place with her inside because he was jealous."

"Well, yes. It's just a theory, mind you, but one you should look into."

"I find it interesting that you were the one who mentioned Donahue being in the same apartment as Suzanne. And you used the term 'torched' when no one had suggested arson was involved. We merely told you they had both died in a fire."

Carlisle waved away Matthias's comment. "I made an assumption. I don't believe that's a crime." He pointed at Cassie. "You brought up this Donahue fellow's name during our discussion of what happened to Suzy. I assumed the two were linked somehow. Perhaps you should polish your interrogation skills."

Before Cassie could say something she'd regret, Matthias asked, "But how did you know it was arson?"

Carlisle heaved a bored sigh. "As I told you before, your girlfriend, sweet little Emma, told me."

"Except, she didn't."

"Of course, she did. If she denied it, she's lying."

Matthias planted both forearms on the table and leaned on them. "She recorded your conversation. I listened to it. She never mentioned arson."

He caught the slightest twinge of Carlisle's left eye.

Farrell Owen, Esquire, placed a hand on Carlisle's shoulder, but his words were directed at Matthias. "This woman you speak of recorded a conversation without my client's knowledge or permission. Certainly, you know I'll never allow it to be played in front of a judge or jury."

"Certainly," Matthias replied smugly. "But we now have him on *our* recording stating a lie."

Owen shook his head. "Inadmissible. Are we done here?"

"Not yet," Cassie said. She shot a look at Matthias.

He caught her meaning and leaned back in his chair. While they'd been waiting for Carlisle's arrival, they'd gone over their strategy. She'd wanted Matthias to excuse himself at this point and leave the room. He'd refused.

He still refused.

She faced Carlisle. "How did you meet Isaiah Honeywell?"

He turned to look at Matthias, a slow smirk developing. "I don't recall ever saying I had."

"Yet you asked Detective Honeywell about his father when we started this meeting."

"Did I? Is that on your recording there?" Carlisle lifted his chin, gesturing toward the video camera in the corner.

"Not everything has to be recorded to have happened." She angled a thumb from herself to Matthias and back. "We heard you."

Carlisle shrugged. "If I did ask, it was a courtesy." He struck a relaxed pose. "How's your family, Detective Sergeant Malone?"

"Enough," the attorney said in a tone a parent might use on an unruly child.

Speaking slowly, deliberately, Cassie repeated her question. "How did you meet Isaiah Honeywell?"

Carlisle shot a look at his lawyer. "I don't have to answer her, do I?"

"Absolutely not."

"You might want to, though," Cassie said. "Considering what Isaiah Honeywell had to say about you."

The smirk faded into a dark scowl. "He would never talk to the cops."

"Enough," Owen said again, this time sounding less like a frustrated parent and more like legal counsel.

"You're right," Cassie said. "He didn't talk to us. But he did give a statement to a member of the press."

Carlisle's eyes widened, but he quickly recovered and purred, "Sweet Emma."

It took all of Matthias's self-control not to lunge across the table at him. The sound of her name in Carlisle's mouth lit a fire in Matthias's soul.

"We're done here," Owen said, collecting his legal pad and pen and placing them in his briefcase.

Carlisle raised a hand. "Not yet, we aren't." He shifted to fix Matthias with a dark glare. "I want this on record. Your father is a stone-cold killer."

Matthias didn't blink. It wasn't as though this was news.

"I have no idea what he's told Emma, but I can imagine. He lies better than anyone I know."

Also not news. "Even better than you?" Matthias growled.

"Oh, hell, yeah. I'll make a statement right here and now. Whatever you think I've done, I didn't. I'm just an easy target. Isaiah? He arranged the shooting at the Clifton house."

"Under whose orders?" Cassie asked.

"Not mine. I'm a businessman, not a killer."

Another lie, but Matthias let it go. For now.

"That fire? I had nothing to do with it either. Isaiah set it. He was afraid Donahue was going to roll on him for the Larson homicide."

"He was?" Matthias asked. "Or *you* were?"

Owen came to his feet and hooked a hand under Carlisle's arm hoisting him out of his chair. "Not another word. Do you hear me? Not. One. Word."

"Fine." He glared at Matthias. "I had nothing to do with Donahue's or Suzy's death, and you have no evidence saying otherwise."

"We're leaving," Owen said.

Cassie stood as well. "He's under arrest."

"And I've arranged for his arraignment in—" Owen checked his watch—"In twenty minutes. His father-in-law will be posting bail at that time."

Matthias rose slower than the others, the attorney's words weighing him down.

"By the way, detectives," the attorney said, "you have no case. If your primary witness is an ex-convict, I will shred him on the stand. The jury will never believe a word he says."

Cassie turned off the recording as Owen and Carlisle headed for the door.

"He's not the only witness," Matthias said.

Carlisle stopped and turned to him.

"And this isn't the only case being brought against you. There's a new witness willing to testify against you in the homicide of your late wife."

The sneer returned. "You wish. There's no evidence against me in any of these so-called cases." He took a step closer to Matthias, leaned in, and whispered, "There won't be any evidence against me when your sweet Emma disappears either."

Chapter Thirty-Three

Emma checked her phone for at least the hundredth time. Still nothing from Matthias. If there had been good news, he would've let her know. Wouldn't he? He'd texted her when Russ's arrest was imminent. Since then, nothing.

Preston strode toward her perch on a different bench in the park. She'd been moving, following the shade all afternoon while still keeping the police station in sight. "Carlisle's being arraigned." Preston waved his phone.

At least *his* informant was keeping him in the loop.

A figure appeared on the sidewalk across the street, walking briskly in front of the station. Emma recognized Mrs. Nelson. The woman was looking in Emma's direction, spotted her, and crossed the street.

Preston saw her approach and met her halfway. "Mrs. Nelson, can you answer a few questions for me?"

"No," she replied in a tone that left no room for debate. She met Emma's gaze. "I wish to speak with Ms. Anderson. Alone."

Preston raised an eyebrow at Emma. She waved at him. "I've got this."

He nodded and wandered off but, she noticed, not very far.

"May I?" Mrs. Nelson indicated the bench on which Emma sat.

She slid over to make room. "Be my guest."

Mrs. Nelson eased down and placed her handbag—Gucci, Emma noted—on her lap. The woman sighed loudly as she gazed toward the station. "He's going to get off, you know."

"Russ? No. He can't." More accurately, Emma couldn't accept it.

"Yes, he can," Mrs. Nelson said flatly. "And he will. I, like you, had hoped he would finally be made to pay for all he's done." She fingered the gold locket hanging on a long chain around her neck. "Well, not all perhaps." She opened the locket and gazed at the photo Emma knew was Havana. "I'm starting to question what needs to happen for my daughter to have justice served."

Emma ached for this grieving mother, as she herself ached for Nell. "For what it's worth, I was told by someone who knows, that he killed Suzanne Foster and Quentin Donahue. The police have traced his involvement in the murders of Darcy Tomasetti and Orlando Larson as well."

"Yes, and I'm quite certain all of that is true, but I just spoke with Elias's attorney, who's representing Russ. According to him, the police have a flimsy case at best. He believes it will never go to court. If it does, he'll tear the prosecution's witnesses apart on the stand." She twisted the leather strap on her handbag. "No, I'm afraid Russ will walk free. Again."

Emma's eyes burned. She blinked and gazed in the same direction as Mrs. Nelson. Kindred spirits, Emma thought. They'd both lost family members to Russ. And if, as Mrs. Nelson claimed, he continued to roam the earth as a free man, Emma would never get her sister back.

She wasn't sure how long they sat motionless, staring at the Erie City Police Department, but pounding footsteps eventually drew her attention.

Preston jogged toward them. "Carlisle made bail."

Mrs. Nelson exhaled. "That would be my husband's doing."

"He's been released," Preston said, his tone apologetic.

"Of course, he has." Mrs. Nelson rose to her feet and looked at Emma. She didn't speak but gave her the saddest smile Emma had ever seen.

"Karma," she reminded the grieving mother. "Just not today."

"Perhaps."

Emma spotted them on the sidewalk, crossing in front of the station from the left. Russ looking dapper and victorious between his father-in-law and the man who had to be the high-priced attorney she'd heard about. Bringing up the rear were Matthias and Cassie.

Mrs. Nelson turned to Emma and appeared on the verge of speaking. Instead, she lowered her face and said, "Good day, Ms. Anderson," before striking out toward her family. Such as it was.

Preston caught Emma's arm. "Come on. Take some photos. I need to get a statement."

She picked up her camera and jogged after him. Capturing an image of a triumphant Russ Carlisle was not how she wanted to end this long, miserable day.

She fell into step behind Preston, who trailed Mrs. Nelson across South Park Row. Mrs. Nelson stopped, facing her husband and son-in-law. Emma couldn't hear what was being said, but from Russ's eye roll, she assumed Mrs. Nelson was telling him and her husband how she felt about what had transpired.

Preston reached them first, his phone in hand. The attorney and Russ turned their attention to the reporter as Emma raised her camera. But before she could bring her eye to the viewfinder, Mrs. Nelson's movement stopped her cold.

The woman opened her Gucci handbag and reached inside. When she brought her hand out, she clutched an object. The bag fell to the ground. For a fleeting second, Emma didn't realize what the woman held. Then the sun glinted off chrome.

Everything shifted into slow motion.

Russ turned his head away from Preston and looked down at his mother-in-law. Emma spotted his eyes widen in terror.

The pop echoed against the concrete structure housing the police station. Russ's knees buckled. Preston leaped back from the sound, as did the attorney. At the same time, Matthias and Cassie launched toward it.

Elias grabbed for his son-in-law as Russ sank to the pavement, his descent only slowed by his father-in-law's arms encircling him.

Screams erupted from the park. Cassie held her phone to her ear, shouting about shots having been fired and ordering EMS to be dispatched immediately. She elbowed in between Elias and Russ, giving Emma a glimpse of the crimson circle blooming across Russ's chest.

Matthias charged at Mrs. Nelson. But she raised her right hand, holding the gun loosely, while clutching the locket in her left. He ordered her to set down the weapon in that gruff, authoritative voice.

Emma knew Mrs. Nelson wasn't going to put up a fight. She placed the gun on the pavement and continued to comply with his orders to turn around and put her hands on her head.

"Emma!" Preston's shout jarred her out of her paralysis. "Take photos!"

She swallowed and lifted the camera the rest of the way to her eye, capturing images of Russ bleeding out on the sidewalk, of Elias in shock at his son-in-law's side, of Mrs. Nelson being placed in handcuffs.

When Emma lowered the camera, she realized Mrs. Nelson was looking at her. With an almost blissful smile on her face, the grieving mother said, "I got tired of waiting on karma."

Chapter Thirty-Four

Matthias expected to have a harder time locating Isaiah, but when he cruised past the property where his old man had taken Emma, the FOR SALE sign was missing. He pulled into the driveway, turned off the ignition, and stepped out of the unmarked Malibu. The late afternoon sun cast the tree-lined driveway in shadows as Matthias hiked toward the house with the lake beyond, placing each step carefully and silently.

A black Camry sat outside the garage. The real estate sign leaned against the foundation, just as Emma had said. Matthias crossed to it and tilted it so he could read the logo, one he now recognized.

EHB Holdings. Boze's holding company that filtered back to Elias Nelson by way of Russ Carlisle. Matthias had done some digging and learned over half a dozen properties in the Erie area were owned by EHB Holdings, including this one. He figured his old man was holed up in one of them.

The sun over the lake set the horizon ablaze with yellows and oranges. Matthias wished he was sharing the view with Emma.

He hoped, once he took care of this business, they would get back to where they'd been before his old man came to town.

The Adirondack chairs remained where they'd been the last time. Except there was a blaze in the firepit and the chair facing the lake was occupied.

Matthias crept closer but was still ten feet away when Isaiah spoke. "Hello, son."

Pissed that he'd lost the element of surprise, Matthias closed the rest of the distance to stand in front of his father.

"You make a better door than a window, boy." Isaiah aimed a thumb at the other chair. "Quit blocking my view and have a seat."

Matthias calculated his options and decided, what the hell. He moved to the second Adirondack and sat.

"There's beer in the house if you want. You can bring me one while you're at it."

"I'm on duty."

Isaiah's gaze slid from the lake to Matthias, taking in his department-issued polo and tactical pants. With a grunt, Isaiah let his head drop against the back of the chair and again turned to gaze at the horizon. "I'd've thought you had a busy enough day and would take some time off."

"The job's not done yet."

He grunted again. They sat for several minutes before he spoke. "You got something to say to me?"

Matthias had a lot to say but knew damned little of it changed a thing. "How'd you meet Russ Carlisle?"

"Friend of a friend."

"Give me a name."

Isaiah pressed his lips into a deep inverted U and shook his head. "Don't think I care to do that."

"What's your relationship with Carlisle?"

"I'm an employee. I fix things. The boy had some problems he needed handled. I solved them for him."

"You arranged to have Orlando Larson killed."

"Nope. I introduced Russ to Quentin Donahue. They had a mutual interest. A mutual problem."

"Larson."

Isaiah didn't reply.

Matthias thought back to the woman who'd grieved Donahue's death far more than her husband's. And her reaction to the photo of Isaiah. "What's your connection to Yvonne Larson?"

"Who?"

"Orlando's widow."

Isaiah appeared perplexed. "Don't know her."

Matthias tried again. "Quentin Donahue's girlfriend."

This time Isaiah's face lit up. "Sexy brunette?" He blew an appreciative whistle. "Stone cold fox, that one."

"What's your connection to her?" Matthias asked again.

"None. She was in the car with Donahue when we had our meeting, but I never spoke to her. Only saw her that once." Isaiah chuckled. "Damned pity, too."

And he'd clearly made an impression on her, as well. Probably not in the same way.

"What about Zane Norris?"

"Russ wanted an extra layer between him and the solution to his problem, so I introduced Donahue to Norris. After that, I stepped back and let them figure it out."

Matthias sensed that in his father's mind, stepping back after arranging a hit removed all culpability on his part. "What happened? Donahue have a change of heart? He was the only one who could connect Carlisle directly to the murder. Besides you, I mean."

"Donahue wasn't too happy about the collateral damage. It was supposed to be just the one body."

"You mean he felt responsible for Darcy Tomasetti's death."

Isaiah appeared on the verge of saying something but reconsidered.

"Carlisle lured Donahue to that apartment on the premise of paying him what he owed," Matthias said.

"That's right."

"Was Suzanne Foster more collateral damage?"

"Nah. More like two birds, one stone."

"Carlisle killed them?"

"Yup."

"He drugged them both, dumped gasoline on their bodies, and lit the fire."

"Yup."

Matthias let a minute or two pass before continuing. "I have some problems with that."

"Oh?"

"First, Carlisle insisted you did it."

Isaiah brought his gaze to Matthias. "Carlisle's a liar."

"So are you."

"Yeah, but he's dead. Hard for a prosecutor to put a dead liar on the stand."

His old man had a point, although Matthias had to wonder how he knew Carlisle had been killed. But he'd address that later. "Here's another problem." Matthias pushed forward to balance on the edge of the seat, elbows on his knees, fingers interlaced. "Carlisle was largely a bully. He'd beat up a woman, but when it came to anyone stronger than he was, he was a coward who didn't want to get his hands dirty. Take Orlando Larson for example. Carlisle would much rather pay someone to do the wet work." Matthias glared at his father. "Like you."

"Doesn't take a lot of bravery to slip barbiturates into someone's drink and then douse 'em with gasoline after they're unconscious."

"Which brings me to my third problem with Carlisle being the killer."

Isaiah waited.

"How the hell do you know about the barbiturates? That tidbit wasn't released to the press. And Carlisle was too canny to share those kinds of details with anyone."

Isaiah's eye twitched. The same way it used to right before he would knock a much-younger Matthias onto the ground. "You can't prove anything."

Carlisle had said basically the same thing, before his mother-in-law had shot him to death. "I guess we'll see how a jury takes to an already convicted killer accusing a dead man who can't contradict him. Speaking of, how did you hear about Carlisle's demise?"

"Friend of a friend."

"And you aren't going to tell me who that is, are you?"

"Nope."

Matthias nodded. He didn't need his old man to tell him anything. Cassie had been digging and discovered that Elias Nelson was well acquainted with one of Isaiah's old cellmates.

Friend of a friend.

Matthias gazed out at the horizon where the sun was starting to kiss the surface of the lake. "Why'd you bring Emma out here?"

The change in topic relaxed Isaiah. "To talk."

Matthias had managed to control himself through most of the day. He hadn't pinned Russ Carlisle to the wall by his throat for threatening Emma, much as he'd wanted to. But now his self-control began to unravel. "To tell her a bunch of lies."

Isaiah gave an apathetic shrug.

Fighting a clenched jaw, Matthias said, "Everything you told her was a lie."

"Well, of course it was." Isaiah turned slowly to look Matthias in the eye, his expression one of loathing. "You can do your damnedest to win back her trust, but no matter what you say or what you do from now on, she'll never be one hundred percent certain."

The old rage Matthias had discovered as a teen and had struggled to keep in check for all these decades, roared to the surface. He climbed to his feet and clenched his hands so tight his knuckles ached, all to keep from reaching for his sidearm. "I should've killed you back then."

"Yes, you should've."

Matthias stretched his fingers and reached toward his service weapon, watching Isaiah's eyes and the momentary flash of fear there. Just like the night Isaiah had killed Matthias's mother. Matthias had taken Isaiah's revolver and aimed it at him. He remembered the tremor as he pointed the muzzle at his father, who was standing over his mother's lifeless body. He came within a hair of squeezing the trigger, and Isaiah knew it.

Tonight though, Matthias didn't unholster his gun. He reached farther back and freed his handcuffs from their case. "Stand up."

"You aren't going to arrest me."

"Like hell I'm not."

Isaiah snorted. "You got nothing on me."

"What I have is a warrant. And now that I know where you've been staying, I'll soon have a second warrant. One allowing us to search this house and your car."

"You won't find anything." But Isaiah's voice didn't hold the conviction it had only moments ago.

"You don't think? It won't take much. You're an ex-con. It won't take much at all." Matthias took a step closer. "Now stand up."

Isaiah folded his arms across his chest. "No."

In the golden light of the setting sun, Matthias could see the muscles bulging in his father's forearms and knew that's exactly what he wanted Matthias to see. Planting more seeds of doubt.

For every hour Matthias had spent in the gym at the station, he knew his father had spent three in the prison gym. They were the same height, the same weight. Matthias might be twenty years younger, but Isaiah had twenty more years of experience.

Matthias took a step toward his father.

Isaiah unfolded and raised both hands. "All right, all right." His tone was conciliatory, but his eyes were even colder than before. He placed his palms on the chair's wide arms and scooted forward.

Moving faster than Matthias would've thought possible, Isaiah rose. His right hand swept down to his side and up. The fading sun glinted off steel. Matthias's reaction was instinctive, his left arm blocking, slamming into his father's right. The bruising impact of flesh and bone on flesh and bone.

Not the white-hot sear of a steel blade.

In one smooth pivot, Matthias hooked Isaiah's arm, pulled him in close, and drove his knee into his father's groin.

A groan escaped the old man as he dropped to his knees.

Matthias grabbed his wrist and twisted, taking the knife from his hand.

From the direction of the house came Cassie's voice. "*Day-am*. And here I thought you might need my help."

"What took you so long?" Matthias growled.

"Well, someone parked their car at the end of the drive, so I had to walk the whole way in."

As Cassie closed the distance between them, Matthias looked down at his father on hands and knees, scooped up the handcuffs he'd dropped, and pressed down on Isaiah's back, forcing him the rest of the way onto his belly.

Isaiah spewed a string of epithets aimed at Matthias, who calmly cuffed one of his father's wrists, forced both of his hands behind his back, and clicked the second cuff closed. He leaned down to Isaiah's ear and whispered, "This time, it's for good."

Chapter Thirty-Five

Matthias stood at his kitchen island, chopping onions, garlic, and red bell peppers. Emma had agreed to come to his place for dinner, and he wanted to create a feast for her. His mother had always quoted the old line about the way to a man's heart was through his stomach. He didn't want to admit he was reversing the cliché to use on Emma, but after the last week and a half, he needed all the ammunition he could muster.

Isaiah was safely tucked away in a jail cell. With Russ Carlisle dead, Elias had refused Isaiah's request for access to his legal team, leaving him with a public defender. He faced charges of assaulting a law enforcement officer on top of two counts of first-degree murder for Suzanne Foster's and Quentin Donahue's deaths and two counts of second-degree murder for his role in the Larson-Tomasetti homicides. Whether or not all of those charges stuck was in the hands of the legal system, but Matthias vowed to stay informed this time. If he had anything to do with it, his father would never step foot outside a prison again.

If Zane Norris's testimony and Darcy's photos of Norris and Isaiah's meeting weren't enough to seal the deal, the plastic bottles of secobarbital found hidden inside Isaiah's Camry's door panels should do it, especially if the lab was able to match it to what Donahue and Foster had ingested.

One part of the case that left a bitter taste in Matthias's mouth was Mrs. Nelson. Elias not only refused to pay for Isaiah's legal defense, but he did the same with his wife. At least the grieving mother had Ms. Ruffino in her corner, although the attorney faced a stiff challenge. Claiming temporary insanity would be difficult considering Mrs. Nelson was as clear-headed as anyone Matthias had ever met. If the case went to trial, he hoped she'd face a sympathetic jury.

The buzzer announced the arrival of Matthias's dinner companion. He wiped his hands on his chef's apron, glanced at the sheet of notepaper on the edge of the island, and headed down the steps. He swept open the door to find Emma huddled under her umbrella, as a steady, drenching rain fell.

"Come in," he said, standing clear.

He wasn't sure if he was imagining her hesitation or if he was projecting his own trepidation on how this evening would unfold. She closed the dripping umbrella as she stepped inside and propped it in the corner, then faced him awkwardly.

He pulled the door closed and debated what to say, settling on, "I'm glad you came."

Her smile gave him hope. "I'm glad you invited me."

He gestured to the stairs and followed her up to his loft. "Pinot grigio?" It felt like a dangerous question. She never drank if she planned to drive back to the campground later.

"Sounds good."

He exhaled.

She sat in what had become her usual spot at the island, drinking her wine and watching him cook. As if they'd made an agreement, the conversation was light, focusing on the food, Emma's annoying neighbor at the campground, the heatwave forecast for later in the week, and news from her childhood friend Eric about goings on in Washington County.

"One of these days," Matthias said, venturing into dangerous territory once more, "you're going to have to take me there and show me where you grew up."

"I'd like that. So would Eric." She sipped her wine. "By the way, I gather you knew about Darcy's cat?"

"Yeah. Cassie's husband's a vet and is trying to find it a home." Matthias grinned. "You want to adopt it?"

"I'd love to, but I don't think it's fair to make a cat live in a seventeen-foot camper. Besides, the kitty has already found a furever home."

"Oh?" This was news to Matthias.

"With Preston."

Matthias nodded his approval. He may have had his doubts about Guilfoyle, but he'd reconsidered after the reporter slugged Boze on Emma's behalf.

Conversation dwindled while they ate, limited to Emma praising his skills in the kitchen. Maybe his mother's favorite cliché really did work in reverse.

After dinner, with the dishwasher rumbling in the background and the rain pelting the windows, they settled at opposite ends of the couch and into silence. All the easy topics had been exhausted. She put her stockinged feet up, and he took them into his lap to give her a foot rub.

"I'm sorry," he said.

"You don't have anything to be sorry for."

"Don't I?"

She scrutinized him with those almost-teal eyes. "I don't know. How much of what Isaiah told me was true?"

"None of it," Matthias answered quickly. Maybe too quickly. "Then again, I wasn't there to hear all he said."

She tipped her head. "Just tell me." There was nothing

remotely accusatory in her tone. "Tell me what happened back then."

It took a couple of false starts, even though he'd anticipated this conversation for days, but speaking slowly, he let the memories pour from his heart. The beatings his father had given him, beginning when he was eight. Watching his mother endure much worse. Then he reached the part of his story that he'd never told anyone. That he'd debated telling Emma. He glanced at her, took in her gentle gaze. Hell, if he didn't tell her just to keep her from leaving, they'd be living a lie.

He drew a deep breath and let it out. "When I was seventeen he came at me with a baseball bat. I snapped. I took it off him and nearly beat him to death. I heard my mom cry out. I'll never forget the look on her face. The sheer horror of what I'd become. I walked out of that house and swore I'd never return. But I did. Twice. Once to beg Mom to come with me. To get out of there, away from him." Matthias swallowed. "She refused."

He checked Emma's expression. Rather than looking appalled, tears glistened on her lashes, her expression one of sorrow rather than loathing.

"I went back one last time. A neighbor had called me to say he'd heard screams over there. When I was almost at the door, I heard the gunshot. I busted in and found Mom on the floor, my old man standing over her with the gun." Matthias choked. "He'd shot her in the head. I took the gun off him and— and— almost shot him. To this day, I don't know why I didn't."

Emma withdrew her feet from his lap and slid over to wrap an arm around his shoulders.

"Instead, I held the gun on him and picked up the phone to call the police."

"That's why you didn't shoot him," she whispered. "You're not a killer." She touched a finger to his sternum. "You're a protector."

"Except I didn't protect her. My mom's dead." All of the regrets and self-loathing he'd kept bottled up for twenty-six years roared over him like a runaway train. "I never should've left her there."

Emma held Matthias, his head resting on her shoulder. She rolled his story around in her mind, trying to imagine what he'd lived through at the hands of his father. She looked at the photos on the brick wall. Matthias on horseback. Matthias in uniform. And his mother, leaning into a barrel on her own horse. Emma had always loved the images. Snapshots from Matthias's youth. She'd never dreamed of the darkness behind them.

Matthias stirred and sat up, turning to face her. "There's something else. Something I need you to do."

"Anything." She meant it.

He rose and crossed to the island, picking up a piece of paper. She thought she caught him palming something else as well. He returned to the sofa, but instead of sitting, he handed her the paper. On it was a phone number.

"What's this?"

"It's Melissa's number. My ex-girlfriend."

The one Isaiah claimed Matthias had beaten. Emma held the paper out to him. "I know you didn't do what your father said."

His expression was doubtful. "I want you to call her anyway."

"But I don't—"

He shook his head. "One of the last things Isaiah said to me … before he tried to knife me … was that no matter what, you'd have some seed of doubt. I don't know if he learned about your past. It wouldn't surprise me if he did."

It wouldn't surprise her either.

"I—" Matthias stuttered. "I don't want that. Please. Call her."

The simple fact that he wanted her to make the call was more than enough to convince Emma, but she nodded and dug her phone from her pocket.

Matthias wandered away as she keyed in the number.

"Hello?" came the cautious greeting.

"Is this Melissa?"

"Yes. Who's this?"

"My name is Emma Anderson. I'm…" She debated her next words. "I'm dating Matthias Honeywell."

"Oh."

Emma explained about Isaiah coming to Erie. About him taking her to a remote beach. About what he'd told her about Melissa and Matthias.

There was a disgusted huff on the other end of the line. "That's a lie. All of it. Listen. Matthias is a sweet guy. But he's a cop first and foremost. That's why I broke it off with him. His career will always come first with him. No woman could compete with his job." Melissa paused before adding, "You may not want to hear it, but I don't believe that's changed."

Emma smiled. "Thanks for your time. I appreciate you talking to me."

"No problem. Tell him I said hello." The line went dead.

Emma stared at the phone. Melissa had ended the relationship because Matthias's priorities involved his work. She'd cautioned Emma off for the same reason. Except Emma already knew that. She didn't *want* to compete with his job.

Matthias's footsteps were so soft she didn't hear him return until he reclaimed his seat on the sofa beside her. "Well?"

She looked at his scarred but handsome face and smiled. "There are no seeds of doubt to sprout."

"Good." He looked down at his closed fist, then held it out to her and unfurled his fingers. Resting on his palm was a key.

It was what she'd seen him pick up when he'd retrieved the note from the island. "What's this?"

"I— I—" he stuttered again. Pressing his lips together, he regrouped. "I know it's too soon for anything more, but I—" He ran his tongue over his lips. "I want you to have a key to this place. So you can drop by anytime you want."

She picked it up from his hand. "You're just tired of interrupting your cooking to come let me in."

He started to protest, but stopped and grinned. "Right. That's all it is."

Emma leaned toward him to press a kiss to his lips. As the kiss ended, she whispered words she hadn't intended. "I love you."

He wrapped his arms around her and pulled her into a deeper embrace, a longer, hotter kiss. "I love you, too."

Acknowledgments

Once again, I have a whole team who helps me create these stories. Without their help, I shudder to think how my books would turn out.

Thank you to Leslie Budewitz for answering my legal questions, Bruce Robert Coffin and Adam Richardson for their assistance with police procedure, and Chris Herndon for offering help concerning postmortems and dead bodies.

I want to thank the owners of Sara's Campground and Restaurant for giving me permission to use their businesses as settings in this series. If you're ever in Erie, Pennsylvania, stop by for lunch.

And thanks to the real Laurie Kassim, my friend who won a contest to have her name used in *Keep Your Family Close*. Since her character didn't get much time on the page of that one, she's now become a regular with a bigger role.

Three of the most important people in my writing life are my critique partners: Jeff Boarts, Liz Milliron, and Peter W.J. Hayes. I couldn't do this without them. They're fabulous authors. If you haven't read their books, I highly recommend them.

I've dedicated this book to my late, beloved agent, Dawn Dowdle, who was responsible for initially finding a home for Matthias and Emma. I'm grateful for all she did for me and all her authors.

I'm also deeply grateful to have landed with Talcott Notch Literary and the amazing Paula Munier, who guided me through the contract negotiation after Dawn passed away. Thanks for keeping the Detective Honeywell series going.

Last but far from least, thank you to Jennie Rothwell and the team at One More Chapter who take my words, polish them to a brilliant shine, and package them so beautifully. I appreciate all you do.

PRE-ORDER THE NEXT DETECTIVE HONEYWELL MYSTERY TODAY!

COMING DECEMBER 2025

When a local Erie vet is shot during a robbery, Erie City Police Detective Matthias Honeywell and his partner Cassie Malone are tasked with pursuing the perpetrators. But as they close in on the truth, a mysterious sniper targets those involved in the case.

News of the shooting becomes local interest and journalist Emma Anderson's instincts kick in. But she doesn't expect to uncover a secret that could cause friction between Matthias and Cassie…

As Cassie and Emma get caught up in a kidnapping plot – will they manage to escape or is time against them?

On the shore of Lake Erie, Pennsylvania, a body lays half hidden, the waves slowly moving it with the rising tide…

In the early morning mist, freelance photographer Emma Anderson takes pictures of the rocky coastline. She moved to Erie to escape a past that haunts her but the last thing she expects to capture is a dead body.

AVAILABLE IN EBOOK AND PAPERBACK NOW

When a badly decomposed body is found in the basement of an abandoned warehouse, Erie police detective, Matthias Honeywell, is called in to investigate.

Meanwhile, freelance photographer Emma Anderson is desperately trying to find her drug-addicted sister, Nell. Then a devastating piece of evidence found at Detective Honeywell's crime scene brings her world crashing down, a driver's license belonging to her missing sister.

In need of her assistance, Matthias asks Emma to help with the case, hoping to solve the mysterious disappearance of Nell Anderson. But in doing so, will the investigation uncover more questions than answers?

AVAILABLE IN EBOOK AND PAPERBACK NOW

ONE MORE CHAPTER
YOUR NUMBER ONE STOP FOR PAGETURNING BOOKS

The author and One More Chapter would like to thank everyone who contributed to the publication of this story…

Analytics
Imogen Wolstencroft

Audio
Fionnuala Barrett
Ciara Briggs

Contracts
Laura Amos
Inigo Vyvyan

Design
Lucy Bennett
Fiona Greenway
Liane Payne
Dean Russell

Digital Sales
Laura Daley
Lydia Grainge
Hannah Lismore

eCommerce
Laura Carpenter
Madeline ODonovan
Charlotte Stevens
Christina Storey
Jo Surman
Rachel Ward

Editorial
Janet Marie Adkins
Kara Daniel
Charlotte Ledger
Federica Leonardis
Jennie Rothwell
Sofia Salazar Studer
Caroline Scott-Bowden
Helen Williams

Harper360
Emily Gerbner
Ariana Juarez
Jean Marie Kelly
emma sullivan
Sophia Wilhelm

International Sales
Peter Borcsok
Ruth Burrow
Bethan Moore
Colleen Simpson

Inventory
Sarah Callaghan
Kirsty Norman

Marketing & Publicity
Chloe Cummings
Grace Edwards
Katie Sadler

Operations
Melissa Okusanya
Hannah Stamp

Production
Denis Manson
Simon Moore
Francesca Tuzzeo

Rights
Ashton Mucha
Alisah Saghir
Zoe Shine
Aisling Smyth
Lucy Vanderbilt

Trade Marketing
Ben Hurd
Eleanor Slater

The HarperCollins Distribution Team

The HarperCollins Finance & Royalties Team

The HarperCollins Legal Team

The HarperCollins Technology Team

UK Sales
Isabel Coburn
Jay Cochrane
Sabina Lewis
Holly Martin
Harriet Williams
Leah Woods

And every other essential link in the chain from delivery drivers to booksellers to librarians and beyond!

ONE MORE CHAPTER

One More Chapter is an award-winning global division of HarperCollins.

Subscribe to our newsletter to get our latest eBook deals and stay up to date with all our new releases!

signup.harpercollins.co.uk/join/signup-omc

Meet the team at
www.onemorechapter.com

Follow us!

@onemorechapterhc

Do you write unputdownable fiction?
We love to hear from new voices.
Find out how to submit your novel at
www.onemorechapter.com/submissions